RAQUEL VASQUEZ GILLILAND

How Moon Fuentez Fell in Love with the Universe

SIMON & SCHUSTER BFYR

New York London Toronto Sydney New Delhi

Library of Congress Cataloging-in-Publication Data
Names: Vasquez Gilliland, Raquel, author.
Title: How Moon Fuentez fell in love with the universe / by Raquel Vasquez
Gilliland.
Description: First edition. | New York : Simon & Schuster Books for Young
Readers, 2021. | Audience: Ages 14 up. | Audience: Grades 10–12. | Summary:
When seventeen-year-old Star Fuentez reaches social media stardom, her
polar-opposite twin, Moon, becomes "merch girl" on a tour bus full of
beautiful influencers and the grumpy but attractive Santiago Philips.
Identifiers: LCCN 2020016455 |
ISBN 9781534448667 (hardcover) | ISBN 9781534448681 (ebook)
Subjects: CYAC: Sisters—Fiction. | Twins—Fiction. | Popularity—Fiction.
| Social media—Fiction. | Dating (Social customs)—Fiction. |
Photography—Fiction. | Hispanic Americans—Fiction.
Classification: LCC PZ7.1.V4 How 2021 | DDC [Fic]—dc23
LC record available at https://lccn.loc.gov/2020016455

To the Vasquez, Villanueva, Tristán, Fernandez, and
Mendosa women and girls:

Katarina, Rosa, Maria Raquel, Ofelia (Nana),
Margaret, Maria Elena (Mom), Jessica,
Aries, Sophia, Daniella, Aria,
and all the ones who came before
and all the ones who will arrive.

May we always recognize our miracles.

My art is grounded in the belief of one universal energy
which runs through everything: from insect to man,
from man to spectre, from spectre to plant,
from plant to galaxy.
—Ana Mendieta

1.

The Wild, Cosmic Beginning
of All Beginnings

EVERYTHING HAS A beginning. And I'm not just talking about things like the shop I ordered my moonstone necklace from, or where it was made, or where the stone itself was quarried. Though that is lovely to think about, isn't it? Perhaps it's from some deep, wild cave pebbled with lakelike stones of moons. . . . But no, that's not what I mean.

I'm not even talking about me, or my twin sister, or *yuck*, the birds and the bees. What I am talking about is everything. I mean, *everything* in this whole wide, wild universe has one beginning. One place where everything, all of matter, converged into a speck one trillionth the size of a period. Let me repeat that, because I can scarcely fathom it myself.

Everything that exists in all the billions of galaxies, including Earth, with our salty, whale-skimmed seas and herds of elephants strewn on the horizon like gray beads and piles of electronic junk gathering here and there since, what, the eighties? And blue-trimmed plates of arroz con pollo and the nearly fuchsia slices of smoked salmon over a bagel and all the smooth and metallic sky-scrapers and the billions of microscopic organisms in a teaspoon of dirt, everything—every last atom and electron and scoop of strawberry cheesecake ice cream—was once a fraction of a fraction of a period. I don't know how scientists have figured something like that out with any certainty, but they have. I mean, if I'd kept reading *Astrophysics for People in a Hurry*, I might know, but I couldn't, not after that sentence. I had to put the book away, and then next thing you know, my library loan was up, and I can't bring myself to touch it again. It's so overwhelming.

I mean, a period! A period! Probably font size ten, too, or something. Can you imagine how heavy that thing was? How, if you'd picked it up, it would've cut a hole right through you? Your mom might have been like, "Oh, Moon, what have you done now?" You know, if she'd cared. And you'd say, "Oh, yeah, just tried to see if I could lift this speck of All-That-Is. I'll be okay." You know, as if she'd care.

Sometimes I think, what if I could go back to the beginning? What would I do? I could try to touch it, that molten-hot little speck, just to say I'd tried. Or maybe I'd look at it, at this beginning of all beginnings, and ask it, Why the heck do the women in our family still have La Raíz? You know, the whole reason why I'm the unwanted, ugly sister. I may allow myself another related question: Why, why, *why* didn't I leave La Raíz in the carved milk jar, right where Mom banished it, on the windowsill in her bathroom?

I can still picture the moment. Despite Mom warning us, with one hand on her Bible and the other basically on the graves of all our ancestors, to never, ever, *ever* touch the milk jar, I got on my tiptoes, grabbed the white bottle, and pulled the top off. And released all the yuck back into our bloodline, apparently. Like a little Pandora-in-training. Of course, nothing happened at first. I spent years thinking Mom outright lied to us.

And then I had sex for the first time.

But that's another beginning for another time.

You know what, though? This whole beginning is super important in the context of, like, my whole freaking life. So . . .

2.

In the Beginning, There Was La Raíz

ACCORDING TO MY mother's brand of Catholicism, at least. When Eve ate the fruit from that one forbidden tree, it cursed all women. One gender being held responsible for humankind's fall from grace apparently wasn't enough of a punishment, so God made sure we were slapped with this wild, uncontrollable penchant for miracles. Not just any miracles. Weird ones. Bad ones, Mom says.

La Raíz, or The Curse as Mom sometimes calls it, was bred out of just about all families. All except ours.

When we were twelve or thirteen, Mom told us some more details on it. "La Raíz comes at first sex," she whispered. The word "sex" was even lower than a whisper, like she basically mouthed it, like saying it aloud would've had the Lord our Father smiting her with lightning strikes or stale café con leche for the rest of her days.

"What happens? Like, what do you mean, bad miracles?" I asked her.

"It doesn't matter. I stopped it myself." Mom was so freaking proud. Her eyes twinkled, her skin smooth with this warm glow, making me think of faraway beach sand picking up the last sunset light. It was the last time I saw her as beautiful. "I took it out of me," she said. "I put it in this."

She lifted the milk jar. Tall, skinny, porcelain, with a tree engraved on it. There were drips of pale gray on the edges of the oak. The artist carved it right down to its roots, serpent-like, coiling into the core of the earth. It was breathtaking.

That was the moment we got the warning, me and Star, with pointer fingers in our faces. "Never touch this jar. It is exactly like the tree of the knowledge of good and evil. And we all know what happened when Eve disobeyed our Holy Father."

Star was absolutely fine leaving it at that. No matter how much I tried to convince her to join me for just a little-tiny-baby peek, she'd shake her head and say, "No, Moon. We're better than that. We're better than Eve."

It wasn't until years later, not till after Dad left, not till after that one glorious and free summer at Tía's in New Orleans, that I opened it. I couldn't help it, which sums up a lot of my very bad decisions. I'm just like Eve. I knew the fruit would be delicious. It would be better than anything I'd ever tasted before, better than sweet plantains fried up until the edges are black and caramelized. Somehow I knew it'd be worth the trouble.

And you know what? That beautiful milk jar? It was empty. So empty, I could've fit a whole new universe inside it, blackberry bushes and singing blue whales and all.

All that fuss for nothing but empty, empty, empty.

Or so I thought.

3.

Moonflowers Are Considered Weeds
in Some Parts of the Country

TÍA ESPERANZA SAYS the reason I'm not assimilated into the family has nothing to do with La Raíz; it's that I'm still wild is all. And apparently that's why I'm not a weed, doomed to be ignored like an endless pattern of flat, dull dandelions. No. I'm the wild, viny moonflower that somehow got sorted into the round red roses, so thick with petals they could be mistaken for orbs. Which sounds nice and all until you realize the rose tender of my life—Mom—is waiting for the right moment when she can pluck me from the bulbous bouquet and give me a good crumple before depositing me in the trash.

That's how it feels about half the time, anyway. In the other half, I'm just Moon Fuentez, twin sister to Star, daughter of Celestina and William (who, in terms of flowers, may as well be literal dirt).

The only thing my sister and I have in common besides our

ridiculous names is our love of flowers. Star receives them—
thick, color-coordinated bouquets that make the classic dozen
roses look like cat litter—from her many, many (many) suitors.
I'm talking waxy lilies that look like they've been dipped in literal
stardust, rare succulents that probably sell for thousands at plant
auctions, and irises, bearded and blue and nearly blasphemous
with their beauty.

And I, Moon, as far as flowers go, I collect them.

In fact, that's what I'm doing right now, a fistful of daisies in
my hand. These are the sort that grow in sidewalk cracks, bursting into dozens of tiny, translucent pink blooms. Their petals
are long and thin like hair, or feather strands, even, like little
miracles. The good kinds of miracles, I think, though I doubt my
mother would agree. She's the sort of lady who pours hot vinegar
over anything that might look like a weed.

4.

The Kind of News Banshees Appreciate

"MOON!" STAR YELLS. At least, that's what I think she says. The wind by the beach right now is so loud, I can only think of it as the most outraged ghost of all time, howling its undead complaints directly into my eardrums.

"Yeah?" I yell back.

"One more!" She walks a little closer. "This time without the cloak." Even this close, about nine feet away, she has to scream.

"But it's so cold."

"Just one." She's already dropped the cloak on the sand, heading back toward the water. I glance down at the pile of pink silk and velvet. I looked it up when the clothing company, Madam Le Blanc, sent it to Star. It costs $12,000, that pile of fabric right there. More than my life.

"Just one," I repeat, thinking if I had a fraction of a period of a penny every time I'd heard that, I'd be able to buy myself a thousand priceless fairy cloaks.

I grab my camera and adjust the settings once more, letting all the light in. The sun has almost set, and I know Star's not asking for a silhouette shot.

She's already posing, which probably isn't obvious to anyone else but me. Her white-blond hair picks up the peach of the sky, and she closes her eyes and lifts her head, smiling against the bitchy ghost wind. Only I can tell she's pushing out her top lip and sucking in her already concave stomach. Even in the dimming light, I can see her ribs. I haven't seen my ribs in so long, they could be swimming around like jellyfish in there for all I know. Exactly like what bright men who fancied themselves doctors thought uteruses did back in the day.

A few people stop and stare at Star, and it's not just because she's the only person out in basically subzero degrees in a swimsuit. It's because she's breathtaking. Even someone like me, who's known her all my life, can't stop looking. Also, they might recognize her. At my last count, Star had nine hundred thousand Fotogram followers. Can you imagine? I couldn't even wrap my brains around it when she hit two thousand. And now, one year later, she's got more people interested in her feta dinner omelet than I will ever have glance at me in my whole pathetic life.

I'm not bitter. I know that's exactly what it sounds like, but I swear, I'm not. I had to let go of feelings like *envy* and *bitter* and *murder* a long time ago to survive under Star's glare. These sorts of thoughts are unavoidable, as though a scientist were observing the scene and listing the facts. Fact: Star is objectively beautiful.

Fact: I am not. Fact: I've been reminded of these facts for as long as I can remember. They're invisible tattoos stretching across my jiggly brown body, permanent because no one—not Mom nor Star nor any random stranger on the street—will let me forget them.

Star makes me take about twenty-four photos, even as she starts to shiver and shake, before she finally grabs the keys and runs to the car. I pick up the cloak and, balancing everything in my hands, I follow her.

In the car, I turn on Cardi B loud enough to make Star bristle. "What the heck," she says, lowering it. But before I can protest, she opens her phone and begins texting—probably Chamomila, her FG BFF. And now she won't hear a word I say, so I hit the gas and get us going.

It's been kind of a shitty week, if I'm going to be honest. Or month. Or life, even. That's why I don't even look at my phone when it starts buzzing in my purse. I don't feel like talking to any-one except a bag of hot Cheetos tonight, thank you very much.

But then Star's ringer goes off and I know it's Mom. "Hey," Star says, picking up right away. "Uh-huh." She snaps her fin-gers to tell me to turn the volume down even more. "Sure thing, Mom. See you." As soon as she clicks the end-call button, she turns to me. "Mom wants us to come home for dinner. She says she has a big announcement."

I swallow my groan. Mom works as Star's publicist and manager. Any and all announcements are related to . . . that.

Last time Mom had a huge announcement, we discovered Fendi wanted Star to model for their new junior line of . . . God, what was it? Dalmatian puppy coats, maybe? Anyway, I think my ears are still bleeding from Star's shrieks that night. The last thing I want this evening is for my entire face to hemorrhage. Then how would I eat my Cheetos, huh?

"Is she cooking dinner? To celebrate?" I ask, even though I already know the answer.

"She ordered pizza. And before you say anything, Moon, she said she got a ton of different toppings this time. It'll last the week with variety."

I just keep my mouth shut and mentally burn some words on the inside of my skull: *Be grateful. Be grateful.* There they join my invisible tattoos of *You're ugly, You're loud,* and *You're a bad, bad daughter.* Unlike the tattoos, *Be grateful* has pretty much lost all meaning through repetition. I should switch it up.

We live in a tall, too-big town house on the edge of some woods I like to call the Forbidden Woodland, even though I'm not sure Mom's ever thought about forbidding me from anything with regard to it. The house is nice, but fancy. Star bought it for us—for Mom, really—and it was Mom's rich white people's dream come true: central air-conditioning; French doors that open to bedrooms our old house could fit into; a dishwasher, sleek and steel and so soundless, I never can tell if it's on or not. I'm grateful for the house, I am. But my favorite part of living there is the Forbidden Woodland, hands down. I glance at its tree-lined entrance as I pull into my spot, all green and full and alive, and Star's out the door before I can even finish parking.

Six pizza boxes pile up on the dining room table. At first glance, it's become sentient, growing eyes and a long lizard-like tail, sharp teeth dripping with marinara sauce. *Eat me?* it screams. *No! I eat you!* And then it attacks, Mom first, then Star. After which I give it a high-ass-five.

Unluckily for me, in real life, the pizza is still crappy pizza. Though I honestly wish I'd never see pizza again in my life, my stomach grumbles at the smell of gooey, warm cheese. Traitor.

"In here, girls!" Mom says. She's got a bottle of sparkling cider in her hands, and I freeze.

"Let me guess," I say as she messes with the cork. "Diego Luna wants to marry Star."

"No." Mom grins. "Though I wish Diego Luna would marry me."

I grimace. "So Diego Luna wants to be her driver, then? Clean her toilets? Lick the sidewalk after her footsteps?"

"Dios," Mom says, crossing herself. "You've been here less than a minute and you're already starting with the vulgarity. I taught you better."

"Mom!" Star's jumping up and down as she walks in, changed into pajamas. They're made of such soft satin, the material floats over her body like pink fog. "Who called this time? Was it Michael Kors? Oh, gosh, was it Chanel?"

Mom's eyes light up when she sees Star. "Let's sit down first."

The way Mom is drawing this out is nuts. "Jesus, Mom—"

"Moon!" Mom yells. More crossing and glares. Next step is a blessing with holy water and then a dusting of ground-up saints' bones, and after that, a kick straight into the cleansing fires of hell at knifepoint, so I put a lid on it and pull a plate.

Jesus, though. Mom wasn't kidding about getting all different pizzas. Each one is covered in toppings I barely recognize. I pick a couple of slices of feta and black olive and what I hope to God are caramelized onions and set them down. After grabbing honey from the cabinet, I drizzle some on my food while Star and Mom sit down with theirs.

Star folds her hands, smiling serenely. She won't eat until Mom spills the beans. Meanwhile, I'm devouring two slices at the same time, layered like a mini lasagna.

"I've been on the phone"—Mom pauses dramatically—"with Andro Philips."

Star screams, predictably. Unpredictably, however, I drop my pizza lasagna and about spit my mouthful out.

Andro Philips is the most beautiful man I've laid eyes on through a touch screen. And I swear to Jesus's chest hair that I am not the kind of chick who loses my marbles every time some dude walks by with his pecs hanging out. It's something about Andro's sun-copper skin, chestnut hair, thick, curly eyelashes, and yeah, okay, a built surfer's bod that makes me all completely breathless. And he's really good with words. I'm serious. His posts make him sexier, if you can believe that. I barely can myself.

Oh, and he's also the founder of Fotogram. He's got three hundred MILLION followers, surpassed only by Beyoncé and Lady Gaga. I'm almost embarrassed to admit—okay, I am embarrassed to admit—that I first joined Fotogram with my own account solely to add one more to that gargantuan number.

And now he wants my sister for something. Not a surprise in any capacity, if I had let myself think instead of react for more than half a second. Almost wasted a good bite of pizza there.

"Andro wants Star Fuentez to join . . ." A pause so long, I nearly grind my teeth into chips. "The Summer Fotogram Influencers for Charity Tour!"

Star gives another bloodcurdling scream, which I attempt to shout over. "But summer is now!" We've been out of school—graduated, even!—for two weeks already.

"Yup. He apologized for the short notice, but apparently the Sapphire brothers dropped out for a family emergency. You and Belle Brix—we met her once, right, in Seattle?—anyway, you two will take their places."

Star visibly shudders at the name "Belle Brix." "Ugh," Star says at the same time I say, "That sucks."

Mom gives me a warning glare. I forgot that "sucks" upsets Jesus too.

"What's wrong with Belle Brix?" I ask, diverting attention away from my vulgarity. That girl single-handedly taught my whole generation—me included—how to perfect the glitter cat-eye.

"It's . . . drama." Star waves her hand. "When do I leave?"

Right. Damn. All summer without Star. What the heck am I going to do?

And then something really close to happiness settles in my chest. I know exactly what I'll—

"You and your sister leave this weekend."

For the first time in ages—years, maybe—Star and I are silent. She stares at me as though I cut all her paper-white hair off with a pair of garden shears. And I stare at her like—like I don't know what. Because I don't know what the hell is going on.

"Oh, don't give me that look," Mom says, grabbing another slice of pizza. "I told Andro that because you're so young—Star, you're the youngest Fotogram star to join the tour ever—you'd need your sister. What kind of a mother lets her seventeen-year-old daughter tour the country alone? Huh?"

I promptly remove that lid off my mouth. "But, Mom—"

"No buts, Moon." Mom gives a glare that says, *I will throw six steak knives at your face if you don't stop.* So I stop. Because I know my mom has really good steak-knife-throwing aim. "Besides, who's going to photograph her on the road?"

My head has dropped so far, I'm practically inhaling pizza grease. "So you're telling me I'm going to spend all summer locked in a tour bus so that I can take pictures of Star?"

Star tilts her head. "As opposed to spending all summer locked in our home to take pictures of me?"

"Hey, I get out—"

"The woods don't count, Moon!"

"Girls!" Mom's voice slices like a machete. I bet she's good at throwing those, too. "You're both going. And no, Moon, you will have more to do than take photos. Andro said he's hiring you to sell merch."

"Merch," I say. God. "Did Andro really say 'merch' or—"

"He's paying you four thousand dollars."

I stop breathing when I realize Mom's talking to me and not Star. "For selling merch?" My voice is all squeaky.

"Yes."

Jesus. What kind of merchandise am I going to be selling? Crack? Live velociraptors?

"Come on, Moon," Star says. "You'll get to see your soul mate in the flesh."

I scoff. "You know I don't care about that." Even though the thought of breathing the same air as Andro Philips is giving me heat rash.

Mom leans back. "I'll let you tell me your decision, Moon. You know I don't make those for you girls." I swallow my snort. "But if Moon doesn't go, neither of you go."

Star gives me a look so devastating, I immediately groan. "Fine."

Mom always says she doesn't make our decisions, but she also fails to mention that she doesn't give us a choice, either. Or me at least.

Another shriek that makes my eardrums want to crawl and hitch a ride to Alaska. I glare at Star and Mom as they hug and dance. I literally cannot remember the last time Mom laid a hand on my shoulder. I'm not sure she's ever hugged me, not even before I learned to talk, when she had zero proof I'd be the bad daughter.

Whatever. I have better things to do.

In my room, I pull up the Fotogram app on my phone. My username is Moonflower, Tía's nickname for me. It's kind of obvious if anyone were going to search for me on there. But no one will, so, moot point.

Andro Philips's FG page is full of healthy meals made of pureed carrots, grilled chicken breasts, and wilted kale. There's the occasional party picture with shimmering celebrities, everyone smiling and looking as though they've just participated in a giant orgy with sparkly fairies and vampires. My favorites are the ones of him surfing, skimming the water like it's made of fabric. Oh, no, actually, I really like the workout ones too. "Damn," I say as he lifts what looks to be a three-thousand-pound dumbbell in a loop. His bicep looks like it's trying to eat his whole body.

I can't believe I'm going to be licking distance from those biceps in less than a week. As the merch girl, I have to remind myself forcefully. As Star Fuentez's invisible sister.

A notification pops up in my messages. It's from Deborah Opal. No idea if that's her real name. *Hey, OMG, Moonflower lady, where are you? I'm dying for an update!* I smile. Opal was one of my first followers when I decided to use FG for more than stalking Andro Philips. And I think an update is something I really need right about now too.

I gather my mystical little suitcase and my camera bag. After pulling a lavender-print hoodie over my head—my favorite, the illustration looks like it's from an ancient book of herbs—I head down the hall. I can hear Mom and Star yapping in Star's room, so I give the door a knock.

"Come in," Star calls.

They're both standing over a massive mountain of clothing that reminds me of one of Maurice Sendak's Wild Things. I recognize the million-dollar cloak hanging out the side of it like a tail.

"Packing already?" I ask, surveying the pile of luggage on Star's bed.

Star waves around a bunch of papers. "There are sixteen whole events. Each with a different theme." As though that explains a need to transform everything you wear into a colossal clothes creature. But I shrug. I guess I'd be more surprised if Star didn't start packing before she was even finished with dinner.

"What's in your hand?" I ask Mom, who's got the papers now.

"The schedule." I make for it, but Mom pulls it away. "We need this, Luna." She gets like this when she's all stressed out, calling me and Star by the proper Spanish names she and Dad should've given us.

"I want to see it when you're done, okay?"

"I'll forward you the email," Star says, picking up a brown jumpsuit covered in gold embroidery. It's one of my favorites.

"Yes," I say before she even asks. "You need to bring that. You know you look like a goddess in it."

Star beams at me. "You should've gotten one too, you know."

"Yeah . . ." Yeah right, I mean. With my hips, I'd look about seven months pregnant with great white shark triplets. But Star's attention is back on the clothing creature, along with Mom's.

Seeing Mom and Star together, it's a constant reminder of how different Star and I look from each other. Because I take after Mom—skin brown as acorns, hair black like basil seeds. A figure as curvy as a mountain range. None of those things is bad. We're not ugly.

But next to Star, we're pieces of trash adrift on an aquamarine sea.

Star's figure is long and willowy and still curvy. Her skin is the color of wheat, and not a single freckle ruins the marble smoothness of it. Her bone structure is sharp and angled, complete with brown doe eyes and a rosebud mouth that's perpetually pink. Her hair is light brown enough that she doesn't look like a mother-flipping fool when she bleaches it white blond. Instead, she looks like she belongs on *Game of Thrones*, with a dragon curled around each shoulder.

The worst part is, you can't hate her. No one can. 'Cause her heart's as sweet as it is covered with Swarovski crystals.

"The only good thing your father left behind is Star's looks." Mom says this all the time, and after she's done, she'll look at me and remember to throw a bone. "Oh, and your eyes, of course."

My eyes. Sometimes I wish I could pluck them out and present them to her, like Saint Lucy. That's the only way I could compete with Star. If I were just my eyes, I mean, disembodied and staring up from a silver platter.

5.

The Story of My River Styx Eyes

YOU KNOW HOW when Achilles was born, his mom dipped him in the River Styx? To protect him from all harm?

That's what happened with me and Star, when we were born. First came Star, pink and small, and then me, big and brown. And Mom dipped Star into some ancient, holy river. One that was big and wide and rushing with bubbling rapids, the color of pale sapphires, smooth stones along its silt edges. Mom sat on one of those stones and dipped Star in the river. Unlike Achilles's mom, she took care to make sure each of Star's heels was consecrated. That's why even Star's toes and ankles and knees and elbows are beautiful.

And Mom, for some reason unknown to me, couldn't love me as much. It was like there was a shallow reservoir of love inside her, and Star took it all. Star drank it all up before I even had a chance. And so when Mom dipped Star in the river, some of the water got in my eyes from Star splashing.

"That's enough for you," Mom must have said, because all the love inside her was already gone.

And that's how my eyes became my only source of beauty. It was an accident, one Mom seems to resent from time to time. They are like tiger's-eye, the stone I mean, all gold and mixed with bronze and little flecks of green. They're not even that special, but against my dark skin, they stand out enough that Mom begrudgingly will compliment me. Though Mom's compliments to me are not like the ones she gives Star. Star's compliments are wide like that river, clear and bottomless. The ones I get are always sharp, like soft tulle wrapped around razor blades.

"You're not dressed like a slob today," she'll say, or, "Your stomach isn't as fat in that skirt," or, "You could be so pretty if you'd keep quiet for five minutes, Moon." Stuff like that.

Sometimes I wonder if my face hadn't been splashed, if Mom would keep me around at all. But then again, who would take photos of Star? Not her, that's for sure. Not Mom.

"I'm going on a walk," I announce.

"Okay," Star says. Mom doesn't even glance up.

"I'll try really hard not to fall on the knife of a serial killer, okay?"

"Mm." Mom narrows her eyes at a black sweater.

"I won't have sex with any trees, either."

"Dios." Now Mom glances at me, crossing herself. "We need to do something about that mouth of yours, Luna." She holds up a leather jacket. "What about this, Estrella?"

Dismissed.

I make my way to the back door.

The sky is lit just enough that I can go in the Forbidden Woodland a little, thanks to my namesake, the full moon.

I guess now's as good a time as any to go over that one.

6.

How Star and I Got Our, to Put It Nicely, Weird Names

MY DAD WAS born in Mexico, but he's got all this European ancestry. Had. Had all this European ancestry. His eyes were like sea glass, turquoise almost in their brightness. And his skin was white people's idea of tan, and his hair was slick and brown, and he even had freckles on the tops of his cheeks every summer. Must be where I get mine from.

And my mom was born in Texas, but she's dark like roasted chestnuts, her hair curly and so black, it won't lighten at the ends no matter how long she grows it. She's short with wide hips and feet, perfect for baby-making and field-working—that's what some white guy on the street told her once, right in front of me and Star.

They agreed to name us Luna and Estrella, proper names, normal names, but something happened when my mom was in labor. My mom was in agony, screaming curse words in Spanish, and one of her nurses hissed, "We speak English in this country."

It wasn't the first time Mom had heard that—I'm sure of it.

But something about being in the middle of having two babies, something about her body about to be split open like an overripe mango, it was like she'd decided that was the last time.

"No," she said when my father started filling out our birth certificates. "They'll be Star and Moon."

My dad didn't think Star and Moon were as pretty as Estrella and Luna, because, honestly, they're not. But I guess he knew better than to argue with a woman who'd just pushed out twins, so he filled out our names as she asked.

Star Celestina, after her. Moon Willow, after him.

"I knew you'd be a star," Mom tells Star all the time. "That's why I named you that."

This doesn't hurt as much as the other stuff, because once, while camping, I was up with my dad watching the moon rise. And he took me in his arms and said, "Look at that moon. Have you ever seen a prettier moon?" And I hadn't, because that moon was full and gold like an ancient coin, glowing with a smattering of fog-like clouds around it. But then Daddy said, "I have! I have!" And he lifted me in the air and told me I was the most beautiful Moon he'd ever seen, and that's why he named me Moon, because he hoped I'd always see the moon and know my worth and place in the world.

This is a story I keep written on an old scroll, rolled up, sealed with red wax, locked in a little trunk in my heart. Sometimes, when Mom gets really bad, I hide in my room and imagine it again, what it was like to be loved, to be tossed up into the night sky as high as that gold coin moon but knowing someone would be there to catch me.

It's a nice feeling. I'm glad I got to know it.

7.

All That Spooky Old-Religion Stuff

I TAKE A breath and close my eyes, smelling the pine and moss and dirt. Though I can't see them all, flowers open all around me. Crocuses and dandelions and salvia, sage and lupine and five-petaled wild roses. There's the white blooms of fruit, too—strawberries, blackberries, raspberries, all wild, their bushes already full of tight green berries. God. I won't be around to taste them, not this summer. Not till August, and by then the asshole squirrels and birds will've cleared them out. Anything left over will taste too much like wine.

Star owes me a lot of freaking berries.

After I wander around for a few minutes, this is what I've collected in my trunk: Leaves, a few pine cones no larger than my thumb. A piece of thread, shiny and silver, draped on a low branch like a strand of moonlike hair. And before I leave the woods, I glance up and spot the mother lode. A hummingbird vine. When in the heckle did that sprout up? It's covered in fine, comblike leaves and star-shaped red blooms. Smaller than a pinkie print. I pull tiny clippers from my bag and I snip two dozen blooms.

I always ask the plant before taking. And I always thank it too. Just like Tía taught me. I don't care how that sounds. Plants have been here for six zillion years longer than us. That makes them sacred in my book.

And now comes the fun part. I sit near the edge of the forest, where backyard porch lights still reach, and spread the treasure, ruffling items back and forth. An empty shell husk here, open so delicately, it's as if a tiny fairy did it with reverence. Pine cones on all four corners. Did you know that pine cones close up when they get wet? Once I spent all day in the forest after a rain, and the cones were boarded up like when Southerners are expecting a hurricane. By the end of the day, they'd all opened up again, slow and in a spiral. That's when I realized that even the things that fall out of plants, seemingly unconnected to any roots or veins, they too are still alive. How amazing is that? It might be even more amazing than all of matter existing inside a fraction of a period.

I arrange the thread in a spiral and the red stars in a crescent, open at the top, like a flat, wide bowl. And finally, I light a bunch of tea light candles, all Dollar Store brand. And then I set up my tripod.

This is why Esperanza calls me wild. She says I'm still doing the old-religion stuff, and that I came by it naturally. Rituals from way back when, before the conquistadors barged in and said, *Hey, you heathens, we're gonna rape and kill you now, mmkay?* Before, when our people were free and did their own ceremonies and spoke to their own gods. Because they wanted to, not 'cause they were forced to.

But I dunno. This isn't a prayer or anything. It's not a spell. I'm basically making something beautiful from all the stuff lying around.

That *is* a prayer, Tía says.

I've got it. Shit, the exposure's so long, I couldn't even breathe near it, but I've got it now. I wink at the viewfinder, like it's my little partner-in-crime, because the photo turned out so perfect. Everything arranged just so, gold under the candlelit glow. It really does look like a prayer.

Welcome to existence, Empress.

After I admire the image in the viewfinder, I look around over my shoulders. Looking for what, I'm not sure. Usually when La Raíz comes, it's when I'm really, really absorbed in my work. But I guess I was too quick for it this time. Thank goodness. The last thing I need today is a cursed miracle.

8.

Maps of Constellations like Cake Sugar

MY DAD WAS an anthropologist, an archaeologist, and an all-around adventurer. It's hard to believe my mom was ever okay with a man like that, but supposedly they were happy once.

Dad would take me and Star camping every other weekend, and once he took us all the way up to Alaska to camp for a whole summer month. I was super into astrology at the time, and Star was such a jerk about it, trying to get me back on the "Christian path." "Daddy," she said to him. "Isn't it ridiculous that some people believe our personalities and futures are in the stars?" She then gave me a long, pointed look.

"Oh, I don't know," Dad responded. We were all sitting by a little campfire, heating up water for hot cocoa, which we'd drink out of Dad's old tin cups. "For thousands of years, all we had to guide us were constellations. We followed them at sea and on land, letting them guide our whole destinies." He shrugged and winked at me. "Makes sense that people still look up for answers on the next steps."

I think about that from time to time, about how those stars we look at, how they looked at our ancestors. How they've been guiding us since we started memorizing their shapes and movements, the way the earth breathes around them year after year. And how it's so weird that stars are so magical, but Star has none of that inside of her. She's like a star whose light got muddied somehow. I mean, Star is beautiful and blessed, but I can't remember the last time she genuinely laughed from her belly. I feel like while I got Mom's looks, Star got Mom's heart. And it makes me sad.

9.

Star Has a Nemesis
and I Didn't Even Know?

STAR BANGS INTO my room as I'm settling down with my cold, honey-topped pizza and coffee. Breakfast, because what else is there? Gravel and Madam Le Blanc cloaks? Even just waking up, she's almost too beautiful to look at. "Hey," she says. "Have you finished editing the beach shoot? They're supposed to go up by tonight, remember."

"On it," I say, minimizing the Empress.

"Wait, what was that?" Star points at my computer screen. "A new art piece? Let me see."

I pull it back up and keep my sigh as soundless as possible.

"Oh," Star breathes. "I love it! This one's my favorite."

"That's what you say about all of them."

"Well, I love them all." She gives me a side hug. "Thank you for giving up your whole summer for me."

I stiffen a little, but gradually I lean in. "Sure, Star."

"Don't forget," she says as she leaves. "Beach shoot. Tonight."

"Got it."

When she's gone, I pull the Empress back up. Madam Le Blanc's cloak company can wait an hour or so.

Even though my whole ass is tingly, I stay in my chair for another minute after I update the cloak photos to write Tía and tell her about the Beautiful Fools Road Trip. A whole summer stuck in a bus with Star and Star clones, I type. Yay.

I have to wait until all the way after dinner to get a moment to check the tour schedule, since Mom and Star have been on my back on editing away the teeniest tiniest muffin top in a couple of the beach photos. I collapse in bed and pull up the email. "Jesus Flipping Christ," I mutter.

So I guess this is the fourth annual Fotogram Influencers for Charity Tour. It started as one big charity event in Los Angeles, to raise awareness about drunk driving and provide resources to families whose lives have been destroyed by drunk drivers—something Andro's always been super passionate about. But somehow, along the way, it's morphed into a giant-ass road trip. Select influencers are invited to tour the country, meet and greet their followers (or fanatics, in many cases), give speeches on things like "aesthetics" and "believing in your dreams—the Fotogram way," and sell merchandise (with all profits to go to Families Against Drunk Driving). I can appreciate the charity support, but man, I am *so* not looking forward to anything else about this trip.

Meet on 6/18 at the Los Angeles Fotogram Fair. Star and Mom are purchasing plane tickets as we speak.

Then, twice a week for eight weeks, there's music festivals and social media conventions, self-help events, and even a wine and cheese festival. We hit up Las Vegas, Portland, San Antonio, Memphis, and after that, each city starts to look like *Blah-blah-blah* to me, so I stop reading and start skimming.

Finally! A list of participants. There's Van Williams. He's a self-made model who's terrified of environmental toxins. Has his own essential oils brand called Van I Am. There's Oak Longsteinson, an amateur free climber. Also, I suspect, constantly high. Chamomila Jones—well, she will keep Star occupied, I guess. They're already FG besties. Cham is, like Star, a religious model, but her focus is on fitness. Thy body is a temple and all that, so one must offer it juice cleanses and kettlebell workouts.

And next is Belle Brix. Self-taught makeup artist. Reinventor of the glitter cat-eye. And Star hates her for some unknown reason. I make a mental note to myself: *Must ask Star more about this later.*

Last but not least is my twin sister, Star Fuentez, religious model. Her focus is on purity. That's why she loves it when I edit her photos to give her an angelic glow, like she's too good to even consider that penises might exist.

At the way bottom of the list is *Merch people: 2.* Like, we don't even get the privilege of names. I wonder if I'll be Merch Girl all summer, if by August my whole body will be erased and replaced with poached-egg-and-avocado-illustrated tanks, faded photo filters, and bamboo makeup brushes. 'Cause that's all this tour is going to consist of. I can already taste it, even without reading a tarot spread.

A shriek snaps me out of my melancholy. I step into Star's room, where's she's scowling at her phone.

"Everything okay?" I ask.

She sighs. "I'm trying to move my hair appointment up, but Shauna's booked within an inch of her life. She's going to squeeze me in too early tomorrow."

"Oh, that sucks," I say halfheartedly. After a beat, I add, "So. Belle Brix, huh?"

Star rolls her eyes.

"No, seriously. What is your beef with Belle Brix?"

Star collapses in the bed. She looks like one of those goddesses in a Renaissance painting, her hair silky and lashes spidery. "Two weeks ago, Belle Brix commented on my laughing-in-front-of-the-barn photos. That I was wearing too much foundation. In fact, her exact words were"—Star pulls up what I'm assuming is a screenshot—"'I could slice a piece of cake from that liquid layer. Tone it down, friend.'" She scoffs. "Like I'd *dream* of being friends with her."

I bite my lips to keep from laughing.

"Moon!"

"I'm sorry. I'm sorry, Star. But that's freaking hilarious."

"No. No, it's not. She's got all the networks to spread nasty rumors about Star Fuentez sneaking foundation. I even trended on Twitter for sixteen minutes!"

"Star, everyone knows you don't wear makeup. Everyone. It's your whole thing, your brand, your life. And Belle Brix's brand is nothing but makeup. She's probably trying to sell some new sponsored foundation or something."

"Yeah, well. It still stinks."

"We'll avoid her as much as we can." I pause. "I noticed Oak Longsteinson on the list." God, saying his name aloud is so weird. How white can a white boy's name possibly be? But Star has been sending him heart-eyed emoji comments for a full year now.

Star shrugs. "Yeah. I guess." Her reaction is a lot more anticlimactic than I thought it'd be. She asks, "Have you packed yet?"

"No."

"Moon. We're leaving in two days!"

"I'll be fine, Mother."

She throws a pillow at me and pulls out her phone. Dismissed.

I leave and plant myself in front of my computer, groaning. FotoDrama isn't helping me to feel excited about this trip at all. At all. I hope to Zeus I don't have to hold Star's head in my lap while she cries, trying to convince her that she's the fairest of them all.

An email notification dings. Tía. I grin as I read.

Think of the flowers, Moon. Think of the flowers.

10.

It Was Fireweed That Made Me Fall in Love with the Whole Wild World

I DIDN'T REALIZE this until we spent half a summer there, but the light in Alaska is wild. Most of the time it's like dusk. There's basically a whole hour of legit night, and even that night isn't quite right. There's still light blue in the sky, like it was dipped in the turquoise ocean and was reluctant to let go. And then, before you know it, it's dusk-like once again, for nearly the rest of the day.

Because of all the light, plants grow so big up there. I saw lupine, graped and violet and blue, as tall as my dad. And Queen Anne's lace, their soft white blooms bigger than my head.

There was one flower that grew about everywhere—tall, its leaves emerald and grasslike, with sunset-pink blooms that gathered in a long cone, opening from the bottom up. I plucked the petals and slid them into my Spanish-English dictionary, the only book I brought for the trip.

"That's called fireweed," my dad told me. He said that it was so named because it sprouted up really fast and full anywhere that had just burned. "After London was bombed in World War Two, it sprouted right through the ashes. Big swaths of pink where there had been so much killing and trauma."

Later on, before leaving, Dad took us to an open market and bought us fireweed honey. When bees drink the fireweed nectar, they make a honey that's so pale, it looks almost clear. Like water that just decided to become thick and sweet for no reason. Star and I ate spoonfuls of it until the jars were basically licked clean even before we got back home.

I still have those petals in my book. They're a little faded and you can see the veins of them really clearly, but they remind me of when I fell in love with the world. That's the moment I realized that anything, that everything, could be holy.

Star makes us stop at the church on our way to the airport for the father's blessing. Despite my feelings for the church, I have to admit that St. Joseph's is beautiful. The walls are built of gray and brown stones the texture of homemade paper, and the stained glass makes me think about pomegranates and strawberries and Granny Smith apples made into light across the floor. I take Star's photo as Father Luke places his hand on her head. "In the name of the Father, the Son, and the Holy Ghost. May you travel protected. And may you be guided with the love of God." He smiles at Star and Mom.

"Now Moon," Mom says. Demands, really.

I furrow my brow. "Mom, I—"

"Now." And just like that, I'm pushed in front of the father.

I'm sure Mom is congratulating herself on behalf of God for whatever sins she's imagining I'm about to be cleansed of.

Father Luke dips his hand in the holy water. His smile is strained as he mumbles the same prayer. I was his least favorite Communion girl, and he probably sank to his knees and screamed thanks to the Lord when he found out I'd dropped out of confirmation classes—and, thereby, Catholicism.

Mom says she knows Jesus will lead my heart back to the church, but I think I'd rather rip out my heart, place it on a dish, and serve it to Father Luke. To be honest, I think, given the option, Mom would rather that too. If only my bleeding out wouldn't look so bad to Father Luke, I mean.

A click has me tilting my head toward Star. She smiles, my camera in her hand, no doubt congratulating *herself* on documenting my big spiritual moment. Probably will post it to all of her thousands and thousands of followers, begging for them to pray for my soul or something. God. I hope she doesn't. Photos of me get the worst comments.

I've packed ten pairs of leggings, a skirt, sixteen tank tops, eleven wrap sweaters, ballet flats and sandals, and two dresses. My clothes can, when all bunched and rolled up, fit in a large makeup bag. Then there's my laptop, my sketchbook, my Spanish-English dictionary, and my art pens. That fills up one book bag. My camera equipment goes into an extra-padded canvas tote.

Every-freaking-thing else—the two rolling Coach luggage bags, Victoria's Secret Pink totes, Kate Spade handbag—that's all

Star. I help her with her luggage, and she exhales with an "Oh, gosh, thank you, Moon" as she heaves one of the larger bags onto my shoulder. I manage a smile even though it feels like I've got Michelangelo's statue of David propped on me while pulling a suitcase that feels like it's been stuffed with many, many planets.

Mom hands us envelopes. "This is for your food plan, and souvenirs." She smiles. I want to snatch both cash bundles from her hand, just to see how much more Star got, but I give her a hug instead, making sure not to touch her with anything other than my hands and forearms. "Thanks, Mom. So thoughtful."

She nods and winces a little, shrinking away from me, digging in her purse for some holy relic. She gets a little teary-eyed as she crosses us with her rosebud rosary. "God bless you."

"Mom," I say. "We're not off to war."

"Luna," Star mutters.

"I'm fine, Star," Mom says, giving me a glare that could cut the pope's dick right off. "And, Moon? No sex." She whispers the last word, like the pope is nearby, listening.

I groan, and once again berate myself for telling Mom when I'd lost my virginity. Such a weird term. I gave it away. It was my choice. Not that the wording would've made a difference to Mom or the aim of her steak knives.

Mom continues. "I'm not raising any grandbabies. Or sluts."

The word "slut" settles into my skin like the fangs of serpents. I speak before I can think of stopping myself. "Could you say it a little louder? I'm not sure everyone here knows I've had a penis in my vagina."

A lady next to me smirks. Mom looks like she wants to strangle me with grenades. I can tell she is thinking really hard about how to react. She can't say what she really wants to because we're in public and people would think ill of her. She finally settles on "You need to go to confession. This week."

The woman next to us rolls her eyes in such a way that only I see it. I hide half a smile.

"I doubt they'll be making any stops at Catholic churches," Star says.

"I don't care! I'll call that Andro—"

"Mom," Star says calmly, with another hug. "We've got to go."

"Ah. Okay." Mom wipes her tears again. "May our heavenly Father protect you."

"From all the penises," I finish.

"Moon!" Mom's teeth are starting to get pointy, so I run away before she can see my grin.

Star jogs behind me as I call, "Amen!"

I can't believe I'm still upright with this whale on my back.

And just like that, we're off to God knows what. *Flowers*, I remind myself. *Flowers*.

Apparently, FG couldn't foot business class, which is so considerate of the multibillion-dollar start-up. Star takes the window, because blah-blah-blah claustrophobia, and I'm in the middle, squished by a long-legged man who's apparently never heard of the concept of personal space.

"What are you, a model?" he asks Star over my head.

Star smiles, but she's reining it in, thank God. Sometimes she likes to enchant strangers for attention, but I am so not in the mood to sit between her giggles and this guy's eye-fucking.

"Oh," Star says. "I'm just a freshman in high school." Oh my good Gandalf, YES. We graduated a few weeks ago, actually, but this is one of the easiest ways to get grown men off her back. I almost laugh at the look on his face—like he's been caught shooting heroin with the devil.

"Ah." He glances at the scar on my collarbone, and his eyes immediately drop to my cleavage.

"Sophomore," I say.

He clears his throat and pulls out a thick book while angling his legs away from us. I grin at Star. The whole "pretend like you're fourteen when old dudes get fresh"—that was all her idea, and it works really well about 64 percent of the time.

Star's got her pillow out and she's already dozing.

I scoff. "I don't know why you always need the window if you're just going to sleep."

"The window makes you sick."

"No it doesn't!" I've got Mom's envelope in my hand, ready for my wallet.

"I thought you got carsick."

Carsick. That was Mom's excuse for wanting Star to be up in the passenger's seat alongside her. But I just say, "That doesn't translate to plane sick, all right?" I pause, bills in hand. "Star.

Why on Middle-earth do I have fifteen hundred dollars?"

She puts a finger to her lips and closes her eyes. "I swear, you are begging to be robbed."

"That doesn't answer my question."

"The meal plan costs fourteen eighty. I guess the rest is for souvenirs."

"Why does an eight-week meal plan cost fourteen hundred and eighty dollars?" I ask. "Little Caesars can feed us for a day with their five-dollar Hot-N-Readys."

Star groans. "The restaurants they made deals with aren't Little Caesars. They're *nice*, Luna. It's an amazing price, considering."

I stare at the wad in my wallet. We haven't had to worry about financial stuff, not since Star made it big. Still, the way Star and Mom throw money around scares me sometimes. Am I the only one who remembers mustard sandwiches and buttered-rice dinners?

"I thought I read we had to sign up for the meal plan online."

"The PayPal thing wasn't working for Mom. Andro said we could pay when we got there."

"You've already talked to Andro?"

"No. Mom did." Star rolls her eyes. "Can I sleep yet?"

"Do you know if the tour bus has a little kitchen or something?"

"How would I?" She pulls on her eye mask. "Good night, Moon."

Now I'm the one rolling my eyes. It's two in the afternoon, genius. I pull out my computer and start some research.

11.

I Am the Bad Daughter
Who Lies and Keeps Secrets

MOM THINKS I'M going to Temple Community College, down the street, so I can continue my unpaid labor of photographing Star. I haven't told anyone yet, but that was never my plan. I've been accepted to Brown, Portland U, and one wild card: Tulane University for their art program. I found out a few months ago I got in, and it took every ounce of willpower to not run through the house throwing fireworks while screaming, "I'm getting the hell out of here!"

One problem. The full ride I got isn't entirely full, because it doesn't cover room and board. Technically, I could ask to stay with Tía, but Mom would never speak to me again, and I don't know if I'm ready to cut ties that hard with her. So I need eight thousand dollars. Or to put down five and work-study the rest.

If I eat next to nothing this summer, I can go to Louisiana. And live on campus.

There's one more thing that's so ridiculous, I probably shouldn't even be thinking about it, but I can't help it.

It costs $265 to get 158 tarot decks printed by Occulette, the best of the best as far as deck printers go. It's the cheapest plan, but the stuff is worth it, according to my research. Thick cardstock, the paper smooth as windless lakes. Nothing is going to bend or peel or crack for one hundred thousand spreads. And that's how a tarot deck should be. Passed on and all so we can have the cards of our literal ancestors.

We can afford it, but I'm pretty sure Mom would rather give Father Luke a blow job than let me contribute to the devil's work. I mean, I haven't asked, specifically, but I'd place a large bet on it.

I can print my decks and live on campus if I can figure out a way to live on cold SpaghettiOs all summer without wanting to cut out my own tongue.

. . . Or not. According to my internet searches, lots of tour buses have kitchens. Some even have full-size ovens and fridges and stuff. Surviving on grilled cheese all summer is an option now. Much better than cold SpaghettiOs, in my humble opinion.

I grab my sketchbook and trail mix and don't look up until the plane rumbles back to earth.

12.

Why Does It Seem Like in All My Beginnings, I'm a Total Jackass?

WE'VE LANDED AND gotten our luggage. Well, I got our luggage. Star approaches the driver holding up the STAR FUENTEZ sign first. He grins when he sees us—or Star, specifically.

"I've been following you since the old house," he says. "God. I can hardly believe I'm talking to you. And you're even hotter in person." He coughs, pink spots high on his cheeks. "I mean, I think it's so cool, that despite everything, you're staying true to God's plan, you know?"

Star responds with a Bible verse or something, and this is the part where I put in my earbuds, stare out the window, and tune everyone the flip-flop out. Except that's the moment my phone chooses to kick the bucket battery-wise, so there goes that grand plan.

The traffic is as stuffed as a Thanksgiving turkey. It takes us

RAQUEL VASQUEZ GILLILAND

forty minutes to get to the bus-slash-restaurant-slash-store, but our driver doesn't notice. He doesn't even breathe. I'm tempted to check his neck for some sort of extra nose or gills or something. "I've been telling my friends, but they don't believe me. No one is going to believe I got to drive Star Fuentez from the airport. Seriously, do you need to stop somewhere to eat? You sure? There's a Port Burger on the way. But you probably don't eat burgers, huh? I mean, you're *Star Fuentez*. Hahahahaha—" And the earbuds go right back in, even with no music, because I'm that desperate. I don't know how Star doesn't regularly scream her face off and then light it on fire. But she keeps nodding, smiling, making this guy feels like he's the first person on earth to reveal his journey back to Jesus to *Star Fuentez*.

When we finally reach our stop, he asks, "Will you take our picture?" He doesn't look at me as he hands me his phone.

He puts his arm around Star like they're old buddies. She leans her head in, toward his shoulder, but keeps the rest of her body a foot away, the classic Creep Alert sign. My instincts crawl out of my body like cobras to see what this guy is being a jerk about. There. His fingers are gripping the underside of her left boob.

I delete the photo immediately and permanently. "One more, except stop fondling her."

"Moon," Star says, but her eyes show nothing but relief.

The guy jumps back like he had no idea. "Sorry," he says, but his eyes are twinkling. I'll bet he's mentally composing a text

46

to every dudebro he knows that he got to grope Star Fuentez. Joke's on him, because now I'm deleting even the proper photos. "There you go, friend," I say, giving him a glare along with his phone. Asswipe.

He sort of wilts under my gaze and stuffs his phone in his pocket. "Good to meet you," he says to Star, then gives me a glance before jumping in his car and driving away.

"Thanks, sis," Star says, hugging me.

Sometimes I wish she'd tell me thanks in front of her fans. Or even just Mom. But whatever. I hug her back and say, "You need to stop posting about waiting for marriage. It's bait for pervs like him."

"But it inspires young girls like me. Like us." Star pulls back to give me a meaningful look, and I know we're both thinking of that time she told me I can be a virgin again if I confess to God and, like, hold a marriage to Jesus or something. I tried so, so hard not to laugh at the time, and it's happening again, so I'm relieved when some girl comes running up, screaming Star's name.

"Chamomila!" Star shrieks, and they hug for eternities, long enough for a new universe to compress and expand and make galaxies and stars and moons and an entirely new conscious species vastly different from humans.

Chamomila Jones somehow looks even less real in person than in her photos. Her body is the bronze of a perfectly applied spray tan, and it's shimmering, displaying toned muscles everywhere.

She's in a sports bra and leggings with holes cut almost all the way up to her perfect butt. I'm not sure what Purity Culture would say about that, but she looks incredible. I can feel my cellulite deepening just by proximity.

"This is my sister, Moon," Star says.

I reach my hand out, but Chamomila crushes me into a hug that probably fractures my spine. "It's so good to finally meet you!" she says into my neck. "I've heard so much about you." I doubt Star spends more than three seconds talking about me to anyone, but I'm sure Chamomila knows three things about me: I'm not a virgin. I don't regret it. And therefore I need to be prayed for.

She releases me (I swear, I choke for air like I've been drowning) and gives my collarbone a long look before turning to Star. "Come on, we've got to get you checked in!"

I touch the spot she stared at with my fingertips—a pink, ugly scar about three inches wide. I bet Star never told Chamomila where that's from. Nor ever will.

In a shocking turn of events, I'm left with almost all the luggage, so I'm certain I look like one of those junk people from *Labyrinth* who trap mountains of garbage on their backs. I have to move so slowly. Like if a sloth and a turtle and floating algae all had a baby, it'd be me right now. If I lose my balance, one of these bags is going to kill me. I'm certain of it.

There's a group of beautiful people next to the bus, all welcoming Star. They're radiating light and drinking green juice and whipped-cream-topped coffee, so I decide to start my own club, the Uglies, population: one. I take the luggage off, one by one, noticing the red marks on my skin from the straps. As long as it's just me suffering, that's what matters. I groan and grab my Spanish-English dictionary from my bag.

Mom, along with cooking and sewing and baking and general well-being-ing, has refused to teach us Spanish. "You're in America," she says. "What do you need to know Spanish for?" Over the years, Mom's tried everything to get rid of her accent. An online class, underpronouncing her *r*'s, and saying the most random phrases, like "Let freedom ring!" and "Always blessed under the US of A!"

Star's never cared to learn, but I took Spanish for my language classes and loved it. And now I spend half my days with my Spanish-English dictionary, trying to find the most beautiful words in Spanish. I've already got a huge list in my sketchbook, with gems like helecho for "fern" and lluvia for "rain" and tierra for "earth" and frambuesa for "raspberry." Everything about these sounds makes me feel more alive somehow. The idea that languages transform and move and become something new, just like people. Imagine. Somewhere, all the way back in the beginning, there was a first word. Who said it? What was it? The idea gives me goose bumps along my arms, neck, spine.

"Luna!" Star says, making me nearly fall over a Coach tote. "What are you doing over here by yourself?" She grabs my arm and pulls.

"But—the bags—"

"Don't worry. Cham says Andro's brother's going to get them."

Chamomila appears out of nowhere like a wraith, making me choke on a piece of air I was trying to inhale. After I'm done coughing up an organ, I turn to Star. "Andro has a brother?"

"Oh, yes he does," Chamomila says, sticking her gorgeous, skinny hip out. She fans herself. "He's even thicker than Andro." She nods her head toward somewhere behind me.

I turn, and my heart sort of jumps up out of my body and slaps my face when I see Andro Philips and the tall and bulk and big-handsome-smile of him, and oh, gosh, did he angle one of those smiles at me? *No, of course not,* I think as Cham smiles back and waves. Silly Moon.

And then, next to him, another guy, as bronze as Andro, but shorter. Like, six foot three instead of six foot five, so still a giant, basically. And yeah, he's solid. Like, his biceps make Andro's look like baby fat.

"Wow," I say, and judging from Star's face, she's got the same reaction going on.

"I know," Chamomila says with a smirk. "It's too bad he's just Andro Philips's brother. Otherwise I'd . . ." She makes a cat-growling sound, or at least tries to. Sounds more like a chicken getting slaughtered to me.

I scoff and turn it into a cough when Chamomila narrows her eyes at me.

"Did you say something?" Chamomila asks me sweetly.

Star widens her eyes to say something like, *Don't embarrass me in front of my friend.*

I shrug. "I thought that was kind of mean. 'Just Andro Philips's brother,' you know?"

Chamomila stares and laughs. "Oh, right, I get it. We Christians always have to defend the less fortunate, right? It's what Jesus would do."

"Are you serious right now?"

"Moon." Star's eyes are about to pop. But so's my last nerve, so I keep going.

"I mean, I'm *just* Star Fuentez's sister to about everyone." Even my own mother.

Chamomila doesn't look the least bit embarrassed. And then she has the audacity to say, "Oh, I'm sure you will accomplish something that will surpass that soon." She shrugs. "Who knows, maybe Santiago will too."

What a little— "Oh, I get it," I say. "When you're just the *sibling* of someone so *accomplished*, you're basically extra-hairy Chupacabra poop, huh? And who would *rawr* at extra-hairy Chupacabra poop?"

"Luna." Star is gesturing behind me with her eyes and fingertips, but I'm not done yet.

"Because any of Andro Philips's siblings would just be *losers.* Just big, ridiculous lo—"

"Luna!" Star's chin is jutting past me, and I spin around with dread falling through my body like dried leaves in a windy autumn forest. And yep, there is Andro Philips's brother. All 150 percent muscle of him, glaring at me like I'm some mud stuck to his shoes.

"You're the Fuentez sisters, I take it." His voice is rumbly, like it comes from his chest, and he won't remove his murder-eyes from my face.

"Yes," Star yelps. "Moon and Star. That's us."

After glaring at me for another few seconds, the guy gives us name tags. "Andro wants you to wear these." He scowls when my fingers touch his. Star and I slap the tags on our chests at the same time, eyes wide. About as twinsy as we ever get. And then she decides to put on the charm.

Smiling, she says, "What's your name?"

"Santiago." His voice is so deep, I can feel it in my feet. "I'm the merch guy."

Merch guy. *He's* the merch guy? The guy who heard me call him a loser. The guy I'm going to work alongside all summer long. "Oh God—" I say, then slap my hand over my mouth.

"*Now* you're praying, Moon?" Star says, echoing one of Mom's lines.

"Just for death, sister," I croak, my cheeks so hot, I could melt a glacier on them.

Santiago gives me one last glare before walking away. I turn to Star and Chamomila. "Please tell me that he didn't hear me call him extra-hairy Chupacabra poop. Please tell me he didn't hear that."

They don't have to respond.

Star's got a finger pointed at me. "If you've cost me this opportunity because you don't know when to shut up . . ."

But I can't think about anything other than Santiago, how under his murder-glare, he looked *hurt*. Shit, shit, shit.

"It's okay, Star," I say. "If Andro says something, I'll volunteer to leave." Now let's pray to Jesus, Mary, Joseph, and the legions of saints and angels that Andro says something.

Meanwhile, Chamomila the Craphead can't stop giggling. "You were sputtering nonsense and he was *right there*. The whole time, he was right there. Star, you didn't tell me your sister was so silly."

"You know what you are, Chamomila?" I say. "You're a—"

"Okay," Star says, jumping in. "I think Andro's calling for us to join that circle over there."

Before I follow them, I turn and see, not more than ten feet away, Belle Brix, smoking a cigar like my ninety-year-old great-grandfather. She's even kind of dressed like him, with a brown button-down top and slacks, though I don't think he'd go for the black leather jacket. And she's grinning at us.

Jesus's toenails, what have I gotten myself into?

13.

The Most Perfect Kitchen, So Dang Close and So Dang Far

"ALL RIGHT," ANDRO says, clasping his hands together. "Why don't we introduce ourselves, grab a bite, and then hit the road? Yeah? Rock and roll!"

His voice is so chipper. I wonder if Andro's ever been tempted to not expect the best. He's so beautiful and successful, it's hard to imagine that he wasn't born with the touch of Midas—everything in his path turning to cold, smooth gold. Or, rather, billion-dollar apps. He leans into Belle Brix, who must've finished her cigar off in record time to join us. "Belle! Why don't you get us started?"

Belle Brix smiles. "I focus on makeup at BelleBrixArt."

Star scoffs next to me. "Makeup isn't art." It's under her breath, but Chamomila and I both hear it, and Chamomila laughs.

"I'm releasing my first lipstick line this season, called Brixsticks. All the colors are available in matte and a glitter blend. I have plenty of samples if you all want to try!"

"I might take you up on that," Andro says to some chuckles, and goes on to the next in line. Oak Longsteinson, who introduces himself as an internationally renowned author, free climber, and entrepreneur. Chamomila describes herself as "willed by God to guide people toward their best health." I want to laugh, but at the same time, I can't. Everything sounds so fake. Everyone has to have a title, a tagline, a logo. It's like we're introducing companies and not real, live people.

And then it's my turn. Andro leans into my name tag and laughs. At first I'm startled—Andro thinks I'm funny? Or funny-looking, more like. But then he says, "Wait a minute—you're not Star!" Then everyone else laughs too.

And maybe it's 'cause we're all nervous. Maybe that's why everyone's losing their minds over something not all that hilarious. But I can't help thinking I'm the joke. *Ha ha ha, of course this size 16 frump isn't Star Fuentez.* And I catch Santiago's eye and he's smirking too, and I think, *Dang. Touché, Santiago.* He must've handed us the wrong name tags on purpose. Which, if that's the case, I guess I'll take it. It's not every day you get to call someone poop and get away with it.

Star and I quickly switch name tags and I say, "I'm Star's photographer. Moon. And yes, that's my real name. And, uh, I'm here to, uh, work in merchandising."

"You and Santi both," Andro says, throwing an arm around his brother. "I have a feeling you two are going to be the best merch team in the nation, right? Rock and roll, right? Let's hear it for Santi and Moon!" And everyone actually claps and cheers, like we the merch people won an Olympic gold medal or something. Well, everyone except for Santiago, who glowers at me, his jaw really sharp under the streetlights, which are flickering on. And all I can think now is if Santiago hating my guts means we'll make a great team, then maybe merchandising should be an Olympic sport. Because we've already won the gold.

After the last person says their spiel, Andro calls us to join him at the restaurant—some fancy lantern-lined French bistro. "You coming?" Star says. "We gotta pay for the meal plan real quick so it's covered."

"I'm not getting the plan."

"What?"

"I'm trying to save money, you know?"

No, I can tell she doesn't. Like, she hasn't even considered the option. I don't know what they're paying her to be here, and frankly, I don't want to know.

"Star," Craptastic Chamomila calls. "We gotta get selfies by the lanterns!"

"Suit yourself," Star tells me. "Meet you on the bus, okay?"

"Yeah, sounds good," I say, but she's already gone, along with everyone else.

And I'm sitting in a half-empty parking lot, hands in my pockets, looking like the world's biggest loser. Because that's exactly what I am. With a deep, dramatic sigh, I make for the bus. Better see what I'm working with.

14.

I Swear, I Didn't Start Out as a Loser

I MEAN, MY parents named me Moon, so even in the way, way beginning, the odds of non-loser-dom weren't all that great.

I think I was five or six when I realized that Mom loved Star more than me. But that wasn't so terrible, even that young. Because I had Dad. He was the biggest, strongest man in the world, and though I knew he loved me and Star equally, I was his favorite. After Star declared she hated camping, he took me and only me. Out into the mountains, wide and snow-tipped and seemingly just as tall as my father.

On those trips, he loved to tell me about beginnings. About how alongside the first people on this continent were animals so wild, it was like they were imagined and not real. Mammoths that made modern elephants look like babies, saber-toothed tigers with teeth longer than ice cream sugar cones. Dire wolves that could probably fit a man's whole head in one of their mouths.

Armadillos the size of a school bus, armored and just as strange-looking as their descendants. They were all huge and ancient and amazing, roaming these lands, leaving footprints so large and deep, a man and child could probably fit inside them.

He always brought honey and cinnamon to make my favorite hot cocoa, topped with toasted coconut marshmallows he got special from the health food store. And when I leaned on him, he never pushed me away. He'd hug me right back, exactly like a parent ought to.

Yeah, once upon a time, Moon Fuentez wasn't a loser at all.

And then Dad left. And everything went downhill from there.

15.

Sleeping with the Flipping Enemy

THE INSIDE OF the bus is a Fotogrammer's dream. Hardwood floor, little windows with sheer eyelet curtains, everything covered in warm fairy lights. There's a reading nook next to the living area, both filled with rugged-yet-chic furniture. The throw pillows look hand-sewn from vintage fabrics, and the rugs on the floor are knit from huge, cloudlike yarn. It looks more like a mountain cabin than a gas-guzzling steel tube-monster.

And there, right in the middle, is my saving grace. An honest-to-God kitchen. I leap inside and open drawers and cherrywood cabinets and find it stuffed with pots and pans—fancy-looking stuff, dark and minimal and sleek. Under the oven is a drawer full of bakeware, which I'm checking out on my knees when someone grunts behind me.

I turn, and my stomach drops. It's Santiago. Of course. As usual, he's glaring at me. He's got his arms crossed, and his biceps look like they're trying to kiss each other, only there's some gargantuan pectorals in the way.

"I'm sorry." It's out of my mouth before I can stop it, and actually, I don't want to stop it. "For what I was saying when you walked up. I was trying to be sarcastic, but I guess it didn't come off that way. I'm such an asshole. I was so angry at Chamomila for being such a wicked witch of the western persuasion, and I was trying to make her see—and my mouth, once it starts, it just keeps going, like the Energizer Bunny on crack. I never know when to shut up—that's what my mother is always telling . . ." I stop because he hasn't even blinked. His glare is worse, which I wasn't sure was possible. So what do I do? I open my mouth again. "My brain did the worst thing possible, which is, it short-circuited. Poof. In a cloud of smoke." And now my brain shuts down, because Santiago isn't giving me an inch. He's not giving me a fraction of a period. Honest to God, he looks even angrier. "Anyway." I swallow and glance down. "I am sorry." I turn and bump my elbow on the corner of the oven. "Shit. I mean. I didn't know this was going to be here, did you?" I gesture around. "And it's all stocked! With really nice-looking stuff."

"The stuff's mine," he says. I forgot how deep his voice is. I have visions of Vin Diesel and Alan Rickman singing Gregorian chants together.

"Oh." It's all I can manage.

"The pans. The spatulas. The utensils are mine too. And the can opener. Everything but the electric coffeemaker is mine."

I wait for him to offer something. Like, maybe that I could borrow whatever I needed. But all he does is narrow his eyes. I'm not sure he's blinked this entire conversation.

"So . . . you're not on the meal plan?" I ask.

He shakes his head. Very slowly.

And for some reason, my response is to nod like my head is attached to a spring. "Okay. So everything's yours. Got it."

"Everything but the coffeemaker."

"Right." I stand and edge around him. I need to get out. With my back sliding across the wall, I say, "Well. Good talk. I'm going to go see a man about a dog now."

Finally the guy drops the menacing look and furrows his brow. I give him a big smile and his brows join together to become one big brow now. That line, about a dog? It's slang from the 1920s. I did a report junior year for English. It means "I have to get whiskey." Which is true. I need a whole bath of whiskey to deal with the shitstorm that today is turning out to be. Too bad I'm still mega-underage.

As soon as I squeeze around him, because no, Santiago didn't even think of moving, I run out and head to the corner store on the other side of the restaurant.

Okay, so the 2-Kwik-Mart doesn't exactly have options. But I grab a basket and do the best I can.

First, yogurts. I add a few packages of the chocolate flavor, because duh. And a jar of peanut butter. And jelly. Bread next, because that's the natural progression of things. Ooh, butter and cheese! Oh, and microwave popcorn, extra-ridiculously buttery. Like, four packages of those in my basket, which is already threatening to overflow.

Fuck, though. If I'm going to manage grilled cheese, I need a pan, since Santiago holds grudges harder than John Wick, the Punisher, and my mother put together. And you know, my mom hasn't spoken to the mailman in eight years, since he once delivered a Weight Watchers brochure. I tried to explain that it was his job, but she threw one of the kitchen chairs across the room, so I hightailed it right out of there like a yelping coyote.

I find a sad, dented little pan covered in some nonstick coating that's probably carcinogenic according to the state of California. But it's all they've got. So I toss it in my basket along with a package of plastic cutlery, since Santiago couldn't be bothered to offer to lend me one freaking fork.

"You did call him an imaginary creature's poop," I mumble to myself. That's fairly unforgivable.

"What's that?" the cashier guy barks.

"Nothing," I say. "Just me, Moon Fuentez, off my rocker already at sweet seventeen. I should retire and sell all my bikinis and yell at the children loitering on my lawn already."

The man blinks. "That'll be $25.98."

Not bad. I bet Star's dinner cost twice that. Though Star, I'm certain, isn't dealing with some old dude staring at her chest. Or, specifically, the wide whale of a scar on mine.

"That looks like it hurt," the guy says.

"Does it?" I ask, but he doesn't sense the sarcasm at all.

"They make creams and stuff for scars now. You should look into that."

I know he thinks he's being helpful. Fine. But did he honestly think that had never occurred to me? That the girl with a giant scar on her collarbone, pink and ugly and raised, had never thought, *Hmm, wonder if there's something I could do about this?*

So I have no regrets about muttering "*Asshole*" before I grab my meals for the next two weeks and get on my way.

Santiago's cooking something that I'd give up my fingernails for. I have no idea what it is, only that it smells so good, I might throw in my camera along with my nails. Might.

But I ignore him as I walk by, even though when I get close enough to almost taste the salmon—salmon!—I want nothing more than to get on my knees and beg for a bite like a dog. I should get a parade for resisting the urge. I put away my dairy products and jelly and frying pan and refrain from drooling all over the polished hardwood floors.

Past the kitchen are the bunks. There's a name tag attached to each one written in a sparkling Papyrus-type font, arrows printed on all sides in mint green. I search for "Moon" on nearly every single bed. I'm beginning to think my assigned mattress is strapped to the top of the bus when I finally find it. All the way in the back, next to the boxes of merchandise. It's a top bunk.

And guess whose name is on the bottom one? Santi-freaking-ago. So, you know, guess I have to fake my death and run away to Montana now.

Sounds like people are back from dinner, so I find Star in the living area. "Hey, got a sec?"

Star wrinkles her nose. "Why do you smell like peanut butter?"

Because I had about half a jar for dinner, that's why, specifically when you were enjoying gold-crusted caviar and platinum lavender mousse. But instead, I say, "Do you think we could switch our assigned beds?"

She narrows her eyes. "But I'm next to Cham."

"And I'm . . ." I lower my voice when I see Chamomila narrowing her eyes at me. Little witch with a *b*. "I'm right next to Santiago."

"OMG, what?" Star covers her mouth and laughs and laughs.

"Please, Star," I say. "He's going to kill me in my sleep."

"And can you blame him?" Chamomila's scooted up now. Shit, I didn't think she could read lips like some government-trained assassin.

"The beds are assigned for a reason, Moon," Star says in her snitty voice she uses when she's trying to impress someone with how resilient she is.

"What reason is that?" I ask.

She blinks for a couple of seconds before responding. "It would be an insult to Andro to rearrange everything." She gives me a long look. "He's already disappointed that you opted out of the meals."

Andro? Disappointed? In me? I was certain he'd forgotten my name immediately after learning it, like everyone else does once they realize I'm with Star.

Before I can ask, though, Andro himself walks in. "All right! I don't mean to break up the party, but I'm going to bed, and I suggest you all do too. We've got our first stop at nine a.m. The Roanland Opera House." He looks directly at me and smiles for a full trillionth of a second. I can't remember the last time a guy made me feel like my atoms were bursting into a whole new existence, so I glance down with what is probably a look of terror on my face.

"Close your mouth, Moon. You're drooling," Chamomila hisses. And Star does her classic fake laugh because yeah, that's not even remotely funny, and I'm not sure how I could hate Chamomila Jones more, but I do. And you know what? My sister's being a big cabbage-head nematode too.

I stand and leave, not bothering to respond when Star calls, "Good night, Moon."

"Oh no," I whisper to no one as I stand in the bathroom, alone, having just brushed my teeth. Because all I brought to wear to bed is a giant T-shirt and tiny shorts, my usual getup. But. It looks like I'm not wearing anything under the shirt. And there are boys here.

I can hear my mother's voice, ringing all around. *Boys have already seen you naked. Why start caring now?*

"Hey, you done yet?" a deep voice rattles right at the door. Great. My nemesis. I take a breath, grab my things, and refuse to look at Santiago on my way out. And he does the same on his way in.

Oh, thank goodness. We're going to pretend the other doesn't exist. I'm really good at that, especially the not-existing bit, so. Yay.

I climb into bed, spotting a pile of books through the open sliver of Santiago's bunk curtain. So Mr. Freeze reads. The bathroom door clicks open before I can spy any titles, so I quickly climb into my bed, which is smaller than his. Makes sense, considering he's the size of an average wildebeest.

I lie back for a moment, feeling the shift of the frame as he gets in. Is it weird to bunk with someone who'd rather watch you eat your own hair than speak with you? 'Cause I'm thinking it's weird. Mega-weird. Weirder than bunking-less-than-twenty-feet-away-from-Andro-Philips weird, though? I honestly don't know. I feel like I'm in an episode of *Stranger Things*, like I somehow got sucked into a universe where everything is upside down and inside out.

My phone gives a little buzz, and I roll my eyes.

Samuel: WTF Moon? Ur on the fotogram tour and couldn't even tell me??

I type back, It happened really fast.

Samuel: **Bullshit. I thought I meant more to you than that.** There are several emoji to indicate he's not completely serious. Which he never is.

Me: **howd you find out, anyway?**

Samuel: **Star's feed. Bejesus, real gold on dessert?**

Me: **Tell me about it.**

Samuel: **I miss you. Can't believe you're not going to be around all summer.**

My fingers linger on the keys a little. Samuel is . . . sigh. He's Samuel. We fooled around once and we've been friends since, though I always get the feeling he keeps in contact with me for the offhand chance we might hook up again. He's never said anything outright, but no one's friends with Star Fuentez's sister just to be friends, you know? They're always after me for something; that's all I gotta say about that.

Finally I write: **Oh, you'll have a lot of company, I'm sure.**

And I am sure. Samuel, star basketball player, lean with big brown eyes, impossibly long lashes, and dimples. He's never short on company of any gender.

Send me a nude.

I snort. In your dreams, friend.

Then I turn my phone off. Before sleep, I imagine that instead of a bus, I'm on a spaceship, blasting through a glittering nebula that still tastes like the beginning of this whole, wild universe.

16.

The First Time I Ever Had Sex

IT WAS AFTER Dad was gone and Mom had spent nearly the whole day yelling at me to stop being such a shitty daughter because I didn't wipe down the living room walls as well as she wanted. And so when Iris Bowler asked me to go to a party with her so she could see if she might catch her girlfriend cheating, I screamed "YES" with the force of a nuclear explosion and snuck out the window after I was sure everyone was asleep.

When I got there, though, all my enthusiasm totally faded away, like a dried-up patch of earth sucking up rainwater. Iris disappeared to investigate her girlfriend's faithfulness, and I was alone, surrounded by classmates I'd rarely spoken to, everyone drinking and yelling and dancing. I walked into the backyard and collapsed right into the overgrown grass, cold and damp against my legs.

"Hey," a boy said. He was leaning up against the house, looking at his phone. I knew him. His name was Mike, so basic, but he had these lovely hands I'd noticed in art class, as though they were made for things like building gorgeous wooden dressers and benches and bed frames.

And I was so sick of everything, everything sucking all the time, and so I walked up to him and said, "Want to make out?"

I ended up right back on the grass, with him on top of me, and everything went so fast. At the time, I really felt like I was ready for all of it. How my body burned underneath his wood-smith hands, how I had to try so hard to not moan when his lips found my neck, chest, belly, thighs. But now I'm not sure. I'm not all that sure I was ready for it in my mind, even if my body wanted nothing else.

He used a condom. It hurt a little, in a sore, full kind of way, and then it was over, and as he lay on top of me, he lifted up a little and gazed into my eyes. And he was so reverent. "That was amazing," he whispered. And I felt like I was worth something, for the first time since Dad left. It made my heart break and repair itself all at the same time, over and over until I was certain I fell in love with this boy right then and there.

And then a firefly landed on his hair, blinking like a warm fairy lantern. "Look at that," I whispered, intending to brush it away. At that moment, ten more fireflies arrived.

"Wow," he said, and before he could even sit up, a hundred arrived, swirling around us in the dark until it felt like Mike and I were planets, spinning in space.

When they landed on us, Mike yelped and jumped up, scratching at his arms and hair. "Are you some kind of witch or something?" he asked, sort of serious, sort of laughing.

"Or something," I said. Because no, it wasn't quite a witch. It was La Raíz. The root that connected me to the sin of Eve, surrounding me right then with such beauty, it took my breath away.

"This is too weird for me," Mike muttered, walking away.

It was too weird for me, too, but at the same time, it felt exactly like what I deserved. I finally had proof that I had released the curse that day I opened Mom's milk jar. Finally had proof that I was the cursed daughter.

As for Mike, I never spoke to him again.

17.

Peach-Stained Lips and a Plum-Stained Head

MY ALARM COMES way too soon, chiming with what I imagine to be copper singing bowls, but they sound a little like cars crashing in my brain right now. It takes me a good four minutes to turn it off.

I peek out of the curtains on my little personal window. We're parked at some resort-looking building, gold-lined, with Greek-looking columns, ivy covering half of it, making it almost look like it came from the woods. Like the ivy just presented it to earth.

I flip open my dictionary and search for "ivy." Hiedra. I let the deep green of it wash over me: pointed leaves, prickly against my skin. Ivy is pricklier than hiedra. Hiedra is a blanket of vinery, covering me as I slip into a thousand-year sleep in the forest.

Hey, you up? I text Star. She doesn't respond, so I guess I've procrastinated enough. I grab my bathroom bag and head down the ladder. Before I reach the last step, I see an enormous arm where my foot ought to go next, and I slip, stumbling onto the ground.

"Motherfucker," I say as my head slams on the hardwood.

My leg is on someone. That realized, it doesn't take me long to recover. In fact, I stand so hard, I see little white planets dancing for a full thirty seconds. Once my vision clears, all I can process are muscles. There's a sea of them, right in front of me.

Santiago is balanced on the floor, shirtless and planking. Apparently, I fell on him and he didn't even notice. He shifts his weight a little, and those cuts along his back do a lovely ripple under his skin, as though he were Poseidon with an ocean wave of a body.

It's early, and now my head hurts, so I probably stare longer than I should. Because muscles. They're everywhere. His muscles are married to all his other muscles, and they have little muscle babies in their little muscle carriers, bunching and rippling together like one big, happy family.

"Can you not walk around me?" His voice is gruff and loud and deep. If I touched my own skin, I bet I'd feel it. But he sounds super annoyed, so I gulp instead, grab my bag, and tiptoe around him on my way to the bathroom.

The door flies open and Oak Longsteinson is there. Shirtless. Of course. Because I'm not flustered enough, apparently. "Hey," he says. "Moon, right?"

I mumble, "Good morning," and when safe in the bathroom, immediately splash water on my face.

Is this what it's like to live with guys? All pecs and happy trails exposed all the time? If so, I'm not ready. At all.

I change quickly into a pale-pink wrap sweater and black leggings. I look in the mirror and groan. Right in the middle of my forehead, a beautiful reddish bruise the size of Alaska. The color of it feels like clippers pinching my legs. I brush my hair in my face and hope that's enough to distract from what is essentially a lake of blood just under my forehead.

There are words I hate, for no reason other than they feel abrasive in my body when I say them, read them, even think them. "Evergreen" is one, though just "ever" or "green" is fine, weirdly enough. I hate "poncho" and "thrash" and "crumb." But if you add an *s* to "crumb," it changes everything. Suddenly the word is soft like snow on my forearms.

I've been collecting words almost as long as I've been talking, or at least, that's what my dad said to me once.

As I join Santiago in the back to unload the merch, I can add another word to the mix of most unliked. "Stubborn." It's an ugly word, one I've never liked, but as I think it now, hot spikes burn into my back.

"I can get that," he says for the fifth time as I grab a box. He tries to pull it from my hands.

"I've got it. Really."

He stares at me, or rather, the bruise on my head for the hundredth time. Most people might say something like, *Are you okay? What happened? Can I get you something?* But not this dude. Or, not if you were a bit of a poophead for his first impression of you. I guess.

He pulls on the box harder and I just give up and let it go, then grab three smaller ones to head up the million stairs flanked by ivy-wrapped columns. And that's when I notice that Santiago is missing his left hand. He balances the boxes perfectly on his forearm on that side, securing the front of the pile with his right hand. I wonder if he was born without it, or if there was an accident or something. I'll never ask, though, because that is rude as flip, even if he is my nemesis.

On his way back, Santiago reaches for my pile once again, but this time I'm ready and jump away. "This is my job too, you know," I say, staring right at his ridiculously gorgeous face.

He stands there, glowering, his eyes flicking to my forehead again. With a huff, he turns and walks off, grabbing more boxes. He doesn't look at me or my head injury for the rest of the setup, and I happily pretend he is made of air as well.

"Wow," Andro says, walking up. Our little merch corner is adorable, thanks to me. I've organized it based on aesthetics, keeping the Andro and FG T-shirts and mugs in the center. I took some of the fairy lights and paper triangle banners from the bus, completing my effort with a candle I found in the bottom of my bag, so now everything smells like clary sage and oranges. Andro beams, which means the whole light of the sun is now in this room with us, and then he frowns, and just like that, the sun bounces away. "What happened to your head?"

My brain feels weird under his black-eyed gaze. "Tripped," I respond, and it comes out a little like a cough. And then Andro's hand is on my face. Let me repeat: Andro Philips is *touching* my *face*. He tilts my chin up and, oh God, he can hear my heart picking up, can't he?

"You don't have any dizziness? Fatigue? Headache?"

I shake my head. I don't trust myself to speak.

"What's wrong with your forehead?" Star's voice rattles in like a broken bell, and Andro releases my face. She and Chamomila have both walked up, arms crossed, faces concerned, but like, not for me, I don't think.

"I tripped." If I focus on them, I can form sentences.

"Over what?"

"The Grinch." It comes out before I can stop myself. Beside me, Santiago clenches his jaw.

"Let me know if you feel off, okay?" Andro is still looking intently at me. Everyone is looking at me, actually. How can Star stand this all the time? All I want to do is turn my eyes into lasers, Cyclops-style, and set everything on fire.

"Andro, how do you like the new shirts?" Star asks in a singsong voice, gesturing to her merch pile. Finally, blessedly, Andro looks away from me.

Star's debuting a lot of new items on tour. There's an assortment of tanks and bracelets that display WWVMD?, which stands for "What Would the Virgin Mary Do?" Along with some of her classic stuff, like soft long-sleeved crewnecks featuring gold font that says NOTHING FEELS BETTER THAN SAVING YOURSELF. Everything white and bright and pure.

"Wow, the fonts are fantastic," Andro says. "Who's your designer?"

"Oh, um," Star says, fingering her hair. "That would be Moon."

Andro flashes me a brilliant grin. "Really? That's great. What font did you choose here?"

"It's . . ." I cough. "It's mine."

Andro looks stunned for a moment. "Rock and roll! It's so good. How long did it take you to make?"

"Oh," Star responds. "Moon just does these things as a hobby."

Andro doesn't look at her. He's still waiting for me to answer, I guess.

"Um. A week."

"You're joking." He glides a hand over one of the shirts again.

Fonts change the texture of words. The one I designed Star's merch in, it makes words feel like silk has bees thrown on it. I originally wanted it for my tarot deck, but in the end it was a little too soft.

"Moon," Star says. I realize I'm daydreaming.

"What? Sorry . . ."

Andro looks concerned. "You sure you're not dizzy?" He takes a step forward, and I, like a mirror, take one back.

"I'm sure," I tell him. If he gets any closer, I will get dizzy, but it won't have anything to do with the head injury.

"Good." He pauses. "I was just asking, how much for a custom font?"

"Oh, I don't know—"

"It's her hobby," Star says again, most helpfully.

"You should charge a lot. This is quality." Again he ignores Star, and the look on her face! I want to take a picture. But she'd kill me by strangulation using one of her WWVMD? bracelets.

Andro smiles again. "It's great that you girls are so devoted to purity."

"Oh, that's definitely not Moon," Star says. "Not anymore."

Everyone looks at me, even Santiago. What the hell? Star is probably the only virgin in a twenty-mile radius and *I'm* the freak? I glare at her, and she has the decency to look bashful.

"Well," Andro finally says. "Great job on the font. Maybe we can talk about something custom for me, yeah? Sometime?" He points at me with both index fingers, and I nod, my cheeks flushed.

But I'm not free from near-constant humiliation yet. Oh, no. Because for some reason Crappy Cham has to speak up right then. "Where'd you get that scar, Moon?" she asks, and now everyone's looking at my collarbone—or trying not to and failing. And like, what the hell is wrong with everybody today? Is this some alternate reality, where no one understands what manners are? "I'm sorry," she adds, looking around like she's just realized her faux pas, which I don't believe for a second. "I was simply noticing . . ." She drifts off, looking for me to fill in the awkward pause, which I don't.

But Star, of course, comes to the rescue. "She fell. It was a bad, bad . . . fall."

"Yeah, I fell," I say. "And there was this knife sticking out of the ground, almost like someone—a lady, even—was pointing it right at me, and I fell on it, like—"

"Andro!" Star practically shrieks. "I think we're almost late!" I have to turn because I can't stop my eyes from rolling. Anything. Star will do anything to keep the status quo, to keep anyone from knowing any little flaw in our lives, to keep the ugliest truth buried sixteen million miles in the earth.

"Right! Influencers," Andro says, and Star and Chamomila straighten their backs. "We've got a meet-and-greet in . . . oh, ten minutes. Let's go!"

I sit in my designated merch-girl chair and bury my face in my hands.

"Wow, Chamomila Jones is a bitch, isn't she? Your sister, too." I peek through my fingers. It's Belle Brix, rearranging her pyramid of Brixsticks.

"Star's . . ." But you know what? Belle Brix is right. Star acted like a real jerk, and for no reason. I mean, I get the scar thing, 'cause that's her MO when it comes to that, but not the other stuff. I don't get any of it.

Belle can read my face, I guess, because she responds, "I know. Can't talk trash about the VM." She holds up one of Star's bracelets. Star insisted on getting them dipped in platinum—the purest, whitest metal.

I smile. I can't help it. I mean, I know Brix is supposed to be the enemy, but right now it feels like the opposite.

"I haven't formally introduced myself," she says, holding a hand out. "I'm Belle. Makeup extraordinaire."

I shake her hand. "Moon. Weed extraordinaire."

"Weed? You mean like . . ." Belle mimes smoking a joint.

I laugh. "No, I mean like dandelions. The kinds of plants that everyone thinks are ugly and tries to kill?"

Beside us, Santiago snorts.

"That is a unique brand, Moon. How are you, Santiago?" Belle asks. He responds by inclining his head toward her, keeping his eyes on his book.

Belle glances at my head. "They make concealer for that, you know."

"Eh. I'm okay."

She looks disappointed. "Don't tell me you're an au naturel girl too."

"No. No, I love makeup. I'm completely obsessed with your glitter cat-eye."

Belle smiles and grabs some of her merchandise. A few lipsticks, eyeliner, other things in shimmery smooth containers, and hands it all to me. "Uh . . . ," I say.

"A gift." She smiles. "For being real," she calls as she turns away to join the others.

"Thanks," I call back, but I think she's too far away to hear me.

And then it's just me and Santiago. I tap my fingers on the table for a few moments. When is the event done? An hour? I check the schedule in my emails. Jeez Louise. Two and a half hours. Thank goodness I brought my sketchbook. I pull it out, along with my watercolor pencils, and sketch flower arrangements.

After, like, thirty minutes, I look up. Santiago hasn't moved a millimeter, and he's still reading that ancient-looking tome. It looks like a regular-size book in his hands, but that only means it's seven feet wide and nine feet long. Ridiculous. But I should be nice. Right? He and I are going to be working side by side as the merch people for the next eight weeks. So I should at least try.

Angling my body toward his, I say, "What are you reading?"

It's a fairly innocuous question, but Santiago sighs like I've asked him to tell me the name of his first crush, his social security number, and the passwords to his bank accounts. He lifts the cover and lets me look at it for all of a trillionth of a second. I don't even get to read more than a word, which is "flavor."

"Is it good?" I ask.

For my efforts, I am rewarded with a shrug.

Okay. Two more hours until showtime. Jesus on a tortilla.

I try to rein in the embarrassment of that awkward encounter. After all, he has no reason to like me. He doesn't owe me anything. I shuffle through my bag, trying to look busy, when Santiago, like he can hear my thoughts, speaks. "We're not friends."

I snap my head up. He's still looking at his hulk book, the muscles in his neck tense.

"What?"

"You and I." He finally glares at me. "Are not friends. So stop talking to me."

Well, I *had* stopped talking to him. I mean, I got the hint, didn't I? Apparently not well enough. He's still looking at me. "Do. You. Understand?" He speaks slowly, like I'm a child. The tone of his voice is burlap scratching at the back of my neck. I want to tear it off and throw it at his face.

"Not friends. I get it." I shake my head a little. And then I can't help myself. My mouth becomes a runaway train. "But I'm really going to miss what we had, you know?"

His glare turns to bewilderment. "You know," I continue. "Staring contests. You marking your kitchen territory like a wolf. Barking at me even. Tripping me this morn—"

"That wasn't . . ." His voice is loud, and he lowers it. "I didn't mean that." And he gazes at my forehead before dropping his eyes back to his book.

"Look, I'm just saying I'm going to miss *us*. You know? We really could've been something, Santiago."

He looks up at me, even more confused. And maybe it's my imagination, but his cheeks look a little pinker than a moment ago.

"You know, like how Thor and Loki were something." I raise my eyebrows. "Or Jesus and Judas."

And then Santiago astonishes me. He smiles. His lips go peach and wide, and his eyes sparkle, making the brown of them even deeper. When his face relaxes like that, he looks warm. *Attractive* and warm. It's so unsettling, I almost prefer when he looks murderous. But then he says quickly, "I'm not Judas. You're fucking Judas."

"Only if they paid me enough silver." I shrug.

Santiago narrows his eyes and tilts his mouth in a half smile, and I know, just know in my bones that it is on.

We don't speak again until the stampede of Foto-fans approaches, so loud, I'm concerned for a moment that we're going to get trampled. Then it's all business, passing items and change back and forth, and I drop a few coins.

"Nice one, Loki."

I'm kind of shocked, but not shocked enough to refrain from responding, "Screw you, *Thor*." I ignore the gasp from my customer.

"I'd rather be crucified."

And now my customer looks genuinely appalled. "Sorry," I mutter, handing her a bag. She walks away in a huff. Turning to Santiago, I say, "What the eff?"

"You started it." He adds "*Judas*" under his breath, and I grin. Our banter continues like this for nearly an hour. I can't remember the last time I've had this much fun with someone.

The one time our energy hits a bump is when a woman walks up and takes a look at Santiago's left arm, staring right where it ends at his wrist. "Oh my God," she says with a huge, unnecessary gasp. "Oh God, what happened?"

"Polar bear," Santiago responds, his voice hard. I think only I notice the pink at his ears and neck.

This confuses the woman for a beat, but then she gives him a look of pity. "You know, you're so *brave*—"

And this is when Santiago shoves the bag in her face and says, "Next."

I think the lady doesn't really care about Santiago at all, because instead of taking the hint, she scoffs, looks at me, and says, "Some people." And waits for a response. Like I'm going to agree with her?

So I say, not kindly, "Ma'am, your transaction's done and you're in the way."

She raises her shoulders, huffs, and walks away, muttering something like, "Kids these days, no respect."

When I turn back to Santiago, his eyes are all soft on me. It's hard to explain. He looks like he actually likes me for a moment. But then he growls, "Back to work, Judas."

"Whatever, jerk-head," I respond, and he tries really hard to hide his grin. I can just tell.

And that back-and-forth sort of summarizes the rest of the day. It's weird, but it feels better to get all that hate out in the open. Like Belle Brix said. It's real.

Everyone's out to dinner at some fancy Peruvian restaurant. Star tried to convince me to go. "It has a star *theme*, Moon! The whole thing is covered in silver glitter and star lights! Perfect for a shoot!"

But I made myself keep an expressionless face as I told her I needed to draw. And save the $173 I'd spend there. Not to mention, fuck doing anything with my jerk of a sister, but I left that bit out.

So here I am, sitting in the living area. Santiago's in the kitchen, cooking up something that smells better than bacon-fried cheesecake covered in chocolate and crack. But we're back to ignoring each other, which, whatever. I've got yogurt and a PB&J and my sketchbook. I will live.

I don't really know all that much about tarot, except that it originated in France as a card game and turned into something more mystical. The most famous version—what lots of people consider to be the original modern tarot—is called Rider-Waite. Which is complete bullshit to me, since the name doesn't include the woman who actually painted each of the seventy-eight cards. Decks should be named after the artist who made them, not the random guy who had a cool idea. In my mind, it's the Pamela Colman Smith tarot, and that's that.

I'm sketching ideas for my next card—the Ace of Wands— when I hear a grunt in the kitchen.

"You okay?" I say without looking up.

There's no response. So I go over and see him pop open this lid of what looks like gray crystal bits, shimmery and beautiful. He scatters them on his plate of pasta.

"Holy heck," I say. "That looks great."

"You sound surprised." I blink because his tone is back to bristly. My neck itches again.

"Are you okay?" I ask once more.

He stares for a second before responding. "Why wouldn't I be?" Again, his voice is sharp. I'm covered in paper cuts.

Is it weird that I feel hurt? I thought we'd struck up a sort of comradery earlier. A hateful one, sure, but not mean-spirited, not like him right now. And I've kind of had it, so I turn around to leave, but then spin again to face him and say, "You know what, Santiago? I apologized. I was a jerk. I don't expect you to forgive and forget it, but since we're working together all freaking summer, surely you could be more like a cloud."

His brows furrow, which is an improvement from the murder-stare. "A cloud."

"Yes. Less like burlap. More like a cloud. Or yarn, even. Though yarn can be really harsh sometimes. Especially certain wools. So I retract the yarn suggestion."

He grunts a little and turns back to his food. "I don't like you."

I walk to the living area and grab my things. "You know what? I don't like you, either. So let's just go back to pretending the other doesn't exist."

"Fine by me," he mutters.

And that's how my evening ends. I spend the rest of the night in my bed, drawing under my cell phone light. When I awaken in the morning, I still have a pencil in my hand.

18.

Reading Cloud Breath and Fox Prints like Cards

I DON'T EVEN know how tarot works. I barely understand myself most of the time, much less this strange and windy way we can communicate with the universe. It makes no sense as to why I'm in love with tarot enough to spend nearly two years making my own stinking deck.

Except . . . I can recall the exact moment tarot enchanted me. Mom was going through some . . . stuff, let's call it. And she sent us to live with Tía. Her sister, Esperanza. And Mom *really* doesn't like Esperanza, would rather give me a big hug than owe her sister anything, so you know she was going through shit.

Tía's house is outside of New Orleans, a turquoise-painted bungalow. And when I say turquoise, I mean literally. She's an artist, and she got on her knees and on a ladder and painted the broken and black veins that the real stones actually have. "Ribbons," she calls them.

Tía Esperanza is my favorite family member, and I feel no guilt whatsoever in saying I love her more than I love my mom. I wish she were my mom. Sometimes I wonder if Mom can sense this and it's why she hates Tía, but I don't know if Mom cares about my allegiance all that much.

Whatever. All I know is I walked in on Tía at the kitchen table, the lamp lit like amber caught in the afternoon light. And spread on the table, these cards, all elaborately painted in the colors of jewels. That's the feeling I got when I looked at them. Smooth, cool jewels, passing over my neck and my arms, my face and my legs. For a moment I was walking on stones, these glowing sunset and moonrise colors beneath my feet like a river, and I actually stumbled.

All of Mom's warnings about the habits of el diablo went out the door. I looked at Tía and said, "Can I?" I'm not even sure what I was asking. Can I get my cards read? Can I grab them and rub them on my arms a little bit? Who knows.

Tía. She knew what I was asking, because she said, "You sure?" I'd never been more sure of anything, even without actually knowing what we were discussing. And thus began my apprenticeship with Tía, the divination apprenticeship. It was the best and worst part of that summer. But that's a story for another time.

19.

Thinking of Flowers
(and Absolutely Nothing Else,
Nothing at All, I Swear)

"WE'RE STOPPING IN about an hour," Andro calls from the front of the bus. Great. I'll have to spend some quality time with my jerk-faced nemesis. But then Andro pops his head in and says, "The Westernly has their own merch they want to sell, so you guys are off the hook for today."

"Cool!" I say before my brain reminds me I'm talking to Andro Philips and I should sound a little less like a loser. "What state are we in again?" But then Andro is gone.

"Don't you have a schedule?" Santiago's voice is somehow quiet and booming at the same time.

"You don't exist, remember?" I respond, but it is a common-sense idea, so I pull up the sched on my phone.

Ah, Montana. My aunt's last email comes to me. *Think of the flowers.* I smile and climb down and head to the bathroom, pretending all the while that Santiago the Jolly Green Giant was never born. I don't even stare when he rolls out of bed without a shirt on and gets right to his planks. Not for even a single second. I swear! Not one.

20.

Okay, So About That Summer with Tía

. . . AND HOW DIVINATION was the best and worst part of it? I'm just going to lay it all out here and get it over with.

First, there are the Rules.

Tía Esperanza's Rules to Learning Divination.

First we must start with twigs and swirls in the dirt and leaves, both fresh and skeleton. We take daily walks in the wilderness—on the banks of rivers and in the deep, dark woods, and see what we see. Learning to listen to the land is the important part.

Then we've got to look up. Pretty much the same thing as rule number one, but with clouds and lightning and wind as it rustles tree branches like hands in hair. The gods of the earth and the gods of the sky are pretty different, though. It's like learning a whole new language.

Then comes tarot. Tía considers tarot to be one of the lesser forms of divination. "Everything is spelled out for you," she says.

Easy for her to say. Even with a guidebook, most of my spreads seem like gibberish to me. But tarot is a stepping-stone for the next step.

The most powerful form of divination uses mirrors. This is the kind I refuse to learn. And I'll tell you why right now.

Mirrors are what ancient Mesoamerican shamans used for divination. There's so much we don't know about our ancestors; thank you, European colonizers who destroyed everything in their paths like literal demons.

But we do know that they used smooth stones made of obsidian, hematite, pyrite. Sometimes they filled bowls with water and read the shapes and stuff in there, but Tía preferred to focus on the stone tradition. And yeah, they gazed right into them when they needed answers.

The best part of that summer at Tía's? Everything. Vanilla ice cream swirled with passion fruit in crunchy waffle cones. How she'd take us to the French Quarter, all filled with musicians and artists, and buy us pralines, all melt-in-your-mouth caramel-sweet. And how she'd let me sleep in the backyard in a tent because that made me feel closer to my dad. All sticky summertime, all blooming flowers in the colors of a sunset at sea, all Tía cooking up something wonderful in the kitchen all the time.

And then I grabbed her most prized mirror stone. Pyrite, wide, big, smooth, so reflective, you could light a room with it.

I should've left it well enough alone, you know? But no, I grabbed the thing and set it on the kitchen table, right in front of the full moon. The most potent moon for talking to your ancestors. But I didn't learn that until later.

I dipped my gaze right inside it, like I was pressing my fingertips into a gold glass lake.

And I saw my father. In the stone, but it was as though he'd stepped into the room. I jumped away from the table and had to breathe, counting to two, three, seven, before I felt okay enough to toss the stone right back on Tía's altar.

Tía walked out of her bedroom, empty water glass in hand. "Moon!" she said. "You look like you saw a ghost!"

I had. I didn't tell her this, but I had.

And *that* was the worst part of the summer.

21.

The Best Omelet in the Known Universe

"IS THAT WHAT you're wearing?" Star asks, not disguising her tone of disgust.

I look down at my brown leggings and peach wrap blouse. I mean, I'm decent, aren't I? This top even covers most of my cleavage.

Star, though, has on a fancy white dress. Its neck is high and square and there's a little eyelet flower design along the edges.

"What's wrong with my clothes?" I say.

"The Westernly is nice."

"Oh. I'm not going in. I don't have to work today."

"I know. Which is why it's perfect for you to take photos of us."

"Star—"

"Moon. I haven't uploaded one of yours in too long. Everyone's been asking why there's an abundance of cell phone pictures lately."

I roll my eyes. "Well, sorry, but I don't want to."

"And why not?"

I sigh. "I'm pissed at you, Star, okay?" There. I said it.

"Don't say you're pissed. You're not a horse." Another one of Mom's gems. I've long given up trying to explain to them that humans also urinate.

"I'm sorry," Star says. And she does look it, her eyes glassy, her lips in a little pout. "Sometimes I forget that you're not proud of your sexual history."

"Well, it's not like I'm ashamed of it," I snap. "I'd just appreciate it if it stayed private." Telling Mom I had sex really isn't worth it anymore. Even now, thinking about the look on her face—eyes and mouth wide like a Gorgon, reaching for her collection of rosaries—that doesn't cheer me up in the least.

"I'm sorry, Moon," Star says, wiping away a tear. "It won't happen again."

It can't happen again. You don't get to unspill the beans. Not those kinds of beans, anyway. They're scattered across the floor now like bugs, shiny for everyone to see. And judge. But I sigh and say, "Fine. But you know it doesn't matter what I wear, Star. No one's looking at me."

Star doesn't respond to that, but in his bunk, Santiago snorts.

"Something funny, Thor?" I ask in his direction.

"Be nice, Moon," Star whispers. "He doesn't have it easy."

"And what on Middle-earth is that supposed to mean?"

But Star ignores the question, looks at my clothes, and says,

"Well, you're not eating dinner with us in that, so I guess it's okay."

"Jesus Christ on a fiddlestick. Can we lay off my outfit, please?"

"I hope you're praying," Stay says in a singsong voice as she flounces away.

"Yes, Star," I call back. "I'm praying for a Jesus sighting on a fiddlestick." And then I mutter, "So I can masturbate with it." Behind me, Santiago starts choking. After affirming that he's not dying, I consider correcting myself, saying I would never masturbate with anything remotely religious. Unless there's a religion that worships human fingers. But I bet that won't make this situation any better. Plus, it violates the whole not-existing contract. So. I throw my bags over my back and get the heck out of there.

Crap, crap, crap. I almost forgot that I freaking hate people. They're everywhere. Screaming for Andro and Van and Oak Longsteinson, shrieking for Belle and Chamomila Jones, and of course, squealing for my sister. I hold my camera up, wincing as another screech digs into my ears like a machete, stabbing me right in the brain.

I love the click my Nikon makes, even though it's artificial. But right now, not even that rain-like shutter can soothe me. *Click*, Star smiling at the masses that surround her. *Click*, someone telling her, "I've been following you since the beginning!" *Click*, people asking Star to pray for them, like she's the pope's daughter or something. But what gets me is she does. She puts her hand on their heads like she's anointing them with the blood of Christ. I've never wanted to strangle my sister more than the first time I saw her do that. Now I grit my teeth and *click-click-click*.

"Hey there," Andro says, and I almost drop the camera. "Oh, didn't mean to startle you."

"It's no problem." I keep my eyes on the viewfinder.

"Let me see?"

Dang it. Nodding, I hand him the Nikon.

"Jesus. You're talented."

"Thanks."

"I'm serious."

I guess I didn't sound thankful enough, so I give him a wide smile and nod. "Uh-huh. Thank you."

"You ever do self-portraits?" Andro looks in my eyes and it's all I can do to stay upright.

"Uh—"

"Moon!" Star bounces over. "Ooh, let me see!" She stops at one where the light is formed around her head like a halo. I knew she'd like that.

"Lovely," Andro says, and Star beams. "You've got a gift, Moon." And Star's smile falls, falls, falls like all those angels who sided with Lucifer. Before she can sing or do a backflip or anything, anything to get his attention back, he checks his phone and says, "Oh, time to meet at the restaurant." He gives me the camera. "You joining us, Moon?"

"Oh," Star says. "She didn't get the meal plan."

"You should come." Andro smiles and puts his hands in his pockets. "Really. I'll buy."

I think Star and I both have the same look on our faces. Like, a mix of *What the fuck* and *Is this a joke?* With a pinch of *Is Andro confused about who is who?* Does he realize he's talking to me, Moon, the ugly one?

I break first. "No, sorry. I've got some flowers to, uh, check out. Flower power." I flash the peace sign, turn, and run, almost knocking over Belle Brix.

"Flower power, huh," she says. "Far out, I must say."

"Oh God," I say, putting my hands over my eyes. "Jesus Christ on a dildo."

Belle cackles. "Oh my God, Moon. You really have to join us for dinner sometime."

"Not tonight," I say, stopping when I see the omelet bar being set up. They're doing breakfast for dinner? My stomach wants to die from jealousy. It literally growls with the force of a thousand whale bellies.

"You look hungry."

"I'm . . . not *that* hungry." In truth, I am starving.

"Why didn't you get the meal plan, anyway?"

"I'm trying to save money."

Belle snorts and then stops. "Wait. You're serious. You're the sister of millionaire Star Fuentez and you're trying to save money?"

"She's not a millionaire," I say. Yet. When Belle gives me a look, I groan. "Look, it's a long story, okay?"

Belle shakes her head. "Meet me on the steps outside in, oh, an hour?"

"But—"

"An hour," she calls as she walks away.

While I wait for whatever an hour will bring, I climb a tree.

According to my internet search, it's a banyan—wide, thick, its arms low-hanging like a spidery earthen beast. Banyan. The word feels like a hammock, swaying under my body, with speckled light pouring in between leaves.

My father said that scientists can extract pollen from deep archaeological sites and learn about what, exactly, ancient forests and meadows consisted of. "Based on pollen taken from the bottom of the Bering Sea," he said on one of our camping trips up north, "we know this whole area had summers full of wildflowers."

What did the first humans think of flowers? Did they ever wonder why the earth so willingly burst into beauty every spring? All those colors making a wide, wild sea on the horizon . . . it must've been pure magic. It still is, really.

That in mind, I pull some wild violets from my pocket, plucked on my way back from the Westernly. I clip a few banyan leaves and arrange everything on a flattish part of the trunk until it feels right. Until the colors pour over me, wet, smooth, and soft, like sand under a passing saltwater wave.

I adjust the settings on my camera and photograph the

Knight of Wands. After, I sling the camera over my shoulder and lean back, enjoying the breeze, not even letting the growls of my stomach ruin my mood.

When I climb back down, my eyes stop at the bus. Santiago's watching me like a creep, eating a sandwich made of truffles and lobster, probably. I give him the finger. He takes a big bite and returns the favor.

"Voilà." Belle sets the plate in front of me. On it? The most beautiful thing I've ever seen. An omelet. Steamy yellow perfection, filled with spinach and cheese and I don't even care what else, because it's food and it's hot and there's no peanut butter in sight. I snatch it out of her hands and groan like a porn star with my first bite.

"And you said you weren't that hungry," she says, raising an eyebrow.

"Shut up." And I stuff another enormous bite into my mouth. "I haven't eaten anything warm in a week."

"Yeah. Tell me about that." My mouth is really full, so she adds, "When you're finished. I'll wait."

Belle's got on jeans, high-tops, and a tank covered in pink glitter. Her makeup looks legit mystical. Like she had it done in Neverland or something. Everything's perfectly contoured, there's a dusting of pink glitter on the tops of her cheeks, and her lips are stained with a strawberry-peach color. You can't tell what's makeup and what's not. That's why she's got seven hundred thousand Fotogram followers.

When I plop my fork down after the last bite, she grabs my plate and pushes it to the side. "Well?"

I groan. "What?"

"Spill."

Truth be told, I sort of don't want to tell her, out of allegiance to Star. But Star has pretty much proved she's got no allegiance to me, so I spill with only a fraction of a second's hesitation, not without considering the word "spill," how it feels like a distant galaxy is being poured over my legs. "So my mom is super religious."

"No shit."

"Right. So, yeah, Star's whole brand is real. My mom really, really, really loves Jesus. Like, really, really—"

"Okay. Mom loves Jesus."

"Her sister, Esperanza, she practices the old-religion stuff."

Belle shakes her head. "Like . . ."

"Like pre-Columbian Mexican-type spells. Blessing of the egg, cleansing of the broom. Et cetera, et cetera."

"So what's this got to do with living on cold bread to save money, when your sister sleeps in a bed made of it?"

I snort. "Well, my mom manages Star and her money. And she would never let me go to college far away. Especially not to a college next to my aunt, who she knows I'd be visiting all the time." I don't mention the tarot card stuff, because that seems like so much to explain right now. "She'd probably literally disown me. She will, I mean, once I do it. Which I will. Thanks to eating cold bread all summer, I can afford to live on campus."

"Wow."

"Yeah."

"And your sister won't lend you the money?"

"I haven't even thought to ask."

"You should. Your sister is a lot of things, but she's generous." Belle's cheeks look a little pinker than earlier.

"I thought you and Star hated each other."

Belle opens her mouth to respond, but she shakes her head. "Ah. Well, we used to be close."

"Really?" I have never heard this. "When?"

Belle lifts a hand. "Oh, a while ago. Hey, do you want me to grab you another omelet before they close the bar?"

"Um, yeah."

And a little while later, she returns with a feta cheese and shallot creation that tastes so good, I want to start a religion worshipping it. Belle laughs when I tell her, but she never does answer my question about her and Star.

22.

Looking for My Future in Cards like Scattered Seeds in a Moonless Night

EVERYONE OKAY? TÍA emails me. You haven't updated your pages.

Tía is the only person who knows about my FG account. Well, besides my 42,868 followers. She's the only real-life person who knows, I mean.

Sometimes I fantasize about telling Mom that I have my own brand and it's got nothing to do with Jesus and everything to do with the creepy old religion. But I can't.

I'm not scared of her. Not anymore. I just know she'll find some way to take it from me. She'll confiscate my camera, my phone, food and water until I'm on the brink of death and have to give up my art. She'd take me by the ear directly to Father Luke so they could pour Jesus's blood on me by the gallon to cleanse me of my sins. And then she'd personally nail me to a cross and parade me in the streets. Think I'm exaggerating?

"Bad people got burned by the church," she told me when

I'd sullied my God-given purity. "You would've burned for this, Moon." And then she lost her shit with kitchen knives.

Later, she did apologize. After I asked the father for his opinion on the matter in front of her. Afterward? "Don't you ever embarrass me in the Lord's house ever again."

Right. It's my fault she implied I should be murdered.

So I dunno what she'd do if she found out about the university housing and the tarot and being right next to her lifelong enemy, Tía. But a public street crucifixion sounds about right to me.

I set my little book lamp and a string of fairy lights I stole from the living area all around my bunk. It's lovely, even with Santiago shifting under me and rumbling and creaking the frame. Still not used to bunking with my nemesis, but it's gotten slightly better the last few days, I guess.

Okay, so most people say you've got to shuffle the cards, thinking about the questions you want answered, and that's fine. But Tía likes to shuffle with nothing on the brain first. She lets the cards surprise her. "Just like with mirror stones," she says.

But I'm going to do this the question way. And my deep, supersecret, desperately loserish question is, *Is Andro Philips kind of into me?*

Even just thinking it makes me cringe. Of course he's not. But he's been so nice, noticing me. Complimenting me. Or, at least, my photography. So I know I don't repulse him. And it makes sense that I'd want to make sure there's nothing more, right?

A three-card spread. The Lovers, the Hierophant, and the

Knight of Swords. I take a breath. It's good to go with first impressions. It feels weird attempting this without Tía, but I've seen her do it enough times. My first impression? Andro just got out of a relationship. One where he felt like he was in love. The Hierophant tells me that Andro is focusing on his business. No secret love for me. Bah humbug.

And I have no idea about the Knight of Swords. Swords represent conflict and butting heads and . . . Oh crap. Who else could this be but Santiago? What is my sworn enemy doing here?

Let's do a one-card spread. Just to see what happens. I shuffle and shuffle and pull one out triumphantly, watching it flutter to my bedspread, where I see, once again, it's the Knight of Swords.

I pull another. Knight of Wands. And another. Knight of Cups.

Seeing them all lined up together gives me a little jolt. Twinkling nebulas sit against my chest and belly, blinking on and off like a thousand suns being eclipsed and uncovered by endless moons.

That's my first impression. A nebula. Otherwise known as a cosmic shitstorm.

At that moment, the bus hits a bridge. I stifle a scream with a pillow and look out the window. Oh, thank the Lord, it's not a water bridge. Those tend to freak me the flip out.

I take several deep breaths and do the only thing I can think of. I take a photo of the spread and email it to my aunt with the words "What the hell is going on here?" That summarizes everything well enough, so with that, I hit send.

23.

Pondering a Human-Formed Nebula

WE HAVE THREE "mini" stops in three days, so it's chaos. Mini stops mean that we park at some amphitheater, unload as fast as possible so we can set up as the influencers give their speeches and high-five their fanatics. Sometimes we put out the very last of the merchandise *just* as the people start to pour in. It's kind of anxiety-inducing. *For charity*, I have to keep reminding myself.

I barely speak to anyone, except business stuff with Santiago as we set up and sell. Occasionally, I let myself stare at him for a beat or two, wondering how on earth this cantankerous bastard is a nebula. Nebulas aren't rude. They don't resemble the Hulk as far as disposition. They're thousands of light-years wide, and they give birth to planets and moons and rings made of dust so beautiful, everything looks as blue as the sea. This whole thing is driving me bonkers, along with the fact of his biceps. I've been estimating what they resemble, and the closest thing I can think is soup bowls. I don't understand how they stay flexed and firm even when he's standing around, not holding anything.

I'm lifting the boxes into the back of the bus when Santiago walks past me, double the amount of what I've got in his arms. After he bends to drop them on the pile, I keep my eyes on his arms. The soup bowls on them, to be precise. How does that even work? Isn't he afraid his muscles are going to come alive and eat him in his sleep?

"What are you looking at, Loki?" he asks. He actually flexes. He flexes his arms! The soup bowls seem like they reach out to touch me. And the idea of touching Santiago is a little much. So, like a total loser, I drop all three boxes right at my feet. One of them explodes and Brixsticks go tumbling all around.

"I was wondering how the hell you even stay upright," I tell him as I bend to grab the makeup.

He looks at me up and down as I lift the lipstick box. "What are *you* looking at?" I demand.

He shrugs. "Just wondering if you get your hair that black from dye or if it's naturally the color of your soul."

"Oh, ha ha ha." I make a face of disgust.

"Moon!" Star says, walking up. Her hair is about as white as it gets at the ends, light honey on top. It bounces from her high ponytail, making me squint as it reflects the sun. "Oh, hey, Santiago." She says his name casually, almost too casually. If I were a cat, my ears would be turning toward her.

"Yeah? What's up?" I say.

"I saw a bunch of blooming wisteria back that way." She points. "I thought you'd want to know."

"Oh." I'm stunned. I can't remember the last time Star has told me something that didn't somehow deflect back to herself.

"Maybe you could bring some back for me? And photograph me with it in my hair?"

Ah. There it is.

She gives Santiago a smile, one of her good smiles. "You think purple would look good in my hair?"

It's a waste of time for her to ask. Everything looks good in her hair. But Santiago gives her a weird look and grunts something that sounds affirmative.

"Sure, Star," I say.

"Great! Santiago, if you want to come to see the shoot too, you should!" And then she walks away, her hair a sun glare in this light.

"What the hell is a wisteria?" Santiago asks me.

"If you were civilized, you would know." I slide my bag over my shoulder.

"Well, you can't leave now."

I put my hands on my hips. "And why not? We're not starting for another two hours!"

"Some people get in early."

I scoff. I mean, it is true that every now and then we get the enthusiastic fan who's convinced they need to get ahead of the crowds, but we're a whole 120 minutes away! Surely he can handle those himself.

Santiago scowls at me. "Andro's not paying you to wander around in nature and shit."

I feel so angry. I know it's irrational, but it's *wisteria*. There is almost nothing in this world that smells better than wisteria. *It's okay*, I tell myself. *You can wait a couple of hours for this.* So I sit down, but not without saying, "You are such an asshole."

"Likewise, Judas." He's got the smirkiest smirk on his face. Honest to God, I have to sit on my hands so they don't reach out and strangle him.

I refuse to even look at Santiago while we wait, much less speak to him. I wasn't sure things could be more silent and weird between us, but they are, and the worst part is it stretches on, pulling us into its tide. Well, that's what it feels like for me, anyway. Santiago looks right at home while silent and broody. He should be a model for some clothing company that sells to grumpy bunnies.

"Luna."

Gosh. I'm so bored, I'm actually hallucinating. Or halluci-hearing. Whatever that word is. But then it comes again, louder. "Luna!"

"Samuel!" I stand, barely noticing that I've done it so abruptly, my chair's fallen over.

"My beautiful full Moon." He says this very suggestively, gazing up and down at me so fast, probably anyone else would miss it.

"Fucking pervert." Except Santiago, of course, who mumbles this under his breath so only I hear it.

Before I can give Santiago a scathing look or a violent smack on the head, Samuel is here, throwing his arms around me, picking me up even.

"Stop!" I scream when he starts twirling me around. But he keeps going, until I feel like my brain is diving down my body, making a break for it. "Samuel, please."

"Put her down." A mean, gruff voice stops both me and Samuel in our tracks. I glance over, and yep, there's Santiago, arms crossed, looking exactly the way I imagine a great white shark does before it rips off the skull of a seal.

"You must be Santiago," Samuel says, not at all flustered as he puts me down. He gives Santiago a smile, a really good smile, and then a wink. A wink!

"Lord," I mutter. "Here we go."

"Moon told me how ripped you are," he says, surveying Santiago's massive arms and pecs and everything else. "How often do you lift, man? Those are something else."

Santiago looks slightly taken aback. I don't know if it's due to Samuel telling him about my fixation with his physique or Samuel's shameless flirting.

"Don't talk to him," I say to Samuel, pulling his arm back. "Just—what the heck are you doing here?"

"Thought I'd surprise you," he responds. "I missed your pretty smile. And the team is practicing right by the city all week. I couldn't pass up the opportunity."

I roll my eyes at Samuel. He can't help but flirt with anyone warm-blooded. Come to think of it, though, he probably would very much flirt with a zombie or a vampire, too.

"Let me take you to lunch?" he asks.

"She can't," Santiago grumbles. "She's working."

"Santiago! What the hell!"

"You can't afford to slack off. Not in the woods, not out with assholes. I'm not going to keep covering for you." He's so mean with his tone. It's like I'm a three-year-old.

"Go grab me something," I tell Samuel. "Bring it here and we'll catch up."

Before Santiago starts complaining, I shoot him a glare. "If you can read your freaking peppercorn bible there, I can have a guest."

"Whatever. Just make sure he doesn't stay long. We have a full house today."

I scoff. "You are such a . . ." And then I see Andro approaching. Santiago does too, and now he gives me an amused look.

"Such a what, Moon?"

"Such an understanding and caring person." I make my smile saccharine. When Andro passes, I lower my voice. "On opposite day."

"Really?" he asks, narrowing his eyes. "That's all you got?"

"No, of course not, you—you big hobgoblin!"

Santiago looks like he's trying not to laugh. So hard. I'm hit with a wave of thrill until I'm nudged in the shoulder.

"Moon."

"What's up?" I glance over while thinking, *Shit, I literally forgot Samuel was here.*

Meanwhile, Samuel's smiling, looking between me and Santiago like he's got a secret or something. Finally he claps his hands together and says, "Red curry good? There's a Thai place down the street."

"Oh, yes please," I say. When I reach for my purse, Samuel waves me off.

"I got this, beautiful." Samuel gives me that devastating grin of his and walks away.

As soon as he's out of earshot, I turn to Santiago and hiss, "What in the heckle is the matter with you?"

"Heckle," he responds. "Did you seriously say that?"

"Stop changing the subject."

"Remind me of it again. The subject."

I'm exhausted with him already and it's still technically morning. I take a breath and unclench my jaw and fists. "Look. I know why you're so mean to me. But don't extend that hate to everyone who knows me. That's all I'm asking."

"You think I'm mean?" Santiago frowns, which makes him look so angry, and yes, mean. And then he repeats it. "You think *I'm* mean?"

And I know exactly what he's saying. I sarcastically called him extra-hairy Chupacabra poop before I even knew that he totally *is* extra-hairy Chupacabra poop. And he's never going to let it go. Ever.

I should get used to this feeling of extreme guilt, thanks to my mom, my sister, and the two-thousand-year history of the Catholic Church. But I'm a wimp, and I'm not, not yet, and that's why my eyes fill with tears. Crap. Why did I have to be blessed with such *sensitivity*? I will them back in, but naturally, the tears don't even think to listen.

"Because I seem to remember . . ." He stands, getting all high and mighty, and then he sees my face. He looks panicked.

"It's not what you think," I say, my voice high and my words fast. "There's mascara in my eyes."

He's still staring. I turn away and face the wall, sniffling.

After a few moments, there's a tap at my shoulder. I jerk back and my head hits something like a belt buckle. "For peach's sake," I say, grabbing my head.

"Are you okay?"

It's Santiago. Of course. It is *always* Santiago. "Great. Thanks. Go away now."

But he doesn't go away. He pulls my hands from the back of my head and says, "You're not bleeding."

Then he walks around and kneels down so we're at eye level. "May I?" He's got a tissue in his hand, which is pretty surprising as it is. And I nod, even without knowing what on earth he's asking, and then Santiago Philips astonishes me. He brings the Kleenex to my face and dabs at the salty wet along my cheeks.

I'm frozen, the feel of the tissue so gentle, it tickles. The word "astonish" comes to me again. It truly is the perfect way to describe what's happening to my cheeks right now. My shoulders, my bones. Every part of me is astonished, the way longtime snow melts with sudden spring.

"I made you cry," he says when he's done. And I guess I'm not astonished enough to keep my mouth shut.

"Oh, you wish, you banana peel."

When I look up at him, he's got a little smile on his face, one that takes that whole mean edge off him and throws it into the dumpster.

"Banana peel, huh."

I shrug. He's still smiling. And now I am astonished enough to keep my mouth shut. Because I can't stop looking at that crinkling sparkle in his eyes.

"Guess that's an upgrade from hobgoblin."

He's still smiling, so I still don't have a comeback. My brain is actually mushy thanks to that smile. But I can't help it. It's only the second time I've ever seen him look anything but murderous.

Just as that thought crosses my mind, Santiago's smile turns into a scowl. Looking behind me, he stands and tosses the tissue into my lap. "Your friend's back."

And just like that, Soft Santiago is gone. I already miss him.

"So you're going to force me to ask," Samuel says through a mouthful of pad thai. We're sitting on a bench near the enormous windows of this building, within sight of the merch tables in case Santiago needs me.

"I'm not making you do anything," I say. "In fact, feel free to not pry into my life at all."

He ignores me. "You know he wants you. You gotta know that, right?"

I almost snort out a spoonful of rice. "You mean Santiago? The guy who regularly wants to kill me? Who thinks I couldn't be more annoying if I tried?"

"You annoy him because he wants you." Samuel leans back and sips his Pepsi. "Man, and here I thought coming here would mean you and I would . . ." And then he makes a rude gesture with his fingers.

"Really? That's why you came? Because you thought I'd give that to you?"

He shrugs. "I wanted to see you. You can't blame a guy for shooting."

Ugh. Boys. "First of all, Santiago has no bearing on my love life. Second, you and I"—now I make the gesture—"were never gonna anyway."

"Not even a possibility, huh?"

"Not at all."

"You're wrong about two things." Samuel is finished gobbling his food down and leans back in his chair. "I would've had a shot, if it weren't for him. Because I can tell how lonely you are."

I scoff. "What does that even mean?"

"But you want him back. That's what's in my way."

"You can leave now." I stand, grabbing my bag.

"Moon, don't be like that."

"How could I not be? You just told me I'd be an easy lay because I'm pathetically lonely, and that's the whole reason why you're here."

He slings an arm around my shoulder, which I fail to shrug

off, because I'm not spilling any of this awesome red curry. "I really missed you," he says, and Lord help me, I want to lean in. I am that starved for human connection. And he knows it.

"Look, I have to get to practice. But I'll be in the next town over all week. Call me if you need it, okay?"

He acts like he's the one doing me a favor. When I don't respond right away, he brightens. I think because he thinks I'm considering his completely generous offer. So he hugs me, and I let him, because I want him to leave as soon as possible.

"Think about it," he calls as he leaves.

And when I sit back down in my spot, I stare and stare at the space where Samuel stood before he left. Because I know only a few weeks ago I would've. I would've fucked him, just to feel an iota less lonely. But now I want something better than that.

It's weird how a human being can change so fast. I feel like I've cast off all my flowers, but now they're busy making seeds. Like I can become brand-new, pure, over and over again.

"What happened to your friend?" Santiago asks when I walk up.

I shrug. "He's not my friend anymore. Let's just say that."

When I glance over, Santiago looks pleased. I'm not surprised. Naturally, he'd bask in my misfortune. At that moment, the doors burst open and the herds of Foto-fanatics stream in. He and I don't speak again until after the last customer disappears out the door. I stretch my back and crack my knuckles. "I'll come help load the truck in fifteen, okay? Now, if you'll excuse me, I have a tree to climb."

"I hope you don't happen to fall and break your face."

I narrow my eyes at him, and he does the same to me. Poophead.

Before I make it outside, I pull out my phone and check my emails quickly. Tía's written back on the Knight of Swords! He's your enchanter. And that's all I'll say about that.

Great, now Tía and Samuel are telling the same lies. Because there's no way on earth Santiago will ever enchant me. Someone else has got to be the Knight of Swords. I guess I'll find out who soon enough.

The wisteria is high. Really fucking high. If I fell, I'm pretty sure I'd break not only my face, but the rest of my skull, and my knees and toes, too. But I try not to focus on all that.

Wisteria smells bright and sweet like vanilla and honey and something in that exact shade of lilac purple (though, thank goodness, they smell nothing like lilacs). I shimmy up the trunk and onto some wide branches, going up and up until I can touch the thick, sinewy vines, rough against my fingers. The way they reach and lift, I imagine them directing the creation of universes. After talking to them a bit, and asking, I reach for the flowers.

Wisteria looks like the curly hair of pale-purple fairies, spiraling lovely and free. Its color is smooth like water, and cold, too. I shiver when I touch it and snip some away.

Tía said we always have to give thanks for whatever we take from a plant. It's alive, like us, and what we have with it is a relationship. And I do. I say "Thank you" before sliding down the way I came, stumbling a little along the way.

And who should be waiting for me at the bottom? None other than my hulked-out enemy, wearing *much* too tight a shirt. His hair is wet, too. He must've just showered and changed. I could see his nipples from across a whole sea in that thing.

"What do you want?" I say, making my voice icy.

"Do you always have to climb random trees whenever we stop?"

"Yes." I glare at him and drop my gaze to the dirt. It's dark. Perfect and clean, the color of something fresh-baked and happy and best eaten with cheese. I drop to my knees and start arranging the petals.

"What are you doing now?" He sounds incredulous.

"I'm preparing a witching circle. So I can hex your dumb nipples away."

When I look up, he's staring at his own chest, but he lifts his head again and he's grinning. Grinning! It changes his whole face, crinkling up his light-brown eyes, his white teeth making his lips look like slices of a peach. Then he says, "Why are you looking at my nipples?"

It takes me only a second to snap out of it. "Are you kidding? They looked at me first."

Again he grins. Again it makes my whole equilibrium flip upside down. The cells of my body tell me that the ground is sky and the sky is ground. I look down at the dirt fast, hands back on the flowers, but I'm halfway expecting to reach down and touch clouds instead.

He clears his throat. "I was wondering how tired you were of popcorn and peanut butter on a spoon."

"I never eat popcorn and peanut butter on a spoon."

"You know what I mean."

"Why? What do you want?"

"If you wanted to use my pans . . ." He lets his voice fade away, and now he looks equal parts angry and bashful, which shouldn't even be possible, yet here we are.

"I have a pan," I respond. I haven't had the guts to use it yet, but the fact is, I do own a pan.

He makes a face. "You mean that Teflon shit that looks like it's been through a meat grinder?"

"Yes."

He makes another face. "I only use cast iron."

"Okay, great. I'll order you a parade."

He clears his throat again and puts his hands in his pockets. His nipples are still about to unravel holes in his shirt, and he shifts his weight from side to side until I can't take it anymore. I sit up and say, "Are you offering your kitchen stuff for me to use?"

"I—uh—yeah, I guess. If you want. Or not. Whatever."

I take a breath and look back down at the Wheel of Fortune. When I look up again, Santiago is already making his way back to the bus.

Jeez. What was that about?

24.

The Second Time I Ever Had Sex

IT WAS A year later, I was sixteen, and Mom had spent all week really getting on my case about my weight. My butt had somehow gotten even bigger, to the point that when I looked at myself from the side, I was reminded of things like wheels of cheese and Alaskan mountain ranges.

"The only acceptable size a woman can get to is a ten," she hissed at me every time I sat down to eat. Mom is a size ten. But when she was an eight, she said the only acceptable size was an eight, so I really doubt her sources on that information.

Either way, by Saturday I was pretty sick of her and myself, the way I'd lock myself in my room and try not to cry all the time. So after everyone was in bed, I snuck out the front door and got in my car, driving around with no purpose at all. I mean, I did go by the cemetery a few times, but I still wasn't ready for that. Not even after years. So eventually, I pulled up at the movie theater, where there was a group of guys hanging out.

One of them, he noticed me. He was like a wild animal, looking for a girl just sad enough. That's what it seems like now, when I think back on it. At the time, I thought he thought I was pretty.

His name was Ryan, and he was a senior at our school. "Hey," he said, draping his long, lanky body over my window.

"Hey," I said. I unlocked the car doors. "Wanna get in?"

It happened so fast. He barely even kissed me, and next thing I knew, his hands were in my shirt and shorts. We ended up in the back seat and he moved, moved, moved like he couldn't have me fast enough, like if he didn't get it within the next two minutes, he'd explode. The only time he stopped was to grab a condom.

So less than two minutes later, he was done, looking so pleased with himself. And I realized right then and there, he didn't care who I was. I could've been any person with a vagina to him, and he would've reacted the same. And I had to knock him off his high horse. I couldn't let him think any of that was good for me.

"You're already finished?" I asked.

And that's when things got really, really bad. He didn't hurt me, not physically. But when I pulled into my driveway that night, my whole body shook and shook and wouldn't stop. My window was cracked open a little and a moth landed on it. Pale green and fuzzy. It slid inside and landed on my chest, like it knew I was about to be sliced open right there.

What I didn't know was that Mom was waiting inside for

me. What I didn't know was that several more luna moths were trailing after me, like I was made of their favorite flowers. What I didn't know was that Mom would take one look at them and know everything I had done.

What I didn't know was that my mother would punish me so thoroughly, for the first time I couldn't pretend to love her anymore.

25.

The Worst Omelet in the Known Universe, and Soon Thereafter, the _Actual_ Best Omelet in All the Universes of All Time

STAR WANTS ME to meet her at the restaurant chosen to host our influencer gods and goddesses tonight. **Bring the flowers,** she texts.

She's wearing a baby-blue sundress, a white knit thing covering her shoulders, because purity. Most everyone's at the table. "Moon!" She gestures to her hair. She's braided and wrapped it around her head in a Grecian headband, the rest of it flowing behind her like a piece of pale silk.

I arrange the wisteria over her ears. When I'm done, she looks like Mab, queen of the fairies. And it makes me smile, because she is so beautiful, and I love fairies.

"Do you want me to photograph you here?"

"Yes, yes," she says, checking the flowers with her phone, adjusting little strands of her hair.

I take a step back, pulling my camera out. Star and Chamomila are side by side, with Van and Oak on either side of them. It doesn't escape my notice that Oak's hand is on the back of Star's chair, and it doesn't escape Belle's notice either. If I had to name the look Belle is giving her, it would be *longing*. What on this green earth is that about? Before I can ponder it too long, though, Star gives me a gesture that says, *Get on with it*.

Oak is telling a joke, I think, because when I pull the camera up, Star laughs. Chamomila adds something spectacularly funny, and Star unhinges her jaw and makes the walls shake with her cackling. It's amazing how much teeth I'm able to capture. *Click*. Star, cackling again. *Click*, Star's eyes wide as Chamomila reveals that she is, indeed, a snakeskin ogre underneath all her lithe musculature. *Click*, Star, shining so bright and pretty, she actually becomes the sun and roasts us all to ash.

Andro's voice slithers around me from behind. "Wow, Moon. Those came out great."

I jump a little, and he laughs. "Sorry, I keep doing that, don't I?"

"It's fine." I get the feeling that he likes making me jump. Kind of a dick move, to be honest.

He smiles at me and I don't know how to act or what to say, so I open and close my mouth like an animal on the verge of death, and he smiles some more, tolerating my demise, apparently. "Can I see the rest?"

I nod, snap my mouth shut, and hand the camera over. Andro clicks through the memory, nodding here, raising an eyebrow there. He stops abruptly, and my hands go a little numb when I realize he's looking very intently at my wisteria Wheel of Fortune.

"Holy shit," he says. "Did you make this?"

My mouth is open again. No sound is coming out again. Finally, just as I'm forming words, Star is right there, saving what's left of my pathetic life.

"Moon makes earth art," she says.

"Wow. Wow." He's zooming in on the wheel. You can practically see the microscopic mushroom network in the dirt. "What do you do this for? A school project or something?" His eyes widen a touch. "Wait, are you on Fotogram with this stuff?"

Star laughs. "Oh, no. Moon hates Fotogram. Like, legit wants to light it on fire and toss it into the sea."

That's right. My sister tells the creator of FG that I want to murder his billion-dollar life's work.

But Andro chuckles in response and hands me back my camera. "I can relate to that. Hey, maybe we can talk tomorrow about that custom font, okay?"

I nod and take several steps back before waving goodbye and promptly running away. When I turn my head a little to see if everyone is laughing at me, I'm slightly dismayed to see, instead, that Star is already pulling Andro back into her orbit. She's giving him a good smile. Not as good as the one she pulled on Santiago earlier, but pretty close. When Star smiles like that, she may as well pull out a microphone and sing, "And oh, you're gonna love me." All the spells she puts on everyone all the time, you'd think she had La Raíz, not me.

I'm so out of sorts, I entirely forget what I'm so pissed about until I finally reach the bus. "Fucking Star," I mutter, leaning my head against the smooth of the outside metal. Fucking Star and playing down everything I do. Star has always made me feel small, but it's never felt this . . . purposeful before.

I'm not taking another photo of her until she apologizes. With chocolate.

At that my stomach grumbles so loud, I think the bus shakes a little. My mood improves immediately when I remember Santiago basically gave me permission to use his kitchen. I can think of only one thing I want. "Onward, omelets," I say to no one, and march right in.

Why didn't anyone tell me that I'd need a degree in astrophysics to make a stinking omelet?

First of all, the eggs stuck. And that whole stuck layer burned up into a thin, black forest of smoke. I scrub the whole mess up, and while I'm doing so, pieces of that piece-of-crap nonstick skillet start scrubbing off. Like metallic dead skin after a terrible sunburn. I end up throwing the whole thing away, pan and all.

Well, Santiago said I could use his precious pans, right? So I grab one of his smaller cast irons. Put some butter on it, heat it up. Whisk the eggs, pour them in, start praying the rosary, light a cone of holy incense . . . and about burst into tears when the omelet sticks again. Smoke pours right up from it, so I scrape it out and put soapy water in the pan, which causes Santiago to jump out of wherever he was hiding to scold me. "It's porous, Moon! The iron is porous. Do you know what that means?"

"Oh, yeah, porous. You can pour stuff on it." I give him a buttery fake smile and flutter my lashes. "Funny, right?"

He gives me a look like he can't believe how unfunny I am, takes over, and finishes washing his pan. I rummage in the cupboard for my popcorn. I throw a bag in the microwave, sit at the table, put my face in my hands.

What am I doing here? What am I doing with my life? I mean, I know I'm getting paid enough to live on campus at my dream school, but anytime I ask myself those two questions, the answer, like a compass, always points to Star. Always. And right now school and my tarot art have been on the back burner, with me, as usual, struggling to keep it on the flames at all. What am I doing here? Taking photos of Star. What am I doing with my life? Taking photos of Star. And what is Star doing? Eating caviar from rare platinum jellyfish wild caught from Siberia. Making friends. Getting every guy to trip over his dick for her, even Andro.

I'm feeling pretty sorry for myself once the microwave dings. Unfortunately, my pity party has an audience. When I lift my head, Santiago's in the doorway, his arms crossed, his biceps looking more like hubcaps than bowls. Ugh. Get those things away from me. I'm not in the mood for that sort of distraction.

I stand and flip open the microwave. "What are you doing?" Santiago asks.

I pause, letting some of the steam out of the bag. "If you're here to laugh at me, I will throw this burning-hot popcorn all over your boobs."

He doesn't even blink. "What happened to your eggs?"

I sigh. "In the trash, man. Can I eat my popcorn in peace now?"

He stares at me for a second, then takes a step forward, grabbing my popcorn and topping my sad little omelet attempt with it.

"What the hell—"

"Get the eggs." His voice is so gruff, goose bumps—against my will—run up and down my arms.

"Why—"

"Because I'm tired of watching you eat garbage instead of food. The eggs, Moon. Please."

Him adding "Moon" and then "please" somehow gets me in motion, even though my goose bumps have multiplied by a zillion trillion. There are fewer stars in the sky by now. I am a whole galaxy of goose bumps, spiraling and swirling into some distant black hole.

"How many eggs of an omelet?" he asks when I hand him the carton. Then he looks down. "What is this junk?"

It's some eggs I bought at a creepy gas station after Belle snuck me those omelets from that one hotel. It says "farm-fresh" right there on the package, but he's frowning at it like it reads "may or may not poison you" instead. Then he pops the eggs in the trash too.

"Hey! I paid good money for that!" A little over a dollar, but that still definitely counts as money last time I checked.

He ignores me and grabs other eggs—his eggs presumably—

which are in a biodegradable container, covered in fancy scripted words like "free-range," "organic," and "meet your egg's makers inside!" That last one makes me think there might be a portrait of God, white-bearded and cuddling hens, and it makes me half smile, even in these circumstances.

"How many eggs?" Santiago repeats.

I started with two in my previous attempts, but now I am much, much hungrier, so I say, "Six."

"Six?" His pretty eyes are bugging out. "Quick question. Have you ever cooked anything before?"

I straighten my back and stare right at his pecs. "I'll have you know, I can make the best grilled cheese on Planet Earth." Until I ate them every day for six months—because yeah, it is the only thing I know how to make—and got deathly sick of them.

"Somehow I doubt that." He cracks three eggs into a bowl. I can barely successfully crack an egg in five whole minutes, but Santiago is just like one of those professionals on the Food Network, getting the job done in seconds. "We can't do much more than that; otherwise it won't heat evenly." He grabs a whisk and goes to town, cradling the bowl inside his left forearm. "Do you want add-ins? Cheese? Onions?"

"Yes," I say, my mouth watering.

He tells me to whisk. Meanwhile, he grabs some Tupperware from the fridge. Onions, peppers, black olives, all already chopped up. "Melt a knob of butter on the six-inch pan," he says, handing me a stick.

I obey, watching the butter sizzle on the black iron, thanking the gods I've watched Jamie Oliver enough to know what constitutes a knob of butter.

Santiago adds a few handfuls of the veggies, then pauses. "You eat meat?" When I nod, he grabs a container labeled TOFU and sprinkles cooked bacon all over the sizzling onions and peppers. "Andro will eat it all otherwise," he says, pointing at the label. I nod. And smile. A little.

He tells me to stir the veggies, and then he whisks the eggs some more. A lot more. It feels like eight hours have passed. Finally he pours them in and they bubble and pop. He turns the heat down and squeezes right in front of me, the back of his thigh rubbing at my hip. I take a step back.

"What's wrong with you?" he says, tilting his head in my direction.

I shrug, not exactly sure what he's talking about.

"I mean, why aren't you being a pain in my ass?"

I know he doesn't mean it literally, but I take the time to check out his ass before saying, "I don't want you to change your mind about feeding me."

His jaw gets really tight, and he starts pulling the egg toward the center of the pan with the spatula. "See that? First we have to spread the liquid around, let it cook evenly."

I nod.

After a couple minutes, Santiago flips the omelet and gives it a satisfied smirk. Because the omelet is perfect. It's absolutely perfect. No flakes of black from the pan, or even any crispy brown spots.

I give him the biggest grin, and he stops smiling entirely when he looks at me. In fact, I must look like a horror-movie clown, because he drops his spatula in the pan, cutting right into the omelet.

"Fuck," he mutters. "What kind of cheese?"

I open the fridge. He's got so many. Cheddar, both sharp and mild, pepper jack, Swiss, and lots of stuff I've never heard of, like Gruyère and gouda and mascarpone? I thought that last one was a cartoon character or something.

"Grab the Gruyère."

"O-kay," I say, but I guess I'm too slow, because then he reaches past me and grabs the bag of white grated goodness. His arm kind of leans on my shoulder, almost pushing me to the floor with its weight. Seriously, how does he not fall over all the freaking time?

"So why aren't you on the meal plan?" I ask. I'm thinking way too much about Santiago's arms and need a distraction.

He scrunches up his nose. "Whatever they're eating out there, I can make better—and cheaper—in here."

I shrug and nod. Makes sense to me.

He sprinkles the cheese on and closes the omelet, sliding it onto a plate immediately. "Voilà."

"Merci," I say. I'm so hungry, I don't even care that he sits with me to watch me eat.

After my first bite, he asks, "Good?"

And I can't help it. I burst into tears.

He looks so alarmed, like he thinks I might spew food and snot in his face, but ventures with, "What's the matter?"

"Nothing. This is the best thing I've ever eaten." Even better than the fancy hotel omelet-bar omelet. Even better than honey on pizza. I haven't had something this wonderfully comforting since before Dad left all those years ago. But when I look up at Santiago, he appears . . . pissed? What the hell?

And then he speaks. "Am I that much of an asshole?"

Not sure I heard that right. "What?"

"That you think I'd change my mind about feeding you? And that you cry when I make you literally the simplest meal in the history of cooking?"

I make a face. "First of all, omelets are really tricky, jerk." That gets me a little smile. "Second, not everything is about you, Thor. Jeez Louise." I put a huge bite of omelet in my mouth, and when I glance up again, Santiago is smiling. One of those big, happy, real smiles that get his eyes soft and warm and his lips wide and peach.

"There you are," he says. "Where'd you go, Moon?"

Before I can respond, he stands really fast, putting things in the sink. "Tell you what. We go half on groceries. I'll teach you how to cook food that doesn't come from a piece of plastic."

"Really?" Then I stop. "Wait. You're going to poison me, aren't you?"

He snorts. His back is to me, but through his shirt, I can see the way his muscles move and stiffen. "I should've let you use the kitchen first thing. Then you wouldn't be crying over a fucking omelet."

I've stuffed the last bite in my mouth, and I'm so happy I rest my head on the table and close my eyes. "Santiago, you may be

RAQUEL VASQUEZ GILLILAND

an impossible, triple-F Jolly Green Giant, but again, not everything is about you." I pause. "Even if your omelet was knock-
you-naked good."

He chokes a little and then laughs. Full. On. Laughing. I'm
not as clear on sounds, but his laugh is like river rocks, smooth
under my hands, just like what his pectorals probably feel like.

"What's 'triple-F' mean?" he asks me when his belly laugh is
mostly controlled.

"Hmm?"

"You called me a triple-F Jolly Green Giant."

Oh. Right. "Your bra size."

I'm rewarded with another burst of laughter. It's lovely, so
lovely, that now I think of warm summer rain, making everything smell alive and green, like a whole wet forest of ancient,
slow-growing lichen. I sit with this feeling for so long, until for
a brief moment I can close my eyes and actually feel it, the fine
laced hairs of mint green all around me. When I open them,
though, I about fall out of my chair.

Because on the window, in the fading evening light, are about
a dozen amber-colored butterflies, fluttering their wings.

"Oh no," I say as several more fly up.

"What is it?" Santiago asks.

"It's the ridiculous, freaking curse! Jesus Louisus!" Now the
window is so covered in butterflies, I can scarcely see the burnt-
orange sky anymore.

"Moon. What the fuck are you talking about?"

132

I'm up, walking along the bus. Every little window is covered in butterflies. I don't even need to reach the driver's compartment to know the windshield is blanketed in a sea of creepy wings covered in owl-like eyes. "The windows," I say to Santiago, who's following me.

"Holy shit," he says. "That's a lot of bugs."

"Whatever you do," I say. "Don't open the window or door right now. They'll go away pretty soon, if past experience is anything to go by." I sit on the sofa in the lounge and put my face in my hands.

"They must be attracted to the omelet?" Santiago says, sitting next to me. He sounds very unsure of that theory.

I may as well just get on with it, right? After all, it isn't possible for Santiago to think I'm any weirder. "No, they're attracted to me. Well, not necessarily me, but this curse in my bloodline."

"I'm sorry. I don't think I heard that right. Because from here it sounds like you said you have a *curse* in your *bloodline*."

"I know what it sounds like. But it's real. It's called La Raíz, and it's been passed down in the women in my family since Eve, supposedly."

"Why 'The Root'?"

I lift my head. "You speak Spanish?"

"My mother's from Colombia."

I drop my head again. "Yeah. It's the root connection to Eve and the tree and the original sin and blah-blah-blah."

When I peek up, Santiago is trying not to laugh.

"This isn't funny!"

"Sure it isn't. You're saying you're cursed to be visited by thousands of butterflies on occasion. You're fucking with me, right? You've got to be fucking with me."

It's hard to explain why I'm so disappointed that Santiago doesn't believe me. I mean, that's the only rational response to something like this. I guess there was this feeling inside me, soft like floating dandelion seeds. The feeling that he'd understand somehow.

"Hey. They're gone now." He nudges me with an elbow. I definitely do not notice how warm and firm he is.

I peek again, and he's right. They're gone. "Great," I say. "Come on. I'll help with the dishes."

26.

The Worst Freaking Part About La Raíz

. . . ISN'T THE BUGS or the creepiness or the all-around what-the-fuck of it. No, the worst bit is how utterly random it is. Since those thousand fireflies descended on me in that damp, grassy yard almost three years ago, I've been trying to figure out this thing's rhyme and rules. Any rule would be nice to know, before being freaking cursed, you know? Surely some woman from Eve's time to the contemporary world would've figured *something* out by now.

But no. The La Raíz happenings are unpredictable. It arrives the first time you have sex, so okay, there's *one* rule we know, but from then on, it's a whenever-it-feels-like-it, free-for-all house party.

It comes when I have sex, but sometimes not. It comes when I concentrate really hard with my tarot cards, sometimes not. It comes when I'm so intent on making art, I don't even notice it until a million ladybugs have descended upon me, and—surprise! Sometimes not!

I learned this the hard way when I was in art class junior year. I hadn't had a La Raíz–related event in months, and I thought I was safe or something, as though for some reason La Raíz had forgotten about my existence, the way we forget how people hurt us if they're nice for a little while. I assumed, somehow, that I was free.

I was working on a painting, of a woman made out of papayas, and I'd started mixing sand into my palette, which gave it this amazing texture. It felt *so* good, like the words "papaya" and "amarillo" and "juniper" all put together. I gave up on my brushes and started painting with my fingers.

The little flaps of wings were easy to ignore at first. After all, everyone was talking, and the art teacher, Ms. Hershner, was playing a soundtrack from some old movie. It was easy to focus on my paint, on the conversations flitting back and forth as though they were the winged ones, and on the tubas and saxophones in the background.

And then this vibrating tickle swept across my back like legged lace. What really alerted me to something wild happening, though, was the fact that someone screamed.

One hundred thousand ladybugs (as mentioned above). I didn't count, but I'm pretty sure that's an accurate estimate. They crawled all over me. It looked like I was made of them, that my arms and chest and back and knees were formed by red, polka-dotted beetles.

"Okay," Ms. Hershner said, all calm, "let's get you outside, Moon."

Everyone stared. Everyone just freaking stared at me, the cursed ladybug girl, as I walked out. Everyone pressed their noses to the windows as I stepped into the school courtyard . . . and *even more* lady-freaking-bugs landed on me.

Ms. Hershner tried to shoo them away, but . . . yeah. They leave on their own terms. It took only a minute for them to whisk away into the sky like seeds in the wind, but let me tell you. Everyone wanted to be friends with me after that. Not.

I can't believe I thought Mom was lying. And now I'm legit *cursed* for it. Like it wasn't enough that I had to be perfect, beautiful, dainty Star Fuentez's twin sister. I have to attract bugs, too. Like a bloom. But not a sweet, nice one. Something big and in-your-face, something you can't run away from fast enough. Like one of those orchids that smell like dead things.

That's me, Moon Fuentez. The flower no one wants to be around, unless you count massive amounts of bugs from time to time.

27.

Andro the Flirt and Santiago the Jerk

WE'RE ON THE road almost all day today, so I stayed in bed for ages, my face against the window. The landscape is getting darker and mountainous. The colors are absolutely thrilling, mixed with the clouds in peach and goldenrod. Everything made of rock crystal, sparkling on the tips of my fingers and the fog of my breath against the glass.

When the bus parks to let the beautiful fools off to break their fast, I brush my teeth and throw my hair up in a giant bun, then drag my computer to the dining table. Santiago is already there, giant book in front of him.

"Hey," I say, plopping down.

"Hungry?" he asks.

I glance up at the clock. "I gotta edit photos for Star, so I can't do our cooking show. I'll just have a bagel."

He rolls his eyes and starts doing the kitcheny stuff he likes to do. I try not to watch. But he makes it really hard. I swear he does it on purpose. His shoulders are so broad, I bet if I were to try to hug them, I'd dislocate my own. And his movements are smooth, too, like, I don't know, a waterfall or maybe a—

"Oh, hey, Moon, was hoping you'd be up." Andro slides into the seat next to me. "What are you working on?"

"We're about to eat," Santiago says gruffly.

"This won't take long. Was wondering if I could commission that font?"

"Uh, okay," I say, pulling my laptop screen down. "What do you have in mind?"

I take some notes as Andro speaks. He talks for a while, using a lot of meaningless buzzwords, like "informational super-highway," "passion," "holistic," and "rock and roll." "Do you think you can work with that?" he asks.

"Uh." He's so close to me, I can smell the woody notes of his cologne. "I'll whip up some samples by early next week. Does that sound good?"

"Sure does." He winks and my stomach feels nervous. We're looking in each other's eyes like . . . I dunno. Doves? Love doves? Do birds make eye contact with one another? It doesn't matter, because a second later Santiago drops a plate in front of me, star-tling us both with its clatter.

"I'll leave you to it," Andro says, standing. "Email me your rates, okay, Moon?" He gives me a card, holding my hand for a split second before disappearing through the door.

Santiago collapses in the seat in front of me, digging into his dish, which looks identical to mine.

"What is this?"

"Breakfast pasta."

I don't wrinkle my nose. I don't. But the giant can somehow sense my reaction. "Just try it," he grumbles. His hair is all mussed this way and that, gold in the sun. And I smile and take a bite.

And then I pretend to faint. "Oh my God." I shove another bite in and ask, covering my mouth, "What's in it? Besides the personal blessings of Jesus Christ?"

Santiago gives me a half smile. "Olive oil, eggs, onions, garlic, Parmigiano-Reggiano. The real stuff, imported." Then his face goes gloomy again, and he stares at his plate so I can't see his expression anymore. "He's got a girlfriend, you know."

"What?" I've propped my laptop back up and have just sent Star her restaurant portraits.

"Andro. Has a girlfriend."

"Oh." Now I'm working on the Wheel of Fortune. "Why are you telling me this?"

"Because he's a big flirt. Really good at getting girls' expectations up."

I wrinkle my nose. Because I hate big flirts. Even in someone as beautiful as Andro. If I were his girlfriend, I wouldn't like the way he gives cute little compliments and lingers in smoldering glances. And of course Andro's a big flirt. Why else would he be so nice to me—me, Moon the Weedy Weed, awkward and loud. *Round*, my mother would add, as though I'd need the reminder. Only this morning, I found another cellulite dimple on my ample thigh. "Figures," I mutter.

"What figures?"

I shake my head. "You know. A decent guy acting like I'm not gross. Figures that it's his force of habit or whatever."

Santiago doesn't say anything for a while. When I look up from editing, he's staring at me, looking about a heartbeat away from ripping my head off. "What?" I take another bite despite his anger, because nothing but God could stop me from finishing this dish as fast and as unladylike as possible.

He lifts his hand. "Why do you always do that?" He sounds so pissed.

"Always do what?" I ask, my tone just as sharp.

He lowers his voice until all I can think about are dark, muscular fairy kings, lurking in magic forests in search of some lost mortal to seduce. "Fish for compliments."

When I process what he's said, my hands weaken and my fork goes to the plate in a clatter. I don't know why his accusation affects me so much, but I'm a dragon now, hard-scaled and breathing fire. "I do not fish for compliments."

"Trust me, Moon. You do little else."

I close my eyes because hot smoke is slithering out of my ears and nostrils. "Santiago. There would actually have to be compliments in the sea for me to try to fish for them."

He laughs and points. "There you go again! You're fishing for compliments about fishing for compliments."

"I'm not . . ." How can I explain this, that when Andro tells me I'm good at fonts and photos? That's the first compliment I've gotten from someone who isn't Tía, or Star trying to make me feel better about her goddess looks next to mine, or a random follower from FG. And how those tiny, no-big-deal compliments Andro gave me, like it was nothing, how precious they are, like raw, sparkling tourmalines tucked away in my pocket. But I can't. The words are getting sharp inside me, and I finally open my mouth and breathe out fire.

"Fuck you. And fuck your food and your cooking show. I'm done."

His eyes widen ever so slightly, but other than that, he keeps his face expressionless. Like he barely even cares. I hate to admit it, but that hurts a teensy bit more than it should.

I know I'll regret canceling the cooking show by the time I get hungry again in four hours, but I don't care. I lock myself in the bathroom and cry for ten minutes as silently as I can.

When I slide back into the kitchen area, Santiago stares at me from the doorframe, one giant leg crossed over the other. "We need to get to work," I say as I load my plate into the dishwasher.

Neither of us speaks as we unload the merch, sell the merch, and pack up the merch again. So we're back to that. And that makes me sad too, so when we finally get back to the bus, the sky as purple and gloomy as I feel, I crawl into bed, hiding. Like a loser.

My phone buzzes a few times, and I ignore it. Finally it starts ringing, and for a moment I think maybe Mom is calling to check in on me. I grab it and sigh, because no, it's not my mom. It's Samuel. I don't answer fast enough to catch the call, so I click over to my messages.

Moon.

Moon.

You there?

Moon.

Luuuuuuuuuuuna.

MOON.

I know I said he's not my friend anymore. I know I said it. But right now, I really, really want to feel good about myself. And a lot of the time, that's exactly what Samuel does for me. And even though I know his compliments aren't in good faith, that reminder doesn't stop me from answering when he calls again. "What do you want?" I ask when I pick up.

"You mean, besides nudes . . . ?"

I scoff. "You're such a—"

"Stud? Catch? Well-rounded gentleman?"

"I was going to say douche canoe."

He laughs. Everything always rolls off Samuel. I wish I could study how to be more like him, minus all the sleaze. "How have you been?" I ask.

"Good. Balling. Partying."

"Who is your companion this week?"

"Companion, Moon? Is that what we're calling it now?"

I laugh.

"I've been spending time with Maury Bodega."

"Wow." Maury Bodega, despite having the name of a 209-year-old bartender, is hot. Like, Philips brothers hot.

"You jealous?"

"Of you, yes. Not of him."

"That hurts, Moon." I smile as he adds, "It's good to hear your voice, Loon."

Before I can respond, the curtain to my bed is thrown open, and I'm looking into the amber eyes of a certain fuming, hulking jerk-face.

"I'm hungry," the giant demands.

I put a hand on my phone. "And what do you want me to do about it?" Even as my stomach growls loudly.

"Kitchen," Santiago says as he turns away. "Now."

My stomach growls again, as though to say, *Oh God, yes, please follow that mofo anywhere please, thanks.*

"What the hell was that?" Samuel is asking.

"Uh." I'm not sure if he's asking about my stomach's or Santiago's booming growls. "I've got to go eat now."

"Moon—"

"Talk soon, yeah?" And I hang up before he's got the chance to charm me. It's weird, but in a matter of minutes, I don't have time for that BS anymore.

I'm weeping over onions. Weeping like an even more devastating version of La Llorona.

"Are they chopped yet?" Santiago barks.

"Of course not." I throw my hands up to gesture to my face. "I can barely see, much less chop. Unless you want me to cut open an artery."

"It would certainly make my life easier if you did." He hands me something soft, and I wipe my eyes, blink a little, and get back to it.

"What are we cooking tonight?" I ask.

Santiago doesn't say anything. Then: "So you're not done with the cooking show."

"I thought you'd figured that out when I started crying over the onions for you."

He snorts a little. A little too smugly, in my opinion. He then barks orders at me, occasionally cutting in to take over, until I'm plating what he tells me is blackened tilapia with a mustard wine sauce and cheese grits with garlic spinach on the side.

When I sit and take a bite, I swear, my eyes roll back into my liver. The fish is crisp and flaky, spicy and salty. The grits, which I seriously doubted were going to be edible, freaking rock my socks. I'd even smack myself in the face for the spinach. I imagine myself on the streets, holding a hand-painted sign: WILL SLAP SELF FOR WILTED SPINACH COOKED BY SANTIAGO PHILIPS.

"So you still want to learn how to cook?" Santiago's got an eyebrow raised, amused by the foodgasm I'm currently having.

I spoon another bite in before responding, and the buttery-cheesy amazingness hits me all over again. This whole meal is a hearth fire, warming my hands and lips and belly. If I close my eyes, I can almost smell the smoke of it.

"Fine," I finally respond.

Santiago tilts his mouth. "Meh, I don't think so."

I blink. Swallow. Blink again.

"You're a pain in the ass," he says, shrugging. "It's a lot of effort, putting up with you. I don't know if I've got it in me."

I keep staring for a full thirty seconds and then say, "You are such a fucking—"

"But," he interrupts, "I could be persuaded if you'd say the magic word."

Oh my God. He's going to make me beg. I spoon a giant-ass bite into my mouth and will my eyes to stop rolling like bowling balls. This. I'll do it for this. Real food, nourishing my body. Self-care. Whatever.

I lift my face and say, "Santiago, will you please teach me to cook." My tone sort of sounds like I'm in a great deal of pain.

He half smiles, and there's mischievous glint in his eyes. "I don't know—"

"Motherfucking ass-pie."

"Did you just call me an ass-pie?"

"I sure did. And you know what, I'm not sure the ass-pie pain *you* are is worth—"

"Okay," he says. "We'll keep up the cooking show. But you've gotta be in the kitchen at six p.m. sharp, unless our work sched-ule dictates otherwise." He narrows his eyes. "Not chatting to boyfriends instead."

I sigh and stare at my plate. Would it be too pathetic and gross to lick it clean? "Six sharp. Got it, Thor."

"No talking to boyfriends while we're cooking," he repeats.

"I don't even have a boyfriend, so you can stop worrying about that, okay?"

His face is so completely blank, I half wonder if he's turned to stone, if he's been a robot this whole time and the system just conked out. And then he stands. "Come on, help me wash the dishes, fisherwoman."

Fuck, I hate this guy. Damn him and his delicious food.

28.

That One Time I Tried to Pray La Raíz Away (Spoiler: It Didn't Work)

AFTER THE LADYBUG incident, I was actually desperate enough to go to church without Mom forcing me to. It was Sunday, after morning Mass had ended. Everyone was making their way to the exits, and I sat in a pew and cried. Wasn't it enough for me to have lost my dad and have a mom like mine? Wasn't it enough that I was destined to be Moon, Weed Extraordinaire? It was quite the pity party, let me tell you.

I thought everyone was too busy to notice me, but I was wrong. Because that's when Father Luke approached. He didn't sit down or anything; he stood super far away, like I had something contagious.

"I heard a disturbing rumor, Moon," he said in that fake-warm voice. The one he used when he was trying to prove to someone—God, I guess—that he had what it took to speak with people he really didn't want to. That some part of him cared. I always thought if Father Luke couldn't convince *me* he cared, that tone sure wasn't going to work with God, but I never had the guts to tell him that.

Right. Back to the story. So he was like, "I heard a rumor," and my response was to laugh. Because of course the father had heard something bad about me. Rumors preceded me, launched and landed all around me, just like bugs. It's the way it is when you're a weed.

You should've seen his face. He couldn't hide his contempt any longer, not after I did that weeping-snotty laugh. "So it's true, then?" he asked.

"What's true?" I said in return. "About the ladybugs or about the fireflies? Or are you talking about the rumors of all the sex?" I wiped my nose with the end of my sleeve. "It doesn't matter. Because you know what? They're all true."

He audibly swallowed, like the way cartoon animations do when they're terrified, and I swear, he used all his power to refrain from taking a step back. He could only say, "You must've angered God very much, to have these creatures be attracted to you."

Yep. An angry God sicced ladybugs on me. I was too tired to say this, though. When I didn't respond, he added, "The confessional will be open until noon. You can do it, Moon. You can atone for your sins. That's the gift Jesus gave us all." And he nodded, the obligatory Save Moon Fuentez speech complete, and walked away.

He walked away before I could ask him how many Hail Marys

it would take to "atone" myself of a thousands-year-old curse in the bloodline. What did I have to do to burn out the original sin, the one that literally belonged to Eve?

But I couldn't. I couldn't even call these words after him, because he stopped a few feet away and said this: "It's a shame you aren't more like your sister."

That was the moment I decided I was sincerely done with the church. No amount of threats from my knife-wielding mother could make me endure that again. *It's a shame you aren't more like your sister.* I'd heard enough from my mom and strangers from the internet. I wasn't going to let some asshole in priest's robes tell me too.

Tell me I'm not as good as Star.

That I'm not as worthy, lovely, charming, or valued as Star.

It's already tattooed on me, in the shape of a fat pink scar on my chest. What else could I possibly need for it to sink in any more? A larger kitchen knife? A sword?

Oh, and praying the curse away didn't work, by the way. Only girls like Star get their prayers answered.

29.

In Which a Wild Nebula Picks Wild Huckleberries (and Is Also a Big Jerk About It)

IT'S WEIRD. WE have the day off, but I haven't seen Santiago for hours. Not that I've been looking for him or anything ridiculous like that. Just, when you've spent the last couple of weeks in close quarters with an enormously grumpy giant lurking about, it's a little weird when he's not there, stomping around and grumping about stuff like hidden preservatives and monosodium glutamate.

I'm googling how long it takes before someone is considered missing when the bus's front door is flung open. The steps that follow shake up the whole vehicle, the whole universe even. Asteroids far and wide are disrupted on their paths. The slow migration of the Milky Way hits a bump like on a dirt road. So I know exactly who it is without looking.

He appears in the kitchen, and I freeze for four whole seconds before I can move again. Because he wears a tight-as-flip tank top and striped running shorts and he's sweaty. Sweaty not in a gross way, but in a *Men's Health* photo-shoot-next-to-a-waterfall way.

He's got a baby-blue Easter basket in his hand, full of berries. Berries! They're small like dried black beans, dark, and the color of indigo mixed with burgundy. They're shiny like beads made of the chert my father used to bring home from archaeological digs.

"What's that?"

He sets the basket on the table and grunts in an especially grumpy manner. He turns to the sink and runs the water.

I grab a berry and pop it in my mouth. "Ugh," I say, making a face. "Are these even edible? Why are they so tart?" I reach for another, because the flavor is already growing on me, but Santiago swipes the basket away before I can get there. "Hey!"

"They're huckleberries."

"Oh! Like Huckleberry Finn. Are you going to make a pie? Please tell me you're making a pie."

"They're for a special occasion."

"Ooh. What's the occasion?"

"Don't know yet," he grunts so deeply, I can scarcely make out what he's saying. This is reason number 399 why Santiago makes me want to throw eggs at him from time to time—his tendency toward caveman language.

"They're ridiculously sour," I say. I don't know why I'm still talking. Guess I'm a little lonely for company.

"They're ridiculously rare," he says as he pours them into a stainless-steel colander in the sink.

"What do you mean by that?"

"What I mean is real huckleberries are next to impossible to cultivate." He shakes the colander as he swirls it under the tap. "You can really only get them in the wild. And wild huckleberry patches need to be burned every few decades, or they won't make berries anymore."

He's smiling as he grabs a pot. "These berries are only here in my hand"—he lifts a few—"all because of their own prerogative. Humans had nothing to do with it." And the treatise is finished. He moves on to what I think is blanching them. All I can do is watch in wonder.

I feel all strange in my chest area, listening to Santiago wax on about huckleberries, how they seem to have the desire to stay as wild as possible. After he went out and picked several cups into a pale-blue Easter basket. It reminds me of my dad, how just talking about things makes them miraculous. "That's beautiful," I finally say.

"Yes," he agrees. "And they won't be wasted on anyone who doesn't appreciate them." He levels a blamey stare at me.

"I appreciate them! They're a little sour is all. I bet they'd bake up real nice in a pie. Hint, hint."

He grunts like a caveman again. I guess the conversation is over.

That night, I'm curled up in a blanket, thinking a lot about my dad. "You've been collecting words since you were little," he told me. "Ever since you fell in love with 'malvavisco.'" Marshmallow.

I still love that word, even more so now because I know it first came from a plant. A really lovely one, growing tall, with pale-pink flowers all along its stalk. Dad, Star, and I found a field of them once in South Dakota. Just like fireweed, seeing those layers and layers of rose-quartz blooms made me fall in love with the universe all over again. A whole sea of flores de malvavisco.

"Santiago," I say. I reach for the handle next to me and shake the bed frame a little. "Santiago!"

"What?"

"What's your favorite word?"

He grunts noncommittally. He's quiet for so long, I think he must've gone back to sleep, when he says, "Ocean."

"Ocean?"

"Yeah. The sound is like a whole wave, if you think about it. The *o* of it curling, and the crashing *c* sound, and the end of it, smoothing out. Ocean."

"You can hear the bubbles, too," I say.

"Yeah." He shifts in the bed. "Why? What's your favorite word?"

"I like . . ." I pause. There's too many, really. "I like 'ambiguous' and 'moss' and 'murmuration.' And 'fog' and 'piedra' and 'caderas'—"

"You have to pick only one, like I did."

"'Nebula.' I like 'nebula,' then."

We're both quiet for a while after that, so I grab my Spanish-English dictionary. Nebulosa. That's "nebula" in Spanish. I like that, too. How it's drawn out a little bit more, making it epic. How it sounds like the name of a benevolent and powerful prince. Nebulosa. I close my eyes, and that's how I fall asleep, thinking about nebulas shaped like humans, hundreds of light-years long, lit up by aurora borealis–like colors all around. I fall asleep wondering what other words a caballero de nebulosas might love.

"I feel like we haven't hung out in forever," Star says, collapsing next to me.

"That's because we haven't." I don't lift my eyes from my computer. I'm actually not touching up photos right now, believe it or not. Samuel sent me this wild computer game download. I'm not all that into video games, but this one is really up my alley. Basically, you kill the bad guys with whatever you can find in your kitchen—spoons, woks, teakettles. Which has proved to be ridiculously cathartic as of late.

"You've been busy." Star's tone is a little accusatory.

I finally look at her. She's thrown over the side of the sofa in our shared hotel room. Her dress is pale pink, the color newborn babies wear, in a lace that reaches her knees and wrists. I already want to scratch at my arms until they bleed, so I glance back at my computer screen quickly.

"I've been working," I respond.

"So have I." Now she sounds defensive, so I hold back a sigh and close my computer screen.

"I know. We've both been working. A lot."

Star lifts her eyebrows. "You've been spending a lot of time with Andro's brother."

"He's the merch guy. I'm the merch girl. Spending time together is part of the job description."

"I told Mom about him."

Great.

"She thinks I should ask him out on a date."

"What?" I basically choke it out, then sputter, then cough.

"You know. Be a good Christian. Because of . . . you know." She whispers the last bit.

I'm going to pretend like she didn't go there. Because the scales are back on my skin, my teeth are grinding, and my chest is glowing with embers. My nails turn into cactus spines, my tongue, covered in poisonous warts.

"You know?" Star asks.

"I don't." I say it through gritted teeth.

"His deformity."

"Don't say that."

"Why not?"

"It's not okay. It's rude." I looked it up right after I first noticed Santiago's disability. "Deformed" is offensive and mean, and lots of other common terms used to describe a disability are too. Stuff like "wheelchair-bound" and "crippled." I didn't want to accidently hurt him, so I educated myself.

But Star just shrugs and says, "What do you think?"

If I say I think it's ridiculous to use a guy to score some Jesus points—actually, you know what? "I think it's ridiculous to use a guy to score some Jesus points."

Star rolls her eyes. "I knew it! You're still mad at me."

It's so weird. My being mad at her has nothing to do with this, for once. It's about her wanting Santiago to be her good-Christian-virgin prop. I bet she's already planning the FG photo shoot. *He's been through so much,* she'd write. *But with Jesus, we're strong together.*

"I said I was sorry." Her eyes are glassy, and when I let out a defeated sigh, she smiles and sniffles. "I hate it when we fight."

"Me too, Star." I sigh again. "But it's messed up to use someone like that. You have to know it." God knows we both should. People are constantly trying to use me to get to Star and use Star to get their own slab of the pie in whatever form their greedy hands can touch. A shout-out on FG, free merch, or even cold hard cash, like that guy who once threatened Star, saying he had nudes. After a whole legal mess, turns out he was lying. Which we knew. But still. No one likes to be a stepping-stone.

Star nods and smiles a bit shyly. "I kind of like him, though."

And my heart feels really, really weird. Like it's stretching, you know? And I cough to try to get it back in place. "Oh wow. Mom approved? Of real dating?"

Star shrugs. "You know she's fine with it as long as things stay respectful."

I snort. My mom has extremely strong opinions on what's considered respectful in the realm of dating. One, of course, is we don't call it dating. It's courting. Husband-catching. Hanging out with the opposite sex, preferably with a chaperone, always knowing your every move is being watched by a very judgy Jesus.

"Will you put in a good word for me? With Santiago?" Star asks.

And I swallow back a much larger snort, because why would Star ever need a good word from anyone? "Look, sis. You know all you have to do is flutter your eyelashes and flash him that dazzling smile of yours—yep, that one." I cover my face like she's shining a giant spotlight on me. "You don't need anything from me. Trust me."

Star hugs me tight, then says, "We have our birthday off. Did you see that?"

"Really?" Somehow I've forgotten I'm turning eighteen in, what? A week and a half? How did that come up so quickly?

"I was thinking we could do what we always do."

"Go to Taco Bell and order one of everything on the dollar menu and gorge, you mean?"

"Yes!"

I wrinkle my nose because I can't let myself get too excited. "What about that raw diet you were doing?"

Now Star wrinkles her nose. "Ugh, no way. I don't want to see raw tomato sauce on raw squash pasta ever again in my life. Besides." She shrugs. "It's our birthday."

"But just us, right?" I bite my lips.

"Of course," Star says. "That's the tradition."

Now I smile. "Really, though?"

"Yes."

"*Really* really?"

"Yes, yes!"

Before I even know what's happening, I reach over and give Star a hug. We haven't done this in what feels like forever, but it's not awkward at all. In fact, if I close my eyes, it feels like we're kids again. Before Dad left, before Mom made such a big deal about how different Star and I look. Before Star became the beloved one.

When I pull away, Star grabs some nail polish. "Pedicures?"

"Only if you brought something glittery."

"You're in luck! Chloe Lander sent one called Disco Ball." She waves the silver sparkles in my face.

"Let's do this, then," I say. And then it really is like we're little kids again, having stolen one of Mom's old CoverGirl nail polishes and holed up in our shared bedroom. We giggle a lot. Talk about everything. Almost everything, that is. I mean, I don't tell her about tarot, and she doesn't mention any history with Belle, but I don't mind. She digs up some fancy chocolates Oak got her, and we each stuff as much as we can in our mouths and fall over laughing because we look like rotten monsters. It's ridiculous, since I bet these truffles are, like, thirty dollars apiece. But none of that matters, because I'm laughing with my sister.

I guess I just repress our earlier chat, because Santiago doesn't come up again in my head, not until I'm in bed, watching the lights of the windows in the hotel across from us. And my stomach feels like there are tiny swords stabbing at it and it's dumb that I would think of Santiago as my friend, like he's the gold inside my dragon's hoard. But it's been a really long time since I've had a friend who wasn't swept up in Star's orbit and it makes me sad. I wonder if it will always be this way. Because right now it feels like it will.

I imagine all of Santiago as made of stars. His firm body mists and twinkles and he is as big as hundreds of light-years. I send him off deeper into space, where he can enchant any girl or star or alien he wishes. Away from me, the lone loser Moon-weed.

It was fun while it lasted.

But also, he was a bit of a douche canoe. So maybe it's a good thing Star's chosen to take him away.

Wish it felt more like a good thing.

30.

My Sister's Nemesis
(Is Actually Nice? ~~And Cool~~)

"MOON," ANDRO SAYS as I'm filling up a cup of coffee at Honey Hut, the only gas station that provides a brownie-batter flavor. "The samples you sent? Ahhh-mazing. I really like the one you called Sun God." Beside me, Santiago snorts. He's too good for gas station coffee, so he's filling up a ceramic mug with hot water for his Italy-imported hot chocolate mix.

"How much for the rest of the alphabet?" Andro asks.

I pause, my cheeks a little warm. I mean, Andro's richer than Zeus, but I don't want to sound like I'm taking advantage. "Forty."

Andro blinks. "Forty *dollars*? You sure?"

"She means four hundred," Santiago grunts.

I nearly gasp. "What? That's—"

But Andro's already got the four bills out of his wallet. "Rock and roll. Email it to me by tomorrow, okay? That's when I need to send it to my designer."

"Uh." I take the bills with my fingertips as though they're covered in aphids. "Oh, uh, okay."

"Hey, Andro," Van calls, and then Andro's swept away into yet another thing. That guy is basically a tornado.

I turn to Santiago and smack his shoulder as hard as I can. He doesn't even blink.

"What the hell was that for?" I hiss. "Four hundred?"

"Give it back to him if it's too much."

"No way."

He smirks. "You at least owe me dinner."

"In what universe—"

"Per my commission, as your salesperson."

I sigh. "What do you want me to cook for you?"

He shudders. "You? Cook? No. No way. Nothing. Never."

I roll my eyes. "You are such a . . ." I stop when I see Star strolling up, her lips glossy in rose-tinted lip balm, the only form of makeup she'll wear, reserved for *very* special occasions.

"Hey, Moon," she says. Then she angles a shy, sweet smile at Santiago. "Hi."

Ah. So it begins.

"I'm going to . . . ," I say, and turn away, but Santiago puts an arm at my shoulder.

"What are you even drinking there?" he asks me, giving my cup a look of disgust.

I glance at Star, who looks mega-confused, and why wouldn't she? She just used, like, half her moves on Santiago—in *tinted lip balm*—and he didn't even say hi back.

"Coffee," I say, shrugging his arm off my shoulder.

"Wait. You didn't finish your sentence."

"What?"

"I am such a . . ."

"Oh, you know exactly what you are."

"Which is a . . . ?"

I narrow my eyes. "You are a nematode. Covered in *wasps*!" Never mind that the concept is physically impossible.

"Is that all?"

"No, of course not, you, you—you dried biscuit!"

And he smiles at me. Like, a legit, real smile. "That's what I thought."

And then it hits me.

Santiago likes it when I lose my temper. He *likes* it. What a weirdo!

Scoffing, I whip around and run toward the counter, cash in hand. After paying, before rushing out the door, I peek back at them, where he and Star are now in line. She's busted everything out. Hair flipping, eyelash butterflying, tugging at the gold crucifix at her chest.

But he's staring ahead, grunting like a caveman, looking for all the world like he doesn't have the slightest interest in Star Fuentez.

But that's impossible. That's impossible.

Right?

"Hey," Belle says. "Is that Hearts and Stars? Looks great on you."

I touch the edge of my lips, which have exactly two and a half coats of the hot-pink matte Brixstick on them. "Thanks." I glare pointedly at Santiago, who's just told me I look like a clownfish.

He flicks his eyes to me with a smirk, so fast that you'd miss it if you weren't looking for it.

"Wanna get some ice cream?" she asks. "There's a Marble Slab across the street."

I pull up my schedule on my phone. "Ah. I can't up and leave the merch."

She makes a face. "Santiago can watch it, can't you?"

"Yeah, right," I say. "Mr. You Can't Afford to Slack Off—"

"Bring me back some." He looks directly at me.

"What?"

"You owe me, remember?"

Oh, right. Well, he did get me three hundred and sixty more dollars, so . . . If he hadn't stepped in, I wouldn't even be considering ice cream right now.

"What kind do you like?"

He shrugs. "Surprise me." And then: "But no fruit!"

"So, strawberry covered in apple pie filling, got it." He flips me off. I return the favor as Belle and I step out.

"Tell me about your art," Belle says the second we sit down. She's got three scoops of cherry cheesecake. I have a caramel sundae covered in whipped cream. So much whipped cream that I can't even see the vanilla ice cream.

"How do you know about my art?"

Belle pauses. "Your sister told me a while ago."

Weird. "Are you going to tell me what happened between you and Star?"

"Tell me about your art first."

"Ugh." I put my spoon down. "Fine. I'm making a photographic tarot deck."

"No shit!" She's grinning. "What's the aesthetic?"

"Flowers and twigs, basically. Whatever I can find in the woods."

"Rustic, earthy . . ."

"Yeah. Pretty much."

"Can I see?"

I shake my head. "Sorry. It's nothing personal. I'm really superstitious about showing it before it's done is all." I don't mention that if I let people I know into this part of my life, it'll become its own wild animal, creeping around with big paws and a long, swishy tail, and somehow my mother will spot it leaping across the lawn. And even though she can't destroy my work, she'll try. Even if it meant killing me.

"So you'll let me see it when it's done?"

"Yeah. I'm close." I can technically do a practice print now, even without uploading my most recent work on the site, which I've been considering more and more. But I don't want to get that deep. I've been talking about myself for too long already. "So. You and Star."

Belle's face becomes gloomy immediately. "Right."

I feel like I'm imposing. "You don't have to—"

"No, it's fine. Just, remember the Sunrise Expo in Portland last year?"

Right. Normally I'm Star's plus-one for events, but that one was so close, Mom decided to go in my stead, in an extraordinarily rare outing. Anything for Star.

"Well. Yeah. She and I hung out a lot. We were close." Belle looks at me pointedly, like she's waiting for me to have a very specific reaction. I feel completely lost, though, so she nods a little and says, "And at the end of the trip, we had a disagreement."

"Over makeup?" I guess.

Belle smiles a little, a sad smile, and nods. "Yeah. Makeup."

It feels like I'm teetering on the edge of something much more personal than I thought it was going to be. I'm not sure whether to dive in or take slow, deliberate steps back to where I was. Luckily, Belle quickly makes the decision for me: "So how's the tour going for you?"

"Not bad," I respond. Could be worse, could be better. At least I'm well fed now. "What about you?"

Belle sighs. "It's all so fucking fake, you know? I want to talk makeup with people, and that, that's fun. But I'm so sick of trying to act like everything about my life is amazing, how if only you'd try harder and support Fotogram, you can be successful too!"

"Yeah," I say, making a face. I know exactly what she's talking about. It's so obvious when Star gives advice on her account. She only uses vague platitudes and Bible verses, which I understand does pull at some people's heartstrings, but it never gets specific, you know? She never talks about anything difficult. Like having a mom like ours, or Dad leaving, or being poor before all this stuff. Like Belle said, there's nothing real.

"Though that's not as bad as the dudes, like, hitting on us all day with the most corniest pickup lines I've ever heard in my life."

"Like what?" I so rarely get hit on, I feel like I'm peeking in on a brand-new world.

"Oh, like . . . 'Hey, thankfully I have my library card, because I am checking you out right now.'"

I snort. "That's almost funny." It's certainly nowhere near as gross as some of the stuff I've seen in Star's DMs folder.

"Not so much when the man is older than your dad."

"Ew. Good Lord. I didn't realize fans that old were coming to the events."

"Well, he did bring his daughter to see Star."

Now I pretend to gag. "God, that's so much worse. Ew. Ew."

"Don't vomit on your sundae and waste your ice cream. At least let me save it."

"No way," I say, before inhaling the last two bites.

"What flavor are you going to get the hottie?"

"What?"

"Santiago."

I make a face, and she adds, "Come on. Don't pretend he's not hot. I mean, he's nowhere near my type, but even I know he's hot."

I roll my eyes. "Fine. He's hot. But then his mouth and his brain ruin the whole effect."

She laughs as I stand and stare at the ice cream behind the glass for a few seconds. No fruit, he said, which I hope means he likes dark chocolate with peanut butter cups. I have the attendant top the whole thing with hazelnut cream sprinkles, which sounds snobby enough for Santiago's tastes.

"I better get to the others," Belle says, touching my shoulder when we return to the merch tables. "By the way, I want a reading from you," she calls. "With your own deck, okay?"

I wave and give her a thumbs-up, then turn to see Santiago's, okay, yes, hot face. I don't know what it is about him that is so freaking gorgeous. It's probably because he's got a sharp, thick jaw and cheekbones for days. Or maybe his amber eyes, which are framed by what looks like false eyelashes. And, right, he's got this perpetual five-o'clock shadow that drives me absolutely bananas because I can never stop thinking about what it might feel like.

Crap. I'm staring like a creep. I start looking around like I'm intently studying everything for the hell of it, not just him.

Santiago's got an expression on that looks equal parts amused and curious.

"What's she talking about?" he asks.

"Nothing. Here, before it melts."

I hand him the ice cream, which he takes a giant bite of. His eyes roll back ever so slightly. "Not bad."

I snort. "Oh, you love it."

"Would be better with some café con leche."

I plop down in my chair, look into his face, and say, "Shut up."

He stares at me really closely after that, not even blinking. He and I, we're having a whole conversation with our eyes. Moon the

Weed and Santiago the Nebula. When he shoves the last bite of ice cream in his mouth, my skin is prickling with goose bumps, but I don't back down from his stare. Finally, *finally* he blinks and says, "What flavor did *you* get?"

"Vanilla with caramel sauce and whipped cream." It's the superior ice cream combination, so I say it with a tone I imagine a queen would use.

He makes a face. "Caramel, though?"

"What's wrong with caramel?"

"The stuff in those big plastic containers with the pumps? That's not caramel. That's corn syrup with synthetic flavor."

"It's delicious," I say. "I could eat a bowl of it all by itself."

"That's because you're sick."

"I'm never buying you ice cream again. You ungrateful oaf." He gives me a half smile and then we both turn as crowds invade our little bubble, bursting it into tiny bits of warm rain.

After we get swept away into sales and bagging and sliding credit cards through our tablet contraptions for a while, a guy walks up with Andro's surfing book. "Whoa," he says when I give him a polite smile. Which makes me frown immediately.

Look, I'm a girl. It's for that reason and that reason alone that I'm vaguely familiar with male attention. Usually all I have to do is direct them to Star, and then I'm completely forgotten, all three parties in their happy space. Star, with the whole earth revolving around her, the dude with probably the most beautiful girl he's seen in real life, and me, back to a weedy, weedy weed.

But Star is nowhere to be found, so I try to keep my gaze down and neutral.

"You're the Moonflower artist, aren't you?"

I freeze. And then I raise my face to see the look of awe on his.

"How—what—"

"It's your hands," he says, holding his fingers to touch the edges of my palms. "Your rings, the scar." He sees my face and gives an awkward laugh. "I'm sorry. I know that must sound creepy as hell. But seriously, you're the best earth artist on Fotogram. Everything you do is so balanced. The color, the composition. You know? How old are you even?"

"Seventeen." I slide his book into a bag, and I can see next to me Santiago watching. Speaking of creeps.

"You applied to art school programs yet?"

I nod. "Yeah, actually. Only one."

"I go to a great program at NYU. Maybe you could apply there too."

I nod without saying anything, because what? NYU? NYU has one of the most respected photography programs in the nation. They accept, like, .0001 percent of students who apply. Okay, maybe that's an exaggeration, but still. NYU is a big deal, and the fact that this guy just casually mentions it? Like he really thinks I could?

"You're not paid to chitchat," Santiago says. His voice is even more deep and gruff, and his jaw is so sharp, I want to use it to file my nails razor-thin so I can claw at his beautiful face. He looks every bit the grump I first met, before I learned he loves hazelnut coffee and tangerine-lemon aftershave and watching the night sky pass through his bunk windows, because as a nebula, he's attracted to nebulas. So I roll my eyes at the dude in front of me as an apology.

He gives me a big smile in return. "I'm Adam, by the way."

"Moon."

He grins. "What? Really? Like, for real?"

I nod. He's actually kind of cute. In a skinny, pale, nerdy way.

He shakes my hand but drops it fast when Santiago barks, "Moon." Jeez. He sounds like the Hellboy version of the Incredible Hulk. I give Santiago a look so sharp, he really should drop dead. Instead, he levels it right back at me. I scoff and turn to Adam.

"By the way," Adam says before he leaves. "You really should post pictures of your face. You've been depriving us!"

I can barely look at anyone for the next ten minutes. It takes that long for my cheeks and neck and chest to stop feeling like they're made of molten caramel. *He probably just meant you have pretty eyes*, I keep reminding myself. *Gotta stay real.*

Santiago doesn't speak to me as we pack up later on. It's not weird, but it's also not normal. Not lately.

Finally I say, "Why are you so cranky today?"

His shoulders stiffen a bit, and he shrugs.

Oh no. I'm not letting it go that easy. "Santiago. What is it?"

"You talk too much," he says gruffly.

It's like he dropped a box of Andro's self-help books on brand building and rock and rolling on my head. I don't know why it hurts so bad. I haven't even known the guy three weeks. I guess, I don't know . . . I guess I thought that despite our open dislike for each other, Santiago and I were something like friends. Not actual friends. I wouldn't tell him about my dad or why I hate bridges, especially ones that go up so high, the skin of the water below looks like another sky. So, no. Not real friends. But maybe, like, halfway there. Okay. Ten percent there. And Jeez Louise, besides all that, I've had enough of people telling me in so many ways to shut up, so someone—mainly my mom—could hear themselves, or Star, better.

Even though I was ready to raise an army to crack Santiago's bad mood open, now I'm at the edge of the battlefield, throwing my sword down. That's what those words feel like, by the way. *You talk too much.* Each consonant is a slick blade running along my neck, not quite cutting, but almost as painful. And so I turn my head and help load the bus wordlessly. He makes tacos for dinner, and I refuse to say anything beyond what's necessary for our cooking show.

"What's your problem?" he asks a couple times. I answer with "Cramps," which I find tends to make guys ask fewer questions, not more.

I barely eat, and as soon as the dishes are clean, I go back to my bunk to finish Andro's font. After that I check out my folder, the one with all my tarot images inside. And once I'm there, that's when I realize it. The Wheel of Fortune was the last one. I've finished the deck.

Holy crap.

31.

So It Looks Like I'm Not the Only Daughter Hoarding Secrets and Lies like Dragons with Their Gold

MY BAD MOOD was like molasses at my limbs and lungs and heart. But now that's all washed away. In its place, flower buds. Everything tight and about ready to unfurl, smelling all sweet like nectar and looking all gorgeous like petals against thick moonlight.

My energy is wild and the group isn't back from dinner yet, so I grab my camera and sneak out the door. I'm pretty sure I see Santiago spying on me through his little bunk curtain. Jerk-face to infinity, that's what he is.

The night is glorious. We're in a parking lot next to an outdoor shopping center, but in the light of dusk, everything is mystical. All bathed in that indigo light, the beginnings of stars and planets dotting the horizon like sequins. The clouds are dipped in rose gold, long and thin like a series of bangles adorning some ancient bride, clanking together because she's nervous and excited and scared.

And that's when I see it. Not quite a butterfly, or a moth, or a hummingbird, but it looks like a mix of all three, flying around in a circle right in front of me. I pull out my phone and do a quick search. It's a hawk moth—brown, fuzzy, with red-lined wings. By the time I look up again, it's gone. Before I turn back to the bus, though, three swarm past me, the buzz of their miniature wings making me shiver a little. And then a half dozen more follow, making me jump out of my skin a touch.

What if there's some wildflower patch they're all heading to? The idea grasps me with heavy, metallic jaws and won't let go, so I slide my phone in my pocket and see what I can see.

There's a line of cypress trees on this side of the parking lot, and it's blocking a lot of the sunset. Everything is still brilliant, though, and magical. Maybe more so because the stars are even more visible here, so vivid in their winks. And then I give a little gasp.

Jesus on a fiddlestick. There's someone *right there*, against the trees. Two someones, actually. From here it looks as though their faces have been melded together so sweetly, so gently, like two cake layers attached with buttercream frosting. I want to look away, to give them privacy, but one of them is too familiar. It's the long willow of her body, the pale silk of her hair. It's Star.

Before I know it, I'm around twenty or so feet away. Enough to tell that when Star pulls back ever so slightly from the kiss, I recognize exactly who she's with.

Belle Brix.

And just behind Star, completely and utterly unnoticed by

them, is a spiral of hummingbird moths. They're waiting, waiting, waiting to be Star's first miracle. I don't know how I know this, but I know it with enough certainty that I'd bet my camera, my computer, and all the fireweed honey in the world on it.

The next time I look at them, it's through my viewfinder. *Click.*

And now, ew, they're starting to move their hands around way too much, and I can't ignore the feeling that I'm invading something precious and wonderful and none of my business. So I turn around and totally break for it, making my footfalls as quiet as possible.

When I get back on the bus, I don't even make it into my bed. I fall onto the sofa, where I hold my camera with trembling hands and stare at the photo again. It's grainy and blurry, but if you knew them, you could tell who it was. You could also make out the little fairylike creatures that surround them, looking like winged autumn leaves that forgot to fall the rest of the way down.

There are so many thoughts happening to me right now. They're just like those hawk moths, buzzing and flittering their fuzzy bodies against my brain. But three thoughts are the most dominant.

One, I am not the only cursed daughter.

Two, Star and Belle are currently making out against a cypress tree in the rose-gold sunset.

Three?

Holy crap.

32.

Sexy Selfies That Are as Slippery as Seaweed

THE PRINTING COMPANY charges a ton if you purchase a single deck to be printed. Because I've literally had next to no time to myself, I haven't finished retouching almost thirty of my images, so I won't even be printing the whole deck. You'd think that would make a difference in the price, but it doesn't. Makes no gosh-darn sense if you ask me.

I really didn't factor that into my budget, especially now that I'm spending more than planned on groceries. Which I'm not complaining about. Santiago might be a cantankerous bastard, but none of that affects his food, which somehow continues to get better. I don't know how that's even possible, but since the day he decided to get pissed at me, we've eaten carnitas rice bowls and lobster rolls and braised beef with all the trimmings. He still acts like he's allergic to me, which is actually fine. I still hate his ridiculously muscular ass.

So I welcome the night we're getting at the Serenade Hotel. It means I'm getting a much, much needed break from Santiago.

And tomorrow I'll be receiving the first printing sample of the Wild Moonflower tarot, minus twenty-nine cards, at least, thanks to the Handmade Sun God Andro Philips Font Fund. I was able to afford the almost-deck and expedite the shipping. Now all I need to do is pray several rosaries it doesn't look like shit.

Santiago's already in the ballroom lobby when I walk in. Talking to Star.

I ignore the lurch in my stomach and act like neither of them exist as I walk by, looking around for Andro.

But Santiago was looking at her with *interest*. Not that I'm going to care. I just didn't realize she was still trying. I mean, didn't she spend last evening with her tongue in Belle Brix's mouth? Why does Star always get to have everything and everyone she wants? But as I said, not going to care.

"Andro," I say when I spot the Sun God himself.

He grins and opens his arms wide. "Moon." For a second I think he might hug me, but then he clasps his hands together. "My designer finished up. The new font will be live tonight." He grabs my room key, presses it into my hand. "Just one more thing, though. I'd love to credit you. What's your website?"

I freeze, my palm up, not quite grabbing the key card yet. "Uh—"

"Mr. Philips." A manager-looking dude approaches.

"Email me," Andro tells me. "Or better yet, text."

I nod, but he's already turned away.

As I walk to the elevator, I plan one last look at Santiago and Star. Jeez. Even their names sound great together. All that alliteration. Then again, Star and Belle do too. Like rock-star princesses.

But yeah, one more look before I stop caring. I tap the up button and casually lean my hip by the elevator doors as I wait, hoping I look like I'm admiring the ugly-as-mashed-potatoes paintings on the walls, the gold foil pressed into the trims of the columns, baseboards, frames. And then I settle my gaze on Star.

She's smiling up at him, intertwining her fingers in her hair as she shifts her weight to her other foot. She's doing a good job of looking adorably nervous. I almost buy it until she flicks her gaze to his left arm, staring right at it for far too long. A surprising wave of anger rolls through me, and I fight hard at the urge to pull her by the hair and yell at her until she explodes into a super-nova of energy. Good Lord. She's going to hurt him and convince herself that she's doing him a favor the whole while.

And as his back is to me, I can't see if her charm is working yet. But then the firm lines of his muscles tense a little, and he turns enough for me to jolt, forcing my body to face the elevator as it opens. The last thing I ever need is a person to know how much I wish I were in my sister's place. And something tells me, if Santiago looks at me right in my eyes, he'll know. Immediately.

But then I make the mistake of turning around to face the ball-room. Just as the elevator closes, Santiago catches me. Though it's a split second, the moment has the weight of whole universes. Eons of universes. The worst part, though, is his expression. It's completely unreadable. I suppose I should be grateful it's not lovestruck like most people when they spend more than three seconds with Star. But him showing nothing, looking at me like nothing, acting like nothing, somehow that makes everything worse.

My normally bottom-of-the-swamp self-esteem is even more sunk. It's not just the muck of the earth, it's inside the muck of the earth in the core of the earth, being punctured with little spears over and over again. You'd think I'd be used to it by now. You'd think my skin would be so thick, it would take a machete the size of a small continent to reach anything that bleeds. Alas, not quite.

When I get to my room, I try everything in my power to feel better. I order room service—a cheeseburger and onion rings. I eat like a barbarian, in bed while watching *To All the Boys I've Loved Before*. But carbs and fat and cute movies don't help. A shower under scalding water with the fanciest hotel soap I've ever seen—I mean, it's got little platinum flakes *inside* it!—doesn't help either.

So when I get in bed, in a white, fluffy bathrobe, I grab my phone and decide to do something really foolish.

Using the camera as a mirror, I adjust my still-wet hair so it's even on either side. I put on some shiny gloss so my lips still look shower-slick. And I loosen my robe, releasing a new world of cleavage. I position myself on the bed, lying on my side, hip jutting out like a mountain, boobs spilling out like a pair of melons. And I snap a photo angling my phone on the mirror wall in front of me, making sure to crop out my face. I take a few pictures, actually, but the first is the best. Funny how often that happens. My robe is riding up my thighs, the white of it making me look like the hazelnuts in Santiago's homemade trail mix. A nice touch.

As fast as I can, before I lose my nerve, I open a new text box and attach the photo. Sending it to Samuel, the ever-requester of nudes. Even faster, I type and send, **your turn.**

I know, I know. Samuel is not my friend. But right now I'm desperate to feel better about myself. Any little scrap of attention. "Like a dog," Mom says. Samuel is my most reliable thrower-of-bones right now.

It takes almost a whole minute for the dot-dot-dot of a message composing to appear, which surprises me. The dots disappear almost immediately, which surprises me even more. I watch the dots appear and reappear for the next few seconds before I groan and throw the phone on the bed. He better have a response after I've gotten my pajamas on.

. . . Okay. There. Pj's on. But those dot-dot-dots are still appearing and disappearing like summer thunderstorms in the south, filling the sky all thick and dark one minute, completely gone the next. Maybe there's something wrong with the service, or my phone. Samuel's usually way more confident than this. He can't ever send thirsty photos fast enough.

And that's when I glance up at the screen and see my life flash before my eyes.

Because.

I sent.

A sexy selfie.

To Santiago.

Not Samuel.

Santiago.

My nemesis. My enemy. The biggest pain in my freaking neck, who's probably flirting with my sister as we speak.

I want to bash my head in with one of his cast-iron skillets. Though there's no one to even see it, my cheeks are aflame. There's nothing to do but throw myself out the window now. I've reached the end of my life-span. I need to summon the *Sims* Grim Reaper, all dressed in a dark cloak and wielding a scythe, who will watch a romantic comedy on TV with my soul after I pass on. A girl can dream, right?

He still hasn't responded, which is a plus. Before the dots can appear again, I type, WAIT.

And then I send a text to Andro. Hey. Which room is Santiago in? Realizing how this sounds at this hour in the night, I type, I need to give him his onion powder back, along with a bunch of nonsensical emoji. A hundred of them, actually.

Andro's response is immediate: He's in 309 right next to me in 310.

I have no idea why Andro included that information, but

before I can think about it for another second, I run out the door faster than I ever imagined possible. I run up the stairs, because I already know the elevator will take too long.

I reach 309 at the speed of light's idea of fast. I'm panting. I force myself to take one long breath after another, then knock on the door. When he doesn't answer, I bang it with my fist.

Finally the door opens. "What the . . ."

But he stops when he sees me, his eyes dropping down my shoulders, then to my waist and hips and legs and feet and back again. CRAP. I forgot that my Moon-is-in-her-hotel-room-alone pajamas consist of a lace-trim tank and short shorts, with a material so thin, I could probably use it to make cheese. I didn't even bother to put a bra on. Or shoes. Jesus on a pancake.

But I can scarcely process this because of what *he's* wearing. Which is no shirt. I mean, there's gray flannel pajama bottoms. But no shirt. I've only ever glimpsed Santiago's toplessness from his back as he planked in the mornings, which, I'll admit under gunpoint, is unspeakably impressive. But his front. Jesus on a pancake.

His pecs remind me of the lake stones I'd skip on as a kid, back when Dad was around to take us camping. And his abs. More stones. More hard-as-stone stones. His arms and shoulders are so daunting, I want to take a measuring stick to them to see if my four-foot estimation of width is on the mark.

And there's his skin, bronzy brass and gold. How does he look like so many metals fused together? And then his smell. Pine. Oranges. Something spicy like nutmeg. And then—

"Can I help you with something?" His voice is sharp and snaps me out of it.

But *his* eyes keep slipping down too, so I cross my arms and say, "Delete it," as hard as I can.

He narrows his eyes, drawing them back up to my face.

"Delete it, Santiago."

He opens his mouth to respond, but it appears he's speechless. So I push him aside and slide in, trying as much as I can to keep my body from running against any part of him. "Where's your phone?"

He holds it up. I think the camera app is on, which he clicks off. And then he pulls it away as I reach for it.

"Who did you mean to send it to?" His voice is cutting.

"Does it matter? I'm asking you to delete it."

"No. You're telling me to. And not very nicely."

After the last few days I've had, I can't help it. I'm halfway to tears already. I bite my lips and glance at the ground. "Santiago. Please." My voice cracks against my will.

He immediately turns on his phone screen, unlocking it. He pulls up the text convo, holds the photo, hits delete.

"You didn't save it?"

"No." He holds the phone out. "You can check it if you want."

"I believe you." I can't look up at him. He's so freaking distracting. Even with my eyes trained to the floor, I'm getting dizzy being this close to him. Lord, I need to go on a date or something. Like, yesterday.

"Is that it?" he asks. I'm being dismissed.

I nod and walk to the door. When I get there, I pause. "Look, I know you hate me, so it doesn't matter what you think of me or what I say." I swallow and let myself look at him. His face has that unemotional mask on again. When his eyes meet mine, though, they soften. Almost imperceptibly. "But I'm not a whore." He blinks in surprise. "I was feeling really bad about myself. So I meant to send that picture to someone I knew would make me feel better." I shrug. "I know it's pathetic, but it's the truth." Pathetic. The truth is, I'm pathetic.

Santiago says a whole lot of nothing. So I start to open the door, and when I'm halfway out, he puts his hand on my arm. "What happened today? Why are you so sad?"

I almost laugh. Instead, I carefully remove his hand from me. It's warm and wide. I don't think I've ever touched him there before. "You can't treat me like shit for days and expect me to be your best bud the second you figure out your actions have consequences."

Did I admit I'm sad because he won't talk to me anymore? I did. I totally did. Santiago blinks and I add, "Sorry for assaulting you with that photo, by the way. I know there were a lot of rolls. . . ." I gesture to my midsection area, but cover myself with my arm again when he drops his gaze down my body so slowly and smoothly, I about shiver. What the flip is that about? "Uh—where was I? Right. Sorry. Photo assault. I'd help you bleach your brain, but I'm going to be kind of busy screaming into a pillow in about a minute."

And then I walk as fast as I can, without running, out the door. I don't hear it close behind me. I don't look back.

My phone is dinging when I get in and my heart does what feels like a backflip. But I huff out a sigh of disappointment when I realize it's just Andro. **That's quite the knock for onion powder,** he's typed. I pause. I guess I did try to break the door down. And somehow, the best lie I could come up with was onion freaking powder. Great. No wonder Andro sees right through it.

But he's added, **Before I forget. Web address? For site?**

I let the tips of my fingers dangle above the little phone keyboard. You know that moment in a movie where the heroine is making a huge decision, one that's going to change the course of her life? That's what this feels like right now.

Mom's going to kill me, I tell myself.

But she's going to find a reason to kill me no matter what, you know? She'll never run out of material to hate the ugly twin, the one who just had to go and ruin her life with a milk jar and release the family curse back into the universe.

But if she finds out about this, there's no way she could think of loving me again.

My fingertips pull away from the keyboard, only for a moment. Only to touch the top of the scar on my chest. And just like that, I make my decision.

Mom would say this whole thing—my art, my sharing it with Andro and the world—was a sign of disrespect. But she's never respected me my entire life. So why should I hide who I am? It's not worth it anymore. It really isn't.

So I send a link to my Fotogram account.

To the founder of Fotogram.

Jesus Christ on a banana pancake.

And now, like the loser I am, I've been lying in bed for thirty minutes, my thoughts vacillating between Star and Santiago talking in the hotel lobby and then to the gold of Santiago's skin, smelling so good, I wish I could catch him on a plate and have him for dinner. Ugh. Not having a boyfriend is making me cannibalistic.

And then a thought floats by, one so preposterous, it literally sends a shiver down my spine.

Santiago's hotel room was all lit up. He was topless, holding his phone with the camera app on.

After I'd typed, your turn.

I decide to put everything behind me the next morning. Yes, I will never be my sister, but I've long known that. Yes, I've lost Santiago's and my . . . whatever it was we had, but then again, I never really had him to begin with. And the fact that Andro never responded last night has me breaking out in a stress rash, but I'm pushing that shit to the farthest recesses of my brain. I push it past my brain, even, into my shoulders and back, until everything is tense and throbbing painfully.

No. Today I'm not going to give a single fuck about the train wreck that is my life. Because my email app has alerted me to the fact that the trial run of the Wild Moonflower tarot deck is here.

It feels like a big event. And, I mean, it is. So I treat it as such, putting on one of the two dresses I packed. It's made of cotton, violet, and it's covered in a pattern of white roses. I tie up sparkly black ballet slippers at my feet and make up my face nice and sweet. Shimmery pink on my eyelids and cheekbones. I add a deeper pink stain to my lips. And leave my hair down, since it's almost always up.

"Moon," Van says when I step out. "Fuck. You look . . ." He grins. "Got a brunch date or something?"

"I guess you could say that." A date. With my tarot deck.

He puts a hand on my shoulder as I pass. "Lucky man or lady or enby!"

Since my tarot deck is not even a person, I give an awkward laugh and keep it moving, not stopping until I reach the front desk.

33.

I Let the Nebula See My Art

I'M SITTING IN the hotel restaurant. The only thing I can afford is coffee, but I don't care, because I'm staring at the box that contains the deck. You know, the project I've been working on for the last two years, minus twenty-nine cards that are still in my computer, awaiting very minor touch-ups.

I glance up, and because just what I need right now is a reminder of last night's awkwardness, there is Santiago, sitting all by his lonesome, in front of enough bacon, eggs, and toast to feed a small herd of elephants.

When he spots me, he does a double take. The way his head flips is almost cartoonlike in its urgency. I bend my head really low, studying the texture of the cardboard of the package. It's got the finest of fibers that catch the window light, looking like tarnished, spun gold.

I almost fall out of my chair when plates are set down with a *clank*. "Hey," Santiago says, taking a seat.

"Hi." My brain helpfully flashes to hips like mountains and boobs like melons, and of course that leads to pecs like river rocks and abs like tree roots, so I return to my new career as observer of cardboard.

"What's that?"

Oh Lord. He's talking to me. "It's—uh—"

"Something to do with your art?"

I snap my mouth shut. And then open it again. "What?"

"Hold on. I wanted to say something else first. I'm sorry." He's staring at my face so intently. The amber of his eyes glows like a bottle passing a well-lit window.

My mouth is still open. Words do not want to come out. Luckily for me, he keeps going.

"I'm sorry for being an asshole. I was . . ." He waves his hand. "I was surprised to hear you're an artist." Now he's the one observing cardboard with the precision of a PhD student. "I wish you'd told me." He clears his throat. "Plus I was jealous."

"Jealous?" My voice has returned at least.

"Of that guy. In line."

Is he saying . . . ?

"I was jealous a stranger knew more about you than I did."

Oh. So not romantic jealousy, then. Ugh, why is my head always lying to me?

"Do you forgive me?"

His eyes are back on mine and they're devastating, though I can't figure out quite how. I think we're having a moment. I think that's how. Because then my eyes drop to his mouth, to his super-pouty peach lips. And when I force my eyes back up, he's staring at *my* lips. God. *God.*

And then my stomach explodes into a growl so loud, probably half the patrons turn to see who let a rabid animal inside.

Santiago laughs, and now probably everyone's looking at him because of how beautiful he is. He pushes his plate toward me.

"Sir, there's a sharing fee."

A server is on top of us, probably been watching us the whole time to make sure the only teens here don't dine and dash or something.

Santiago doesn't look at her. Instead, he looks at me and says, "You like waffles?"

I nod, already with a mouthful of bacon.

"She and I are going to share waffles, too, then." He pauses, then adds, "With caramel. And extra whipped cream." When I blink in surprise, he adds, "On the side."

"There's a sharing charge."

"Heard you the first time." This time he levels his classic glare right at her. She scowls right back as she turns and walks away.

"You don't have to be rude to her," I say.

"She was rude first."

"You don't know what kind of morning she's having, okay?"

He sighs and just looks at me, which makes me all kinds of nervous, so I frantically clasp and unclasp my hands and say, "I thought you hated caramel."

"I hate shitty caramel. Let's see if theirs is any good." He takes a sip of my coffee, then makes a face. "Too much cream."

"Good thing it's not yours, then, you coffee-thieving hob-goblin."

And he smiles at me. "There you are."

"I'm only forgiving you because of the waffles," I snap.

He smiles even bigger, and I almost drop my coffee. "What's in the box?" he asks.

"You guessed it. My art."

"Tell me about it. I want to hear." He's got faint pink spots under his cheekbones. "I mean. If you want."

"I want to." I say it quickly and without thinking, and then the truth of it hits me in the chest, like a tree has fallen right through me.

I want Santiago to know about my art. I want him to know about my dad. I want him to know everything.

To distract myself from the log lodged in my breastbone, I rip the packing tape off the cardboard, pull out some Bubble Wrap, and there, in a little box, a bit larger than a stack of playing cards, is my deck. My hands tremble. This is nearly two whole years, all printed on and wrapped up in cardstock. Also, Santiago doesn't hate me again. For some reason, both these facts fill me with equal amounts of trepidation.

"Moonflower," he says, murmuring the words on the front of the box.

"It's my aunt's nickname for me."

"Moonflower." He gives me a shy smile and a nod at once,

like he's approving it. "So what is the Wild Moonflower tarot?"

I take the deck from him, trying not to pass out when our fingers touch. God. I think my blood sugar is low. Where in the heck are those waffles?

I take a breath and tell him about my Tía Esperanza and her herbs and altars, how she taught me to read things three summers ago. "She made me start with twigs at first."

"Twigs?"

"Yes. Like, a walk in the woods? She made me read the forest floor." He's staring at me so seriously, I feel as though I'm on the verge of either melting or exploding. "And then I graduated to clouds."

"So the cards are the finale of fortune-telling?"

"Actually, no. Mirror stones are the finale."

"Mirror stones."

I nod, and at that moment, the waffles appear. Santiago's still looking at me like I'm revealing the world's greatest mysteries. Then he snaps out of it, thanks the server, and grabs one of the empty plates. He sets a steaming waffle on top. "Butter?"

I nod again. Seems like all I can do, just bob like a tree branch in a rainstorm. He starts spreading the butter. "You don't have to—" I begin.

But he shakes his head and finishes smearing the butter. And then I shake my head when he gestures to the syrup. He doesn't even ask about the caramel and cream. He adds a dollop of the whipped cloud and then takes a fork and drizzles on the caramel.

Santiago is so graceful when he's doing anything food related. He makes me look like a headless chicken by proximity, and all I'm doing is sitting here, thinking too hard about the caramel that's fallen on two of his fingertips. He hands me the plate, and then! Like he could hear my dirty thoughts, he dips his fingers in the bowl of caramel and brings them to his mouth with a little sucking noise.

I haven't even had a bite yet and I'm about to choke.

And he makes a big face. "That's such shit. You like that?"

I take a bite, finally. And groan. It's delicious.

"Fucking corn syrup," he growls, reaching for the bottle of real maple syrup. His grumpiness is adorable, which means I must be drugged or something. But honestly, who gets upset over corn syrup like this? Santiago Philips, that's who.

"For the people in my real life, my aunt and Belle Brix are the only ones who know about my project. And now you."

He picks up the cards, putting them to the side one by one after careful examination.

"Crap," I say, groaning. "I mean, you and my aunt and Belle *and* Andro all know."

"Andro?" Santiago's voice has an edge to it.

"He wanted my website, to credit the font. And I only have a Fotogram account. I sent him the link last night."

"Your sister said you didn't have an account, though." He clears his throat. "Way back when. During our first event, at the opera house."

"She did?" I mean, I thought I had that whole scene burned in my brain from the trauma of it. After all, that was also the precise moment she outed me as a dirty, deflowered slut. And I don't remember any information about Fotogram and me coming up.

"I asked her if you had one," Santiago says.

Well, that's weird. But I just say, "Yeah, she doesn't know about it. It could be bad if my mom found out. And Star would definitely tell her."

Before Santiago can respond, Andro appears and plops a hand on my shoulder. "Are these them?" he asks, picking up the cards from Santiago's hand. "Christ. These are amazing. I spent an hour reading your posts last night. I want to proposition you."

I forgot about the detailed captions behind all my photographs. "Uh, okay," I respond, and then stuff a half a waffle in my mouth, because I'm smooth like that.

"How do you feel about reading for the tour?"

I almost gag up that half waffle in one cough.

"You could sell your decks. Not at every event—some of them are booked to the limit. But Jonestown, and Austin, and St. Louis, I think, would be great. Especially because Austin has that great, relaxed boho aesthetic going on."

"My deck, though—I haven't uploaded all the cards to Occulette yet. I still need to retouch a handful before I can really sell them."

"That's fine. You can use those"—he points—"to sell pre-orders. And read people's futures with whatever deck you like."

Finally I swallow. "Can I think about it?"

Andro nods. "Let me know by the end of the week, okay?" He glances at my dress. "You look nice, Moon."

Santiago gives a saber-toothed-tiger-sounding growl, and Andro jumps away. "Right," he says. "Just let me know, Moon. Text, email, whatever. Rock and roll?" I can only nod. The words of the English language haven't returned to me yet. Because what the flip just happened? Andro Philips propositioned *me*?

"If you do it, your sister is probably going to find everything out," Santiago says as soon as Andro is gone.

"Yeah."

He gives me a weird look. "What's with your sister, by the way? Did you tell her I'm into her?"

"What? No! Of course not!"

He narrows his eyes. "You sure?"

"Of course I'm sure. Why would I tell her that?" And then I pause. "Everyone's into her anyway. She doesn't need the endorsement."

"Not everyone." Santiago doesn't take his eyes off me as he says it.

And as though her ears were ringing, Star appears from deeper in the restaurant, flanked by Chamomila and Van. I grab my cards and shove them in the box, then throw the whole thing in my bag.

Star's dressed in that bronze jumpsuit I love, with no makeup but gloss, her hair flowing in waves like white gold. Suddenly I feel like Oscar the Grouch, or some other creature who decided to try on a dress they'd found in the trash.

Star lights up when she sees Santiago, then pauses when she sees me, like I'm not allowed to dine with him or something.

"Hey," she says, her smile stunning.

"Hey, Star," I say.

Santiago nods once, then turns around to look at me again.

I know about you and Belle, I think to Star. *And you need to make up your mind on who you really want.*

Star clears her throat. For the first time ever, she doesn't look exceedingly confident. "I didn't know you guys would be down here today."

"We shared waffles," I say, as though that explains it. Santiago is back to his usual mode of impersonating a statue.

"Santiago," Star says. "You got a minute?"

"Actually—" he says, but I stand up so quickly, I nearly knock the table over.

"Sorry," I say, grabbing my coffee mug before it topples. "I need to go."

Star shoots me a look of gratitude, but the fact is, I'm not doing it for her. There's no way I'm going to sit here and stomach her and Santiago flirting with each other. I'm not going to let my day get ruined for this.

I reach in my purse, but Santiago says, "I got it." I ignore him, but he says even more gruffly, "I got it, Moon."

"Thanks," I say, even more unkindly. "See you guys later."

I don't look back. When I'm in the hotel room, I take photos of my cards on the shelf by the window, next to a collection of smoky quartz I had in my bag. It almost distracts me enough from the tree trunk in my chest, which is now somehow splitting *me* into firewood.

I force myself to focus on all those reasons I used to convince myself to share my Fotogram account with Andro in the first place.

Mom will always find a reason to hate me.

I can't hide who I am.

None of this is worth it anymore.

I sit on the bed and scroll through my notifications mindlessly. I can only focus on what's happening on the inside. Half of me is giddy. Half of me has a broken heart. But all of me feels like my decision is the right one.

I already know what I'm going to tell Andro. I just don't know how I'm going to deal with the backlash.

I'm editing a long text to go with my FG tarot post. People have been waiting to preorder for a year or more and . . . and now they can. I had to make a large deposit at Occulette in order for them to, which hurt down to the roots of my teeth, but it's done now. Now I've got to get the words exactly right. My brain hurts from reading the same lines over and over again, so I joyfully turn off my screen when there's a knock at the door.

"Yes?" I say, opening it. My mouth drops when I see my sister, looking devastated, with tears spilling over on her cheeks.

"Star! What happened?"

It's a shock to see Star upset. For-real upset, not just the pretty sort. It's hard to cry when people bow down to you, hoist you on their backs, and wave palm leaves covered in gold dust. I haven't seen her weep like this in years.

"You told him something bad about me, didn't you?"

"What? Who are you talking about?"

"Santiago." She's perched on the sofa, dabbing at her eyes with a tissue. "What did you say to him?"

"I didn't tell him anything." Except that she was everyone's type, but she already knows this and certainly doesn't need the reminder, even now.

"He . . ." She gasps a little. "He said he's not interested in me like that."

"He *what*?" At first I'm incensed on her behalf. Who the hell tells Star Fuentez that?

But then I warm up. The hairs on the back of my neck prickle, and my feet feel a little funny and imbalanced. Santiago. That's who tells Star Fuentez that. She's actually not his type.

Yeah, he basically told me that at brunch. But I thought he was being nice. Star's loud sniffle reminds me otherwise.

"You sure you didn't tell him all my flaws?"

"What flaws?" I ask. Besides her bitchiness at the beginning of the tour, Star is so sickeningly sweet, it makes me want to vomit all the time. I can't ever stay mad at her. I can't ever stay jealous of her. She's been my only friend and constant in my life, the only one who knows what it's like to have a father leave without warning, who knows the extent of Mom's cruelty. Even if she isn't there for me like I want her to be, or need her to be, Star is my best friend.

But a part of me wants to turn up the radio and freaking dance. Dance. Because Santiago Philips doesn't like her like that.

And an even more jerk part of me wants to cheer because Star has finally been rejected. I want to throw a tissue at her and snarl, *Doesn't feel all that great, does it?*

But I put an arm around her instead. "Hey. I didn't know you were that into him." *Especially considering you seem a hell of a lot more interested in a certain makeup artist*, I add in my thoughts.

"I'm not," she says, wiping her eyes and standing up straighter, nudging my arm off. "Not like how you feel about Andro, anyway."

"I don't like Andro." I scrunch my nose a lot. I realize I must look like an elderly tortoise and only then do I stop.

"But you think he's hot."

"He's good-looking. But now that I know him more, I see him as a friend."

"And Santiago?" Ah, there it is. I was wondering why she was bringing Andro into this. It was a segue. And her tone is a touch accusatory for my liking.

"I hate his guts," I respond. "And he knows it."

Star nods slowly, then more confidently. She seems satisfied.

"Well, I thought something might've been happening with you and Andro. He kept asking me about your art this morning. Something about cards?"

Shit. Shit, shit, shit.

I make the split-second decision to rip the bandage right off. "You know those earth art pictures I've been working on? Well, I've had them printed on a card deck."

"Oh?" Star wipes her eyes. "Can I see them?"

Well, there you have it. My hopes to avoid all tarot talk out the window. I hand the partial deck to her wordlessly, sitting back as she fingers the cards. I refrain, with great difficulty, from opening the window, climbing out, and starting a new life in Greenland. I mean, the backlash had to start sometime, right? Why not now?

Star raises her eyebrows. "These came out incredible. The quality . . ." And then, "Oh." She's got her hands on the Ace of Swords, and I guess it's obvious enough. She smiles at me. "It's amazing. I knew it was good, Moon, but seeing it all together like this?"

I fold and unfold my hands. "You're not . . . ?" *Freaked? Appalled? About to throw me on the church tabernacle?* "Mad?"

"Why? Because they're divination cards?" She sighs. "Look, I admit I'm not excited about that. Because you know Jesus wouldn't be excited over that." Apparently, Star and I have different versions of the Bible, because I don't remember Jesus's opinion on "divination cards," but whatever. "But I'm going to support you, okay? Because I think Jesus would be okay with that."

"So you're not going to tell Mom?"

"Of course not," Star says, as though she hasn't betrayed me to Mom before. She eyes my collarbone and forearm, like she's remembering the same thing. "Of course I won't tell."

Now it's my turn to about faint from shock. "Really?"

"Of course." She smiles, but it's one of her creepy sewn-doll smiles. "I'd never tell her something like that, Moon. We both know how she is."

Ah, so the smile is just accompanying some revisionist's history. At least her voice sounds normal. Whatever. "I have your word, then, Star?"

"You have my word," she repeats solemnly, adding a hand to her heart for effect.

I breathe out a long, slow exhale I didn't realize I'd been holding inside of my bone marrow. "Okay. Thanks."

"So Andro wants to promote your work?"

"He's thinking of adding me to the tour." As Star's eyes widen in alarm, I add, "You know, as a little side show. Only when it doesn't take away from you big-timers. Besides, my deck isn't even complete yet. I can't use it on the tour until I upload the last couple of dozen images." I immediately hate myself for the impulse to make her comfortable over my good news. I've been doing it my whole life, it feels like. When is Star going to grow up enough to realize that me having my own glow isn't stealing from her light?

Star does a fake little chuckle, but her relief is evident. "Oh, come on, Moon." She's relaxed again. Our places as number one and number zero have been reconfirmed. "So you and Santiago aren't—"

"No. Never. Not in a million, trillion years." Why can't I stop? Why can't I stop reassuring her?

"Good. Because Mom has been asking about you and boys—"

I groan. "There's no one, Star. You know better than anyone." I pause. "And there's no one else for you?"

Star laughs. "Of course not. No one here is as pious as I require." She's examining the pearl-pink nail polish on her fingernails so very closely.

Pious. I think of her and Belle making out and getting to God knows what base against a cypress tree. "You sure? Some of the people here are really cool. It's an artistic, creative bunch."

"Well, I doubt anything will develop, but if it does, you'll be the first to know."

Bald-faced lie, right to my face. But I can't be mad. Star's not ready to tell me about Belle. When she is, I'll be right here. After a few seconds, she smiles. "Are you ready for our birthday?"

"Oh, Go—I mean, goodness, what? What day is it?"

"You forgot our birthday?"

"No, I mean today." I click my phone. "Just three days away. Holy crap."

"I really need to do a shoot for it," Star says. "The big eighteen and all."

"What kind of theme were you thinking?" And as she goes on about platinum jewels in her hair and disco balls, my brain wanders to thirty minutes ago, when she claimed she's not Santiago's type. The memory has marked my brain, like when you slide a napkin in a book, except it feels a lot like a spiny cactus arm. It won't let go, not when she leaves, not when I pack, not when we're back on the bus, stopped for dinner, Santiago teaching me how to poach eggs, acting all normal, like he's not the first person in all of history to not bow down in reverent prayer at the attention of Star Fuentez.

"You're really quiet," he remarks once we've sat down with our food—bowls of poached eggs in homemade chorizo salsa that's been simmering all day. On the side, Brazilian cheese bread, which tastes like it was blessed by Jesus Himself.

"Sorry."

"Don't be sorry." He makes a face. "Do you realize how much you apologize to everyone?"

I do, actually. "That's what you get when you were a disappointment from the womb."

"That's ridiculous," Santiago says. He sounds almost angry.

"Look, I'll prove it to you." I grab my phone. "Mom has emailed, texted, and called Star every day since we began the tour." I scroll through my incoming calls and texts, showing him. "See, nothing. I got nothing in all this time, from my own mother."

"Your sister concerns her more."

I shake my head. "That's true. But only because I don't concern her at all."

"That can't be." Again he sounds pissed and incredulous. Which makes anger fill up in me, like pouring red wine into a Moon-shaped pitcher. Why does he think I'd lie about something like this?

I hit some buttons on my phone, hard, then tap the speakerphone on. Mom answers on the fourth ring.

"Moon? Is she okay? Is Star okay?"

"She's fine, Mom. I was just calling to talk. How are things?"

Mom pauses. "Normal. The father was asking about you girls."

"Oh. That's nice."

There's crickets for a few seconds before Mom says, "Is your sister around?"

"No. She's at dinner."

"Oh. Well, let her know to give me a call when she gets in, okay?"

"Okay, yeah. I will." She starts making humming noises, like she's about to say goodbye, so I quickly ask, "Mom, can I tell you a little about my day?"

She sighs and, after a long while, says, "Moon, I don't know why you always try to provoke me. Especially this time of year."

"What time of year?" I've never heard her complain about the seasons before.

"It's been six years this month—"

"Gotta go, Mom. Bye."

I return to my food while Santiago watches me in silence. There's a tic in his jaw, like he's grinding his teeth. And his face is a little pink, and not from blushing. I think he might be furious, actually. I groan. "Look. I'm sorry. That was . . ." I bury my head in my arms. "I hated you thinking I was a liar."

"I didn't think—"

"Yeah. You did."

He sighs. "I didn't realize it was as bad as you said."

"It's much worse, actually. But I don't want to dwell. That's never gotten me anywhere. So." I lift my head and look right at him. "Are you going to be a chef or something?"

Santiago blinks. "A chef?"

"What do you mean?" I ask. "You cook better than anyone I've ever met in my life."

"Whatever," Santiago grumbles. He sounds like an old man. A hot, young, angry old man.

"I'm serious. You should have a blog. Or write a cookbook."

"Oh yeah?" he snarls. "So what's my *aesthetic*? The miracle food of the one-handed chef?"

I freeze, my food positioned halfway to my mouth. "Of course not."

"But you think that's a good idea." He sounds like he's had this fight about one thousand times before, and he's primed and ready to win it this time. But, honest to God, I don't have the energy for this.

"Forget I said anything. I won't bring it up again."

"No, I want to hear you say it."

"Say what?" Good Lord, what is his problem?

"That you think I should capitalize on this." He waves his arm around, glaring at me, like I didn't just freaking try to give him a compliment.

"Your brand, clearly, is big, hulking jerk."

"Good one." His voice and expression are still hard, proving my point, basically.

"Santiago, damn it." I take my dishes to the sink. "You're the flipping best chef I've ever seen. And the Food Network is my favorite flipping channel. You're even better than Jamie Oliver, and I gotta say, I want to do a lot more than eat that guy's food!"

"Jamie Oliver is the human version of an American bulldog!" Santiago bellows.

"He's not even American!" I yell back. "He's from England!"

"Fine! English bulldog, then!"

We're breathing at each other, like we've both run half a marathon with skyscrapers strapped on our shoulders. And then I see it. His mouth is all contorted and his eyes are squinty on the edges. He's trying not to laugh. And he's failing.

Which gets me going too. It feels too intimate or something, to lose it while facing him, so I face the kitchen counter and laugh until I'm weak, until I fold over and I'm practically lying down on the smooth quartz.

And then something warm is draped on my back. Santiago.

His arm. That thing must weigh seventy pounds. I'm smiling, but when Santiago drags his hand to the small of my back, my smile evaporates. In fact, it feels like my smile has moved to the space under his hand, tingly and hot.

"I'm sorry," he says. "I know I'm an asshole."

"You're not an asshole," I respond, somehow, because it's really hard to think when he hasn't moved his hand yet. "You're like me when I'm pissy. Except, all the time."

He chuckles again, and his hand shifts so that something— his palm maybe?—has reached the skin exposed from where my shirt rode up. I lift my head like I've been electrocuted and promptly bang it right on the bottom of the cabinet. "Mother—"

"Are you okay?"

"Yes," I say, even as I feel the drip of something warm and thick run down my temple.

"Jesus, you're bleeding." He's grabbed a bunch of paper towels, and now he holds them to my head.

"I'm fine," I say, but all I can think is, *I-need-a-boyfriend, I-need-a-boyfriend, I-need-a-boyfriend right-now right-now RIGHT-NOW.* That's gotta be the explanation as to how Santiago makes me feel all warm and tingly all the time. Even now, with his hand on my head, I'm blushing. Blushing.

He grabs the first aid kit mounted on the side of the kitchen cabinet. He opens it but has a hard time with the little antiseptic ointment.

"Here," I say, and I pop the top off. I make to put some on my fingers, but he stops me.

"You didn't wash your hands."

"Bossy," I grumble, and fight the urge to sink against his fingers as he cleans the wound and rubs the ointment in. Finally the bandage is on.

"You sit here." He points to the dining table. "I'll do the dishes. You look kind of flushed."

Flushed. I think I'm about to explode more like. From not having a boyfriend.

And then the bus touches ground with a freaking bridge.

I nearly jump out of my skin when I see the lights reflecting on the water out the window. A bridge, a freaking ridiculous water bridge. Just my luck.

Thankfully, only a few seconds pass before we're back on the regular road. My hands tremble so badly, I have to grip the table. I need to distract myself. So naturally, I turn and watch Santiago as he washes the dishes.

According to my mother, girls should not have horny thoughts or feelings. If you do, there's something wrong with you. Not that I ever needed anything else to remind Mom there was something wrong with me, but . . . She thinks the only way for sex to be okay is if it's coerced between a husband and wife. As in, the husband must wear the wife down until she—soul, body, and mind pure as an angel—relents.

I looked it up, and actually, that whole situation is also called marital rape. Which is bananas to me. My mom thinks getting raped by coercion is the good, godly way to get laid.

But I can't help feeling guilty. I don't know why it's hitting me now, but I can just see Mom, knives in hand, facing me with her wild, judgy eyes.

I'm calm enough to talk again, so talk is what I do. "I've been with three guys. Had sex with, I mean. Do you think that makes me a slut?"

The muscles in Santiago's shoulders tighten. He puts the last pan on the drying rack. "Where's this coming from?"

I shrug. I'll be damned if I'm going to tell him it's from me wanting to jump on him like he's covered in caramel sauce.

He turns to me. "I don't think girls are sluts. I don't care if a girl's been with a hundred guys. She's not a slut."

I make a weird sound and try to cover it up with an "Oh."

"Who called you a slut?" he asks softly.

I can't look him in the eyes. "Everyone," I respond finally, because it feels like the truth.

"Well, you're not." He turns to grab the little towel to run over the wet pans. "Those guys, though. Are you still dating one of them?"

"No," I say. "I mean, I wasn't even dating any of them."

"Huh," he grunts. And then everyone returns from dinner, and I rush to change into my pajamas to get away from the noise.

As I lie in bed, the streetlight glow flowing over me like little shots of copper, I can't help but stare in wonder at my whole life.

The idea that I'm not a slut. The very idea. It makes me want to scream and cry at the same time. The intensity inside me shakes the earth. I inhale the whole universe and a new one is breathed out again. Inhale, exhale. Creation, destruction, creation again.

Mom loved it in the show *Jane the Virgin* when Jane's abuela crumples up a white flower and says that's what happens when a girl has sex. "She's right," Mom said. "A woman who does it turns brown and ugly like that flower. You can't ever be beautiful again, not to any man's eyes, not even Jesus's."

Mom and Jane's abuela forgot something about flowers, though. The blooms become seeds. And eventually a whole new plant, producing a whole new bouquet of fresh, white flowers.

With each breath, I am new. I'm a seed, I'm a flower, and then I'm a seed again.

And that's exactly how God made it work.

34.

The Big Bridge Scares Me
Straight into Outer Space
(Right into a Warm, Twinkling Nebula)

ALL THIS LIFTING boxes, setting up, packing, lifting boxes again all the time is getting to me. As in, I'm flipping starving. All the time.

We had lunch an hour ago and here I am, about to pop some corn, when who should get in my way but the grumpiest, hulkiest boy I've ever met in my life.

"What are you doing?" he asks, crossing his arms. I try to get around him to the microwave, but Santiago shifts his ginormous body and now everything is blocked.

"Move it, will you? I'm hungry."

He responds by grabbing my popcorn and tossing it into the trash way across the room like a pro basketball player.

"What the—"

"Do you even know what hydrogenated oils are? And why you shouldn't be eating them?"

"Santiago, I am freaking *hungry*."

"Sit down, then. I'll make you a snack." He says it so grumpily, you'd think he was telling me in detail how he was going to kick my ass, not cook me up something probably wonderfully delicious. What a weirdo.

I sit at the table, pretending to sulk a bit, when the bus door opens and Belle Brix appears. She's wearing wide-leg jeans, a white tank, and checkerboard suspenders. If I wore that outfit, I'd look like a clown. Meanwhile, Belle Brix looks incredible.

"Hey," she says, plopping next to me. "How have you been?"

"Not bad. How about you?"

She shrugs. "Not bad myself." She looks right at me. "Hey, do you mind if I see some photos you've taken of the tour lately?"

I frown. "Sure. Just let me . . ." I pull up my computer and let her scroll through my most recent edited work.

"Wow, you're good," she murmurs as she scrolls. "Is this one of your own artworks? That you told me about?" She points to a labyrinthine arrangement of ferns and seashells. The Star, with the leaves arranged in a seven-point star.

"Yeah," I say.

"You're amazing. I mean, I knew you were good from Star's feed, but . . . damn."

"Thanks."

Belle and I smile at each other for a moment and then she clears her throat. "Are there even more recent photos?" She looks away. "I'm thinking of one within the last few days. Near a forest of tall, skinny Christmas trees?"

212

Busted. My cheeks feel like they're the color of sun-ripened strawberries. "Uh—"

Belle lowers her voice. "Look, I saw you walking away and you had your camera. If there's a photo, I want to see. I just want to see."

I nod and pull up my supersecret folder of pictures that reveal deep, shocking secrets about my sister. There's only one file inside. I double click and let Belle look.

The photo is beautiful, almost unnaturally so. The light between the cypress trees angles in on them like thick strands of hair. Each of the hawk moths behind them is lit with its own little lick of that light. They look like they're surrounded with floating candles.

"The second or third time we kissed, Star noticed the bugs closing in. That's when we had our big fight. She stopped talking to me for months, until right now, until the tour started."

My mouth drops open. "Star's known for that long that she has La Raíz?"

"I guess."

And she didn't tell me. Jesus on a hockey stick. I mean, I can understand why Star wasn't ready to reveal she'd been making out with Belle Brix, but all this time, I could've known I wasn't the only cursed daughter. Doesn't she know what a weight lifted that would've been to me? Seeing those moths around Star, light-years of universes were flung off my shoulders. Light-years.

Belle sighs. "Don't—don't show this to her, okay?"

I shake my head. "I won't. I'm not going to say anything until she's ready to tell me."

Belle nods. "Thanks."

I pause. "I'm sorry. I know this is an invasion of your privacy. I'll delete it—"

"No, don't. Don't, okay? I'm glad you took it. I'm glad there's proof that this whole thing, that this whole love, isn't just in my head."

I nod as Belle stands and makes her way to the front of the bus. "I need my reading, Moon!" she calls with a smile.

"Soon!" I say back.

Belle Brix is in love with my sister. Holy crap.

And at that moment, Santiago plops my snack in front of me. "What's that?"

"Cheese and crackers."

"That's cheese?" I point to the wheel that's lopsided and steaming and covered in jam and nuts.

"It's baked brie, and you're gonna love it."

He's right. I love it. And though I'll admit it only to myself right now, baked brie can kick microwave popcorn's ass any day of the week.

Star and I've always gotten each other the most cheesy birthday gifts, all to do with our ridiculous names. One year she got me a moon lamp, another, a Moon in My Room. I've gotten her star candles and cookie cutters and coffee mugs. So when I spot the globe in the middle of the truck stop store, I grin immediately.

It's like a snow globe, but instead of a village, inside someone painted the night sky. All indigo, with a white church propped next to a tiny forest. I like that the forest is there. I want it to remind her of me, now, and maybe in the future, when one day she's super-beyond-FG-famous and married and teaching her sixteen children the sign of the cross.

I shake it, and star-shaped glitter flutters around, and the whole scene looks completely full of miracles. As they settle, I can feel it on my skin. Cool, smooth, like polished gemstones, each star hardened and captured as it fell to Earth.

The price is kind of steep, though, for what is essentially a unique snow globe. She's my only sister, I remind myself. The only one of the two people in my nuclear family who doesn't actively hate me.

"That's pretty," Santiago says behind me. I nearly drop the dang thing in a jolt.

"Don't scare me like that," I say, pulling it to my chest. He's got some green stuff in his hand. "What's that?"

"Mint. They have fresh herbs here. Can you believe that?"

I curl my top lip as I say, "Oh."

He scowls. "What the hell is wrong with mint?"

"I've never been the hugest fan of it."

"Ever had tabbouleh? Tavuk kebabi?"

"Uh—what?"

He sighs. "Ever had mint in something not sweet?"

I make even more of a face, because savory mint? What the fresh hockey stick is that?

"Stop making that face. I'm making tavuk kebabi tonight." He waves the mint right at my nose, dispersing its cool scent. It travels down my spine like ice water. I want to shiver from it.

"Great," I respond dryly. Santiago's never been wrong when it comes to food I'll like, but there's a first for everything, I guess.

"Y'all ready for Huntsville tomorrow?" Andro pops up as he does, like a freaking jack-in-the-box, placing a hand on each of our shoulders. I almost drop the globe again. Lord. Stealth and scaring the shit out of people must be a genetic trait, I guess.

But then I realize what he's saying, and my face falls. Ugh. That means the Sterling Pyke Bridge is today.

We've gone over thirty-two little bridges on the trip and about four medium-size ones. The little ones just sent a jump to my belly; the mediums have me going to bed to deep breathe without letting everyone realize I, seventeen-year-old Moon Fuentez, am more scared of bridges than I am of spiders, zombies, and luna moths combined.

But today is the big one. Sterling flipping Pyke. It's 468 feet tall and nearly a mile and a half long, lined with metallic tracks, so I will definitely feel when the bus meets it. I won't be able to get in bed and put a pillow over my head and pretend it's not happening, not like with the mediums. With how sensitive this bus is, I'll probably feel the tires rumbling over each metal slab as though they were notches in my spine.

It's not even happening and I can already feel my stomach

turning around and around, like it's suddenly morphed into a windmill.

Santiago's talking to Andro, but he keeps glancing at me. "You up for reading tomorrow?" Andro asks me, all smiles.

"Sure thing," I grit out. If I were clutching the globe any tighter, it would shatter, sending shards deep in my palms. I'd be sent right to the hospital and I'd miss the Sterling Pyke, so. Maybe that would be preferable. No, no, I know it's not, but crap, this sucks. This really sucks.

Andro says his cheerful goodbyes, and Santiago is immediately in my face. "What's wrong with you?"

"Nothing."

"Moon, you're fucking gray. You look like you're going to hurl."

"I'm not." But the little choke in my voice doesn't seem to convince him.

"Is it the mint? Do you really hate it that much? Because—"

"No, no. It's not the mint."

He stares at me, his eyebrows lifted and jaw clenched. His lashes are extra curly today, reminding me of neat little spiderwebs, and I count nine light freckles on his nose. His lips are peach as ever, and this close, I can see a tiny dip in his top one. I bet that would feel nice to kiss, if I were even thinking about being interested in that sort of thing.

Santiago has the opposite problem of Andro. The more I get to know him, the more good-looking he gets. Like right now, for instance. He's pissed I won't open up to him. There's curiosity mixed with that, and concern, too. He should have the weirdest look on his face. But of course not. He looks like a freaking god. Why didn't his parents name him Zeus and get it over with? Because with that smoldering glare he's giving me, with that water-smooth skin and those mountainous biceps, just "Santiago" isn't cutting it anymore.

"What?" I finally snap.

"Nothing. You say it's nothing. So it's nothing."

I'm relieved he's letting it go, so I turn away. And then he grabs my arm. He's not forceful or anything. But his grip is firm. "Just . . . if you need to talk . . ."

"Okay." I don't want him to finish the sentence. I don't want him to discover how fucked up I am and why.

I pay for the globe and a bagel and coffee. Decaf. Because I don't think I'm going to need any extra jolts of energy today. "Hey, Star," I say once we're all back on the bus.

"Hey," she says. She and Chamomila are poring over an FG account on a tablet, of someone who is red-haired and gorgeous and apparently really into green smoothies.

"Got a minute?" I ask.

Star lets out a big sigh and exchanges a look with Chamomila. "We're really busy, actually."

I clear my throat. "I was wondering if you know about Sterling Pyke? The bridge? We're going over it today."

"And?" She's so sharp, I lift my head back a little, like I'm stepping away from a hammer to the face.

I close my eyes and inhale. "It's . . . you know—"

She smirks. "You mean you're still not over that phobia of yours?" And she and Chamomila snicker. "Oh, come on, it's a joke, Moon."

"You're scared of bridges?" Oak asks. "That's cool. I'm scared of beautiful girls. Or actually, they're scared of me." He grins, putting an arm around Chamomila, and everyone giggles.

And with that, a joke so absurd I'm not even sure if it was a joke, I leave. Not without noticing the regret in Star's eyes, but it's too late for that now.

The windmill in my belly is turning so fast, I can feel each woosh of air gliding along my whole body. It's like there's a tornado coming. And there's nowhere I can go. The only person who would understand has thrown me under the bus for people who vastly misunderstand the concept of humor.

It's another hour before the bridge is in sight. I've been reading in bed. Or trying to. Really smutty stuff. Like, butt stuff and cane stuff and tree stuff. Stuff I can't fathom being into, stuff I read to gross myself out, but not even that was enough to distract me. Ugh.

There are daggers reaching out of the river. Brassy and shining so bright in the afternoon sun. There is an army awaiting, a Trojan horse of a bridge hiding people who are going to hurt me. I have to run away. I have to get away. But there's nowhere to go.

My ring rattles against the window. That's how I realize I'm trembling.

"Moon." Santiago knocks at the top of his bunk. I feel the reverberations under my calves. "Quit that, will you?"

I snatch my hand from the Plexiglas, but then the shivers ricochet from the ring into the rest of me. It's convulsing now, my body, these wild, rocky shakes, and I feel like I'm watching from outside myself, wondering how on earth this came to be. I am a cabinet filled with the fancy Christmas plates, unhinged, and there's an earthquake. Things are breaking.

"Jesus, Moon. What the hell are you doing?"

Well, add mortification to terror, because apparently my ample body is rocking the bunk as though it were a whale leaping into the shining seas.

"Sorry." I grit it out as I climb off the bed. I barely manage to get off the ladder, with plans to curl up into a ball right next to the merch boxes. But when I sort of thrust my way there, head down, I hit a boulder. A wall. A pile of rocks, hot and hard and dry. Also known as Santiago's chest. For the love of God, does he Gorilla Glue pieces of concrete to himself regularly? I want to poke him, to see if there's any give whatsoever. Then I glance up at his face, and he looks kind of pissed, but that's being quickly surpassed by widening eyes. "What's the matter, Moon? You're shaking. You're shaking."

I open my mouth to respond. I have no response, actually, but my body is going to provide one for me. Before either of us can figure out what that's going to be, we reach the first metal grate of the bridge, and it's a sound that shouldn't exist, period.

That tire-on-metal scrape, Lord. Lord. What ends up coming out of my mouth is a shriek. And then I open my arms and leap on Santiago.

I don't even get a moment to freak out that I might hurt him with the force of my bones and flesh and everything else. Which is fine, actually, because he doesn't budge. His arms go right to the backs of my thighs, and he holds me like someone threw a quilt at him, not a girl who can, at times, squeeze into a size 14.

"Hey," he says, soft, right next to my ear. My face is buried in his neck, and it's all I can do to keep from sobbing. He sits on the bed and now I'm in his lap, but all I can do is focus on the little jump the bus makes on every fucking metal scrape. We're running over metallic bodies every second. Every fraction of a second. Body, body, body. My spine does this little spasm with each one.

He leans back a little, pulling an arm off me somewhere, and I want to say how sorry I am, but I can't; instead I dig my nails in his shoulders as we go over a *thump-thump-thump* particularly violently, and then he pulls me over him.

And now we're in his bed, with his arms around me tight, and his hand is rubbing circles on my lower back.

"Hey, hey, it's okay," he says, his grumbly, rumbly voice vibrating in my temple, neck, chest. "Breathe, Moon. Slow. Like this." And as he demonstrates, his rib cage lifts mine. In, up, out, down. I feel like what's-his-name when he leaned on the torso of a triceratops in *Jurassic Park*. In, up, out, down. Again and again.

And the weird thing is, it calms me. His breath, the in and the out, the up and the down. By the time we go over the last metallic body scrape, I feel halfway normal. I sink into him and stretch my legs out. My head is on his chest, on what I think is the side of his triple-F pec. My left leg is on the bed, the other turned in so that it's over his. My arms are still clutching him as though he were the rock cliff against a free fall into outer space. I cling until my arms get numb and tingly, and then I nudge him so I can move a little.

He lifts his torso for a second, so I can put one arm bent between us, the other across his stomach. I watch it as it rises and falls with his breath. My arm, my thick brown arm, looks like a twig on the belly of an ancient dinosaur. If that dino had about twenty abdominal muscles stuffed in the space six would normally be.

He keeps rubbing my back, and then he says, "You better now?"

I nod. I'm not sure I can speak, seeing that my throat feels like it's made of chopped soda cans.

"You ready to talk about it?"

I shake my head.

"Okay," he says, and he shifts me a little so that we can both face the window. There're big, rolling clouds surrounding us, the color of spilled black-violet ink on white paper, all mixed together into a dusky purple, a color that makes my hair stand up.

"My dad drove off a bridge six years ago," I say. "On purpose." It's barely a whisper, but he hears me. I know it by the way his body tenses under mine. "It's been six years and I don't understand why he did it. Why did he choose to leave me like that? How could he?"

Santiago resumes the circles on my back. "He was cheating on Mom," I say. "He was cheating and she found out and she said she'd leave him and take us far away. She said he was worthless and she threw things at him. And then he left and . . . that was it."

"I'm so sorry, Moon," Santiago murmurs. "But you have to know he didn't choose to leave you. He had depression, or something like that. People don't just do that from out of nowhere."

I sniffle. "Yeah, he was depressed, I think." Especially toward the end, after he lost his job at the university. All he did was sleep, and some days I don't think he ate anything at all. I don't like to think about those memories, though. So I rub the tears away and take more long breaths. "Thanks for being here for me."

Santiago grunts. Back to caveman-mode, I guess.

I push up from him a little bit. "Look," I say, pointing out the window. "Poppies!"

"Papis?" He sounds confused, and a little breathless. My hand is pressed into one of his pecs, the other pushed right next to his hip, as I try to manage a cobra-like yoga posture in this tiny bunk.

"Sorry," I say, shifting my hands and body away from him. It's hard, because he's so massive. I don't know how he fits in this bed without me all in the way. But then he reaches out and grabs my arm, and then I'm back on top of him, only closer, way closer than I was before. I can feel his breath on my forehead. I'm looking directly into his lips, for God's sake. His lips look like they've been kissed. Like they are so made for kissing, they're perpetually swollen and peach, their outlines kind of blurry.

"Moon," those lips say, and I kind of jump.

"Yeah?" I sound absolutely desperate for something, but I have no idea what.

"What's a poppy?"

"Oh." I lift my head, back to the window. They're gone. "Damn it. You missed them."

"You didn't answer my question."

His lips graze my head. My temple. His voice is inside me. It's uncomfortable but not in a bad way. It's a lot like the band of rain clouds tightening in out the window, darkening and darkening until they can't help but burst. Goose bumps echo over my body, up and down, like a current. A water current, an air current, or drops of actual currants, cold and small on my skin.

Crap. He's still waiting for an answer. Only he looks less "waiting" and more amused. He even has those lips formed in a half smirk.

"What was the question?" I ask, and he smirks even wider while it comes to me. "Oh. Flowers. Poppies are flowers. They grow wild in this part of the country."

And then Santiago lifts his torso up, balanced on a forearm, and he reaches over to tuck my hair behind my ear. "Flowers, huh." He says it in a way that makes me think we're not talking flowers at all, like we were never talking about them, in fact.

And then we lurch. Or, rather, the bus lurches as it rounds into what I imagine is our dinner destination. And I fall against the wall.

"You okay?" His hand is on my waist now, and Lord, why is it so warm? Does he hide a space heater in here somewhere? Has he been dipping his whole body in front of it without my knowledge?

"Yeah, yeah. Sorry. I'm a klutz."

He pauses, looking at me as the bus parks. "You okay, though?" And now he's not asking about my clumsiness.

I nod. "Yes. Thank you."

And then I look out the window. At the corner of the gas station, a poppy winks at me, the red of it slick like wet silk.

"You can talk to me, you know." Santiago's voice is slick too but more like a forest in a fog, gliding down my back. "About anything."

"Okay." I nod again.

He stares at me again and licks his lips. I am not prepared for the way my insides get gooey at the sight of his tongue. There's not enough air, I decide. We're much too cramped on this bed. I climb over him to get out. "Thank you," I say. My face is red, maybe as red as that poppy out there, but I can't figure out why. Is it because I almost fainted over driving on a bridge? Or is it

225

because I had to rely on Santiago—my literal archnemesis—to help me out? Or is it because of how effectively he did it? Too effectively. So much so that I don't want it to stop. My body is currently screaming at me to get back in the bunk, now. For what, I don't know. To be honest, I don't want to know.

When I stand and look at Santiago again, my eyes become traitors and practically leap out to glue themselves to his lips. "I gotta go," I say. My voice sounds so clipped, like it's coming out of my chest rather than my mouth. And when I look over his shoulder, back at the window, my voice wilts down into the core of the earth. Because there, right there, is a moth. Not just any moth, but a luna moth. The same sort of moth that followed me home the night of the knives. It's huge and hairy and the color of a pale lime, and I swear I can see its little beady eyes staring at me.

When Santiago glances behind him with a puzzled look on his face, it snaps me out of my terror. My voice rises once more to say this eloquent line: "Uh. I'll be back." I grab my purse from the top bunk and run.

35.

And I Mean, I Run (Straight into La Raíz, Because That Is Just My Luck)

I DID TRACK in school, so this isn't an unheard-of thing, but I'm not in my gear, I don't have Maluma singing about his hot girlfriends in my ears, and without a sports bra, my boobs are bouncing so much, I wince from the pain.

I'm running. Running from a boy.

I've never run from a boy before. Mostly I run to them. Anything for a scrap of attention. "You're like a dog," my mother has told me. "Except I have to feed you." Which, Mom's obviously never owned a dog before, but still. That one really stung. What Mom tells her daughter that? What human tells another human that?

Santiago doesn't think I'm like a dog, I bet. He doesn't even think of me as a whore. And the way he looks at me. He looks at me the way people look at Star. But better. Because there's no hint that he wants to get something from me. He looks at me like

I'm perfectly lovely, and funny, and beautiful just as I am, and that is all enough.

It's the weirdest thing that's ever happened to me. And once I had an eagle land on my car in the middle of the day. I swear to the Lord in heaven. It looked at me right in my eyes, like it had a message for me. Still haven't figured that one out, sorry to say.

I barely realize I'm heading straight for that lone red poppy out there like *it* has a message for me.

I run even harder until I reach it, and when I do, I gasp, because just beyond it, behind the gas station, are mountains, gold in the setting sun. They look carved from a jeweler's bench, set with emeralds here and there for all the trees. And right before me, right here, a field of poppies. All rubies and garnets and red jasper, dappled pink in the light.

There's an invisible thread pulling me in. I am a piece of wool, brown, about to be stitched to a great cosmic blanket. Or maybe I'm a petal stuck to a spiderweb, one tiny fabric-like spot making a whole universe undulate like wisps in the wind.

And I plop right in the middle of it, leaning back to look up at a sky that reminds me of the hand-sewn prom dresses a designer sent Star a couple months ago, teal and periwinkle and lapis lazuli, the shimmery hints of stars beyond thin, tulle-like clouds. The red of the poppies surrounds me, their heads bobbing soft, sometimes touching at my arms. I can't decide if I am in an ancient red sea or being swallowed by a whale made of jewels and dresses that will never belong to me.

"Hey."

My eyes are closed, but I'm so used to Santiago's voice crawling over my skin like satin, I don't startle in the least. "So these are the poplar flowers?" he asks.

When I do look at him, he's smiling, like he's got a secret, and I'm immediately breathless. I manage to rein it in a little and say, "Poppies."

"I know. I'm just messing with you."

I knew that, but Santiago's smile makes it hard to mess around. As well as speak in general. And move. And breathe.

He has a seat next to me. Great. "Got your cards with you?"

He gestures to my purse, still slung on my shoulder and lying next to me. "Uh. No, sorry. I left them in the box in my bigger bag."

"Too bad. Was hoping you'd give me a reading." He says it casually. Almost too casually.

I push my torso up. "You ever had your cards read before?"

He shakes his head. "You'd be my first."

I fall back down. I'm too weak, too exhausted, too breathless to run and grab the cards. So I say, "How about a mirror-stone reading instead?"

"Mirror stones, huh? I thought you said you hadn't worked up to those yet."

"It's not that. They just kind of . . ." Terrorize? Horrify? "Intimidate me."

"Okay. A challenge, then."

I reach in my purse, to the tiny, almost secret compartment.

Before I left my tía's that one summer she taught me divination, she gave me my own onyx stone. "I don't know what happened between you and mirror stones," she said, "but you two need to make your peace."

Maybe now's the time for peace. I pull the stone out. It's almost perfectly circular, and there are tiny gray veins on its edges. It looks ancient and holy, like Tía pulled it out of ruins on one of her travels to Mexico. Wouldn't surprise me if she had.

"Do you have a question?" I ask. "Like, something specific for me to focus on?"

He shakes his head and shrugs. "Let's see what comes up."

I turn the stone over and over, looking, letting my eyes unfocus a little. Looking, looking, like Tía does, but I have no idea what for . . . until the whole universe, the one out there and the one inside me, feels all calibrated together. Like a tiny piece of quartz and a watch, tuned and rhythmically counting from this moment till forever, and all I have to do is reach my hands in and touch any time I'd like.

"Can you touch the stone?" I ask, placing it facedown in a wild grass patch between us. He scoots a little closer and tentatively brings a couple fingertips to it.

I look up at him when he releases his touch. "Sometimes weird things happen when I read. I hope that's okay."

He scoffs. "Right. Your curse."

I roll my eyes and say, "You can be quiet now." Because the last thing I want to do is explain exactly why attracting zillions of bugs from time to time is, indeed, a curse.

And I look. And I blush. Because there's snowcapped mountains and stone phalli and lilies. Sex, sex, sex. Each image is its own composition, coming in and out on the stone, like fog, like long-ago memories, wrapping around my brain with one distinct message.

The reading is about sex. It's about a guy who meets someone full of mysteries and secrets and then they bang each other's brains out.

I have two warring thoughts as I evaluate the reading some more. One, I hate this woman. I keep getting images of her with hands all over Santiago, and I want to kill her. But the fact is, she's into her sexuality, which means it's not Star, who'd rather have her heart shot with an arrow than engage in anything remotely sexual. Or at least that's what I thought, before I saw her wrestling tongues with Belle Brix. Still, this person's vibe isn't Star-like at all. Maybe it's a girl I've never met before.

Santiago's never talked about a girlfriend. Maybe it's some guy I've never met before. Maybe this is why he didn't go for Star. Oh God, he doesn't like girls. What if he doesn't like girls?

It doesn't matter. My heart is already broken, so it doesn't matter.

Okay, my secondary thought is taking the reins. Which is, how the hell do I tell him—

"You're going to be having a lot of sex in your near future." Well. Like that, I guess. Thanks, big mouth.

His mouth opens for a few seconds, but all that comes out are almost-coughing sounds.

"That's good, right?"

He sputters, and now his cheeks are pink. Pink! Almost as pink as the crepe myrtle's fuchsia petals outside of Tía's home.

And then a new thought occurs to me. "Oh, sorry, are you celibate?"

"Celibate?" His voice is loud, too loud for a conversation in a field.

"You know, you don't engage in sexual—"

"No. I'm not celibate."

"Oh," I say. "Well, that's great, because all I see is sex. All kinds of sex. Very amorous vibes going on here."

Now his neck and ears are just as pink as his cheekbones. "Does it say who—"

"Uh, well, her hair kind of goes this way, and she's a bit round here. Does that sound like someone you know?"

"Uh . . . is that supposed to sound like a person?"

"Yes! God! There's hair . . . and sort of hips here—"

He grabs the stone and examines it closely. "I feel like I'm looking at my baby cousin's ultrasound picture."

"Oh, you . . ." I grab it back. I don't feel so awkward anymore, and his cheeks are a little less rosy. I take a breath and place the stone back down. This is okay. This is easy, even.

"So is there anything else besides hot sex in my future?"

Hearing him actually say that word. Now *my* cheeks are heating up. "Uh . . ."

A dragonfly lands on the stone. "Well, there are people in your way, as far as what you want to do with your life."

"Okay."

"And you're going to have some heavy opposition, which will force you to stand up to all of them."

"Uh—Moon?"

"Hold on. I'm almost done." A dragonfly lands on my hand and I lightly shake it away. "So after that . . ." I finger the stone, turning it over and over in the grass, where more dragonflies have gathered. "You have to stay firm about what you want, you know? You . . ." And I stop. Because I've looked now, and Santiago's holding his arms out stiff, and his spine is so straight and still.

There are dragonflies all over him. And I mean all *over*. They're sitting in his hair and on his shoulders, perched on his bare forearms and hand and the soft black T-shirt over his torso. One moves across his jaw, and he breaks into just the biggest smile, which makes me feel so weird, like my whole body is made of dragonflies and they want to fly all over him too. Like he is the center of the Dragonfly Universe.

"It's La Raíz?" he whispers.

I swallow and nod. "Yes. It's the curse."

"I don't believe you." His tone tells me different.

"Oh?" I pick up the stone and slide it back in my pocket. It's weird, but if they come when I'm slipping my hand into another time and I stop my reading? That makes them scatter. Nothing else but that. "There."

The second I say the word, the dragonflies, each and every

one of them, leap up. They hover around us for a second, long enough for us to hear the whisper-buzz of their beating wings, long enough for me to shriek a little, and then they decide, all at once, to fly away. And we watch all three hundred thousand zillion billion dragonflies slide over the poppies, in the warm sheets of sunset light, like a murmuration, like they're made of nothing but magic.

"Okay," Santiago says, still staring at where the dragonflies disappeared. His eyes are so wide, and when he looks at me, he doesn't even blink. "I might believe you now."

36.

The Stuff I Don't Like to Remember

YEAH, TOWARD THE end, Dad wasn't doing well. Once I found him in his office crying so hard, he could barely speak.

"Daddy," I whispered. I curled into his lap and hugged him. I initiated a lot of hugs back then. I thought if I hugged him hard enough, I could hug that sadness away, you know? "Maybe you could go to a doctor," I said to him.

He never acknowledged this. Instead, he said, "Maybe if I got a dog, it would help. You wanna get a dog, Moon?"

Uh, yeah, what eleven-year-old girl doesn't want a dog? But Mom put a stop to that right away. "I'm not taking care of you all and a dog."

I want to blame her for what happened. If it hadn't been for Mom, he might still be alive, right?

But after he was gone, it was like his sadness stayed around and went right inside Mom. Her skin turned gray, almost, and her eyes looked as though someone had punched her over and over again. This was in the old house, when our rooms were really close together, so Star and I heard her weeping almost every night. She'd talk to Dad sometimes too.

"I'm like this because of you," she'd scream. "You did this to me! You made me into a piece of shit!"

This is what I try to remember when Mom makes me feel worthless. That somewhere deep down, she feels worthless too. It's not like it erases everything she's done to me, but remembering that she's a wounded human sometimes helps a teeny-tiny bit. Only sometimes, though.

And when I get to thinking about all this stuff, I can't help but wonder, What if Dad hadn't done it? I mean, not the cheating. I don't care about that. That only proves to me that my father was human. That he made mistakes. Just like me.

No, what I mean is, if he hadn't driven off a bridge. If he'd left Mom for whoever had stolen some of his heart. What if he could've taken me, you know? Imagine it. Me, Moon Fuentez. Instead of my eleven-year-old heart shattering into so many pieces it may as well have been dust, I was tucked up and rescued to a new family. With a stepmom who maybe wouldn't have loved me, okay, but there's no way she'd have hated me as much as Mom did. And does.

I could've gotten away, you know? From the hurt, the pain, the knives. I could've been safe, treasured, and loved.

But he chose to leave me. Forever.

I could smack myself for this sometimes, but every now and then I feel more hatred for my dad than for my mom. I wish it weren't this way, but it seems as inevitable as the light lime of a luna moth's wings, smooth, smooth, smooth like a sky.

37.

La Raíz Strikes Again (Also, Jealousy Becomes an Emerald Mask and Covers My Face for Nearly a Whole Day)

"EXPLAIN THIS CURSE to me some more," Santiago says after dinner. (Yes, the tavuk kebabi was good. In fact, it's better than mozzarella sticks, chocolate lava cake, and hot Cheetos all together, which is a high, high compliment in my book, but Santiago very much disagreed.)

Santiago continues. "I've been thinking about it and I can't wrap my head around it. Stuff like that"—he points outside—"happens to you regularly? For real?"

"Yes." I groan. I ate too much, so I unbutton the top of my jeans. Class act, I know.

Santiago's drying his precious skillets as he turns to face me. "But . . . *how*? How is it even possible?"

"I don't know. I wish I knew, though, because maybe then I could predict it. And stop it, you know?"

"Why would you want to stop it?" Santiago sits across from me. "Why would you ever want to stop something like that?"

I close my eyes for a few moments, and when I open them again, Santiago is closer, like I'm about to share something wild and mystical with him. And maybe I am. "La Raíz first comes when a girl has sex for the first time."

"You make it sound like it's a bad thing."

"Well, it is a bad thing, isn't it? It's a punishment for becoming impure!"

Santiago looks at me like I've just grown antlers. "Look, I know your sister and family are really religious. But sex isn't inherently bad. This . . ." He points out the window again. "How could being visited by dragonflies once in a while be a punishment?"

I shake my head. I don't know what to say.

"It's one of the most lovely and . . . amazing . . . and wild . . ." He drifts off. I've never seen him so full of conversation. Santiago is now a nebula of words. A nebula-dictionary, letters swirling around him like shimmering stardust. He's always been beautiful, but right now I can't take my eyes away. Can hardly take a breath, even. "This isn't a curse, Moon. Trust me. It's not."

And that's what I think about when I get in bed. What if my whole life, Mom has been wrong? About the curse, about Eve, about everything.

Maybe sex isn't inherently bad.

Maybe when Eve ate the forbidden fruit, she became something different in a good way. A woman capable of taking risks and becoming free.

Maybe La Raíz isn't a curse at all. Maybe what's in my bloodline is actually magic. Maybe along the way someone just mistook magic for sin, and that misunderstanding, that's what's been passed on and on, from the first woman down, down, down to me, Moon Fuentez. The girl who was once the ugly twin and now, now I don't know what I am anymore. All I know is I'm like Eve. I'm changing at every moment. Becoming something entirely different, all in a good way, I think. I hope.

Andro's ordered a fancy table and setup for me and my readings. It's lovely, covered in tasseled fabrics in the colors of flowers—warm paintbrush and echinacea alongside iced-lavender cosmos. "You like it?" he asks, grinning. "I told the venue about your aesthetic, and they ran with it."

"It's gorgeous," I respond. "Did they mention . . . the cost?"

"Don't worry about it," Andro says. Behind me is a snort.

I turn, and there's Santiago with a couple of our merch boxes balanced in his arms.

"Oh! I didn't realize you were already unloading." I rush up, but he shakes his head.

"You're busy today."

"Oh, please. It's not starting for another hour."

"Actually, I need you at the table in fifteen, if that's good, Moon?" Andro says, causing Santiago to give me a victorious smirk.

"Yeah," I respond. I jog to the cart and pick up a box. As soon as I'm upright, Santiago is there, pulling it from my hands. I grab another box, but before I'm halfway to the merch table, he huffs, marches over, and—you guessed it—steals the merch away. "I said you don't have to," he grunts, not kindly.

My skin and muscles are all tense and I roll my eyes, going for another box. When Santiago comes back, I zigzag like I'm being attacked by a shark. "Stop it, okay? I can help you a little before I start."

"Why are you running like that?"

"Because you're coming at me like a wild animal! See? Look at you! You're circling me like a shark! With your long legs and your . . . your sharp teeth!"

"Moon."

"Just stop it, okay? I can help if I want!"

"Moon, you only zigzag from alligators. Not sharks."

"Oh, that's what you say now! Because you're trying to pin your bad behavior on alligators!"

He thinks he's sneaky, trying to distract me with chitchat so he can reach in when I'm least expecting it. I run the other way.

"When's the last time you saw a shark run, huh?" he asks.

"That's exactly what you shark sympathizers want us to think! But I'm onto you!"

By the time he gets to me again, I'm breathing heavy. This box must be the one with literal bricks in it. He takes it from me, places it on the ground, and then does something astonishing. He wraps his arms around me. It takes a total of eight seconds to get over the shock, and then I slide my arms around his waist, tight.

"I get annoyed when I see my brother flirting with you," he

says into my hair, and just like that I'm in shock again. This time it takes me twenty whole seconds to recover.

"Andro definitely wasn't flirting with me," I finally say.

"Right." My chest is squished up against the top of his stomach, and I can feel his voice all grumbly there.

I snort and take a step back, breaking up the hug a little. But I keep a hand on his waist, and he still has an arm draped on my shoulder. All this touch makes me want to jump, or shiver, or do something unspeakable that would undoubtedly freak and gross Santiago out. "You said he has a girlfriend. So who cares if he flirts or not? It's not like I have a chance anyway."

I meant it light, like a joke. Like, ha ha ha, no one ever likes me. But as I'm saying it, I know, I know for some reason that it's the exact wrong thing to say. Santiago's face confirms this. It grows taut, and he drops his arm, which just reached my lower back.

"What? What is it now?"

He shakes his head. "Nothing."

"Moon!" Andro is gesturing wildly for me to go to my fabric table.

"Go," Santiago says. When I don't leave right away, he repeats it much more sharply, like he's now a rose, covered in spines of thorns. "Go, Moon."

So I go.

Jeez Louise, I should've charged one hundred dollars a reading. Because the line. The line is so long, I keep fantasizing about lassoing it up and dragging myself to something warm and soft and very far away, like my bed, or a hammock, or the planet Mercury.

I was nervous at first, but now I feel . . . kind of numb. The cards are all starting to look the same. And if one more person asks me to pose for a selfie, I'm going to unhinge my jaw and swallow this entire event whole. "Only fifteen more minutes," I keep telling myself.

A teen sits down, with her mom, I'm assuming. "I don't know if you remember me," she says. "I'm Maritza Reyno?"

"Oh my gosh!" I say. "Maritza as in Marilunar?" Marilunar was one of my first followers, and her feed is really cool. She knits moon-shapes into delicate tapestries people probably spend fortunes on to hang on their walls.

Maritza beams and laughs. "I can't believe you remember my handle. Mami, she knows my handle." Her mom nods and smiles. "Mom's really excited because you read things that look like nature. She said that's how she was taught to read, by looking in the woods."

"Oh my gosh!" I say. I'm so excited, I barely stop myself from jumping up. "That's how I learned! That's how my tía taught me!"

They talk animatedly in Spanish for a few minutes, and a couple of girls behind them start rolling their eyes. "Can't believe we're behind these freaking Mexicans," one comments. The other cackles. I glare at them, but they don't even notice me.

"Can we have a reading for the two of us?" Maritza asks.

"Yes, yes, of course. I've never done a joint one before, but I'll try. Sit down, okay?"

I pull the cards: the Sun, the Ten of Wands, the Three of Swords. Everything around me slows and pours into this one moment: me, these cards, these people. And I feel *connected*. I don't know why, maybe because they already understand how to read twigs and light and leaves. But this reading, right in front of me, it brings me to some holy space. The sunlight is dappled and turning orange on my arms, hands, the cards. Everything feels alive, you know? The grass under my bare feet, almost blue in color. The wind, blowing the little baby hairs escaping my ponytail around. The cards, each one full of more than what it is. And that's when the first red feather arrives.

The fluff of crimson falls twirling, like a dancer, right onto the cards. And I know, down to the constellations of my cells, that something's happening. So I look up.

Little red swirls dot the sky, getting closer, closer. All wispy-edged and ruby in color. All feathers, none bigger than my pinkie finger. All fuzzy like snow clouds.

"Mira," Maritza's mom says slowly, her voice a whisper of wonder.

And then they both reach up, and we're covered . . . we're all covered in the speckled fluff of red.

"Did you do this?" Maritza asks, holding her hands up, smiling. A feather lands in each one.

"No," I say, but she and her mom start thanking me. Like I

completed the reading, like this had anything to do with my will. And with tears in their eyes, they leave, and then there are those snotty girls behind them, each taking red-feathered photos.

"Oh, look, we're up," one says.

"Sorry, no," I respond. "I'm closed."

"What?" One girl puts her hand on her hip. "But that's not fair. You're supposed to be open for another seven minutes."

"Sorry, I am under a contractual agreement that I can't read for racists," I say, and God, it feels good.

Especially when one makes a face and says, "My father will hear about this."

And then I get to say, "Okay, settler! Bet your father is a bigot too!"

And I slide my cards in the pack and run toward the merch table, stopping cold when I see Santiago, arms crossed, a pleasant expression on his face as he talks to a girl. A really pretty, really thin girl, and she's typing in her phone in a way that makes me think— oh God—now he's reaching for his phone. They're exchanging numbers. They're texting already, right now, as they stand in front of each other. They're probably typing messages like, **Fall wedding?** And, **I've only ever wanted two kids but I can be persuaded to have 3.5.**

She's touching his arm, his bicep, the place where my head fits absolutely perfectly. And then she places her hand right at his jaw, like she wants to kiss him.

But I guess Santiago has Spidey senses when it comes to me

watching him with a girl. Because he turns and our eyes are locked and his mouth drops open, brows furrowed. He looks guilty. And there's no reason to be. I'm not his girlfriend. I'm barely even a friend. I'm just Moon Fuentez, the ugly twin, the one with the jiggly thighs and belly, the girl he can barely manage to not hate all the time. So when Andro approaches and says, "You taking a break, Moon? Perfect. Let's grab some lunch."

With a great deal of fake enthusiasm, I say yes.

I wondered, but now there's confirmation. I no longer am attracted to Andro. Andro Philips, the guy who I thought was the most beautiful human on the planet. All the way up until I met his jackass of a brother.

"So here's the thing, Moon," he says. "When you need a break, let me know, or let someone know, and we'll arrange it. If you leave an event early—even a little early—we get a lot of complaints."

"Sorry," I say, after swallowing a huge bite of sandwich. It's got slices of fresh mozzarella, heirloom tomatoes, and basil, and there's a little dish of balsamic reduction to dip it in. I have no idea what balsamic reduction is, but it's tangy and sweet, and I wish Santiago were here, because he'd explain everything to me and maybe even promise to teach me how to re-create it. Then again, he's probably planning his wedding to Willowy Fairy Girl, so yeah. Good thing he's not here.

"No worries. I know you're just getting the hang of this. Anyway, now that I got the business talk out of the way . . ." He pulls out his phone. "Talk to me, Moon. How in the hell did you pull this off?"

On his screen, there's a photo of me looking up and smiling, my hands lazily spread on tarot cards, feathers falling all around me like rain, the cloth and fabrics and my hair rippling like light on water. It doesn't look real. It shouldn't be real, really, but here we are.

I swallow again and shake my head. "I didn't do it." Technically the truth. "It just . . . happened."

"Just happened? Are you kidding? You're not, are you?"

I shake my head, and then Andro laughs with delight. He flicks his phone screen some, and then he shows it to me again. "It's the top Fotogram story of the day."

"What?" I say. "What?" Not even Star has been at the top before. She got second, once, when she replaced her silver purity ring with a Cartier engagement ring, but this, this, this. I can't even find the words. Except: "Holy shit."

"Look, your following has jumped to almost eighty thousand. In a single day! That's one of the biggest in such a short time in Fotogram history."

"Holy shit." And not just, *Holy shit, that's a very large number.* But also, *Holy shit, there's no way Mom doesn't know by now.* Or, if not now, then she will know very, very soon. Lord, I need a distraction. I'm already biting my lip hard enough to taste blood.

But then Andro distracts me. "Startles," really, is the word, because he leans forward, and for a moment of horror, I think he's going to wrap his hands around mine. I let out an exhale when he leaves his hands on the table, near mine but not quite touching. He gives me a sly smile, like we're sharing deep, sneaky secrets. "I want you to become our headliner, Moon."

"You what now?"

"I want you to headline the rest of the tour. There's only four stops left. And I've never seen potential like this before. You could have a couple of million followers by the time we're done. Ads, endorsements. Your own income."

"Just like Star," I murmur. Something I never, ever thought I'd say about myself.

"You'll be front and center as far as ads, posts, merch."

"I don't have any merch."

"Sure you do. Finish up the Wild Moonflower tarot. We'll have them expedited to our next stop."

I wince. "You're assuming I'll actually sell them."

"Moon." This time he does let his fingers graze my hand. "You will sell them. I already had people asking where the tarot cards were today."

I gulp. "They're kind of pricey unless you do a bulk order."

"I want to order a thousand."

I drop my fork. It clatters on my plate, but I don't tear my eyes from Andro's face. "Did you say one *thousand*?"

"Yup."

"Oh." Everything feels really weird. Like, I don't even know words anymore. The things on my plate don't look like food.

They're now a collection of colors. The windows are little portals into new universes of light. It's like I've never even seen the outdoors before. The light, the blue of the sky, the clouds. The silverware, the flecks of pepper on this cheese, the pink of my fingernails. Everything. Everything is so new, I feel like I'm seeing it for the first time. It takes me almost a minute to reground myself.

Because an order like that would pay for all four years of university housing. And then some.

Because an order like that would mean I'd finally be free from Mom and Star. All thanks to my art. All thanks to *me*.

"So what do you say?" Andro smiles.

And then the ball drops.

I think of how much I hated everything today. The lines, the snarky comments from racist girls, the fact that I couldn't even read properly until I felt emotionally connected to a querent.

And then Santiago, with the beautiful, willowy girl, texting their wedding colors to each other. Baby names. Hamptons vacation-home layouts.

I don't have it in me to be an influencer. I can't. I'm too emotional, too all over the place, too jealous of girls talking to Santiago, too distracted to balance dozens of people trying to talk to me at the same time. Lord, I have a throbbing headache right now, and that's from one day of this. If I were to headline the rest of the tour, I'd be comatose by the end of it.

And not to mention what Mom would say. I can hear it now:

You're so greedy, you had to take, take, take everything: sex, sin, and now your sister's spotlight? Then I'm sure she'd end it with some creative name-calling, involving the words "slut" and "whore" and "very bad daughter whom I never deserved."

And Star, God in heaven. She'd never forgive me.

"I can't," I say, pulling my hands back. "I'm sorry, Andro. I'm an introvert. I'm the girl much more comfortable behind the camera, you know?" I frown at my half-finished meal. "I'm not good at that stuff. It makes me anxious and exhausted."

Andro nods. "Yup, yup. Look, really. I get it. You're a lot like Santiago, or our mom, even. They need their alone time."

"Your mom, too?"

"Oh, yeah. Santiago, he's got his whole quiet personality from her. She's much better at words and writing, you know."

Maybe that's why Santiago gave his number to that girl. He liked her enough to write to her. I mean, he's never texted me. He couldn't even manage it when he thought I'd sent him that thirsty boob photo.

Andro's phone buzzes. "Speaking of Mom." He laughs and does an impersonation with a high-pitched voice: "Alejandro, where are you? Did you eat lunch? When are you going to get a girlfriend?"

I laugh and then furrow my brow. "You don't have a girl-friend?"

"Uh, no." Andro shrugs. "Not for a bit. Been kinda busy."

"Of course." I do this weird chuckle, even though I don't

know why I'm doing it. "It's just, Santiago told me you did. Have a girlfriend, I mean."

"Huh." Now Andro looks amused. "Well, no, not for almost a year."

"That's a weird thing for him to say, then."

Andro shrugs. "Oh, I don't know. People do all sorts of things to protect their, ah, investments." And he immediately looks guilty, like he's said way too much, but the fact is, I have no idea what he's even talking about. "So, no to readings. But you're still up for being Merch Girl, right?"

"Yes, yes. Of course."

"And you're still cool with me selling the decks?"

I pause, thinking of my mom. *Remember,* I tell myself. *Hiding who you are isn't worth it anymore.* All those pep talks I gave to myself before must've worked, because I actually feel good about this. I feel good about becoming who I'm meant to be, no matter what my mom will think.

I straighten my spine and offer a half smile. "How many did you want me to order again?"

"A thousand."

I bury my face in my hands. This. Financial freaking independence. That's going to be so fucking worth it. "That number doesn't even sound real."

"So that's a yes, I take it?"

"Yes." I want to cry. Gosh I'm emotional today. "Yes, yes, yes. And thank you."

When I get back, the line to the tarot table is gone. Andro said I could join the merch table, but Santiago's sitting there looking like a sullen little boy. And everything feels funny. Off-kilter. Like the earth's become hollow without any of us knowing and, at any moment, we could slip through right into the middle of it.

I inhale and walk up to him. "Hey."

He whips his head around, then schools a look of disinterest on his face, giving me a nod.

And just like that, it hits me.

Santiago is into me.

It's so obvious, I almost sway under the weight of all the evidence in my memories. The earth cracks under my feet as I think of them all.

How he scoffs when I make a joke about how blobbish and unattractive I am, as though he of thinks me—all of me, size 16 jiggles and all—as unspeakably beautiful. How he gets mad when another guy is flirty with me, even if it's just Andro. How he held me during the big bridge. Like I was everything precious in this world.

But maybe he doesn't like me anymore. Because I've been so dense, you know, saying things like, *I don't have a chance with your brother*, as though I ever really wanted his brother. Andro may as well have ceased to exist the first time Santiago smiled at me.

And now I'm speechless. What on earth am I supposed to do now? Say, *Hey, I think I've finally figured out you have a crush on me and it doesn't freak me out at all!* No, no, no, that's definitely not what I should say.

Star sort of saves me. Sort of. The way she walks up, her hands on her hips, her hair uncharacteristically frizzy on the crown. "I need to talk to you, Luna. Alone." She's doing a perfect imitation of Mom when she's mad enough to hurt me, but since we're not alone, she has to appear somewhat in control of her murderous impulses. You know, pass for someone who wouldn't stab her own child if she were mad enough.

The only other time Star's looked at me like that was when my computer deleted all the photos from the redwood shoot we did last fall. She'd worn a Navajo-inspired print from a white girl designer in Manhattan. So I honestly feel like my computer eating those photos right up was an act of karma.

This, though. I don't know what on earth I've done. She looks like she wants to grab me by the hair, drag me to a ditch, and push me in. We walk a little while away from Santiago, and then she speaks.

"What's this about you headlining the rest of the tour?" She's breathless.

"Uh, what?" How does she know about that already?

"You went to lunch with Andro, right? Chamomila was around. She heard him talking about it." Her cheeks are splotchy and pink.

I sigh and close my eyes. "Star. He asked me to headline, yeah, but I said no."

Star's face is ugly for the second or third time in her life. "Right. And what the heck did you do to make him offer that?"

I open and close my mouth. Is she saying—

"We all know what kind of girl you are, Moon."

I reel back. "And what's that supposed to mean?"

"It means, even if you did turn it down, you're still somehow the number one Fotogram story of the day."

"Because of the freaking feathers! La Raíz, Star, remember? Did you not see—"

"What exactly were you doing with Andro before that lunch? Because you know when Mom calls, she's going to want all the details."

I close my eyes once more. It's the knife thing all over again. Only this time Star's the one wielding the weapons and the target is my back. And it hurts. It hurts because Star's the only one who knows how far Mom has gone. Not even Tía knows that.

"By the way," Star adds. "Tomorrow Oak is taking me out to Le Chateaubriand. So we can cancel our shitty Taco Bell plans."

And that marks the first time Star has cursed in ever. Ever. And it was at me. For daring to exist and do stuff, essentially.

"You just can't believe that I'd be more successful than you on my own. I gotta say, Star, unfounded accusations like that are most unchristian. It's not what Jesus or the Virgin Mary would do." I want to tell her I know about her and Belle. I want to tell her that I've never seen her happier, genuinely happier, almost ever. That it should be Belle taking her out to dinner, not slob-bering Oak. The words don't make it out, though. Even with how mad I am, I can't do that to her.

Star stares for a beat and then walks away. I can console myself with the fact that her hair's frizzy crown has grown several inches since she started antagonizing me. It looks good. She looks human, you know? But she'll hate it. In fact, she's smoothing it down already, like she knows her mortality is being revealed or something. The fact that she hates it, that's what matters to me right now.

"Why do you let her talk to you like that?"

These are the first words out of Santiago's mouth. A chair has appeared beside him. I plop down and put my face in my hands. "Fuck," I say, but it comes out like, "Hmmpth."

"I'm serious." He sounds serious, and furious.

I'm cringing. "You heard what she said?"

"I didn't need to. I could see that shit from all the way over here. You don't take a single piece of shit from me, but you let her fucking pummel you on a daily basis."

I lean back in my chair. I feel like I might cry, so I look up to help the tears slide back in. "You don't understand."

"Explain it to me." He puts a hand on my knee, making his voice gentle. As gentle as a voice made out of a gravelly dirt road can be, I guess.

"Not now. Please." The tears are almost back in, but my words break a bit. He squeezes my knee and thigh a little. I am so hyperaware of his hand and the warmth of his skin. I wonder if he'll put his hand on Tall and Willowy like that.

"Okay. Maybe after dinner?"

"Maybe," I say. We're staying at a hotel tonight, so no, I won't even be near him after dinner. But it's sweet of him to offer. So sweet I might cry again. Jeez Louise, what is wrong with me?

I get my answer right before dinner, staring at the crimson stain that has reached the inside of my jeans. Thank God no one saw that, unless they were staring mega-hard at my crotch. I don't know why, but knowing I've started my period doesn't help me much. It makes everything worse, in fact. I burst into tears and shower and change into my pajamas.

Santiago has all the food on plates when I get out. He smiles when I reach him.

"You cooked without me?"

"I was hungry."

"This is the second dinner in a row—"

"I'll text you the recipes."

The gratitude overcomes me, in waves of linen, a little sharp, because of the recent memories of him and his willowy wife, but mostly soft, on my back, cheeks, neck. Willowy wife or not, if it weren't for Santiago, I'd still be eating spoons of hydrogenated peanut butter and poisoning myself with knockoff Teflon cookware. So I lean over to him, placing a hand on his shoulder. The muscles contract under my hand. And the moment I kiss his cheek, he gasps a little but tries to hide it with a grunt. I lean back again, and the look he's giving me, like I've just handed him gold. And I know that the leggy wife has no chance. None at all.

And then we eat, and now that I'm in the light of the kitchen fairy lanterns, he can see how red my eyes are, and probably I'm close enough for him to hear how snotty my nose is. He slides his arm on the table, the one he wraps with the gray cloth, and says, "You're the only one who hasn't asked about it."

"About what?"

He lifts his arm.

"Oh." I glance over. I never let myself stare. Especially not after I acted like a total cabbage-head when I first met him. I thought really hard about if I were him, what I wouldn't appreciate, you know? And that would include staring, talking about it, acting freaked out and pretending not to be. Treating him like he wasn't normal. He's a really moody, grumpy, hulky, hot, thoughtful, generous boy. That's it. Well, that's not quite it. He does have this ridiculous superhuman power of getting hotter every time I look at him. Especially when he planks shirtless in the mornings. And sometimes, in the evenings, I do stare at him, all of him, when he's doing those wild handstand push-ups against the wall by our bunks.

"Why?"

I blink away thoughts of how taut Santiago's forearms are during his push-ups. "Why what?"

"Why haven't you asked about what happened to my hand?"

I swallow. Dinner tonight is arroz con pollo. It reminds me of my mom. The good times, when she still cooked, before Dad left. "I thought if you wanted me to know, you'd tell me." I gesture to my chest, to the scar on and below my collarbone. "Why haven't you ever asked me about this?"

He stares at it for a moment, and then his eyes run up to my face. He smiles. It's a . . . I don't know. A sad smile, I want to say. "I thought if you wanted me to know, you'd tell me," he says finally.

We talk about little else besides cooking-related subjects. It's Switzerland for us as far as conversation. Neutral ground. Garlic goes well with everything, but it especially does justice to tomatoes. Santiago says it's because of the natural umami flavor in tomatoes. You don't need much else in arroz. Tomato, garlic, salt, pepper, chicken. The simple ingredients make something so good, it almost hurts to eat.

On the side, he's fried up sweet plátanos, almost black on the edges of the slices, so the starchy sugars caramelized. He finished them with gray salt, something fancy from some French sea.

"Isn't it amazing?" he's saying. He stands, grabs the little glass container of salt. "This, coming from those old salt marshes in Guérande. It made it all the way here. Into this kitchen. Into our bellies."

"It is amazing," I say. I take the jar and tilt it. The salt is made into flakes and little crystal chips. It looks like jewels. Gray diamonds. "They're beautiful."

When I look at Santiago, his eyes are dark and twinkling. I don't think it's just the lantern light. "Yes," he says, looking from the salt back to me.

I clear my throat. "That girl you were talking to today was really pretty."

"What girl?"

"You guys had your phones out . . . exchanged numbers. . . ."

"Oh. Her."

"Yes. Her."

He smiles at me and leans back, taking the salt jar back. "She wanted to know Oak's Fotogram handle."

"Huh," I say. He's still smiling at me. Tossing the salt jar, catching it, over and over again. It looks like a single marble in his giant hand.

"What?" I finally snap, standing. I grab the dishes and walk to the sink.

"I didn't realize you were watching me so closely today."

"I wasn't."

"Oh, really." He stands and takes a couple of steps toward me. When I turn around to give him a glare, I almost jump back. He's so close, our arms are touching. And then he takes another step closer. My right side is lined up with his left, from the fronts of our legs to our bellies and chests. I feel everything when he breathes, when I breathe, when I sway a little from light-headedness. He lowers his face until his lips reach the shell of my ear. I shudder. "You were all the way across the lawn and you still noticed me."

"Sounds like you knew exactly where I was," I respond in nearly a whisper. There are goose bumps on my neck, sliding down my back like salt. "I'd say you were the one watching me way too close."

He leans down a little more, and I swallow a gasp. His face is an inch from mine. His mouth, more specifically, is an inch from mine. And he smiles and says, "Not close enough, I guess." And he lifts the plates out of my hands and takes them to the sink.

As soon as feeling has returned to my feet, I go to grab our cups. And then I gasp for real. Because there is Star at the front of the bus, looking like I stole something from her. Looking like I stole her whole life and hid it in a milk jar. She turns and runs out, and there is Chamomila, fucking *smirking*. "We were going to see if Santiago wanted to go to dessert with us. But I guess y'all are busy."

Santiago looks up and frowns. "Yeah. No thanks."

Chamomila makes this humming noise and shoots me a knowing smile. Like I want drama. Like I'm orchestrating it for her entertainment.

I scowl and glance out the window. Out where Star is wiping her eyes. Like she hasn't had everything her whole life, like this isn't just about her for once, for *once*, not getting something she wants. Imagine if she'd grown up as the ugly one, the one Mom likened to a dog, the one the whole school rumored to be as loose as the Grand Canyon. And Santiago is her side crush! Her this-will-look-good-on-Fotogram crush. And the sight of me with him makes her break down in the parking lot.

Star wouldn't have survived a trillionth of a period of what I've gone through. It wouldn't have been possible.

38.

How Star and I Are Quilted Together in a Whole, Wild Constellation

YOU LET HER fucking pummel you on a daily basis. Santiago's words echo in my brain and skin and bones. I know I blew him off about it, but the fact is, I don't know how to respond to that, or to the question underneath it. Why? Why do I do this to myself?

I think of Star, how when we were little, we wouldn't go anywhere without holding hands. How when I had my first broken heart in the ninth grade, Star and I took the bus to Taco Bell and that's when the tradition started, eating all we could from the dollar menu with ten dollars. How at the end of the day, when our phones and cameras are off, Star and I are the only ones who really, really get each other. We're the only ones who *know*. Know what it's like to have Mom with the way she is, to have had our dad, to have had our hearts ripped into pieces the day he decided to die.

There's so much that connects me to Star, beginning from in the womb, when she and I were little specks in a dark, watery galaxy. Now I imagine it like thread: we're stitched together by the truth of who we are and where we came from. There's so many strands of string between us, it's like a thousand constellations. It's a quilt of planets and space stuff, all twinkling and bright when no one is looking.

As for me and Mom, I don't know. I don't know why I let Mom pummel me. The kindest she's ever been, to me, is indifferent.

I don't care about losing Mom.

There's almost no stirring inside me as I realize it. My footing is solid. This feels like home, like the truth.

I'm better off without my mother.

What I do care about is if I lose Mom, I'll lose Star, too. And then who will I be without the other half of my constellation quilt? Who else knows me like Star? Who do I connect with as deeply as my sister?

I'm not sure I want to know the answers to these questions. I certainly don't want to think about them anymore, so I don't. I put my earbuds in and turn up some music so loud, I can't even hear the beat of my own heart.

39.

I Finally Free My Red-Feathered Wings

IT'S EIGHT AT night. Thank goodness we were close enough to the hotel that I could hole up in my room right after dinner. Which is where I've been, basically, for the last twenty minutes and am going out of my mind a little. The fight with Star is biting at my skin. Like I'm covered in horseflies. I keep reviewing it, thinking about phrases she said to me. *We all know what kind of girl you are.* I should've said something else. I should've smacked her. I should've decapitated her with my mind.

Santiago was right. Even if we have a quilt of constellations between us, I can't let Star talk to me like that again.

My phone buzzes. Mom again. It's the third time in the last hour. And she only ever calls if she needs to threaten me or make me feel like shit. Which means Star has definitely spoken to her, lying about Lord knows what. I sigh and click open the call.

"Moon."

I cringe. The tone of her voice is enough to slay me.

"Yes, Mami?" Unfortunately, my diminutive use of "madre" doesn't help.

"What would your father say?"

Ouch. So that's where she wants to take this.

"He would've never favored you if he knew what a worthless slut you were going to turn out to be. What were you thinking? Seducing your sister's crush? What were you thinking? You weren't, that's what. I've always known you'd be that kind of woman. Just like that whore your father had—"

"I would've cheated on you too."

"¿Qué?"

"What he did wasn't right, but I would've cheated on you too. I would've done anything to get away from you, Mom. You are the worst person I've ever known." I can't believe how calm I feel, finally telling Mom what I think. Finally telling her the truth.

"You want to know why I act the way I do with you?"

"Yes, Mom, my scars and I would *love* to know."

"Why do you love throwing that in my face? When I already told you, I wouldn't have had to do it if it weren't for you."

"Bye, Mom."

"Moon, if you hang up now, you may as well never come back home. Never again."

I stare at my hotel room for a moment. The only sound is the hum of the mini fridge. It slithers around me.

So I've been okay thinking about my life without my mom.

But what Star did to me today? Those knives in my back? I'm beginning to think I'm better off without my sister, too. And that's how I'm able to say it, with no hesitation, my voice steady.

"Okay."

And then I hang up.

40.

How the Worst Birthday in the Known Universe Became the Absolute Best

ONCE, WHEN I was eight or nine, Dad woke me up. It felt so late, but probably it was, like, nine thirty at night or something. "Moon, come on," he whispered. "Let's go." We hopped in his truck, where it always smelled like coffee and dirt and the metallic tang of old tools. I loved it in there.

We drove into a dirt road in a forest, bumping and jumping wildly with each rock the tires hit. Finally he stopped, reached in the back seat, and pulled out two hard hats—one for me and one for him. He took me into the forest, to a little clearing marked with yellow caution tape. I still remember that tape so vividly, how it moved in the wind under the moonlight.

We climbed down into a hole and stood with walls of sediment all around us, lit by the moon and the lights on our hats.

"This was where our ancestors met in the summers," he said, "thirteen or fifteen thousand years ago." With gloves, he picked up some dirt and showed me little pieces of chert, this really hard rock people used to shape into weapons. "These are the leftovers of their work. They'd come here to feast"—he pointed at a pile of bones poking out of the dirt—"and party, I imagine."

I laughed. "That sounds fun."

"Bet it was. The days were long and warm, the fields filled with wildflowers. I bet ancient people loved summer. I bet everything seemed full of hope." Dad seemed so sad as he said it. So sad. I didn't really understand why until much later.

"So we're looking at stuff that old, for real?" I asked.

"Yes. That old. Imagine it, Moon. Every day we walk on ancient history."

"That's a little creepy."

And that made him laugh and laugh. "Yes, I suppose it is."

"Can you bring me here tomorrow, too? When it's during the day?"

"Can't do, kiddo. You're not even supposed to be here now because of liability issues." He gave me a big smile and helped me climb out. "But when you're eighteen, you can come to all my excavations. Deal?"

"Deal." I remember saying that word so well, how the silver-edged moonlit forest swallowed my voice, how my dad's arms felt good and strong as he carried me back to the truck.

I am eighteen years old today.

Nothing feels all that special about it anymore.

Which is why I am hiding in my bunk on the bus while Star

and Oak and whoever else go and eat platinum-dipped cheese-cake champagne bath fizzies while laughing their asses off about what losers all their siblings are.

My phone buzzes and my heart sinks a little when I see it's Tía. Which is ridiculous because I love Tía. But Mom hasn't called, not once since the big fight last night.

"Hello?"

"Happy birthday, Moon!"

I plaster a big smile on my face. "Thank you, Tía."

"Got any big plans?"

"Uh, not really. We're still on the road."

"You should do something, though. Make a cake. Or even just buy a piece from the gas station. Couple of candles, make a wish . . ."

"Good idea. Maybe I'll make a hummingbird cake."

"There you go."

We chat a bit longer, but I think Tía can tell I'm not in a chatty mood, so she lets me go without prying too much.

As soon as I hang up the phone, a growl emanates from behind me. "What the fuck is a hummingbird cake?"

I close my eyes and take a long breath. "It's just a cake, Santiago."

He doesn't respond for a second, but then he says, "Wait. It's got pineapple? Bananas? Pecans? All in the same cake?" He sounds appalled and disgusted in that unique form of judgment he's so good at. "Well, you can't make that in my kitchen. I forbid it."

"Fine." I don't feel like arguing.

"What's wrong?"

"Nothing. Shut up."

Of course he climbs up instead, pulling open the curtain so I have to see his beautiful face.

"Why were you going to make the gross cake, anyway?"

"I was never going to make a cake, okay? So you can stop freaking out now."

"Why'd you say it, then?"

Sometimes I wish I had the foresight to film our interactions. Just so the next time someone calls Santiago silent and stoic, I can pull it up and say, *See? He's actually a raving banana peel if you get to know him.*

"I wanted to get off the phone. That's why I said it."

"But why'd you say that specifically?"

"Because it was pertinent to the conversation, you giant troll! Jeez! Go back to your hole in the ground. And do everyone a favor and don't come back out."

"You want to know what I think?"

"Not particularly."

"I think that you said it specifically to get my attention. I think—"

"Oh my Lord." I turn over, put my hands on his shoulders, and stare at him right in the face. He's startled enough to stop speaking, thank you, Mary Magdalene. "It's my birthday. It's my birthday and I feel like shit, so to stop my aunt from asking too many questions, I told her I'm making our favorite cake."

He blinks. "It's your birthday?"

I groan and collapse back in the bed, turning my face toward the window. "Yes."

"Are you not doing something with your sister?"

I groan and put my pillow on my head. "No. Go away, please."

And miraculously, he does. Or, at least he climbs down, and then I don't hear him anymore. I keep the pillow over my head in case he decides to get back to torturing me. But he doesn't. I lift the pillow a little to see if he's near, but I think I'm all alone now. "Pathetic," I mutter. Not even my nemesis wants to antagonize me on my birthday. And before this mood turns into a full-on pity party, I close my eyes and pretend I'm on a spaceship. A human-size vessel, shooting through the Milky Way at the speed of light. I am enclosed in warm metal, and there is nothing around me but iridescent starlight. Starlight is my only company for the rest of my days.

I guess I doze off at some point in outer space, because the next thing I know, someone is shaking me.

"Hey."

"Mm."

"Hey, Moon."

Crap. It's Santiago. He's changed his mind about ceasing fire for my birthday.

"What do you want?" I croak like a frog.

While I clear my throat and cough, he says, "Get ready. I'm taking you out."

That stops my coughing. "What did you say?"

"Get dressed. I'm taking you out for your birthday, all right?" He jumps off the ladder, and I swear, the whole earth shakes. "Or you can lie in bed like a loser. All the same to me."

"Go away." I feel like a broken record. But there's no way I'm letting that jerk take me out for my birthday. Where would we even go? To the dump, I'll bet. He'd make me get all dolled up so he can drop me off at the local waste management like a piece of garbage.

"Moon! Hurry your ass up!"

"No." But for some unknown reason, I lift my torso and roll toward the ladder. My feet make their way down. I don't know, I guess I'm ready to be tortured today. It hardly seems like things could get any worse. Why not see how far Santiago takes it?

But then a warm thought arrives: *He likes you.* And I guess I'm so used to shitting on myself all the time that I totally forgot. So . . . what if I want to see how far Santiago takes it in a different way? In the way that he *likes* me. In the way that he thinks I'm pretty, maybe. Or he likes that I make him laugh with my ridiculous name-calling. Or the way he looks at my body sometimes—he doesn't see my rolls and cellulite and everywhere I jiggle. Or maybe he does and he likes that, too.

Why was it so much easier to assume he hated me? Christ. I need to stop thinking and get dressed.

I grab the second dress I packed, white and covered in a small sunflower print. Tía says it's from the nineties. She's the one who gave it to me, so I guess she would know. I like that it's a wrap dress, that I can tie it at the smallest part of my squishy waist and let my hips and butt jut out like some ancient fertility goddess. Plus the white makes my skin look so dark and bronze. I love it.

I let my hair down, kind of wild from my nap, but whatever. Just let me call it beach waves. And then I add pink pigment to my lips and cheeks. I decide to skip the eyeliner because Santiago starts banging on the bathroom door. "I'm hungry," he grumbles.

"When is that not the case?" I call back as I apply some perfume oil, a blend of lemon and coconut. I guess with a boy the size of Santiago, he's gotta eat constantly to maintain all that body. Doesn't make it any less annoying, though.

"Moon, I'm going to leave—"

I push open the door and put my hands on my hips. "You're going to leave what?"

He's too busy staring at my waist and my hips. Told you they're a force in this dress. But I snap my fingers. "Up here, perv."

He actually has the nerve to take his time dragging his gaze back up. I cross my arms and ask, "Are you done yet?"

"You look good."

I furrow my brow, even though a hundred thousand butterflies have crept into my stomach between his ogling and the remark. I'd always thought I was too big and too loud and too much to be beautiful. But Santiago, even with that simple compliment, makes me feel like I'm the prettiest thing he's ever seen. How does he do that?

And, for some reason, this is how I thank him: "Where did

you learn how to give a girl a compliment, huh? Clown school?"

"Be quiet." He says it without any malice and then he takes my hand. "Come on."

Santiago Philips is holding my hand. Santiago Philips is holding my hand across the bus, through the parking lot, until we reach what I assume is a taxi. He lets go of me to open the door and rests his hand on the small of my back as I climb in. By the time he's inside, I feel hot and nervous. *It's because you need a boyfriend*, I scold myself. *You needed one, like, yesterday.*

And also he likes you. And yeah, that's really the source of all my nerves, if I'm honest. Which I don't want to be, because I can scarcely handle just the thought of someone like Santiago liking someone like me.

Santiago gives our driver an address, and then we're off. He doesn't say much on the way, and neither do I. In fact, I turn into a right hypocrite, because all I can think is Santiago looks good. Really good. His slacks are tight on his thighs as he sits, and I can see the slabs of muscle in the moving sunlight. When he asks me to help him roll up his sleeves, I may or may not stop breathing for a few seconds. Thick forearms, all exposed and firm. It's like he knows all my weaknesses.

The driver pulls in front of a two-story, redbrick home. The front yard is filled with dogwood trees, all blooming pretty in white and pink. There's a huge front porch lined with wooden rocking chairs and lit with big yellow candles. "Is this your house?" I ask incredulously.

"Sure," Santiago responds. "One of the twelve I own." He holds out his arm and I grab it. Jeez. Is there any place on him that isn't hard enough to smash bones against? If we're ever at war, I know exactly who's going to be my personal body guard.

The door opens and a man in a suit smiles at us. "Mr. Philips? Ms. Fuentez?"

"Yes," Santiago responds. "I've reserved—"

"The Magnolia table. Yes. Right this way."

The fellow leads us inside a warm, empty living room upstairs, featuring a stone fireplace surrounded with oversize brown furniture. Just beyond is a huge room that's basically a restaurant. There are tables and people, the clinks of glass and silverware. We end up on an open balcony where a single table stands, covered in a peach cloth and white cloth napkins and wineglasses and an ornate carafe of ice water, wet with condensation.

"Thank you," Santiago says, and pulls out a chair. It takes me a few seconds to realize he means for me to sit in it.

"Do I trust me?" Santiago asks as he takes his seat.

"What? Why do you ask?"

"Answer the question, Moon."

Do I trust Santiago? I mean, can you trust a guy who hates you? But also shocks you with random acts of sweetness?

"Mostly," I respond.

"Enough for me to order your birthday dinner?"

I shrug. "Sure. Why not."

"We will have the hazelnut-crusted grouper," Santiago tells

our server. "On the side, grits with white cheddar and the sautéed garlic peas."

"Very good." As soon as the server leaves, I lean over and make a face. "Grits? Peas?"

"You said you trusted me." He lifts one shoulder.

"These grits better be as good as yours, that's all I'm saying."

"When did you last have grits before mine? How were they prepared?"

I shrug. "Camping with my dad. I hated them, so he added jam so I wouldn't starve."

"Jam?" Santiago looks like he might gag. "No wonder you hate them."

"Sometimes I'd put in a spoon of peanut butter."

"That's even worse. My God."

"Hey, I was nine."

"You never talk about your dad." He sips his water, but everything about the delivery of the question is careful.

"There's not much to say."

"What's your favorite memory of him?"

I smile. "He used to take us camping in Alaska. Everything about that was my favorite. Fireweed—my favorite flower—grows like crazy over there. My dad used to press them in his books, and for my birthday one year, he put the dried flowers in these beautiful frames. . . ." I trail off, looking down at my silverware. "It's been a long time without him. Sometimes I forget he was ever around. Which makes me feel like such a shitty daughter."

"That's normal," he says. "Believe me." And before I can ask how he knows, he says, "So why are you such a shitty cook?"

I roll my eyes and smile.

"What?"

"Just, could you go thirty minutes without insulting me? Is that even possible?"

He bites his lips, and when he releases, they're almost fuchsia. "Fine. But only because it's your birthday."

I snort. "Thirty minutes of civility on my birthday. Wouldn't want to spoil me, huh?"

"Exactly. So, why are you such . . . an *inexperienced* cook?"

"Good one." Now I'm sipping my water carefully. "Well, after my dad left, my mom wasn't okay. She had issues. She couldn't take care of us. She stopped cooking completely. And she forbade us from learning, for the most part. She didn't want us to end up as maids or something, I guess."

"Why would cooking make you become a maid?"

"I don't know. Mom's logic has never been that strong." I shudder. "Lord. It was like a prison until Star and I learned how to drive. Probably that's why I started hanging out in the woods so much."

Santiago looks at me for a long moment and clears his throat. "I'm sorry you went through that. I wish I'd—"

But then we're interrupted with dinner. And, Lord, it smells so good. So freaking good. I want to rub even the peas all over my body.

I start with the fish, then the peas. "Oh my Lord, this is good," I say. "Oh my God. This is so good."

"Try the grits, Moon." Dang it. I'm caught.

"Fine." I take a small bite into my mouth and . . . and then I basically fall out of my chair. "Holy. Goats."

Santiago smiles. I grip the table so I don't topple over. Good God. His smile is better than this meal, and all the meals he's ever made put together.

"Told you." He shovels a huge spoon of grits in.

"They're even better than yours!"

"Let's not get carried away."

"Ha ha." I pause with my fork in midair. "So how did you become such an . . . *experienced* cook?"

He shrugs. "You know, it's . . . kind of a similar story to yours. My mom got really depressed about some stuff . . . and she stopped cooking. And I was thirteen. Growing, like, an inch an hour or something."

"So you were even hungrier than you are now."

"Yeah."

"Jeez Louise. How were there no food shortages from that time period?"

"Be quiet." He's smiling, his plate is empty, and he's leaned back. I can literally see the ripple of abs through his shirt, and I look down at my plate with what may be a flush at my cheeks.

"Anyway, I started cooking. But I didn't want to only eat box mac and cheese and frozen pizza. I was concerned about health, too, so I learned how to make vegetables that tasted good. It went from there."

We chat a little more about food, and Santiago tells me, "What really got me into gourmet stuff . . ." He stops, like he's said, or almost said, some big secret or something.

"What? What got you into it?"

"Well . . ." He ends his incomplete sentence with a shrug.

"No, now you have to tell me." I gasp. "Oh my gosh. Was it Jamie Oliver? It was Jamie Oliver, wasn't it?"

"It was not Jamie Oliver." He sounds so grumpy, I can't help but giggle, and this softens his face. "It was salt."

"Salt?"

"Salt."

I'm confused. "What's so special about salt?"

"What's not special about salt is the question."

"Explain it to me."

"Explain what?"

"Don't pretend you don't know what I'm asking. I want to know about salt."

The server comes by and asks about dessert. I want cake, because it's my birthday, after all, but Santiago shakes his head and gives him a platinum card or other, and I'm not going to be greedy, not when it's already been the best dinner of my life.

"I'll tell you about salt in the car," he says.

41.

Salt Made Santiago Fall in Love with the Whole, Wild World

OUTSIDE, THE TAXI awaits. Santiago opens the door for me again and slides in after I do, close enough that I can feel the warmth of his body along my back. "Are you cold?" he asks when he sees me shivering.

"No. Tell me about salt."

"So you didn't forget."

"Santiago. Stop stalling."

"Fine." He takes a breath and exhales slowly. There's a fine mist of rain on the car windows, and with the violet of the evening light, I feel like I'm on a new, beautiful planet, just me and Santiago to work out our fears and hopes and dreams with each other.

"Salt," he begins. "There are these types of salts called finishing slats. Salts that are spectacular in some way. Flaked, flavored, you name it. You add it to the meal after it's done cooking."

"Cool."

"My mom saw my interest in cooking, and for my birthday she bought me a pack of finishing salts. A dozen of them." He grins. "I couldn't believe how a little pinch of this gave a fish a whole new angle, flavor-wise. I went on a quest. Sort of. I wanted to know what made salt so special." He clears his throat and looks a little unsure, but keeps going. "Human civilization was basically built around salt. Mines and seas and shit like that. I mean, no one thinks about it now because salt is plentiful and cheap, but it was once this incredibly rare and valuable thing. It was used as money all over the world." He smiles and takes a breath. "The oldest European city was based around salt. To this day, you can still visit the salt routes in Europe, which go back to the fucking Bronze Age." He runs his fingers over my hand, eventually holding it. I hardly want to even breathe. Everything about this moment is so unbelievably perfect.

"Salt's been the reason for wars, battles, revolutions. And it's so beautiful, this little crystal. Everything that's alive depends on it. We depend on it right now, and we don't even realize how much." He shrugs. "Anyway, that's my big salt talk."

"That's amazing," I say softly. "Like, how could something so common be so magical? But maybe everything is magic and we just get used to the magic or something."

He's eyeing me curiously. "So you're not going to tease me?"

"Why would I do that?"

"For being a salt nerd."

I burst into laughter. I laugh and laugh until Santiago scowls, but I can tell it's a pretend scowl, because his eyes smile right along with me. "I never thought of you as a nerd before. But now I know."

"Stop that."

I bend over from laughing, and when I lift my torso, I'm somehow way closer to him. I stop laughing immediately, and his face is all serious too. I don't know what to say, so I default to babbling. "I'm glad you told me, though, about salt. I never would have guessed. Not in a million years. And now I know we basically eat magical crystals on a regular . . ." Oh gosh. He looks like he wants to kiss me. His eyes are locked on my mouth like freaking dead bolts.

"Here we are," the driver barks, and I jump when we come to a sudden stop. In front of us, the tour bus—big, silver, reminding me way too early about reality.

"They're not back yet?" I ask, because it's eight and all the lights are off.

"They'll probably get their stuff later tonight. Birthday party."

Right. The party my sister is having without me. Reality sinks in even more, to the point where my weightlessness drifts away with the breeze. When I climb out of the car, my feet feel like they're stuck in the mud.

Inside, Santiago stops in the kitchen. "Why don't you sit down," he says.

"Why?" I ask, but then I just do it. These mud feet weren't getting me much farther anyway.

"I made you something."

"You did? Really?" I can't stop the big grin on my face. "No one's made me anything since my dad and the fireweed pictures when I was eleven."

"Right."

"I'm serious, you jerk."

Santiago responds by sliding a pie in front of me. I smile. "It's a pie."

"Nice deduction there. You should be a private investigator."

I ignore him. The pie is golden, the edges hand-pinched, and there's a crimson sauce oozing out of the holes in the middle. "It's beautiful." I furrow my brow. "Wait, is this huckleberry pie?"

"Yes."

I look up at him. "But you . . . you said you needed to save those for something special."

"Yes."

Lord, I'm slow. It finally hits me that he's calling me special. Or, my birthday, at least. "Wait—"

"Here." He jams a knife into the pie and cuts me a huge piece. He reaches for the ice cream in the freezer and rolls a scoop on top of the warm, gooey slice.

"Thanks." I watch as he does the same for himself, and then he has a seat next to me, turning off the kitchen lights behind me. Now the only lighting is all the fairy lights, warm and magic all around us. He waits until I take a bite first.

Santiago raises his eyebrows at me in a silent, *Well?*

"Oh, come on," I say. "What do you think? Have you ever made anything that wasn't absolutely perfect? Lord."

"So you like it?"

"I'd give my life for it."

Santiago chuckles and the sound is so, so, so lovely. I want to keep the momentum going, you know? So I say, "It's amazing what you do. What you've accomplished."

He freezes, then looks at me. "What do you mean?"

"I mean, most people our age are trying to figure it out. What we want to do. I certainly don't have a clue. But you are doing it. You've mastered, like, food. Completely."

"It's especially inspiring with only one hand, right?"

He sounds mean and sharp. I blink. "I mean, I guess?" I don't know what to say. I wasn't even thinking about that. After several long seconds, I say, "All right, I'll bite. What is your deal right now?"

"Nothing."

It doesn't look like nothing. His jaw is firm and he's shoveling the pie in with way too much force. He's going to cut his tongue or something.

"Everyone thinks I'm amazing. An inspiration. Blessed." He gives a little chuckle. "I didn't know you did too."

"That doesn't sound . . . bad to me?"

"Of course it doesn't!" I jump as he raises his voice. "You aren't missing a fucking appendage. You don't know what it's like for everyone to look at you and feel so uncomfortable that all they can do is heap praise so they feel better about themselves."

"That's not what I was doing. You don't see that? I wasn't even thinking about your hand."

"Sure."

And he angles his body away from me, and that's it. I'm dismissed. This whole evening, crumbled to dust. But I'm not done yet. No way in heckle. I stand and say, "Can you possibly, for one second, get your head out of your ass?"

"Excuse me?"

"You heard me. I'm sorry that people are so shitty to you. That they condescend to you like that, calling you an inspiration and stuff. But all I meant was, you seem to have your shit together, you know? You are literally the best chef I've ever met, and at the age of nineteen? What the hell. How is that fair? And me? I take photos, okay, but only because I was commissioned at fourteen to become my sister's personal photographer. I have no idea what I'd be doing if my life didn't revolve around her." I swallow. "Anyway, I'm sorry that's how my compliment came off. That's not what I meant at all." I dump my pie plate in the sink and turn away.

"Where are you going?"

"To my bed."

"Why?"

"Because . . ." I wave my arms around helplessly. "It's my bed?"

He sighs, stands, and gestures for me to follow him. "You can't sleep in the bunk tonight. No one else is going to be here. We're parked at the Evelyn Hotel, remember?"

"Oh," I say. "Right." We did two medium-size cities back-to-back the last two days. I totally forgot we'd be staying at yet another hotel so soon. "Well, I've got to get my bag." Santiago is behind me, and he lifts my tote before I can reach for it. "You don't have to . . ." But, as usual, he doesn't listen to me.

We get our key cards from the front desk without speaking to each other, and the silence continues as we get in the elevator, until I have to break it.

"I'm sorry. I was insensitive with my wording. I'll do better next time."

"I'm sorry," he says. "For jumping to conclusions and losing my temper."

"It's fine."

"It's not. I ruined your birthday."

"Oh, don't be so dramatic." I whip my head around and smack his shoulder, then curl my hand into a fist. "What on God's green earth is going on there? Do you wear shoulder pads made of diorite?"

He just smiles at me. "So your birthday isn't ruined, then?"

"Of course not, Santiago. It's the best I've had in a long time."

He walks me to my room in silence, and when we get there, I gasp as he bends to kiss my cheek. The pads of his lips are way, way softer than what I've been fantasizing. Lord.

"Happy birthday." He pauses. "Loki."

"Oh, go to heckle, Thor."

"Banana peel."

"Salt nerd."

We smile at each other for so long, it's like this moment becomes a whole new universe, like this fraction of a second has been compressed to a trillionth of a period and we're about to burst. I don't know how or when, but Santiago and I are going to explode. We'll become the dust of ancient planets and suns and moons. We'll both become one whole, sparkling nebula, thousands of light-years long.

And then the moment is broken by an old dude leaving his room, coughing his brains out.

Santiago blinks and clears his throat. "Good night."

"Good night," I say back softly.

And I am not ashamed to admit that I let myself watch his backside for nearly his whole walk to the elevator. What? It's my birthday present to myself.

42.

Spending the Night with a Nebula (Is So Much Better Than I Ever Imagined)

WHEN I CHECK my phone again, I nearly drop it, because I have forty-eight missed calls, all from Mom. I should probably be freaking out. From the previews of the texts I've got from her, it doesn't look like she's trying to get in touch to wish me a happy birthday.

But that threat she made about me never coming back? It didn't scare me at all. In fact, it was too good to pass up.

My skin is all tingly. And I can't seem to stop pacing. I don't want to be alone right now. So I wrap my pj's in the white hotel robe and slide on the fuzzy, cardboard hotel slippers. And I head down to the elevator.

Room 1416. I stand in front of it for a full minute before knocking. When Santiago answers, he doesn't look surprised. Pleased, but not surprised.

"I haven't gotten a photo text," he says.

"Right," I say. I don't know what else to say. His arm is now on my shoulder.

"Moon. Are you okay?"

I take a breath and pull my robe open a little at the top, where my scar gleams in the low light. I don't know why it had to heal so dark pink and silvery. "I'm ready to tell you about them."

Santiago nods and opens the door wider. When I walk past him to go inside, my shoulder and hips graze him ever so slightly. His smell, that ocean pine forest, comes around me in a soft, warm cloud. Everything about Santiago makes me feel safe. Little roots are growing out of the bottoms of my feet, all the way down to the other side of the earth. That way I never stumble again.

At first we're sitting in bed, but then I yawn and he leans back, pulling me on top of him. My head fits in the cup of his neck. My hand fits across half of his stomach. His arm is along my back, his hand wrapped around my hip, his other forearm along the top of my thigh.

"I have cramps," I mumble. "They suck."

"I'm sorry." He moves his hand up to rub at my lower back in circles. It feels amazing. I sigh and melt into him.

"I told you I've had sex with three guys, right?"

"Uh-huh." I can feel the deep of his voice to the bottoms of my feet, rattling at the roots there.

"Well, the first guy was nice. I thought I loved him. But he turned out to be . . . basic, I guess." I clear my throat. "The second guy was a huge jerk. All because . . ." I sigh. "I didn't like it.

He thought he was some kind of sex god, but afterward, I asked him, 'You're already finished?'"

Santiago chuckles, and I smile a little. "Yeah, he was not happy. And he said I didn't like it because I was a whore. He said I was as loose as the Grand Canyon."

Santiago's whole body goes rigid next to me. It's like he's planking while snuggling me in bed. "What an asshole."

"I know. Even more so because he then told everyone at our school. Grand Canyon became my new nickname."

Santiago is even tenser. "What's this asshole's name again?" Like he's going to do something about it.

I smile up at him. "I love you for asking that." His eyes go all soft and he resumes the back rub. I sink even farther into him. "Anyway, I got back at him. I told everyone that it wasn't my fault that his penis was as skinny as a strand of hair. After that everyone started calling him Spaghetti Dick."

Santiago laughs, and it shakes me, the bed, and probably the whole floor. He uses his whole body to laugh. I love it. I want to kiss his neck, so I keep talking. "Anyway, right after I had sex with him, my mom found out. Because of La Raíz. She knew I'd gotten into the milk jar, that I'd had sex—she knew everything because of a handful of freaking moths." There's silence for a couple of beats. "You don't know my mom. To her, purity is . . . It's the only thing worth living for. She'd rather have had me kill someone than sully myself before marriage."

Santiago makes a scoffing noise, so I lift my head to look right in his eyes. "I'm serious. Those are the exact words she said as she threw all the knives from the kitchen at me."

His eyebrows drop, and his mouth goes open. "She *what*?"

"I don't think she meant to cut me. It's not like she's a trained assassin or something. First was the wrist, as I covered my face." I lift my arm to show him the scar. "And I thought after the blood came, she'd be done. So I lowered my arms. But she wasn't done. She had one last knife, the sharpest one, and it stuck in me like I was made of avocado or something.

"And I screamed and screamed, and she screamed, marched over, and pulled it out of me. She moved it around because it wouldn't slide out nicely." I wince. "That hurt way worse than the original stab." I shake my head. "But actually, the thing that hurt me the most was after she put gauze on it and stopped the bleeding and all that, she looked at me, all calm, you know, right in my eyes. And she said, 'See what you made me do?'

"And before I could argue, she said, 'If only you hadn't turned out to be such a dirty girl. Then this wouldn't have happened.'"

Santiago's body is so tight, I think I could slide a paper over his stomach and end up with one of those folded snowflakes you make in kindergarten during the winter.

"You didn't get stitches?"

I laugh. "She said if I told anyone I'd gotten cut, even a doctor, and how, she'd say I did it to myself and have me committed somewhere." I shudder. That happened to my cousin Lucia, after her father found out she'd had a pregnancy scare.

"That's such fucking bullshit," Santiago says. His voice is a growl; I can feel the clench of his jaw at my temple. I love that he's so angry on my behalf. I'm not used to it. I could get used to it. But I brush this thought away.

"It was an accident," he says suddenly.

"What was?" I ask just as I realize he's talking about his hand. "Oh. God."

"Yeah. My sister and I were in her car. She was driving. We were going to her college. She had some cheerleading thing, and my parents and Andro were going to meet us there. They were doing lawyer stuff for Fotogram, back when it'd started to explode."

"Right."

"Well, a drunk driver T-boned us. Didn't even hit us that hard. Just swerved into our lane, but it sent us flying. Rolled over into a ditch."

I'm looking at him now. I can't not look at him. But his gaze is somewhere between the windows and the sofa. He's in another universe right now.

"My hand was crushed to pieces. At least it was my left one." He chuckles like he's been told this a hundred times and he still can't believe people would be that thoughtless. "My sister died a week later. The head injuries were too much."

"Oh my God," I say. I grab his forearm, tight. "I had no idea. I didn't even know you guys had a sister."

"No one talks about her anymore." He swallows. "She had both legs amputated before . . . you know." He pauses with a long, shaking inhale. "And for a really long time I wished she'd lived because she would've understood. So that I wouldn't have been the only one." He does this strange, grief-laden chuckle. "How fucking selfish is that?"

"It's not selfish to want your sister back."

"For those reasons, it is."

His eyes are glassy and he grimaces when one tear trails down his cheek. He lets go of me to wipe it away.

"You're not selfish for wanting to be less lonely." And then I lean up and kiss the place where his tear was.

Santiago lifts his hand and holds my face so gently. "You're—you're not a whore, Moon. I know I've said this before, but I guess I need to make sure you know it again. Your value isn't about that. About sex."

And now I want to cry. "Okay. Thanks." It sounds so lame to say. But I can't think of anything else. He glances down at my lips before sliding his hand down my neck, to my shoulder, settling it on my hip.

"I applied to culinary school." He says it all casual. Like it's no big deal at all.

"What?!" I sit up fast. "Are you serious? That's, oh my gosh, awesome, Santiago."

He grunts, but there's a faint smile on his face.

"What are you grumbling for?"

"My dad isn't going to like it. He already thinks I waste my time with all the cooking I do."

"What? Has he not tasted your cooking before?"

He smiles a little. "Mom has. She gets on his case all the time. Once, she heard him making a comment to me while I was making pico de gallo, and Dad slept on the sofa for two weeks."

"Well, yeah. She's experienced the foodgasms. She knows there's no way in the world you're wasting your time."

He gives me a weird look. "That's a pretty messed-up way to put it when we're talking about my mom."

I laugh. "Well, I hope you're fine with me talking about your culinary talents that way. Because I have, to about everyone."

He grins at me. "I don't mind giving you foodgasms." His voice is real deep and guttural. It's got me tingling down to my ankles.

And the double meaning of his little confession has me breathless. And my brain, it's scrambled a little. So I have to try really hard to make my next question make sense. "Why does your dad think it's a waste of time?"

Santiago lifts his left arm. "Because of this."

"That's absurd," I say. "That's so absurd."

"It's—he doesn't think anyone will hire me. But I'm as fast as any other chef. I just need time to prep first."

"You're going to be an amazing chef," I declare. "And chefs have cooks prep for them, anyway. Where'd you apply?"

"The Culinary Institute of New Orleans."

"Oh my God," I say, punching his arm. "That's where I applied!"

"You applied to the institute?"

I laugh. "No, I applied to Tulane. It's right near my favorite relative's house."

"Your aunt?"

"Yep. I love her." I pause. "That's so weird that we both applied to schools in New Orleans, huh?"

He blinks, like he's just considered it. "You're right. I mean, what are the chances?" But then he shrugs it off. "I don't know if I'm going to go yet."

I gasp. "What? You have to, Santiago. You have to."

"It's expensive."

"And . . . I mean, isn't your family well-off?"

"My family, yes. But not me. Andro said he'd pay for it, but . . ." Santiago shrugs. "That feels like cheating."

"It's not," I say. "He can afford it, and you can pay him back if that's important to you. Santiago." I put my hand on his. "It'd be foolish not to. Trust me, the world needs your freaking delicious food. Okay?"

We don't say anything for a while, just sorta look into each other's eyes like . . . like I don't know what. Like in a way that makes me feel like I've lunged off a cliff, but it's only a little scary and a lot of something good. Like this view of the sky and stars, so close I could taste the spilled-powdered-sugar clouds, makes it all worth it.

"You should read my fortune again," Santiago says.

Because I don't ever want to leave, I say, "Yeah! Sure."

43.

The Third Time I Ever Had Sex (Also Known as, the Last Time I Ever Had Sex)

STAR'S ONLY REAL boyfriend was Bryan Finnigan. And I use the term "real boyfriend" lightly. He'd come over, and Mom would coo all over him and pretend we were this perfect family. He and Star would hold hands during dinner, and then he'd leave, and that's pretty much how their whole relationship went. I'm not sure they were ever alone together, to be honest. Mom's idea of the perfect courtship.

After the night of the knives, I was walking around school, trying to hide this massive bandage on my chest. "What happened to you?" Iris asked.

I said it without thinking. "Pissed my mom off." I forgot I'd even said it, that's how flippant it was to me.

Next thing I know, I'm in the counselor's office. Mrs. Blaine said, "We heard a disturbing rumor, Moon, and we wanted to make sure you were okay." She gestured to my collarbone. "Did someone hurt you there?"

My mouth opened, but sounds couldn't come out. My voice became a black hole, sucking everything into it.

And then the door opened and Star came in, all smiles. "Is everything all right, Mrs. Blaine?"

"We wanted to make sure everything was okay at home, Star. Especially since Moon has this scary-looking injury. . . ."

"Oh, that." Star laughed. "You didn't tell her, Moon? Moon's always climbing trees, which she should stop because she's so clumsy. But she just fell out of a big tree." Star shrugged. "That's all."

Right. Just fell out of a tree, directly into the knife Mom held pointed right at me. But I couldn't say this. My voice was still a black hole. It had absorbed the whole school and town and sun, and now Star, Mrs. Blaine, and I were floating in outer space. My feet, my chair, nothing had the ground under it. Nothing was solid anywhere.

Mrs. Blaine laughed too, because Star had put her right under her spell, and said, "Moon, you need to be careful out there. You're a little old for climbing trees!" And we were dismissed.

Star never said anything about it. She acted like that was the truth even when we were alone.

But I couldn't pretend. I could hardly stand upright around Star anymore. My own sister, you know? My own sister.

So that night, I found Bryan Finnigan and I fucked him.

It was a lot easier than I thought it'd be.

I heard them have their big fight the next week. Star loves to talk on speakerphone so she can straighten her hair at the same time, but I guess this time she'd forgotten that the walls of our home were thinner than skeleton leaves.

"Aren't you tired of living a lie?" He asked it over and over again. She started screaming for him to shut up and eventually hung up on him. There was a bang after that, I think from her throwing her phone across the room.

I wondered what that lie was, and now that I've seen her with Belle Brix, I think I might have a clue.

But I still feel dirty, to use my mom's word, about Bryan. He called me a lot after that, and he actually seemed sweet and genuine in his interest. But I couldn't. I'd slept with someone for revenge. I mean, he definitely wanted it, and to be honest, so did I. I was certain this made me a slut for real.

But now things have changed. It feels like a whole new universe being born again, like wildflowers into seeds into flowers, on and on from ancient times until now. And I can be anything in this brand-new world. Absolutely anything I choose.

44.

Back to My Night with the Nebula

IT FEELS LATE, but it's only ten. I feel lazy, so I grab the mirror stone from my bag and plop down again. "What do you want to know?"

"Actually, why don't you read for yourself?"

"Ugh. That's really hard."

"How so?"

"It's really easy to focus on what we want. To interpret everything on how we wish it was, would be. Like . . . to not see what's really there."

"Confirmation bias."

"Yeah. All the biases."

"Well, just try, then. Why not try?"

"Ugh. Fine. I'll take a tiny peek." I rub my fingers over the stone, and the images come really fast. The moon, the rose, the weed. And then a star, right over the moon, eclipsing it.

"No way," I say, rolling my eyes.

"What?"

"My sister. She's going to betray me." Hasn't she done enough of that already? I guess not.

"Huh. That doesn't sound like biased reporting."

"Yeah."

"It's also not surprising, is it?"

I shake my head. "But she's never done anything deliberate before, you know? Like, premeditated. She's never done something on *that* level."

"Are you kidding, Moon? All she's done since you guys got here is try to humiliate you every chance she gets."

I open my mouth to object, and then I close it. Because he's right, of course. I close my eyes. "She has everything. She's beautiful. Everyone adores her. . . ." I shut choking out of my voice. "And Mom loves her." That's it. That's the worst of it.

"Your mom's incapable of love, Moon. I mean, I know I can't say that for sure, but no mom could do what she did to you and be able to know what love is."

"That still doesn't change the fact that everyone else loves Star."

"Star's shallow, Moon. That's why."

"What do you mean? Because Star really is religious. She really believes all that."

"No, she doesn't." Santiago says it matter-of-factly. "If she did, she wouldn't treat her own sister like shit all the time."

Again, I can't think of anything to say. So I sigh and put the mirror stone away. What a crap reading. I guess it's better than seeing your dead dad, though.

"Stay here tonight," Santiago says. And I freeze as he keeps talking. "I swear, I'm not trying to be creepy. It's just . . ." He turns over so he's staring right at my face. "I hate sleeping alone since the accident. And I'm tired of listening to Andro snore when I sneak in his room."

I smile and say, "I'm sorry, again, for all you went through."

"Yeah. When we're home, I make Andro share the room with me. It's so embarrassing. I'm like a four-year-old."

"It's not embarrassing," I say. "Let me get my things from my room, okay?"

I decide to keep on my baggy T-shirt and shorts. He's seen me in them enough. I pack my bag up and return to Santiago's room, knocking lightly at the door. When he swings it open, I have to try really hard to keep my eyes above his neck. Because, of course. Of course he doesn't have a shirt on. He's trying to make me blush, faint, and turn into dust on purpose. I swear.

He slides into bed first, and then I get in. He pulls me to his body just like earlier, my head in the nook of his neck. I'm nervous, so I start talking. "What's with these muscles, huh? Are you trying to make every male-attracted person within a thirty-foot radius hit on you?"

He laughs, and it feels so nice. "I learned early on that other people are a lot less likely to bully you about missing a hand if they think you could beat the crap out of them."

I swallow. "Oh. I'm sorry."

"Don't be."

"I've never done this before."

"Be in bed with a guy?"

I turn to him. "Be in bed with a guy without him expecting something."

He runs his hand along my back. "You don't have to ever do anything—ever—with me. Even if you change your mind about sleeping here. That's fine."

"Right," I say. "I don't have to do anything besides the cooking show, right?"

And he laughs again, and this is how I fall asleep, to the warmth of everything that is Santiago Philips.

When I wake up, I feel peaceful. I don't know why, because everything, frankly, is imploding. My mom might literally murder me the next time I see her. Star thinks I've stolen Santiago right out from under her. And . . . and . . . that's actually it. Because everything else kinda rocks. My tarot sales are through the roof. My FG has almost a couple hundred thousand followers at my last check. And then there's Santiago. His arm is draped over me, but that's the only place we're touching. I knew he wouldn't, but it still kind of amazes me that he really didn't try anything last night. Knowing any sample of teenage guys has skewed my expectations, I guess. Or maybe they're normal and maybe Santiago is exemplary.

I put my hand on his forearm, just above his wrist where it

ends. Usually he wraps his arm, but right now it's open. The skin is pink there. I wonder if it still hurts him. If he gets those phantom limb sensations you always hear about.

Gently, I lift his arm off me and place it on the bed. The sheet is stretched across the continent of his shoulders, but I can still make out about every valley and ridge and mountain of muscle.

I stretch and run to the bathroom. I don't want to look or smell like a sweaty old antelope when he opens his eyes. After freshening up, I walk out and grab my deck, the unfinished Wild Moonflower tarot sample. I stand by the windows, where the morning light is thickest. In this sun, I feel like I'm ancient. You ever think about that? How that same sun lit up the sky for all your ancestors, for the very first humans, for every creature and bug and beast that has roamed the planet. The sun is so old, and every day we go about in it like it's nothing. Which is fine, too. We don't need to bow down and hold a three-hour service to it. It's just amazing to think about every now and then.

I grab the deck and shuffle. There's only one question on my mind and it's the Knight of Swords. The man who was going to enchant me, according to Tía. Is it Santiago? Is it really him?

"Hey," Santiago says. It's almost like he heard my thoughts.

"Hey." I turn around, and there he is, sitting up, the sheet at his waist, his magnificent triple-Fs on full display. "Good morning," I add.

He smiles at me, his face still sleepy-looking, his hair all mussed. "You reading?"

I nod. "A little spread."

He points to the bathroom. "Do you need—"

"No, no," I say. "Go ahead."

I turn around because I don't want him to feel self-conscious about, uh, morning wood. Also that would be really awkward.

As he's in the bathroom, I return to my cards. And I think about Santiago, about how perfectly my body fits alongside his, and I choose one. It's the Knight of Swords.

And yeah, I guess I should've known.

Only now the card seems softer to me. There's less of an emphasis on conflict and more on the ability to cut through bullshit. It feels kind of hot in here, so I open the window a crack. The air outside is dry and cool, and I resist the urge to stick my face out the window and sing a high note.

"What do the cards say today?"

That you're my Knight of Swords. That you're into me. That you don't think I'm as attractive as a slug. This line of thinking, though, gets me on a really pessimistic route. Because I remember when we first met, how he played that little cruel joke on me with the name tags. Even though I deserved it, I can't help but think that if Santiago were the knight—my knight—he wouldn't have made me feel so bad about my looks.

So I laugh a little and say, "Hey, remember when we first met and you mixed up mine and Star's name tags? Ha. That was funny."

"Why is that funny?" he asks, stretching. His shirt rides up a little, exposing the line of hair under his belly button.

I look away and say, "Well, it was a good joke, you know? Having me wear Star's name tag."

He wrinkles his nose. "Yeah, I never got that joke."

Now my mouth wants to drop open. "But you're the one who did it! How could you not get the joke?"

He shakes his head like I'm spouting nonsense. "Explain to me this hilarious joke."

I shrug. "You had me put Star's name on. Ha ha. The ugly, talks-too-much and laughs-too-loud sister is wearing the perfect, beautiful angel's name tag."

Santiago look stunned, which stuns me a little in return. "That's why everyone thought that was funny? What assholes."

I furrow my brow, ignoring the weird butterfly in my belly that gets frantic when Santiago comes closer, so close that I can smell the toothpaste he's just used. I angle my body so it's facing the window and not him. That's a breeze whistling in, and it feels amazing on my arms, my chest, my face. I cough a little before I can say, "Well, why'd you do it, then?"

He sighs and crosses his arms. "You really want to know?"

Oh man. This can't be good. But I nod anyway.

"That girl Chamomile Tea, or whatever, made those name tags for everyone. And she had me pass them out. She'd tell me a line about who they belonged to, 'cause I basically knew no one. I still can barely remember everyone's names." He sits back on the bed, facing me. Lord. I don't know if I've ever seen Santiago nervous before.

"Anyway, she told me that those two tags were for Star and Moon. At first I thought she was joking, because, you know, your names." I nod. Lots of people think they're fake. He continues. "And she said, 'These are for the two girls over there with all the pink luggage. Star is the hot one.'"

We stare at each other for a few moments before I furrow my eyebrows. "Is that the end of the story? I don't get it."

He laughs. "You're seriously going to make me spell it out for you?"

"Apparently I need it spelled out for me."

Santiago groans, puts his hand on his mouth, rubbing at the stubble there. "I thought you were the hot one, Moon."

I feel like I'm not in my body for a moment, and then what he said slaps me right in the brain. "What?"

"I'm not saying your sister is ugly, so don't yell at me about that, all right? I just—she's not my type."

"And I am?" I can't seem to make my jaw close. I mean, it's one thing to think, *Santiago might be attracted to me*. But it's quite another to hear it from the person himself. I glance down at myself—at my roundness, my jiggliness, the rolls and dimples and wide of everything, from my hips to my feet. And then I say, "But just because of my eye color, though. Everyone thinks my eyes are pretty."

"I didn't even know what color your eyes were back then, Moon." Santiago gestures to the deck behind me. "Pick a card. Pick a card on what I feel for you."

I can't speak anymore, apparently, so, with a shaking hand, I slide a card from the deck and turn it over. It's the Two of Cups, which is a card that basically screams, *You're in a passionate and respectful relationship*. And the image I arranged on it is a moonstone surrounded by fuchsia blooms. It reminded me of a heart. Basically, there's a moon in a heart. Like I'm inside of Santiago's heart.

"What's it say?" he asks. He's trembling.

I swallow. "It says I'm your type."

He smiles and so do I. And then the wind picks up through the windows, and a dragonfly sails in. It's purple and electric. It hovers between me and Santiago for a moment before Santiago holds out his hand, and of *course*, of course the dragonfly lands on it. "Hey, buddy," Santiago says softly, and he takes it back to the window to set it free. And the second he turns around, I'm there. It's like my feet do it on their own, but not really. Because every cell of my body wants it. Wants him.

And apparently, he feels the same. Because he says, "I want to kiss you."

"Okay," I say.

And then he's bending way down and I'm reaching up, and it's so soft at first. Like we're testing each other for something— what, I don't know. Well, I do know. I'm still half-afraid he's going to pull back with a camera and say, *Gotcha!* But he doesn't. Instead, he opens his mouth a little, to slide my bottom lip between his. He keeps it really gentle like this for a while, and

I realize he's waiting for me to decide what's next. All the guys I've kissed before have rushed the tongue and the hands and the fondling, like they were trying to get away with as much as they could before I stopped them.

So I'm the one who slides my tongue in his mouth. I'm the one whose hands end up in his hair and then over the firm planes of his chest. Only after all that does he slide his hand down my waist and over my hip, across my lower back until he pulls me forward, until it feels like everything is pressed together. And it's so weird, how I feel. Warm and shivering at the same time. Like, even though I've had sex before, this kiss with Santiago is pretty much the hottest thing that's ever happened to me.

I don't even realize I'm pushing myself against him until he falls backward on the bed. He pulls me on top of him so smoothly, we don't even break the kiss. It's like we choreographed this.

He's hard against my thigh, and instead of feeling dread about what he'll want from me, I *like* the idea of him being turned on. It makes me tremble even more.

Finally he stops it, breaking apart. "Holy shit, Moon." His voice is so raspy and deep and breathless.

"Sorry," I say.

"What are you sorry about?" he asks, angling his head so we can look right at each other.

I shrug. "None of it, actually."

He smiles a lazy, wonderful smile that makes me want to kiss him again immediately. "Me either." He clears his throat. "But we should take a break. Um, yeah. That was getting . . . I was really . . ."

And I grin. "Oh, I see. Okay."

"Yeah."

"You don't want to keep going?"

He gives me a look like he's in pain. "We have to be on the bus, like, five minutes ago."

"What?" I jump up. "Crap!"

"I texted Andro. It's fine."

"I've got to get dressed, though." I take my clothes into the bathroom. Just because we made out and dry-humped a little doesn't mean I'm ready for Santiago to see all the places I'm soft and jiggly.

I don't have any time to do anything special to my hair, so I braid it really fast and pin it to my head. I put on yoga pants and a lavender wrap top. And minty lip gloss. In case of kissing.

Which we do. Because the second I leave the bathroom, he looks at me up and down and says, "Beautiful." And I can't help it, I run and sorta jump on him, and then he stands and carries me like it's nothing at all, right to the edge of the fancy-carved dresser. And I wrap my legs around him and kiss him deeper. He pulls back a little and licks his lips. "Is that mint?"

"Yes. And before you get all uppity about it, it's real mint extract. I checked."

He chuckles and lowers his lips toward mine, but before he reaches me, his phone buzzes between us, in the front of his thigh against the inside of mine. He makes a guttural groan. "It's probably Andro. We should get a move on."

"Okay," I say. "But let's not act romantic in front of everyone yet, okay?"

He frowns. "Why?" His voice has a slight edge to it.

"Because Star has a massive crush on you and she made me swear there wasn't anything between us, when there actually wasn't anything between us. And now she thinks there probably is, but I'm not actually totally sure on that yet."

He scoffs. "Seriously? You're still trying to protect her feelings?"

"I just want to tell her first. About us."

We're out the door and walking into the lobby. I realize I'm making a lot of assumptions, so I add, "I mean, if you want there to be an us."

He gives me a look like I've lost it. And then he stops me right before we reach the bus. "I want you to be my girlfriend. Is that clear enough? I want you to be mine and no one else's. If you want me, too."

"Yes," I say, but before I can respond any further, the bus door opens and there is Andro. "There you two are! Hop on, hop on. We're behind schedule."

"Sorry," I say, and Andro looks from me to Santiago and back again, a half smile on his face.

"Ah," he says. "It'll even out. Say, little brother, is that lip gloss on your face?"

"Shut up."

Andro looks like he wants to keep on pestering Santiago, but he shakes his head instead. "We've got seven hours today, and then we'll be in St. Anne's. Rock and roll!"

"Sounds good," I say, following Santiago to the back. Star and Chamomila sit on the lounge sofas. Star won't look at me, but Chamomila gawks and looks away quickly when I make eye contact, the telltale sign that folks were talking shit about you.

I decide to ignore it. There's too much for me to think about right now. The thrill of kissing Santiago is still around me, tingly and magical like the hovering glow of fairy lights. The bullcrap with Star is burlap. Covering and chafing at my arms and neck. I resist the urge to scratch. Better to focus on the magical.

"Oh, and, Moon?" Star says, like we were just talking. "Might want to check your messages."

I turned my phone off after Mom called a thousand times in a row, and the last thing I want is to turn it on, but I do anyway, because I'm a masochist. I wait until I'm out of Star's and Chamomila's sight. Don't need to give them any more shit-talking fodder.

There are a dozen new missed calls from Mom. That's . . . that's probably more than she's called me all year, if you don't count the times she calls to talk to Star because Star isn't answering her phone.

"What's up?"

I guess I look as glum as I feel. Santiago's just walked in from the bathroom and is leaning against the doorframe.

"All these messages from my mom. I don't want to listen to them."

"So don't."

"You don't get it. It'll drive me wild if I delete them without hearing them first."

He says nothing for a few moments, studying me. Then: "Do you want me to listen with you?"

"Oh my. No. You don't have to. It's not going to be pleasant."

He shrugs. "Come on." He gestures to the expanse that is his bed. So I sit in it, my legs hanging over. I hit play on the voice mail app and close my eyes. I think I'm already tearing up a little, and Santiago puts his hand on mine. It's so sweet, I want to cry more.

"No daughter of mine has ever hung up on me. The disrespect! You'd better call back. Within the hour, Moon."

"Ah, so you're too good to phone your mother. Don't know where on earth you got that idea. Probably from my brat sister! I shouldn't have ever let her take care of you!"

"Oh, I know what you're doing. You're out with that boy, the one Star fell for. Of course you'd lure him right now into your bed. Nothing is ever enough for you, Moon. I don't know what I did to deserve you for a daughter."

"All I'm saying is, you might want to rethink coming home, m'ija. What if my knife slips—"

Santiago grabs the phone right out of my hands. "That's enough." And then he deletes the rest, all at once, with a few swipes of his giant fingers. He turns back to me. "You can't go home anymore. Not after that threat."

I shrug. "She threatens me all the time, though." But I'm shaking. She's never brought up the knives, not like that. She's never admitted that she'd premeditate something like that.

Santiago puts his arms around me. "You can't go back home."

"I know," I say. And the fact is, it's something I've known ever since Dad left. Ever since Mom first gleefully made me feel like shit. And it's the first time I'm really, really admitting it to myself.

Did Star know what was on those messages when she told me to listen? Good Lord. What would the Virgin Mary do, indeed.

When the tears come, I let Santiago hold me tighter.

"What is she talking about?" I say while sniffling. "What she did to deserve me? What did I do to deserve her? You know? Why do I get to have a mom who thinks it's okay to abuse her kid?" And I briefly wonder what it'd be like to have a mom like Santiago's, to have someone who even goes against her husband to make sure her son feels worth something. And I cry harder, getting his shirt all wet and snotty, but I don't think he cares.

And we lean back in bed and I tug his shirt up and lower my mouth onto his smooth brown nipple. He sucks in a breath and goose bumps flare all over his chest. But then he stops me. "Hey, what are you doing?"

I swallow. "Kissing your body."

"But you're still crying." He sits up, and his shirt comes back down most of the way. "Hey, look at me." His voice is gentle and firm somehow. And I do. I look right into his eyes, amber in the sunlight pouring in through the window. He takes both of my hands. "I don't want us to fool around while you're sad. Okay?"

I look down. He puts his fingers along my jaw and lifts my head up. "I'm telling you this because it's important to me that you have me because you want me. Not because you need a distraction."

"That's pretty much how it happened with the guys I've been with." I don't know why I'm telling him this. I guess it's like I'm at church, confessing something. Except, I want Santiago to know exactly what he's getting into.

"That's fine," he says. "But I don't want to be your escape. I want it to mean something more to you."

"Yeah. Me too." I sigh and collapse on top of him. "How are you so comfortable to lie on? Your body is harder than the exterior of this bus."

He laughs, and I lift my head up. "Seriously. Real talk. I'm probably never going to look as beautiful as you."

He helps my head back down against his shoulders. "You're more beautiful than me without even trying."

"But I'm squishy."

"I like squishy." To prove his point, he lowers his hand to my hip and squeezes. And I can't help but smile. He *does* like my body. He wasn't lying. He thinks that I'm beautiful! Without even trying! I mean, he must, right? He said it, after all.

"I want to kiss you again," I tell him.

"Why?" He's smiling.

"Because I like you. And the way you make me feel. And I want to."

I guess this works for him, because he leans toward my lips. And we spend what feels like forever kissing. And yeah, I get a bit eager, putting my hands under his shirt and touching all the places he's firm, which means everywhere, basically. And he cups my face and then my shoulder and then all my squishy bits—the side of my ribs, my hips, my thighs, my chest. When I try to dip my fingers into the waistband of his boxer briefs, he stops me. "Everyone's right there," he says, laughing and breathless, like he can hardly believe me, but not because I'm slutty. More like because he loves how much I want to do things with him. And then we both angle our bodies toward the window and watch the whole world spin in it. The little spots of cerulean sky between bright clouds, the canopy of trees, all pine, larch, cypress, their tall green enveloping the whole earth with their needles.

"What do you want for dinner tonight?" Santiago asks.

I smile. "I'm cooking tonight."

"Oh?"

"We're having pizza."

45.

Pizza and Honey like Alaska and Fireweed

I HALF EXPECT Santiago to take over at some point during the pizza-making process, but surprisingly, he lets me have control. He doesn't say anything when I knead, spread, and prebake the dough like the directions say. I spoon on the sauce and add the five-cheese blend.

"Any toppings?" he asks. "I have chopped bacon, peppers, olives."

"Those all sound good to me," I say, and he hands me the Tupperware, and I add an even layer. The pizza is beautiful. If I do say so myself.

The only time Santiago tries to say anything is when I place the honey on the table he's setting. "Please tell me that's for after-dinner tea."

"It's not for tea."

He and I participate in a staring showdown for almost five seconds, and then finally he breaks. "No." He shakes his head, trying to hide his smile. "No way."

"Yes way."

"That's not for pizza."

"Yes, it is. Furthermore, I've eaten everything you've made without complaint."

"That's because everything I make is good. And . . . makes sense." He lifts the jar of honey with a grimace on his face. It's some fancy type from New Zealand, according to the label. Belongs to Santiago, of course. "Explain to me, please, why are we going to ruin perfectly good pizza with this?"

I sit down next to him and then decide that's not close enough, so I slide onto his lap. He looks a little surprised at first, but then he slips an arm around me and smiles. "You're trying to butter me up."

"I'm trying to honey you up," I correct, and he laughs so hard, the whole bus shakes.

And then he's kissing my jaw and neck and I can't think, so I start rambling. "My mom has a mental illness. Or a lot of them." He stops kissing me and then rests his jaw on my shoulder. He hasn't shaved today, so it's a little prickly. It makes me think of all those pine needles just outside.

"Before Star and I joined the tour, Mom went with us to church. Star wanted us to get blessed so we'd stay out of the path of darkness or whatever. And that was the third time she'd left the house since my father died. It'd been almost six years." I swallow. "She shook all the way there, and to the airport, too. But she refuses to talk about it." Santiago runs his hand on my back, around and around like the way a leaf falls in autumn. "Mom was really poor growing up. We were really poor when we were young, too, especially after Dad. And Mom had this great idea, from when she was little, I think, that happy, rich, successful families ate pizza all the time, I guess. It's what they show in pizza commercials. So when we got my dad's life insurance, she put some into Star's blossoming Fotogram career, and then she started her tradition of ordering a massive amount of pizza once a week to last all week."

I rest my head back on Santiago. Now we're ear to ear, his short, soft whiskers on my cheek. "She stopped cooking completely when Star started making a shit ton of money. And gosh, it used to be so good. She'd make enchiladas and arroz con pollo with bone-in chicken. Not all the time, but when she did, Star and I loved it. But once we had more money, Mom said she wasn't going to cook like some nanny anymore. And so Star and I lived on pizza pretty much until we started driving. And after a while, I got so sick of it, I added honey. It made it so different and much better. That's my favorite way to eat it since."

"That sucks," Santiago says after a beat. "It sounds like your mom couldn't handle losing your dad."

"She wasn't . . . all that great before. But yeah. She definitely got worse after."

Santiago kisses my earlobe. "Was she always this cruel to you?"

I nod. "Yeah. It wasn't always direct cruelty, but more like, she didn't have any love left over for me after loving Star."

"I'm not sure she ever loved Star, though. From everything you told me."

"You said that yesterday . . . but I've been thinking about

it. She gets Star better birthday and Christmas gifts and spends hours with her, choosing outfits and having debates on whether newer, younger influencers can hold a candle to Star—"

"Is any of that really love, though?" Santiago asks. "Has she ever done anything for your sister that didn't ultimately benefit her in some way?"

When I think back, the feeling of being stunned comes over me like sheets of ice. I'm at the end of a glacier, and it's being peeled away like an onion. Because . . . no. Star is not a person to Mom. She's a thing to show how great Mom is. She's Mom's proof of Mom's own beauty, Mom's proof of piousness, Mom's proof of great motherhood. And most of all, she's Mom's paycheck. Star is Mom's little object. And deep down Star knows it. That's why Star treats me like crap too.

"No," I finally say. And then the oven timer dings.

"Ah. The witching hour has arrived," Santiago says, but he's grinning. And when we stand, he gives me the biggest hug.

His serenity is visibly disrupted when I plate our pizza slices and reach for the honey. "Just one bite," I say. He nods with grave solemnity.

We sit, and he closes his eyes as he picks up the pizza, and then he bites. His face is expressionless as he chews and swallows, and then his eyes light up. "No fucking way," he says, standing and pointing at the honey. "No fucking way that's the most delicious pizza I've had in my life."

I couldn't stop my gleeful, gloating laughter if I tried. "I told you! I told you!"

"You did," he says, grabbing the honey jar.

"Don't go overboard," I say. "I learned that lesson early on. There's a very specific honey-to-pizza ratio we're aiming for."

"Is this okay?" he asks, drizzling the honey on in half-inch lines.

"Yeah. Perfect." And I grab the jar and do the same to mine.

And we talk and talk. I tell him about the wild history of weeds, and he tells me about the difference between sweated, sautéed, and caramelized onions. We both talk about all the ways high school sucked and what it's like to have a sibling infinitely more beloved for all the most shallow, superficial reasons.

"Once," Santiago says, "this girl spent two hours talking to me about her mom's Swedish meatballs because she saw I was reading a Julia Child cookbook, and after all that, she slides what I think is her number into my hand, right? And kisses me on the cheek, disappears into the sunset. And when I open the slip of paper, it says, 'Please have Andro follow me,' with her handle spelled out. I think it was igotbunshun, if I'm remembering right."

"No," I say. "No. Two hours? On Swedish meatballs?"

"You know, I actually got into Andro's account and blocked her from it."

"No."

"I did. Petty as fuck, but . . ."

"I don't blame you," I say. "Once I was out with Star and Shauna, her hairdresser. We were all in Shauna's convertible, top down, cruising after Star had her roots bleached. Shauna is gorgeous too, by the way, and blond, like Star. They honestly look more like sisters than Star and I ever will." I take a breath. "So there was this old lady selling roses on the street, right? And I saw her approach this guy in his Lincoln next to us, and then he saw Star. It's always the same when they see her, you know? The short circuit. The complete failing of the brains. And he called the old lady over, and bought flowers, and pointed to our car. And she came over and handed Shauna and Star a bouquet each."

Santiago swallows. "None for you?"

I shake my head and laugh. "Not even that old lady saw me. I mean, growing up around Star, it's . . . easy to get used to not being noticed. But that was the day I realized for sure that I was invisible."

"Like hell you're invisible." Grumpy Santiago is back.

"But—"

"Stop. Stop judging yourself based on how jerks react to your sister."

"But you just were saying, because of Andro, that you understood—"

"I mean, yeah, I get it. But . . . you're not invisible, Moon. People look at you when you walk into a room. That's . . . not the definition of a weed." I try to interject, but he doesn't let me. "And besides your beauty, you're fucking talented as shit— photography, earth art, even freaking divination. I mean, who the hell else can read the future in twigs and rivers and shit?"

"Tía does," I say. My cheeks are on fire right about now, though, even as I say it. "Thanks." And then something clicks in me as I look around. "Wait a second. Where is my camera?"

46.

In Which the Star Eclipses the Moon

I RUSH TO my bedside, but my camera bag isn't even there. "Shit." Santiago helps me rummage through the boxes. We're looking behind the merch boxes when Belle walks in. "Hey. Are y'all doing inventory? Because I'm missing a box of the Corally Coral Brixsticks."

"I'm looking for my camera," I say, the urgency making my voice a little more high-pitched than I like. Lord. I hate looking and sounding weak.

Belle gives me a weird look. "Oh."

"Oh what? Have you seen it?"

Belle's furiously going through her phone. And then stops. "Was it a Nikon?"

"Yes," I respond. "And what do you mean, 'was'?"

Belle turns her phone so Santiago and I can see the screen. And there's Star's feed. "What the . . ." I say, pulling the phone out of her hand.

Star has a new series up, something called *Destroying the Root of Evil*. And in the photos, there's—oh God, no. There's a picture of her taking a freaking sledgehammer to my camera. My. Camera.

"She's still out at the campfire behind the restaurant." Before Belle's even finished talking, I'm tearing out of there. "Moon," she and Santiago call, and I slow down only to hand Belle her phone back.

"I can't believe it. I seriously cannot believe this," I say. "That's a four-thousand-dollar camera, and Lord, the lens cost more than double that! And she just, what? Got tired of all the gorgeous fucking photos I take of her or something?"

Neither of them responds. I march right up to the restaurant, Belle and Santiago behind me. I make it to the deck. Sure enough, there's Star, Chamomila the Bitch, and all the beautiful, jerk-faced Fotogram influencers. Arriving at the same time, because of course, is Andro. "What's going on here?" he asks when he sees my face.

"Why'd you do it, Star?" I say, ignoring him.

"What'd she do?" Andro asks.

"Destroy my camera." I'm still staring at Star, though, who's staring hard right back at me. Like I owe her something. Like I owe her a single fucking thing.

"Mom consulted with the father, Moon, and we're all concerned that you are on a bad path."

I blink. "And was it their idea to take a sledgehammer to my camera? Is that what the father advised?"

"She got your laptop, too," Chamomila calls, and my knees weaken. Because, God. Because that means the last images for the Wild Moonflower tarot are lost. My camera and my computer stored my only copies, and I want to kick my own ass for not backing them up somewhere else. But I want to kick Star's ass way more, because how could I have predicted this?

I'm vaguely aware that Chamomila and Oak and probably a bunch of others are holding their phones up, recording. They're probably freaking livestreaming, the fuckers. Anything for clicks.

"That was Mom's idea." Star's hands are clasped like she's in prayer. She tosses her hair and gives me an angelic smile. Something tells me she's more than slightly aware of the cameras too.

"Well, that makes sense that it was Mom's idea, I guess." I'm ready to go. All of a sudden I don't want to be the subject of some trending hashtag.

"And why's that?" Star's got her hand on her hip. Another hair toss. And I'm just so, so, so, *so* done with all the fakery. That's the only explanation for what comes out of my mouth next.

"Because when I heard from her yesterday, she said she'd cut me with her kitchen knives. Again."

Star's eyes widen, and then she starts and stops a sentence about eight times. Finally she settles on: "Thou shalt not lie."

And I laugh. Because honestly? "Because it's only okay when you and Mom get to do it, right?" I turn to go, but then I stop. Turn around. Looking at my angel sister, I gesture around. "None of this is what Mary would do. You realize that, right?" I can tell she doesn't. So I end with the kicker. "You and Mom are exactly alike. Religion is whatever you want it to be that day."

But Star isn't done yet. As I walk back around the restaurant, Santiago and Belle still with me, she comes running. "Santiago," she calls. "She's not who you think she is."

I scoff. "Go back to your people, Star."

"Has she told you her nickname? The Grand Canyon?" Star laughs as I freeze. It's like knives are being thrown at me all over again, but this time they hit my arms, legs, belly, everything, everything all at once. And Star keeps going. "Did you know she slept with my boyfriend *just* because she was jealous of me?"

I turn around. "Did you look through my pictures before you smashed my camera, Star? Because there's one in particular you might've seen. One with you and Belle Brix, if I'm remembering it correctly."

Star's face is ashen green. "I don't know what you're talking about."

"How could you forget? It was so . . . What's the word I'm looking for? Lovely. It was just lovely."

"Shut up, Moon," Star yells. I've never seen her this out of control before. "Shut up, Grand Canyon."

"Just thought you should know that's not the only copy of that photo. Would be a pity if it were, oh, I don't know. Leaked?"

"Moon." Belle is holding my arm with tears in her eyes. "Don't."

That slaps me out of it. "I'm sorry," I say to her low. "I would never." And I turn to Star. "Did you know the weirdest thing about that photo, though? Star? Behind you. You don't even know it, but behind you was a cloud of moths. Hawk moths." I pause. "They were beautiful. You know what? I'll send you a copy, how's that?" I pull the photo up on my phone. Yeah, I saved it there from my camera. Because when you've been the ugly, worthless sister for as long as I have, it really helps to have the reminder that you are not the only one who's got La Raíz. And I send it right to Star. "There! Now you can admire it yourself!"

"Liar! You're a freaking, heathen liar! Santiago," Star says, fuming. "You should check her Fotogram account. See who she follows. See her tagged pictures. She's not who you think she is."

Santiago gives her a hard look for so long that Star shrinks back.

"Star," I say. "Fuck off."

"Check her account!" Star repeats.

Finally I get away. But only because I run.

"Moon," Santiago calls. He's jogging too. To match my mood, the sky is filling up with swirling gray clouds. Way in the distance, there's the spread of lightning, a rumble of thunder. Perfect.

"I can't believe she went there. I can't believe she called me Grand Canyon." I want to cry, but I am too furious. I want to scream, but that isn't working out either. Santiago's phone does its text thing, but I ignore it. "I thought she knew, you know, how much that destroyed me. How kids at school taunted me with that for so long." My breath is bananas. So I take a few calming ones and turn to face Santiago.

But Santiago isn't here. I mean, he is there but he's also not, staring at his phone with the oddest expression on his face. Almost like he's been gut-punched but trying to hide it as hard as he can.

"What's the matter?" I ask.

And in response, he turns his phone to me. There, a text from Star. A photo of me and Andro from lunch the other day, on the day of the red feathers. We're at the table and we're laughing. From that angle, it looks like he's holding my hands even though he never did. That moment was innocuous. But this photo, it does look romantic. It looks like we're on a date. Still, it's not like we're making out or something. Everything can be explained, you know? There's no reason for him to believe this indicates anything deserving of the rage currently emanating from him right now.

"She says you've had a crush on him for years." He's staring. The gut-punch in his expression is gone. Now everything is hard, cold, just like when we first met. I feel like he's already gone, left from my life. My heart and head and everything hurt.

"I don't like Andro like that anymore."

"Only because he wasn't into you, though, right?" Santiago points at the photo. "Or at least you led me to believe."

"Andro and I had lunch because he wanted to ask about the Moonflower decks, Santiago. About selling them. That's it."

"Then what is so fucking funny?" Santiago's voice is loud. It kind of scares me. There's a fine mist of rain all around. I think both of us barely feel it.

"We're friends, Santiago. Barely that, even."

Santiago's at his phone again, and this time he's pulling up Fotogram. "What are you . . . ," I begin, but stop when he jumps to my account. I haven't checked everything the last two days. I must have thousands more followers now. But Santiago's not interested in who's following me. He clicks on the only person I follow.

Andro Philips.

And then Santiago's eyes are on me, and Lord, the look he's giving me is half killing me and half making me want to punch him in the face. His face that's saying, *I should've known.*

He won't hear me. Because all he wants to hear is Star. Story of my freaking life.

"Can you explain this?" he's saying in his hard, mean voice, and I'm shaking my head. There are tears on my cheeks, but they probably look like raindrops.

"It doesn't matter what I say, does it?" I respond. "You're choosing Star. You're choosing to let her manipulate you."

"Maybe it's you who's been manipulating me, Moon. This whole time. Maybe when I first met you, that was the real you. The one who said I was just a loser—"

"Please don't say that," I whisper. And he doesn't. Sure, he grinds his teeth and stomps away. But at least he doesn't finish that sentence.

Once, on one of my dad's digs, his team uncovered a cave that hadn't been opened in something like eleven thousand years. They finished the work right at lunchtime, so everyone took their breaks then. Everyone except Dad. He had to know right away what was inside that cavern. That's my dad for you . . . so excited about old things. Wonder where I get it from.

The Columbian mammoth stood up to fifteen feet tall. Its bones were so big, Dad said he couldn't make out what he was looking at for a good five minutes. It amazed him, he said, how much this thing still had a presence. Even though it'd been gone for so long, it was like its spirit was still there.

The best part, he told me, was what he remembered right after that. *He* was the first to enter this cave in eleven thousand years. In all that time, this mammoth had been alone, sleeping peacefully deep inside the arms of the earth. And now, all the way here in the Holocene, it had its first visitor, my dad, William Fuentez.

Dad said it was the most sacred moment of his life. He felt like he could speak to all the ghosts inside the cave. He said he knew I'd get it and I did. I felt the same thing when I wandered in the thickest part of the most wild forests. Like trees and moss and vines and bone, like for a few seconds, we all could speak the same language.

Right now I want that more than anything. I want to speak the language of ghosts so I can cry to my dad. But as I grab my mirror stone and reach and reach and reach into the land of the dead, I feel nothing. There's nothing but a rock in my hand.

How many times does it seem like what I need the most is never there? The answer is too many. Way too damn many.

47.

Running Away like the
Swirling, Shimmery Milky Way

MOM'S CUT OFF my cell phone service. I don't even blink when I realize it. I just throw my phone in my bag and pack up. They're not back from the restaurant yet, but someone could show up at any minute. I have to hurry.

Seriously, what the hell did people do before cell phones? I can't even pull up my web browser to google the answer.

I walk to the nearest intersection and follow the restaurant lights. It's still sprinkling, but both the lightning veining across the sky and the thunder that follows seem to be getting closer.

There's an Applebee's, a Friday's, a Taco Bell. That last one makes my heart hurt a little. Memories wash over me, colder and sharper than this rain. Me and Star, seeing who can eat the most tacos in five minutes. Me and Star, talking about all the ways we could help Mom be less Mom over our cinnamon twists and oddly good Taco Bell coffee. I wonder if I'll ever have that with her, or anyone, again. That messy intimacy. That casual closeness. That quilt of constellations.

I know they might look for me in these restaurants, so when I see a bus, I chase it down. When I walk up, the driver is rolling his eyes as he pulls to a stop.

"Can you tell me when we reach somewhere with a hotel? A cheap one." He grunts as I put my dollars in the little machine and pick up the quarters that bang out. I grab a window seat and count water droplets running down the glass until the engine revs up. When the bus pulls back onto the road, that's when I let out a deep, big exhale. And with it? All my tears. The ones for Santiago, who I still can't believe, but even with all that, he's got my heart.

For Star, my best friend, whose hands are still shattered with my past and my future.

And I cry for my mother. Not really for her, but what could never be. A warm woman, who smiled for real at me. Who cooked for us and could leave the house, who had it in her to forgive me.

And then my father. By the time I get to him, I feel like I should be out of tears, but it's like I've had a refill or something. My eyes are the ocean. My face is the land. My cheeks, filled with rivers and puddles and ponds. Why does the world gotta hurt so much? How much did my dad hurt that he couldn't take a second more of life? My daddy, my daddy, my daddy, my daddy. I miss you. I miss you. I miss you.

When I saw how Mom got with Star's money, I opened my own bank account. Inside, my life savings of every cash birthday and Christmas gift along with proceeds from the photos I'd sometimes sell online. And thank God I had that foresight, because I don't know what I'd do right now, in front of this hotel clerk who is literally in the middle of straightening her hair. "Sign there," she tells me as the smell of burned hair thickens around us.

The hotel looks like many, many murders have been committed here, so when I get into the room, I check the bathroom, the shower, and the tiny closet for serial killers. Once I give myself the all clear, I push a dresser in front of the door, turn and click on the TV. And, of course. The first channel to come through is the Food freaking Network. But I leave it on, even as I eat my sad, plain, cold bagel for dinner.

After a moment of watching Jamie Oliver whip eggs and insist salt can be added only after they're nearly cooked (it messes with the texture? Apparently?), I realize I have no idea where the flip I am. I mean, the hotel says we're in Green Village, but that means nothing to me.

I spend some time trying to envision it. We just left that one place with the big willow. We're on our way to . . . what was it? And then it hits me—I passed by a very sad-looking business center downstairs, which had several ancient-looking laptops. I push the dresser away from the door and pretty much rush out.

When the search engine finally loads up, I type in "Green Village, Louisiana." Click enter. Look and look and gasp a little. I'm thirty miles east of New Orleans. Thirty miles east of Tía Esperanza's black-veined turquoise home. I can hardly believe what a relief it is. I clasp my hand over my mouth to keep from shrieking. Maybe things will be okay. Maybe they will.

I sleep so deep and for so long, when I awaken, I feel like I've been drugged. Like I've been uprooted from one life, planted in the next, so fast and violently that I'm gasping for air and water and nutrients.

The first thing I do is call Tía, praying all the while that she'll pick up. It rings two, four, eight times. Just as I'm about to hang up, there's a click, then her voice. "¿Bueno?"

I can't talk right away because I'm crying. "Hello?" she tries.

And then I say, "Tía, Tía, Tía, it's me. It's Moon."

"Moon? What's the matter? What's happened? Is it your mom?"

That's the sort of mental go-to for all of us. We're always half-scared Mom is going to lose the rest of her mind and go do something, well, something like Dad did. So I say immediately, "No, no. Mom's okay. It's . . ." And then I cry some more.

"Talk to me, m'ija," Tía says softly. I can already feel her words in my hair, soothing me. In a way Mom never has, would, or could.

"I fell in love with a boy. One that Star had a crush on. And she got so mad, even though I'm pretty sure she's in love with someone else." This is the worst place to begin, but I can't stop now. "And Star, she—she broke my camera and my computer, and she told Mom I'm still a whore, and she made that boy hate me. He hates me, Tía. He hates me in a way that makes me think he was looking for a reason to hate me." I inhale. "And do you remember how I got those scars on my chest? When I fell off that tree?" I sniffle. "Well, that's not how it happened. It was Mom. She found out I had sex because of La Raíz and she cut me. And I'm scared to go home, because she hates me more than anyone. And I'm stuck in a shitty hotel, alone, and I want you to come and get me, but I'm scared I'm not worth getting, so I'm afraid to ask." My voice is whispering now. Whispering and cracking.

"Where are you?" she asks. I tell her. I read it from the crappy hotel stationery.

"Room number?"

"One twelve."

"I'll be there in one hour. Don't move." She pauses. "Even if you were in Alaska—even if you were on another planet, Moon—you're worth getting."

And after that, I feel kind of stable. I walk to the little dining area with the cold continental breakfast and grab a yogurt and a lemon poppy seed muffin. Santiago would take one look at this buffet, drag me to the bus, and whip up some eggs Benedict or something. But I can't think too hard about that, not right now.

When I decide to visit the business center again, I inhale a little sharply when my messages finally load. There're three emails, all in a row. From Santiago. They read:

Subject: Moon

Where are you?

Subject: Seriously

Seriously, where the hell are you?

My heart is all hopeful until I read the subject line of the last email, which goes: Forget it. And that's it. That one has no actual email in it. So, that's great.

There's also another email, from Andro. He has the decency to write more than a line.

Subject: Off to Asheville

Hey Moon,

We saw you packed and assumed you took off. Seems like your phone's not working. I wanted to apologize. I should've stepped in. I saw her with your stuff and I should've stopped her.

Anyway, let us know you're okay, all right? We're all worried. Especially Santiago.

Star is off the tour. If you want to come back, let me know.

Andro

I guess I can relieve Andro of his worries. So I write back, Hey, I'm okay. I can't go back, though. Thanks for thinking of me. —Moon

I don't know what else to say. Well, I know what would be truthful:

I'm in love with your brother. He broke my heart because he thinks I'm in love with you. Which makes me want to punch him in the neck a little. Or a lot. Mostly a lot. Lol. —Moon

I decide that's a little too much information and send the original message.

Santiago and I were together all the time for so long, it feels ridiculously weird to have him not be right next to me right now. I miss him so much, it feels like I'm grieving a real loss. Like I'm addicted to the gold of his skin, the way he always smells like oranges, how he is so closed off except with the people he really trusts. But he'll never trust me again, so what's the point in missing it?

Maybe I really, seriously do love him. Maybe that's what this is.

As I pack my things, I see something glint from my bag and I fight hard at sharp tears. It's the snow globe I got Star, like a fool, thinking she wasn't going to be such a fucking nightmare and ruin my life. I think about throwing it out the hotel window, just for the satisfaction of hearing it break into a zillion pieces. Then I think about shoving it in the toilet. But each of those options means someone's going to have to clean it up, and unlike her, I'm not a spoiled jerk. So when I leave my room, the snow globe simply fills the tiny trash. Even without breaking it, it seems fitting. Everything, right now, is trash.

Tía arrives in her baby-blue Oldsmobile. "It was the closest color to turquoise," she said when Star and I laughed at her about it. As soon as I get in, she slides toward me and kisses my cheek.

"I talked to your mother," she begins, and I stiffen because Mom has this magical gift of changing a story so everyone feels bad for her somehow. Once, when Star cried because Mom wouldn't let her spend the night at her BFF's house, Mom made it so that by the end of the night, we were apologizing to her. I don't even know how I got sucked into that one, but that's Mom's superpower for ya.

But then Tía's words are "You can't go home again."

I swallow. "Is that what she said?"

Tía laughs. "No. But you know her." And I finally exhale. Because Tía knows Mom better than any of us. She gets it.

"I want you to apply to Tulane. They have an extended deadline for their art program." She glances at me with a smile. "I happen to know you have an incredible portfolio at the ready."

I smile and look away.

"What's that face for?"

"I already got accepted there. Way back in April."

"¿Qué?" Tía screeches. "And you didn't tell me!"

"I was trying to save money for housing."

"Why would you . . ." And it's like the puzzle pieces fit in. "Oh. Your mom wouldn't have let you stay with me, huh?"

I shrug. "It doesn't matter what she thinks now." I glance at her. "If you'll have me. If it's okay. If you don't—"

"Of course. I've already cleaned the guest room, Moon. It's yours."

My eyes are filling with tears. "Thank you."

"Why don't we stop by Best Buy on the way home?"

"Okay . . ."

"Every artist needs a camera, no?"

And now I'm sort of gasping, but it's a happy gasp. With more tears. "Really? But I don't—it's too much—"

"I want to get it for you. And you're not going to talk me out of it."

As I wipe my eyes, a whole new life cascades around me. Like, maybe I am currently shattered into one hundred thousand pieces, but that's not the end. It's a whole new beginning, you know? It's that moment before the universe expanded, when all of matter is the size of a trillionth of a period, all hot and full of nothing but potential.

I could be someone who isn't always and completely eclipsed by my sister and kicked down by my mom. Who could I be? The skyline whips by us, the clouds white. Everything feels new right along with me. Who could I be? I could be anything. No, scratch that. I could be everything.

48.

A New Home, a New Universe

I ALMOST WEEP again when we pull up to Tía's turquoise house. It's the only place I've felt safe since Dad left. And now I get to stay here for much, much longer than a single summer.

It's a two-bedroom, one-story bungalow, all put together with slabs of concrete. Tía painted everything inside the color of terra-cotta, and when I was little, I imagined opening its door was like cracking open a real turquoise to find butterscotch oozing inside.

So there's that deep burnt orange, but it's offset by green. Leaves, specifically, of all the plants everywhere. Tía has a half dozen different kinds of pothos, the jungle vine that grows incredibly anywhere it doesn't get too cold. Its arms reach dozens of feet, and she pins them all over the walls like art—big, heart-shaped leaves glimmering emerald against the burnt orange. Some are speckled white, others lime green. Some are long and skinny and teal, reminding me of blue serpent heads.

And then there's the ficus tree, the yucca, the fiddle-leaf and the avocado and lemon trees, the snake plants, tall with each leaf thick and tapered like an arrow. And then the orchids, all in the kitchen, each one from a dude Tía dated before I was even born.

"Tell me about Orchid Man," I say as she prepares coffee for us.

"Why do you like to hear about him so much?" But Tía's smiling. She loves to hear about him too, I think. "He was the son of a very wealthy man. And children of that wealth, they don't know what to do with themselves." And I nod, thinking about Andro and Santiago. They were incredibly wealthy even before Fotogram became the entity it is today. And they both do seem a little lost in different ways.

"And one day, he was in Guatemala, and he found an orchid. A monja blanca. And . . ." Tía sighs. "Who knows what makes us fall in love with the universe, Moon. For me, it was paint. For this man, it was orchids." She pauses long enough for me to think. Who knows what makes us fall in love with the universe. For me, it was fireweed. For Santiago, it was salt.

"And when I ran into him ten or so years later at La Merced Market, that's how he courted me. With . . ." She lifts her hands, gesturing to the orchids that surround her. Not all are in bloom, but the ones that are, they're stunning in a way that shouldn't be earthly. White with pink tongues, orange and red with a little lick of blue, like a real flame. And then one so purple, it looks black except for where the afternoon light hits it.

"But you didn't want kids," I say, finishing the sad story before Tía can.

"Right. I knew that wasn't the path for me." She smiles, and it's mostly a peaceful one.

And then the guilt almost swallows me into its multifanged mouth. When Tía hands me the coffee—sweet and pale with cream—I stare at it for a long while before she says, "What is it, Moon?"

"I'm sorry," I say. "You said you never wanted children, but here I am, being that burden you never wanted."

Tía stares at me for a moment, before saying, "You know, that summer after your father passed, I tried to get custody of you and Star."

I'm gaping. "But—"

"But your mother said no, and if I ever wanted to see you again, I'd drop it." Tía frowns. "I should've tried harder. I know how your mom is, Moon. I mean, I didn't know she had taken things that far. . . ." She gestures to my collarbone. "But I knew with your father around, you'd all be protected to an extent." She sighs. "And after. Well. I should've tried harder. A lot harder." And she puts both hands on mine. "You're not a burden, Moon. You're my prayers come true."

I should be hugging her now, but at the mention of my dad, I flinch a little and try to refrain from balling my hands into fists.

"What is it?" Tía asks.

"Dad," I say. "Just—sometimes it hits me all over again." I

can't help the way my eyes fill with tears or how my voice cracks like papery leaves under snow. "I don't understand how he could leave me like that. Leave me with her."

Tía takes a long breath, placing her hand on mine. She glances out the window and then back to me. Her eyes look shiny too. "I was on antidepressants for years, Moon."

I blink. "Oh. I didn't know that."

"That's because you're the only person who knows now, besides my doctor."

"Is this the hot doctor?" I ask, sniffling. Tía always brags about her appointments.

"The very one." Tía smiles a sad smile. "After I lost my position at the art gallery and broke things off with Esteban—remember him?" I nod. He was Tía's longest relationship at seven years. "I felt hopeless. Like all that badness, it wouldn't end. Couldn't end." She leans back in her chair. "It's hard, being human. It's too easy to get pulled under by what makes us ache and bleed and cry. But I know, without any doubt, Moon, that your father adored you. He wouldn't have done what he did if he felt there was another away. And it was mental illness that made him think there was no other way."

We say nothing for a while. The only thing that can be heard is my sniffling. Tía stands and opens a nearby dresser drawer. From inside, she pulls out a long prayer candle. "For grief," she explains, and as she lights it, she adds, "Your father's not here, but you'll be okay with that someday. You'll never stop missing him. Your heart will never completely repair. But you'll be okay with everything, as imperfect as it is." The candle flickers with her breath.

I take a deep breath, close my eyes for a few seconds, then open them. "So, I'm your dream come true, huh?"

Tía smiles. This time, it reaches her eyes. "Of course."

I swallow. "Star, though."

"Star is welcome here. But it sounds like she already made her choice, as far as her mother versus everyone else."

Star. Reminds me of Santiago, of his face as he pulled up my list of who all I followed on Fotogram. And I don't want to think about either of them anymore. So I say, "Did you have sex with the Orchid Man?"

"Moon!" I've never seen Tía look bashful before.

"You don't have to tell me. I was wondering is all."

"Okay. I know your mother told you a lot of crap about sex."

And I snort. "Remember, that's how I got this." I point to my scar. "She'd found out about my having sex."

"Shit, Moon." Tía shakes her head. "First of all, there's so much you have to unlearn." She takes a breath. "And so I'll be honest with you. Yes. I had sex with the Orchid Man. Lots and lots and lots and lots—"

"Okay," I say, covering my ears. "We're already in TMI territory."

"We did it at the beach—"

"Tía!"

"In his Porsche—"

"Oh my Lord."

"At church—"

That startles my hands off my ears. "Wait a second. Did you say 'church'?"

"An old one. We did it among the ruins."

I cover my ears again. "I don't know if that's better or worse than what I was thinking."

"Rule number one to your unlearning. There's nothing wrong with sex."

I drop my hands. "On an intellectual level, I know this, but . . ."

"I know it's going to take time, especially after all you've been put through." Tía stands. "Come. Let's make a list of everything you need for your room."

The guest room faces the west, so the sunset lighting is magnificent, she reminds me. There's a brass frame on the full-size bed, a dresser that's about chest-high, wooden, and ornately carved. There's a large knit laundry basket the color of the sea.

"I don't know what else I could possibly need," I say. I want to cry, for probably the millionth time today.

"Well, let's begin with a phone," Tía responds. She turns. "Let me start lunch and then we'll figure the rest out!"

I take one long breath and raise my arms to open the curtains a little bit more. And immediately jump back.

Of course a moth sits on the screen to greet me. Of course it's a luna moth.

Weirdly enough, I'm not as creeped out as I thought I'd be by this. I stare at her for a few moments, and she stares back. It feels like we know each other. Like that tentative, awkward shift before someone turns from an acquaintance to a friend.

"Just don't get inside my room, please," I tell her. "I'm not ready for that yet."

As though she understands me completely, she lifts her gorgeous, watercolor wings, and then she flies away.

Tía and I make a list of what I need over rice and beans and fried plantains, and then we go shopping. We pick up a phone. And then clothes, she insists. "You need more than a 'gym wardrobe,'" she tells me. It's her gift to me, she says, to make up for not being there. I tell her the camera was enough, but she shakes her head. "I could never make up for it, not really. So you're getting some clothes whether you like it or not!"

Just by picking me up, she's made up for everything a thousand times. But I let her. And by the end of the night, with the whole of Target's juniors' and women's summer wear in bags lined up in my room, I feel rich, richer than a queen. And I'm grateful. I am. But I already know this is when I'll feel what I've lost the most—at night, in bed, the emerald curtains drawn tight.

Mom and Dad and Star. Santiago. More than half my heart, just like that, set adrift at sea, with nothing to guide them but old constellation maps that are so tearstained, they can't be deciphered anymore.

But I think of Tía's words again. That somehow this will all be okay. Though it feels impossible, the message, the letters, they all settle into my hair, my cells, the marrow of my bones. One day I'll be okay. Maybe now, maybe even now, I already am.

Tía's at work, at the bank. She's not around to get on my case for moping everywhere, so I try to distract myself every which way I possibly can. I turn on the television and watch reality TV for twenty whole minutes. I open my camera and take photos of Tía's orchids. Every hour they're a new color thanks to the kitchen light. They almost kill me with their beauty.

I fry cheesy tortillas and stuff them with guacamole and lettuce and sour cream. And it makes me sad, because even the idea of this meal never would've come so naturally if it weren't for this summer's cooking show, starring me, Moon the Weed, and him, Santiago the Nebula. But then Santiago, the thought of him, it starts a little smoke at my fingertips. Because I'm not sad anymore. I'm freaking mad.

When I sit in front of my aunt's computer, I open a Word document and write "How dare he" about eighty times. How dare he. How dare he believe Star's bullshit. How dare he think I was capable of using him to get to Andro. How dare he write "Forget it" in that flipping useless email. The one I still can't bring myself to delete.

How dare he give me a speck of hope only to take it away, ripping my whole heart in half in the process. I feel like a seed, you know? But not in the good way anymore. I'm dry, almost an empty shell. I was so close to water that I could smell it, and then bam! I rolled away, straight into a desert.

When I tell Tía this, she wrinkles her nose. "Don't let anyone feel like they're the one who's supposed to save you," she says. She's spooning sugar into our café Cubanos, served in little white cups on little white saucers, everything lined with hand-painted roses. The serving ware makes me feel solid, more so when I put the cup to my lips. Like the porcelain somehow connects me back to the earth from where it came.

"You can only save yourself," Tía continues. "This doesn't mean others can't help you. But if you're looking for them to give you your worth, to give your life meaning? They will always fail you."

I groan. "Yeah, yeah. Girl power and all that."

"It doesn't only apply to girls, Moon!"

"Okay. That's true. So how do I save myself?" I ask, half expecting her to respond with something wise and mystical sounding, like, *Only you can know the answer to that.*

Instead, she says, "Get to work."

"What?" My little café is frozen in midair. "You want me to get a job?"

"You have a job," Tía says, pointing to my camera, which is currently stashed in the bookcase. "Get back to it."

"You mean posting on my Fotogram? The earth art?" I already know that's exactly what she means.

"Yes." She leans back, daintily sipping the café, her pinkie finger extended like a princess.

"But—"

"But what?"

"I lost so much, Tía. Months of work. It's going to take me forever to complete my deck. And I'm not even sure that's what I want to do anymore."

"So?"

"And Star's on there still. And they're probably posting videos of our fights. Probably editing them to make me look like the villain. And there are Star trolls just *waiting* for me to—"

"So go on another platform."

I sigh. "You make it sound so easy, Tía."

She sets her cup down and puts a hand on mine. "Look. I don't want you to go online if you're going to get bullied. If you need to wait until this blows over first, then wait. But you gotta get busy, Moon. All you did today was sit around and moon over that boy—"

"I did not—"

"Make art. And when you're ready, share it again. The world needs your talent, Moon. This world needs *you*." Tía stands and leans to kiss me on the forehead. "Get busy, Moon."

Make art. Okay.

Tía's backyard is a jungle and we're on this little hill in the neighborhood, so we get the best views of the sunsets and the moonrises, through big palm and live oak and sugar maple leaves. I set my tripod up and take a long-exposure photo of the dimming light on her garden. All dark shadows blotted with little spots of sunset light rays. Makes me think of topaz, scattered across the forest, each stone glowing like a lantern.

I go inside and pour myself a glass of mint tea, and when I go back out, the moon is rising, its light so thick, streams are pouring between all the dimming topaz lanterns.

The beauty startles me. It startles me like La Raíz did each time. Like this right here *is* La Raíz—an unexpected and unpredictable miracle. And I set the shutter for as long as it will go, and then the moths arrive, fluttering right toward Tía's arbor, covered in moonflower vines. They dance like spirits, I think, almost forgetting what it was like on earth when they were alive, and just like that, an idea falls into my head, so strong that it feels like someone smashed an egg right into my hair. I can even feel the yolk sliding into my neck. But I ignore the slimy sensation. I go inside, I go to the computer, and I do exactly what Tía said to. I get to work.

49.

How to Meet a Cute Boy at the Library (Even If Your Heart Is Still Broken like a Cracked Seedpod)

CINDY SHERMAN WAS one of the first artists to base her whole work on self-portraiture. It's kind of hard for me to imagine in the age of such easy selfies, but her work was seriously revolutionary at the time. Up until then, humans had made art, lots and lots and lots of art, on the female body, but 99.9 percent of it was based on the male gaze. Which means the portrayal of women focused only on the parts that mattered most to men. Boobs and thighs and seductive looks. Subservience, Madonna/whore categorizations, sinners, and subjugation. There were a few lady artists who broke the mold, but Cindy Sherman was the first as far as selfies go. And she did it way, way, way before digital cameras and Photoshop and filters. I mean, she used film. She literally developed that shit in a darkroom. She didn't get to see if a photo shoot was successful or a load of crap until after all that work. What a badass.

Searching through Cindy Sherman's portfolio online isn't enough. It feels wrong, even. Her work was meant for paper, you know? So after procrastinating for almost two weeks, I borrow Tía's library card and head out.

I find the section of photography books pretty easily. They're all mostly massive. I grab one on Cindy Sherman, then a few more that catch my eye. By the time I'm walking to sit at a table, the pile of books in my arms reaches my nose.

"Hey, you need help?"

I guess I must look like I'm going to topple over because there are hands grabbing the first five or ten thousand books.

"Thanks." I look over the guy as he places the books on the table.

He nods and looks up at me, and his jaw sort of drops a little. It's a look I've seen exactly one zillion times when it comes to guys first seeing Star. But I've basically never seen it directed at me. He must recognize me as Star Fuentez's sister. Or maybe he knows my work like that one guy in Colorado.

"So you're a photographer?" the guy asks.

Am I? For so long, I was just Star's camera girl. That was switched up recently into merch girl. A slut and a whore and a bad, bad daughter according to my mother. And to too much of the world, I'm a dark and thick and exotic girl, glanced at and forgotten like a weed.

So it takes me a second to respond. "Um, yeah. Well, yeah."

And he grins, and I realize how flipping cute he is, with his chestnut hair, freckles, and big green eyes. "Me too," he says, reaching out his hand. "I'm Marco. No jokes about the pool game, please."

I laugh. "Well, I'm Moon. No jokes about whether or not I'll moon you, please."

"For real?" he says, holding my hand a touch longer than necessary. "Seriously, your name is Moon? As in . . ." He points up.

"Yup."

"I bet there's a wild story behind that name." He grins again.

"Uh. Well, not wild, exactly." Just my dad being poetic combined with my mom being stubborn.

We're shushed by some old lady, and we turn to each other and silently laugh a little.

"Why don't I take you out Friday and you can tell me all about it?" Marco whispers.

The first thing I think of is Santiago, and my heart hurts a little. But I mentally shake it off. I've got to move on sometime, right? "Get busy," Tía told me. So I nod and say, "I'd love that."

The thing with Cindy Sherman is she embodies personas in her work. In one, she's a naive-looking housewife, gazing up at the camera from her kitchen floor, where she's picking up spilled groceries. In another, she's positioned herself in front of a painted landscape, like she's a painted portrait done in the 1800s, bonnet tied up on her hair and all. Sometimes her makeup is done clown-like; sometimes her face is completely distorted with it. Nothing is really beautiful, not in the traditional sense of the word. But the way she owns the space of the photo, the way she doesn't care to smile. It's powerful.

And it leads to other artists. Painters like Frida Kahlo and Artemisia Gentileschi. All women who did the selfie before the term "selfie" was even a thing. And it seems kind of lame and sexist that once lots of women started taking pictures of themselves, it started to be called "selfies." Something people like to mock, to dismiss as a symbol of vanity and narcissism. But what they used to be is self-portraits. That's what they are still, in fact. It's all kind of messed up.

My absolute favorite artist I've discovered is Ana Mendieta. When I look at her earth art, or self-portraits, or anything she's done, it makes my whole body want to shiver like I'm getting ocean waves of déjà vu over and over. In one photo, she wears nothing but white flowers in front of an ancient Mesoamerican tomb. In another, she stands in front of a huge tree trunk, arms up, covered in wet dirt. She looks like a mud goddess in it. These in particular are from a series called *Siluetas*, and I spend hours looking at each one, trying to figure out which is my favorite. I think it may be the one of a woman's body carved in the sand, covered in red ochre. That one reminds me of ancient cave paintings. Or something even older than ancient cave paintings, maybe something even older than flowers or ochre or mud.

On Monday night, I wait for the sunset to arrive, bringing its little drops of liquid topaz. And I set it all up in Tía's backyard: my tripod, a white sheet to reflect light, a collection of magnolia blooms from the neighbor's yard. And I take off my clothes and lie in the grass, the sticky evening dew kind of cold at first, making me gasp.

Then I place the magnolia flower right over my crotch. It's huge and covers everything important and then some. And then I scooch down so I'm under my camera, reach for the remote shutter release, and press the button.

At one point, I push the camera farther away and add more magnolias over my chest. I swoop my hair to the side, fan it out. And then slide my finger over the button. *Click, click, click.*

"What in the hell are you doing out there, Moon?" Tía's voice is ringing through the backyard.

"Don't look!" I call back. "I'm only wearing flowers!"

"It's a little late for that," she says. "Get dressed and come inside! I brought some pastelitos from la panadería!"

Well, that gets me moving. I pull my clothes on, pack up, and sprint to the house.

"What kind?" I ask.

"Guava."

Oof. My favorite.

"Want to tell me what you're doing outside in your birthday suit?"

"Self-portraits." I pour cream into the coffee Tía sets in front of me. "But not porny," I clarify. "Artsy."

"Can I see them?"

"No." I pause. "Sorry, it's just . . . I'm not even ready to see them yet."

Tía smiles. "When you are, Moon, let me know, okay?"

50.

Making Art like Warm Southern Rain

I SPEND THE next three days taking portraits. In one, I drive to the river and stand in front of a massive banyan tree. I braid a belly chain made of switchgrass, and I photograph my bare stomach. Enormous, ancient tree on one side; enormous, ancient river on the other. I would've gotten more work done if some old asshole hadn't started catcalling me. "Hey, sweetheart, lift your top a little higher, would you?" Why are men so gross?

When I get home, I borrow some of Tía's inks and paint my feet in the backyard, all warm in the sunlight. My feet are so dark, even in the thick afternoon, but I try to stop my brain when it goes on to bring up images of Star's small, pale, dainty, and always pink petal–polished feet. No, instead I stare at my own even harder. And then I paint Cōātlīcue, goddess who gave birth to the moon and all the stars on my left foot, and on the right, I paint Xochipilli, god of flowers. Aztecs did not portray their gods pretty, or what we think of as pretty. Their gods are flat, wide-eyed, strong, and snarling. That's exactly how I paint them. Fierce and wild. Just like me. Just like the animal that is my body.

I get the hose going and I wet the side of Tía's garden, where there is nothing but blue chicory plants, until the mud is thick. And then I slap my feet right on there. Some of it splatters onto my skin, making the ink on Cōātlīcue and Xochipilli smudge a little, but it looks cooler, in my opinion. I lift my camera from my neck and start snapping.

And then I spend the rest of the day exactly like that. Barefoot, muddy, watering all the plants—the breadseed poppies, the sweet and sour marigolds, the roses, all blooming in pink and yellow and crimson. The enormous bromeliads that line the house, the way they hold water in their reservoirs like little teacups. The morning glories, the hummingbird vines, and, of course, the moonflowers.

When I get inside, I tiptoe around, wipe my feet on a dirty towel, and slip my SD card in Tía's computer, clicking *yes* when it prompts me to upload new photos. And I close my eyes.

Everything is tight—my shoulders, my jaw, my calves, even. I can barely open my eyes. I don't know why, but it feels like I'm about to dive off a plane into nothing but misty clouds for miles and miles.

But then I look, and everything sort of goes into a state of pleasant shock. My photos. My body. My rolls and my dimples. My face, even. It all looks . . . okay.

Better than okay. The effect I was going for, the idea of my body as its own land, its own borderlands, came out so much better than what I was even imagining. There, my hips in the emerald grass, looking like a bronze hill, with the magnolia right in the center. And there's another, me in the aloe, looking like a woman made of stone. And then my soft belly, between the ancient tree and ancient sea, wearing a chain of long leaves. And it amazes me, because those leaves are also ancient, made by those groves of trees and their mothers and their mothers and on and on and on. Everything, everything is part of a lineage. Everything, everything is ancient. Just the thought of it is a wave of warm salt water along my head, my spine, my thighs. Goose bumps prick along my arms and belly and chest, and I minimize my photos and start googling.

One hundred and seventy thousand years ago. That's when the first anatomically modern humans roamed the earth. I knew that from Daddy.

Three hundred and eighty-five million years ago is when the first banyan trees appeared.

Nearly five hundred million years ago—like, holy crap, what kind of number is that, anyway?—is when plants first appeared. This is when I push my screen down and go back outside.

The sky is thick with rainstorm clouds on one side—dark, slick, about to burst with water. How long have clouds roamed the earth? And rain? And wind? I take a moment and watch, you know, *feel* those old-as-dirt formations and migrations. We are all ancient. And it's bananas to me, how the holiness of this earth was attempted to be contained in a church, forcing people to feel bad about the sacred and ancient and wild of our bodies, our senses, our glorious impulses to make mistakes, some of which turn out to be the best things ever.

Like my mistake to go on the Summer Fotogram Tour. That all led me here, staying at Tía's for as long as I need to, weeping under millions of years of rainstorm clouds because they're all so fucking beautiful, you know? And even though I don't want to, I wish to all the ancient lineages on earth that Santiago were here with me. He'd get this. He'd feel it too.

But he's not here. It's just me, barefoot, my eyes closed as the rain begins. It's just me and I'm finally beginning to feel that is enough. That I am enough.

"I spoke with your mother," Tía tells me at dinner.

I'm showered and in my softest gray sweatpants and a T-shirt. We're in front of our latest favorite takeout, the pollo a la plancha combo from La Granja down the street. Arroz, frijoles, chicken cooked with a thousand onion slices until it's sweet. Santiago would love it, I think.

Now, though, my appetite dwindles a little. "Uh. Okay." I wait to ask a lot of things. *Why did you talk to her again? Don't you know she's a mess? Don't you know what she's capable of?* But I keep my mouth frozen shut.

"I thought she may want to hear that you were doing okay here. Just in case she—"

"Gets a personality transplant? Decides to become a decent human being? Discovers that she actually is capable of loving her fat brown daughter?"

Tía shrugs as she slices her maduros into perfect quarters. "Maybe I shouldn't have. Pero . . . I don't know. I guess I'm a sucker for giving family chances."

Now I'm cutting my maduros into intricate pieces. "Well. What did she say?"

"I'm not sure you want to know."

"I bet I can guess. She called me a long list of nasty names. Probably things like 'ungrateful whore of a daughter.' And then demanded I come home where I belong."

Tía sighs. "That summarizes it. Except after all that I told her the only way she'd see you again would be if she came here and apologized to you. Far away from my kitchen and its knives."

A wave of giddiness comes over me. "Really? You said that?"

"Really."

"And what did she say to that?"

Tía snorts. "She hung up on me."

I'm tearing up. Just a little bit. "Thank you for saying that. And for believing me."

"Wish I could do more." Tía moves her head and arms and hands. "Ah. Let's shake off this bad energy, huh? Tell me about your date tomorrow. Is he hot?"

I laugh, and all of a sudden I'm hungry as heckle. And Tía and I talk and eat until we're stuffed, and then she has the audacity to bust out passion fruit–vanilla ice cream, which we eat on the back porch in the topaz of the setting sun. And I think, this is all I ever wanted from my mom. But I can have it with Tía. And maybe new, future college friends. And, who knows, maybe even Marco. I can choose who I surround myself with and make sure they deserve me. Because maybe that's thicker than blood, you know? Maybe love is thicker than blood.

51.

Quite Possibly the Worst Date in the Known Universe

I'M IN A YELLOW-ochre dress, the color of almost-ripe mangos. It's an A-line, flares a little, and shows off my brown calves and braided flower sandals. I put on some peach lipstick and gloss, braid my hair over one shoulder. And then I feel like I'm ready for my first date A.S.—After Santiago.

"He's here," Tía says to my door.

"What? But that's, like, fifteen minutes early!" When I check my phone, though, I see that he's exactly on time.

As I step out, Marco smiles really big. "Wow." And then he pushes a bouquet out. Daisies, and mostly pretty, but . . . ones that are electric blue and pink. They're kind of sticky on my hands, and I realize it's because they've been spray-painted with glitter. "Wow, I love flowers," I say, because it sounds like a compliment and it is also not a lie. Marco smiles some more as Tía takes the bouquet.

"Que bonito," she says, but her nose is wrinkled. "Have fun, Moon. I'll get these in a vase for you."

"Do I have a curfew?" I ask.

"Just text if you're going to be after midnight," Tía says. She smiles at Marco. "Nice to meet you, Marco."

"Nice to meet you, again, Esperanza." Marco is the picture of perfect manners. He even kisses her hand. When he looks at me, Tía raises her eyebrow from behind him, and I swallow a laugh. I can't tell if she's impressed or thinks he's trying too hard. I think it might be a little of both.

Marco wears a black-and-red button-down shirt, jeans, Converse sneakers. "You look gorgeous," he tells me as he opens the door for me. He drives a sleek, low-to-the-ground car. I think I heard Santiago once telling Van that he drove a Mercedes G-Class. Something rugged, but also expensive. Probably a birthday gift from Andro or something.

"I thought we'd go do something kind of quirky," Marco says. "There's this new restaurant downtown called the Vine Box. My buddy says it's incredible. They grow all their produce on the rooftop."

"That's awesome," I say. Santiago would definitely be intrigued.

"So, you going to an art school in the fall?"

"Yeah, uh. I'm going to Tulane."

"Really?"

"Um. Yes."

"You sure you're going? Tulane University? For art?"

"Yeah. I'm sure. Or else I'm hallucinating the acceptance email in my in-box." I chuckle, but Marco doesn't look amused at all.

"That's a really hard school to get into."

"Is it?"

"Yeah. A buddy of mine, he's tried twice in a row." He looks over at me. "Guess they must have a specific quota they need to fill."

It's been two minutes into our date and I can already declare it extraordinarily unsuccessful.

"Maybe you could apply to my program too, over at the university."

"Oh wow. Maybe." Super-weird offer, for me to apply to a school much less prestigious than the one I got accepted to, but whatever.

My response improves his mood for some reason, and he smiles. "So I want to get to know you, Moon. Tell me what got you into photography."

I don't want to mention Star this early in the game, so I say, "Oh, well, I first got into portraits and then documenting earth art. And now I'm kind of getting into self-portraits."

Marco does this little impatient nod, and the second I'm done speaking, he inhales real big. "Right, well, what got me into it was film. I'm really kind of a film buff, you know, British New Wave, Italian neorealism. And then from there I got interested in photography, you know, Robert Frank, Alfred Stieglitz, David Bailey."

"Oh," I say.

"But for film, you know, I don't only watch really obscure movies you've never heard of. I also love Quentin Tarantino, Paul Thomas Anderson, Woody Allen."

"Woody Allen?" I say. And I mean it as, *Really, you support Woody Allen in this year of our Lord?* But he mistakes the question for pure ignorance.

"Wow, you haven't heard of Woody Allen?" He laughs. It's kind of ugly. "Man, we really need to catch you up. Maybe a movie marathon. My place, next time."

There will never be a next time, but I don't know if I'm safe enough to announce that yet. I check the clock. We've been talking for a total of seven minutes, and I already want to open the door and roll into the bayou to escape.

"Oh man, I know just the films. First we'll do all the Woody Allen classics. *Annie Hall, Hannah and Her Sisters . . .*"

I think I'd rather eat a pile of roasted DVDs. I give him a big smile and say, "Wow." Because wow. Marco doesn't notice the sarcasm in my tone and goes on to tell me the whole life and career of Mr. Allen. Ugh.

The Vine Box is dimly lit and there's a whole wall covered in the names of their craft beers. Marco orders a pale ale as he starts educating me on microbrews. "This one, this one tastes like it was made in someone's backyard, you know? Like it's got hints of birch and cumulus clouds." He grins and seems to bask in how deep and artsy he is. "Try it," he says.

"I'm eighteen," I respond.

"One sip."

He already drank from it, so at least I know he didn't drug it. I take the tiniest sip in the history of assholes pressuring girls to do stuff they don't want to.

"Good, huh?" he says, and the only thing I can think is it tastes like it was actually made in someone's bathtub, with left-over bath- *and* dishwater. But instead of saying all that, I make an excited-sounding *mmm* noise.

Our conversation stalls until our food arrives. I have hope it's going to save this date, but when the plate of pasta is placed in front of me, Marco looks at it and goes, "Wow, that's a lot of carbs." He ordered chicken and waffles, but I guess he gets a carb pass or something.

It's a margherita pasta dish, with gooey-looking homemade whole-wheat pasta. I swirl some on my fork and get it in my mouth, and my eyes water with the fight to spit it out.

"Oh man. You can taste how fresh it all is, can't you?"

I sure can. The pasta tastes like soggy, half-ground wheat. The mozzarella is good, but it can't save what is essentially a bowlful of spiceless Weetabix cereal.

"Everything okay?" he asks after wolfing down half his plate.

"Yeah, of course. I wasn't expecting it to be cold, you know?"

From the look on his face, it seems like he wasn't expecting that, either. But then he sort of smirks and says, "Well, the ingredients are so fresh, you know? Rooftop garden? It hardly even needs to be cooked."

"Or to be salted," I say, and he nods enthusiastically.

"Exactly."

I eat all the cheese and tomatoes, slowly, while Marco goes on and on about really obscure films I've never heard of. And all I think about is how Santiago would hate this restaurant so freaking much. He'd yell at them about French gray sea salt or even just regular table salt and pepper, and then he'd sweep me away and angrily make me mac and cheese with truffle oil or something. And serve it while it was so hot, I'd be able to warm my hands over its steam before eating.

I time Marco to see how long it takes for him to notice I'm not speaking. He never does. He speaks for thirty-eight minutes after I finish what I can and then asks for the check. At least he pays, I guess.

He walks me back to his car. I have my phone in my hand, on a screenshot of my last message from Santiago. *Forget it.* It's there to remind me when I start to miss him too much. Like right now. Like all the time.

"Are you in the mood for dessert? Or did you have too many carbs for dinner?"

For the love of everything, why is this dude so fucking hung up on the amount of carbs I'm eating? I want to tell him he ought to have shoved his chicken and waffles up his dick hole, and by the way, he owes me a thousand carby meals for making me suffer through that pretentious restaurant and crappy conversation and his implications that I need to limit carbs in the first place.

But the thing is, I can't. I don't want to make Marco mad,

especially when I'm in his car. Boys can get so jerky when a girl is real with them. That's why so many girls just put on a smile and play nice. We are literally trying not to make a dude so mad, he'll punch us, or kill us. And then guys pretend that's not a thing. Marco seems pretty nonviolent so far, but I once went out with a notorious Nice Guy who banged his fists on the wheel and screamed his face off when I said I thought it'd be best if we were just friends.

So instead of telling him off, I say, "You know, I better get home, if that's all right."

Marco furrows his brows. "But your aunt said—"

"Right, but I feel a little sick. I'm sorry. I guess I'm not used to fresh ingredients." He looks like he might argue some more, so I add, "I'm trying not to hurl as we speak!"

Well, that gets his mind off dessert. He looks a little crazed as he asks, "Do you need me to pull over? Do you need me to pull over?"

"No, no. I'm stable. For now."

"I'll get you home, okay? God, let me know if I need to pull over."

Ah. The ol' potential vomit. Gets 'em every time. Once I had a guy question it, but all I had to do was gag a little and he freaked too, just like the rest of them. One of the best parts about the vomit act is there's no way you're getting an after-date kiss.

True to the tradition, Marco about pushes me out of his car without so much as a peck on the cheek. "Sorry about that," he says. "We'll have to do dessert another time, okay?"

I cover my mouth and nod as I quickly make my way to the door. He squeals his tires as he makes his getaway.

The vomit act is probably the most effective. Then there's the just-got-my-period-with-reeeally-bad-cramps one, which I learned works well from it happening for real. That one is great because most guys are such babies about periods, plus it eliminates the chance of them getting any action, so they stop putting any effort into pretending to be decent people in the first place.

I'm so lost in thought about how shitty it is for girls to date that I barely notice the strange car in the driveway. It's so dark, I almost convince myself that I'm just mistaking Tía's Oldsmobile for something huge and sharp and shiny. But no—Tía's car is actually in front of this thing.

I approach it slowly, maybe like how someone would tiptoe around an ornery beast. What if it belongs to Tía's Orchid Man? How romantic would that be, after all these years?

Only then do I notice the logo. It's a Mercedes. Goose bumps trickle down my back and arms like long coils of small snakes. I rush to the front door and stuff my keys in the lock, pulling the door open with such force that I'm mildly surprised it doesn't fly off.

Tía sits on the sofa, coffee in hand, and opposite her, on the edge, tears on her face and shaking, is my sister.

At first the shock is just the fact that Star's here. And then another wave of shock comes over, and it's the fact that she looks like shit. There are half-moons under her eyes the color of winter shadows. Her hair has a half inch of mousy brown roots. Her skin is blotchy—pale, pink, red.

"What happened?" I ask. But I think I already know the answer.

"Mom." Star's voice is shaky. "I guess . . . I've been reading a lot about it. I was the golden child. You were the scapegoat. But then you left, and she couldn't handle not having a scapegoat."

"Did she cut you?" I want to run to her. She's so pale and sick. But I don't know. It's like my whole body isn't sure if it can trust her again.

Star shakes her head. "No. Just throwing stuff. Books. My computer. My, uh, television." I gasp because that's an eight-thousand-dollar television. It's massive. I don't know how Mom could lift it, much less throw it. Star takes a shuddering breath and continues. "Every day. Every day she lost it and threw things, screamed. It's like she can't pretend to love us anymore."

"Well, she never pretended to love me, Star." I know it sounds ridiculous and bitter to say, especially while she's falling apart, but I'm not ready to act like Star and I were ever on the same level as far as our mother goes.

"God, I know, Moon." And that's odd, so odd, hearing her take the Lord's name in vain. "I should've defended you. Especially with the knives. I was so scared of her, though." Star looks at my scars. "I've been the worst sister." She's sobbing now. "And I'm not saying that because I'm trying to make this about me, okay? I'm saying that because it's true and I'm sorry."

"Okay," I say.

"Can you forgive me?"

I sigh, and when I look down, my hands shake. "Of course I forgive you, Star. You're my sister. You're my best friend I've had most of my life." I shake my head. "But it's going to take a long time before we're close again. I have to make sure I can trust you."

Star nods slowly. Her eyes are red and her face is puffy and her skin is magenta on her cheeks, like spilled ink. She still looks beautiful. But for the first time ever, I don't hate her for it. "That's fair," she responds.

"So are you going to stay here?" I ask.

"If . . ." Star looks at Tía. "If—"

"Well, you can't go back home," Tía responds. "But Moon has the guest room. You'll have to sleep on the pullout."

I open my mouth to say she can share with me, but Tía stops me with a single look. *It's time for her to learn a little humility*, she says with her eyes.

"Thank you," Star says. "That's perfect."

"Does Mom know you're here?" I ask.

Star's eyes well up. "She probably does now. We left while she was at church, praying for your and my souls."

"We?" I say. "Whose car is that?"

Star sniffles. "It's Santiago's. He drove."

Star and Santiago. Star and Santiago alone in his big, ugly Mercedes for who knows how many hours. I didn't know they even were close enough to arrange their own personal road trip. But I guess they didn't waste any time, did they?

Probably because he was eavesdropping, Santiago steps into the opening of the kitchen, facing us. He's staring straight into my eyes and it hurts me right in the middle of my chest. He looks beautiful. All tall and gold in Tía's chili-pepper lights, in a linen button-down top and jeans. "I made tea," he says, and lifts a mug to me, like an offering, but . . . but . . . Star and Santiago. In a car. In a hotel room. Both beautiful and glowing and smiling. The image of them happy and laughing together comes so vividly, it takes my breath away, and I stand up.

"I'm going to bed." I look at no one as I say it. I look at no one when I walk to my room, when I open the door, step in, close it behind me. Inside, I think nothing as I undress and take the flowers out of my hair, and I think nothing as I brush my teeth and ignore Marco's texts asking if I'm okay and when will we get dessert. I say nothing until I get in the shower. And that's when I speak, but I'm speaking with wild, blubbery tears, and I slide down the silver and teal fish tiles and just try to keep it quiet.

When I get in my bed, there's a few knocks on my door, but I pretend not to hear them. And when I go to sleep, it's to the faint sound of rustling paper. I think that's why I dream of a darkroom, under the red glow of those developing lights, dipping memories into the water, pulling them up and each one is ruined. I guess that's how broken hearts go.

52.

How a Letter Wraps Around My Whole Heart like a Vine

I'M SCARED TO leave my room in the morning, but my growling stomach and the smells of Tía cooking breakfast force me to cave. I open the door a little, peeking.

"He's at his hotel," Star says. She's on the sofa with a book in her hand. She looks a little better from yesterday, but still tired.

I bite my lips. "Okay."

She raises her eyebrows. "Like you weren't looking for him?"

"Whatever." I roll my eyes and walk to the kitchen, where Tía hands me a plate of tacos filled with cheesy eggs and fried plantains. "Thank you."

"Gracias," she corrects. "You two need to learn Spanish while you're here."

"That wasn't one of your rules before."

"Well, it is now."

"Gracias, then." The word is warm. I think of a family, cooking around a hearth fire. There's smoke. Laughter. *Gracias.*

I sit down and Star joins us. I'm not really sure how to act around her, but she doesn't seem to mind. She knows exactly what questions are flying around in my mind like vultures.

"I was at Mom's, locked in my room, trying to figure out how I was going to get out. She'd pushed furniture in front of the door."

"Christ," I say. Star winces a little, but she doesn't chastise me.

"Well, I got a text from him that night." She picks up her phone and shows me. **Hey, Star. It's Santiago Philips. Do you know if Moon has a new # yet?**

"Ah," I say, and then I force half a taco in my mouth.

"Well, I told him some of the situation. And that I was pretty sure you were here, in New Orleans. He offered to get me. Said he wanted to see you anyway. I climbed out the window in the middle of the morning."

"What about the rosebushes?" Mom planted giant climbing roses outside of all Star's windows to protect her purity from would-be rapists.

"I put on a pair of your boots and several layers." She clears her throat. "Basically, I started packing the second she started. I knew I couldn't stay there anymore. I brought a bag of your stuff, by the way. And that old bottle of Daddy's cologne you kept. And the pressed fireweed, in the photo frames."

Okay. There's something in my eyes right now. "Thanks."

"And yeah, it was a thirty-hour drive. We came straight

through, stopping only to sleep, basically." She pauses. "Did you read your letter yet?"

"What letter?"

"The one Santiago slid under your door last night."

I'm in my room in what feels like an instant. I must've walked right over it—because yeah, right there. An envelope. *Moon* is scrawled on it in small, neat handwriting.

Because I'm starved, I don't open it yet. Clutching the envelope like it's holy, I walk back and return to my plate and mug of coffee. "Well?" Tía says.

"I haven't read it yet."

"Don't leave us hanging," Star says.

"I need a minute first." I grab my food, walk back to my room, and sit on the bed. After a couple of more bites, I open the envelope.

DEAR MOON,

   I FEEL LIKE THE BIGGEST JERK IN
THE WORLD. AND THAT'S BECAUSE I
AM, I GUESS. I THOUGHT YOU WERE
TRYING TO GET CLOSE TO ANDRO
BY BEING WITH ME BECAUSE, I
GUESS, WHEN ALL IS SAID AND DONE,
I DIDN'T UNDERSTAND WHY A GIRL
LIKE YOU WOULD EVER WANT ME.
YOU'RE TALENTED. BEAUTIFUL. FUNNY.
AND I'M, WELL, YOU KNOW ALL ABOUT
ME. I KNOW I REALLY BLEW IT WITH

YOU, BUT I WANT TO MAKE IT UP
SOMEHOW. I'll BE STAYING AT THE
OLDE TOWN INN.

I'll BE UP FRONT. I WANT TO
TAKE YOU OUT. COURT YOU. All THAT
STUFF. PLEASE LET ME . . . AND IF
YOU'VE CHANGED YOUR MIND, I MEAN,
THAT WOULD SUCK, BUT THAT'S OKAY.
I STILL WANT TO BE FRIENDS, IF
THAT'S OKAY WITH YOU.

THERE ARE SO MANY AWESOME
PLACES TO EAT HERE. WHY DON'T
WE MEET AT ARNAUD'S TOMORROW
AT SEVEN? EMAIL ME WHAT YOU
THINK. OR NOT. IT'S All UP TO YOU,
MOON.

—SANTIAGO

I rush out to the kitchen, where Tía and Star are finishing their coffee. "So you and Santiago aren't together?" I ask Star.

"What?" Star says. "Are you kidding?" When I say nothing, she smiles. "He won't even look at me unless I'm talking about you. The only time he spoke to me was to remind me of all the times I was shitty to you." Her eyes water a little.

"Wait, so he was a jerk to you?" That's not what I want either.

"No. No. He told me exactly what I needed to hear."

I lift the letter, looking over his blocky handwriting again. "He wants to meet me at Arnaud's tonight."

"Ah," Tía says, raising her eyebrows, and at the same time Star squeaks and says, "What are you going to wear?"

I blink for a second, staring at Star. "Are you really freaking serious right now?"

Now Star's the one who looks confused. "But—he's trying to get you back, right? Why wouldn't I want to know what you're planning to wear?"

I scoff. "Um, maybe because the last time I saw you, you were destroying my camera and livelihood? You were telling Santiago what a slut I am? And then you made him believe I wanted Andro instead of him?"

"Why do you sound so mad?" Star asks. "You said you forgive me."

"Just because I forgive you doesn't mean I'm over it."

"That's exactly what forgiveness is supposed to—"

"Girls." Tía's voice is quiet and firm. "You both have things you need to work out. Clearly. But we're not at your mother's house. I won't have this dissolve into a screaming match." She stands. "You talk. With inside voices. I'll make more coffee."

Star and I watch her go. When we look back at each other, we each fidget in our seats, in the exact same way. We're practically mirror images of each other.

"You tried to ruin me," I say. "That's not something I can just forget, okay?"

Star nods. "Okay. Yeah. I get it. I did some really crappy stuff to you."

I scoff. "Really crappy stuff" is certainly putting it mildly.

"One of the things I don't get is why you did it. Why? Why did you go out of your way—"

"Because I was jealous, okay?" Star's voice is loud, and she lowers it when Tía *tsk*s in the kitchen. "Because I am jealous of you."

"You. Are jealous of me. You."

Star nods.

I huff. "This isn't a joke, Star."

"I'm not joking. Not lying. I really was—and am—jealous." Her eyes are getting big and glassy. "For so long . . . you were you. And I was me." It's kind of a vague beginning, but I get it. She was Star Fuentez, the virginal FG influencer. And I was . . . me. Moon the Weed. Star wipes her eyes as she continues. "And all of a sudden, you were getting noticed. And not because of what designer you were wearing or how you braided your hair or how many Bible verses you've memorized or . . ." She sniffles. "You were noticed because of your art. Because you're funny and smart. The things you'd say. And your tarot deck." She takes a breath. "It hurt when you didn't tell me about that. Why didn't you tell me about your Fotogram account? How could you let me find out about it when your story, with the red feathers, hit number one?" She blinks back tears. "I felt so ridiculous. And *betrayed*."

"You would have totally freaked, Star."

"No, I wouldn't have. I would've supported you."

I shrug. "Sorry. That's really hard for me to believe."

"Okay. Yeah. That's fair, given my behavior."

We both pause as Tía places café con leche in front of us.

"Gracias," I say. Star echoes me.

"Right," Star says, and takes a sip. "So. I was jealous and I saw that you were getting close to Santiago. And I—I know that must make me sound like such a sinner. But I wanted to get him. I wanted control back. That was it. I felt so out of control."

"You wanted to put me in my place as the ugly, weedy sister."

Star rolls her eyes. "Moon, you are not—"

"But you know what I mean."

"Well, whatever I was trying to do didn't work. He really likes you. I swear. I think he's in love with you, Moon." She shrugs. "And I was terrible. I know. But I thought—I thought if people realized how great you are, if you realized it, that you'd leave me. That I would be alone."

"What are you talking about, Star? You—you've always had everything. Everyone. Thousands of fans and followers and friends. And Mom. Like, I would've never left you if you hadn't been so cruel. But don't kid yourself, or me. You wouldn't have been alone."

Star shakes her head. "All Mom cares about is money. Even my friends . . . even Chamomila. All they care about is access to one-point-four million followers. Everyone's only waiting to cash in, as far as I'm concerned. When you left, Moon, I realized you were the only *real* relationship in my life. You're the only one who ever cared to protect me from the creeps. Who even thought of doing that." Star shrugs. "I don't want to lose you. I get that you can't just let it go, but I promise you, Moon, I'm going to try to be a better sister to you."

I get up and sit next to her and lean into her, and she leans into me, and then we are hugging and crying.

"I want to be a better sister too," I say. "So if you have feelings for Santiago—"

"I don't. I promise. I don't." Star pauses. "But I do need you to promise me one thing."

"What's that?"

"Let me help you choose your outfit for tonight."

I groan. "What the hell, Star?"

"You dress a little too—"

I give her a look.

"*Casually* most of the time."

"Fine. Help me dress. Whatever."

Star cheers and Tía pops her head out of the kitchen like it's pure coincidence and she wasn't eavesdropping the whole time. "Ya? All good now?" She sits. "So you're going to give him a chance?"

I shrug. "I don't know."

"Come on. You have to. You have to," Star says.

"Don't pressure her," Tía says.

"I mean," I say. "I guess I'll go to hear what he has to say."

"Not in that, you're not," Star says, gesturing to my goat pajamas.

"Well, duh."

"Show her," Tía tells me. "All those clothes we got, eh?"

"Ugh, fine," I say as Star claps her hands together rapidly. She runs to my room before I can even finish my last sip of coffee.

"Have some patience, would you?" I call.

"Oh my gosh! What about this brown jumpsuit?" she calls back.

I groan, and Tía smiles like she knows I'm only pretending to be annoyed. Because . . . you know what? It feels good to have Star be interested in me for once. Like . . . she's invested in me or something. Like she cares.

So I let her dress me. In distressed denim and my pale-pink wrap top. In an ochre dress of Tía's patterned with tropical-looking leaves. Finally, I put on the brown jumpsuit. "That's it," Star says. "That's what's going to make Santiago's eyes explode right out of his head!"

"God, let's hope it doesn't come to that," I say. But yeah, I know I look good in it, because the belt hugs right where my waist is smallest, making me appear like an hourglass. But there's still a part of me that keeps wanting to glance over my shoulder to measure the rolls on my back, to see if the cellulite on my butt is visible through the fabric. The kindest thing I think is, *I look chubby.* But Santiago liked it, didn't he? He liked all the thick, soft, wobbly parts of me, so much that when I let him, he couldn't keep his hand—or mouth—away.

But he didn't like it enough to fight for me. . . . That's what he's doing now, though, right? Fighting.

God, I'm so confused. Now I feel like I just look bad.

Tía knows what I'm doing. "Stop," she says, lightly smacking my hip. "His eyes will be nothing but ash."

And she's right, of course. Santiago will melt when he sees me, not just because *he* thinks I'm hot . . . but because I actually *am* hot. I hide a smile as I look at myself again—hourglass, jiggly, dimpled. Beautiful.

"Yeah, he's going to pass out for sure," Star says, smiling, then looking around. "Where's your jewelry?"

Star and Tía decide to put bamboo hoops in my ears and on my hands, with my brown leather sandals and my coconut bag. Everything on me is some form of bronze or brown or deep gold. "You look amazing," Star keeps reassuring me, but seeing myself in the mirror, I feel conflicted. I know I look good. I just feel like I might be trying too hard. Like I come off as desperate.

Tía scoffs when I say this. "That's because you've been raised to think a woman dresses up only to attract a man. Consider this—maybe a girl dresses up for herself? Hmm? Ever think about that?"

Which makes me feel much better, actually. Because all this, it's not for Santiago. It's for me.

53.

Actually, This Might Be the Worst Date in the Known Universe

I SPOT HIM first, standing at the front of the restaurant. Everything is sticky-humid. Everything smells amazing. Everything is blue and orange and glowing with gas lanterns, little tongues of flames hovering around like fairies.

And Santiago. So freaking handsome, it's not fair at all. He dressed up, maybe for himself, too. He's got on a cobalt-blue button-down that looks a little too tight over his broad shoulders. His gray slacks are lightly pin-striped. Black dress shoes so shiny, I can see the lanterns reflected on them, little fairies flitting at his feet.

And then he sees me and there's, like, a thousand different emotions on his face. I don't get a good read on each one. There's maybe surprise and relief, maybe hope, and maybe—Lord—longing? But then all that zips up nicely into something vaguely pleasant.

"Hey," he says when I get close.

My whole body wants to hug him. I want to melt right into

him, take him to my bed and snuggle for hours. And then kiss for hours. But then, you know, the fact that he thinks me whorish enough to seduce him to get Andro. And all the crap that comes with that.

I guess he senses my restraint against touching him, because he tilts his head rather than reaching for me. "Shall we?"

I follow him through the epic Arnaud's. I actually looked up some of its history online. It's literally over a hundred years old. Once, a European dude mocked me for thinking one hundred years was actually old. I couldn't say it at the time, but the reason we have so few old things here is because European conquerors destroyed it all. So I'm allowed to feel awe and wonder right now at a whole hundred years, a whole lifetime ago. I mean, really. Back then was so different, it was like a hundred lifetimes away.

I feel like if things were normal between me and Santiago, he'd be telling me all about Arnaud's now, probably some supersecret historical information that only chefs would know, with that same joyful tone in his voice that I first heard when he told me about salt.

Now, with things anything but normal, we say nothing. He leads me to the back of the restaurant, where there's a server. "Mr. Philips," he says. "Ms. . . . ?"

"Ms. Fuentez," Santiago finishes.

The server nods and smiles and reaches to pull my chair out, but Santiago beats him to it. "Are you ready for the menus, sir?"

Santiago nods, and I sit down, suddenly acutely aware that I haven't said a single word since I got here. A trickle of fear nips at the back of my neck. What if I've lost my voice? What if I can't say anything for the rest of the night, or ever again?

"Thanks for meeting me here tonight," Santiago says. There's nothing wrong with his voice, that's for sure. It's still the same, deep, flipping sexiest tone I've ever heard in my life.

"Do you like oysters?" he asks next.

I shrug and do a really weird head movement that's basically a combination of a nod and a shake.

"You ever had them before?"

I shake my head.

"Want to try a couple?"

I shrug and nod at the same time. Santiago drops his menu. "Are you ever going to speak to me again?"

I open my mouth, then close it.

"So that's a no?" He takes a breath while I try, and fail, to not freak out. And he stands, and for one super-freaked-out moment, I think he might leave me there, all alone, in my brown-on-brown-on-brown outfit. But he stops once he's next to me. "I want to hug you," he says. "Can I?"

My hands, arms, knees—everything—shake. I nod. His hand is on mine and he helps me up, and then his arm is around me. First on my shoulders, then the other at my waist. It takes me a few seconds, but finally I raise my arms and clasp my hands around his hips. He rests his chin on my head. When he speaks, I can feel the rumble of his voice on my cheek and throat and collarbone.

"I'm sorry. I'm such a fucking fool." He holds me for a long while. After a minute I relax enough to sink into him. His muscles are firm against all the squishy bits of me.

His hand reaches my hip and squeezes. I squeak like a mouse.

"Ah, so you can speak," he murmurs into my hair.

I'm stiff again. I take his hand off my hip. "Look." Taking a step back, I glance up at his face. How can someone look so beautiful in the freaking dark like this? If anything, his cheekbones and lips and ambery eyes are heightened by all the shadows.

I swallow. "Okay, yeah, I'm not exactly sure about all this. About you. The fact that I'm here isn't a yes. It's . . ." I run a hand on my hip, where everything still tingles. "It's a maybe I'll give you a chance to be friends. And then maybe more. Or maybe not. I'm not sure yet."

He looks slightly devastated, but then he nods. "I respect all of your choices." He gestures to the table. "Can I compliment you?" he asks as we sit.

"Why wouldn't you be allowed to compliment me?"

He shrugs. "I guess—maybe my compliment isn't exactly a just-friends sort."

I swallow. "Well, in that case, maybe wait a bit, okay?"

He nods, looking down at the menu, cheeks and neck red.

"But," I add. "Maybe a friendly version of that compliment would be nice."

"Is that so?" He gives me a half smile. And then his eyes drop to my ribs, then back up again. "Sorry." He shakes his head. "I didn't mean to look—I mean."

I clear my throat. "The compliment, Santiago?"

He's biting his lips when he looks back up at my eyes. "You look . . . nice."

It's amazing how a simple, even boring compliment can carry so many other words behind it. He may as well have said, *I want to eat the oysters we ordered off your body. That's how nice you look to me.*

"Thanks," I say. And then I let my eyes drop to the wide of his shoulders. I remember exactly what they feel like in my fists. And then I say, "You look nice too." Translation: *Yes. Eat dinner off me. After I have a go at you first, though.*

"So, oysters," I say, and somehow, that doesn't break the tension. "Are they as slimy as they look?"

He smiles and chuckles and, Lord, okay, the tension wavers, but there's something else between us. Relief? Happiness? Alegría? That was my word today from Tía. It means something like joy. Alegría. It settles around me like dust, warmed and red from some distant, ancient desert.

"A little. Maybe." He picks up the menu. "We can try them for an appetizer, along with mushrooms Véronique. Does that sound okay? For dinner, I was going to order gumbo."

"What's all in that?"

"It's a Creole dish. You cook it in a big pot all day. Like it's a potion or something. Start with sautéing the onions, garlic, green pepper, celery. Add the shellfish, the sausage." He shrugs. "Some chefs put their own spin on it. A little okra or greens."

"You ever made it before?" I ask.

"Not yet. But I want to. Maybe this will inspire me."

I nod. "Okay. I'll have the same thing."

"Yeah?"

"You make it sound irresistible." I shrug. He does that to virtually all food, really. It's his superpower.

The oysters arrive with the mushrooms, and neither of them are half-bad, but I definitely prefer mushrooms. And then the gumbo is presented, in wide, big bowls with a decorative taupe trim. Santiago digs right in, but I go much more slowly . . . and you know what? It completely rocks my socks off. Everything mixed together, the shrimp and chicken and sausage, all in that brown broth, over perfectly cooked rice. Lord, I can't finish it fast enough.

"This is incredible," I say, and Santiago beams and then I almost drop my spoon. So I guess my not-talking instinct has been transformed to my default make-things-as-awkward-as-possible one.

"So you and Star road-tripping. How was that?" Yep. Awkward as flipping possible.

He frowns a little. "It was fine. She was worried about you." He coughs. "And me, too. I was worried. About you."

"Were you worried? Because your email—"

"Right. I was worried. I tried . . . not to be worried. That's what happened when I sent you that douchey email. Sorry about that." He clears his throat. "Your aunt said you were on a date yesterday?"

I shrug. "It was no big deal, just this guy I met at the library."

He's frowning again. Deeper. "Yeah. You sure bounced back."

And right as the words spill from his mouth, I realize my heart is still wide-open broken. Because that deep ache returns, right at my chest. Right where I maybe *love* him . . . But I'm not ready to think about that too hard yet. I don't drop my spoon, but I do place it back in the bowl a little harshly. "And what's that supposed to mean?"

He tilts his head. "What?"

"What do you mean, exactly, by I 'sure bounced back'? Like I'm some ugly hag-girl who should've been waiting for you by the door in case you decided to change your mind about me? Or did you mean it like, 'Wow, guess you really are a whore.'"

"Holy shit." Santiago's arms are up. "This—I didn't mean—"

"Sure you didn't." I stand and throw my napkin on the table. "Sorry, Santiago. But this isn't going to work out."

"No, Moon." He stands up. He's following me. "Moon." I open the beautiful iron-and-glass doors to the restaurant courtyard and frantically scan for an exit.

"Moon." Santiago's hand is on my arm. His voice is a deep, gentle silk all around me. "Why are you pushing me away?"

"I'm not." I whip my arm back. "I'm just remembering what a jerk you are."

He holds his arms out. "I'm sorry. I'm sorry. Can you come back inside? Let's have dessert, okay?"

I almost say yes. Almost. But he was so quick to believe the absolute worst of me, you know? How do I know that's not going to happen again? How do I know that once I give him my heart, he's not going to rip it into chunks and, like, pee on it before leaving to take some Star look-alike on a date? It's too hard. I already feel like a mess and none of that has even happened. So I turn and walk away, fast enough that he doesn't see my tears.

Tía takes one look at me when I step through the door and she's on me instantly, arms around me tight. And then there is another set of arms. Star. "What happened?" Tía asks when I pull back.

I start to shake my head, but she stops me by saying, "Look, Moon, I know your mom never wanted to hear anything you had to say. She never cared to know about your life. But that's not familia. She wasn't familia. Understand? I'm your family." She looks at Star, who nods. "And that means I want to know. I care. Okay?"

"Okay," I say. "But I think I'm going to need a lot of passion-fruit ice cream first."

We're all on the porch, bowls of ice cream in our hands. Tía has cut open a passion fruit and scraped the sweet, jellylike insides on top of the vanilla. "And for you, Moon." She holds up a passion-flower.

I've always loved passionflowers. They look like they belong on another planet, with their wild, curly stamen shooting up like antennae, reporting back to the mother ship, alongside their first layer of petals, which are long and springy like curls. And they come in the most gorgeous shades of purple and pink and white. Beautiful and weird. My kind of creature.

Tía plucks the petals and shreds them over my ice cream. "It'll soothe your nerves."

"Flower medicine," I say.

She smiles. "Flower medicine."

And then I'm crying again, and I tell them everything between bites of ice cream, and it's so surreal, to be the center for once. To be the one looked at and listened to. It seems like the whole universe has leaned in. The clouds move away so the face of the full moon is there, bright, pale blue. The birds are quiet. Even the wind has become gentle. Combined with the passionflower and fruit and ice cream, it's all a balm to me. A weighted blanket, filled with everything I love. Flowers, humidity, thick waxy leaves, mud on my bare feet, Mexican bingo cards, passion in fruit and in bloom on my tongue.

"So what's the problem?" Star says. "You don't want him. You told him. It's done, right? Now you can move on."

Tía *tsks*. "Star, it takes more than that to move on. There's emotions, memories, hopes to process and grieve."

"Right, but once she's past that."

"The problem is I'm in love with him," I announce.

There's silence for a moment. An eerie sort. Like, the wind is so quiet, it's like wind was never even invented. Then Tía and Star erupt.

"What?"

"Are you serious? Are you sure?"

"But does he deserve that love, Moon?"

"Are you sure? Well, you need to freaking tell him, then, Moon!"

I shut my eyes and cover my face with my arms. "Too much information. I'm glitching."

"Take a breath," Tía says. "Let her breathe," she tells Star.

I lower my hands. "Okay, to answer the questions that processed. I'm sure. I mean, I'm mostly sure." I don't have a filter on right now. Hazard of not being used to people listening to me for more than four seconds. "He—he's . . ." I take a breath, looking at the hibiscus to my left, swaying in the breeze, which has decided to rebirth itself. All around us, the moonflowers are beginning their slow unfurl.

"He sees me. He made me feel—made me realize that what I contribute to the world is valuable. That the space I take up is mine and worthy of me." I shrug. "When we first met, I was such an asshole. And then we butted heads like rams and then, bam, kindness." Santiago snorting when I got down on myself. "Thoughtfulness." Santiago insisting on the cooking show. "Attraction." Me smiling at him, and his sentence is completely interrupted and gone. I frown. "But then again, he was so quick—"

"He was so quick to think you'd want Andro instead of him, just like you thought he wanted me instead of you," Star finishes.

I blink. "Well, it's not exactly—"

"It's exactly that. The same. Having Andro as a big brother makes him insecure. You having me—and I'm sorry for taking advantage of it—but you having me made you insecure. And you both completely projected your insecurities on each other."

The truth is bitter. I swallow and nod slowly.

"So now what?" Tía says. "Do you think you can let what he did . . . ? Do you think you can let it go?"

I sit for a little while. Half my ice cream is left, already a gooey puddle in this heat. "I don't know," I finally say. I sound pretty miserable as I say it too. I want everything to be clear, right now. I want to know everything, to be sure about everything. I want all the universe's secrets to be poured into my lap, a pile of little sentences folded up into letters, sealed with waxy blue stars.

"Sleep on it," Tía says. "Take all the time you need. He can wait."

"Really?" I ask. "You mean you can't make my decision for me real quick?"

"Not how it works." Tía laughs. "How nice that would be though, eh?"

This is the thought that stays with me a little as I slide under my covers. If someone could make my decisions for me, would I want that? Would it really be easier?

At first, yeah. But . . . if I couldn't make my own decisions about something, would I really deserve the outcome? Would I need to earn Santiago's friendship? Or kisses?

Great. Now all I can think about is Santiago's kisses. I go through lists in my mind—everything I will need for college. Books. Supplies. Tomorrow, Tía and Star are going to the store to get Star her phone. I guess Mom cut her off too.

But I keep going back to Santiago. His lips, specifically. Then I groan and punch a pillow. "Sleep," I say. "Just sleep on it." And that's exactly what I do.

54.

The Fourth (and Fifth, Sixth, and Seventh) Times I Ever Had Sex

WHEN I WAKE, it's late. There's a note in the kitchen. *Breakfast burrito in the fridge. We'll be back after lunch. —Tía*

I try not to think about Santiago. About kissing him. About loving him. Needless to say, the effort is futile. The best I can do is get on with my day as fast as I can, filling it so that he doesn't seep in the edges of my brain too much. After all, he's still all over my heart. And there's nothing I can do about that at the moment. So I eat as quick as possible, then jump right into the tub when I'm done.

After I'm showered and dressed and fed, I get on Tía's computer and start planning my next self-portrait photo shoot. My room has slowly become my muse. I've moved some of Tía's orchids in here, along with a couple of pothos vines. On corkboards nailed into the walls, I've pinned photocopies of my favorite images. There's Cindy Sherman, of course, and, like, every image of Ana

Mendieta. Also the work of Helen Levitt, Cyndi Brown, Ivette Ivens, Kirsty Mitchell. There's so many women out there, being amazing in every way. Is it weird that I think I can join them somehow? I'm beginning to think it's less and less weird, and more and more what I was made to do.

My empowering thoughts are interrupted by a weird sound. Like someone is dragging their sharp nails on glass just outside my bedroom. "What the—" I'm cut off by a series of four thumps. Big thumps that make me think of things like Godzilla's reign of terror.

Oh God. It's a rapist. Or La Chupacabra. Or La Llorona. Any way I can spin it, it ends with me in a bath of my own blood. So I do what any person interested in self-preservation would, I think. I grab Tía's biggest cast-iron skillet lid—the one with the sharpest spikes—and tiptoe to the door.

A huge, dark form appears at the front window and I almost drop the lid. I can't do anything about the gasp I emit.

"Shit," I hear from outside. Oh God. It is a man. Scarier than La Chupacabra. That's for sure.

But the tone of that voice was . . . familiar. Images wash over me. Cheese grits, huckleberry pie, fancy New Zealand honey, gray-gemstone salt.

Salt!

I run to the door and throw it open with such force, glass bottles and jars rattle all around me. Why are there glass jars rattling—but then I spot him. Impossible to miss, what with his tall, hulky frame. Santiago's frozen with a look of guilt on his face.

"I'm sorry," he grits out finally. "I'm leaving now."

"Wait. What are you doing here? Why are there . . ." I stop speaking when I take in the bottles. The jars. There's ten, twenty, God. There's, like, fifty jars set up on Tía's porch, filled with water and . . . and . . .

"Fireweed." My voice is breathless as I take it all in. Because . . . no, I'm not dreaming. Tall stalks of fireweed are everywhere around me. Pink, petaled, perfect.

"What—how—wh—" I can't form words. The combination of Santiago and fireweed has destroyed my faculties.

Santiago walks back over, slowly, hesitantly. He's in jeans and a white shirt. Somehow the casual, simple clothes make him look even more godlike.

"I'm sorry. I know you don't want anything to do with me. I didn't mean for you to find me here."

I'm going between the fireweed and him so fast, I probably look like I've just snorted a mountain of cocaine.

"I contacted a guy in Alaska. Found him on this message board. He had to mow his field, but it was filled with fireweed. He, ah, mailed them to me. Wrapped in ice packs, to keep them fresh. I—uh, even though you don't want me, I didn't want to leave without giving them to you."

"They're beautiful."

"Yes." He's staring at me. He blinks, like he's been abruptly unhypnotized. "I should go."

"No." My voice is all choked up. "No. Don't. Please."

"Are you sure?" His hand's in his pocket. He's moving his weight from side to side. I'm worse, trembling from my jaw to my ankles.

Yes, I want to say. *I am sure. Come here and hug me. Don't ever leave.* But when I open my mouth, this is what comes out. "Will you help me move them into my room?"

"Okay." His answer is quick. Gruff. "I have a pallet. . . ." He wanders to his car and returns with a wooden box in his arms. Together we fill it with the jars. The fireweed blooms are so tall, they bump and slide against one another. We can only fit a few at a time.

It takes us five or six trips, him carrying the box and me balancing three bottles in my arms. My hands shake a little and I spill some water on my yoga bottoms.

We survey my room together when we're finished. My bed, covered in a quilt with a print of hibiscus, pink and red and white. The walls, green, the exact green of the trees that line Tía's backyard. And now the fireweed. Real fireweed. The sweet berry and bergamot-like scent surrounds us in a cloud.

"I love you." My voice is calmer now. Grounded. "That's why I pushed you away."

Santiago stops breathing for so long, I wonder if he's going to faint or something, but then he inhales, takes two giant steps toward me, and his hand is on my face. "Tell me I can kiss you now." His voice is sharp and crackly.

"You can kiss me now," I say. It's just a whisper, but he hears me well enough, because he bends down low and then his next inhale is with my mouth on his.

The kiss is gentle for all of four seconds, and then everything is open and wet and warm and so, so good. We go backward until my shoulder blades hit my door, shutting it with a bump we both ignore. In fact, he shoves himself at me harder with his hips. A strangled sound comes out of me and he pulls back fast. "Did that hurt?"

"No." I'm breathless, but I don't even care. I put my hands on his neck and pull him in, back to my mouth, so I can suck on his delicious lips.

I basically rip his shirt off and stare at him for a moment, letting myself really look, unlike all those other times he's paraded his chest in front of me. He's so firm everywhere, and there's a fine sheen of hair in the middle of his chest that tickles my palms a little. The more I touch him, the faster his breath goes. "You're perfect," I say, and then feel kind of basic, because isn't that a cheesy thing to say to a boy you're about to have sex with?

And Santiago chuckles and says, "All except for this, huh?" and he lifts his left arm. He's trying to be light, but I can feel the pain in the joke. It scatters around me like dropped glass.

So when he goes to kiss me again, I put my hands around his face and make him look in my eyes. "No." My voice is firm and final. "Santiago. You are perfect."

And he stops breathing again, but before he passes out, he kisses me so hard. We're on the bed now, and I don't even know how we got here. We kiss more, we lose more clothes, until all I'm wearing is my moonstone necklace and all he's wearing is a condom. And he's on top of me, waiting.

"Are you sure?" he asks.

"Yes." I am emphatic.

He stays still, looking at me. His eyes are dark and a little bit scared. Finally he says, "I've never done this before."

"Oh." The surprise leaves my mouth before I can control it. "Well, there's not much to it, really. And the first time isn't a big deal to guys."

His jaw is a little hard. "It's a big deal to me."

"Oh."

He swallows and says again: "It's a big deal to me, Moon."

I open my mouth and spill my heart. "This is a big deal to me, too." Now I swallow. "A really big deal."

And then it's happening. And I sort of stay still a little, because he's so beautiful, his muscles rippling like water, each movement a stone's throw into a wide lake. After a minute he stops and I furrow my brow. "What—"

"Are you okay?"

"Yes . . ."

"You're quiet."

"I am?"

"You don't like it?"

And I smile and say, "You feel nice, Santiago."

He pulls out and leans on his arm next to me. "And you

feel fucking amazing, Moon. That doesn't seem equal."

"What? You think I feel good?"

He scoffs and then raises his eyebrows. "Wait, you're serious?"

"I mean." I take a breath. "You don't think I feel like . . . the Grand Canyon?"

His face, he gets it now. "No. Christ. No. You feel like . . . I dunno. A glove. Or an agnolotti pasta."

And now I'm snort-laughing. "Oh my Lord. You just called my vag a pasta noodle?"

"Not a noodle. Agnolotti."

Okay. We're both laughing now. And when we stop, he says, "When I touch you, you get loud." He reaches toward me and proceeds to prove his point enthusiastically. "But it wasn't like that . . . when I was inside you."

"Sex is weird," I respond. "It's always just nice."

And he nods and I can tell he's thinking hard about this. And so he pulls me on top of him and says, "You ever tried it this way?" I shake my head, and he rests his hand on my hip. "I want to try. Is that okay?"

It feels . . . deep at first. I'm a little embarrassed because I can't hide my jiggly bits from up here. But then I watch Santiago's eyes, and it hits me. He *likes* my jiggly bits. He loves them. He almost can't stop watching them. If I jiggle extra hard, he groans a little and tenses up like it's all almost too much. And that gives me the confidence to forget about what I look like and focus on how I feel.

I try a lot of different things—angles, speed—and then something clicks. It's warm, and warmer, and then hot. Santiago makes me stop three times so he can collect himself. But eventually, and suddenly, I'm a fireweed burst into bloom, all pink and peaked in some ancient Alaskan field where wildflowers have bloomed every summer for eons. And now I get it. I know why everyone is so obsessed with sex.

And so Santiago and I do little else for the rest of the morning and into the afternoon. He puts me on the desk, on the edge of the bed. I make him hold me against the wall, and then I get on top of him again, because that's now my favorite.

And I know Mom would say I'm disgusting, and a whore, and a heathen for doing this. For loving it.

But you know what's kinda funny? After the third or fourth time, Santiago turns off all the lamps and opens the curtains so we can see the light pouring through like milk. And then he's on top of me, everything gold about him even golder, and he puts his hand on my belly and says he can't believe how soft I am, and then he stares at me with this expression of awe, and then he kisses just above my left breast over and over again, because that's where my heart is.

And this I know, as he's next to me in bed, arm thrown over my hips: today might be the holiest day of my life. Because of this, of him. Because of me.

I'm exhausted in the best way. My bones are weeds. My hair is sea grass. My limbs are tender leaves of butter lettuce. I don't even move when I hear Tía and Star return.

"Should I lock the door?" Santiago asks.

At first, I don't care, but then I realize I don't want anyone to see his glorious body but me. I'm completely greedy for him to be mine, all mine. So I say, "Yeah."

After the lock clicks, he starts dressing, and I whine, "What are you doing that for?"

He grins but says, "Your aunt will probably want to talk, right? I want to be dressed for that, if you don't mind."

"Whatever." But when Tía starts knocking, I don't want to be naked either. So I put on my bra and underwear, squeaking when Santiago pinches my love handles. "Stop pinching the jiggly parts."

"I like all your jiggly parts."

I knew he'd say that, but it doesn't make it less thrilling to hear.

He kisses my hand. "I think this has been the best day of my life."

I laugh. "Because of all the sex, right?"

"No." But he smiles. "Well, yeah. But it's because of you. Being with *you*."

I blink. "How are you so sweet? When I first met you, I thought you were the grumpiest piece of—"

He squeezes my hip again. "I'm still the grumpiest. Don't forget that."

And then he holds his arm out and we walk out my door.

"You're back," Tía says to Santiago. She's on the sofa with a cup of café con leche. "That didn't take long."

I feel a prickle of shame. Even though I know Tía didn't mean it that way, I feel like it's something Mom would tell me. My hair mussed and lips swollen and the taste of Santiago's skin still in my mouth. *That didn't take long.*

Tía reads me instantly. "I didn't mean it like that," she says warmly. "I'm glad it didn't take long. Now maybe you'll stop moping all the time, huh?"

"Tía!" But I'm smiling.

"I'd like to cook dinner for you," Santiago announces. "And your family." He looks up at Tía shyly.

Tía smiles. "Why not? The way these girls eat, I could use the break."

Santiago smiles so big, my stomach does this wild flip-flop. I know I've thought this a zillion times by now, but dang it, he's so flipping handsome. How does a guy like him want anything to do with a girl like me?

"I need to get groceries," Santiago says. He turns to me. "Wanna come?"

"Uh, yeah." I grin. "Just like the old days, huh?"

"Yeah. A whole three weeks ago."

I start to slide my shoes on but stop when I see Star sitting in the kitchen. "You wanna come?" I ask her.

"Hmm?" She's looking intently at her phone, but I can see even from here that it's not on.

"Come. With me and Santiago. To the store."

"No way. You guys need your alone time. I'm not going to disrupt that."

"Don't be like that." I grab her hand. "Come on."

"Moon." But she follows me and sits in the back of Santiago's Mercedes, quiet. In the store, she opens up when Santiago asks her opinion on things like scallops and mollusks, and then she and I laugh as we debate on who is worse in the kitchen.

"I've never burned grilled cheese before," I say.

And Star says, "Well, I don't put honey on pizza like a barbarian."

And even though she's smiling, her eyes are still sad as we joke and talk. So when we get home, Santiago asks me, "What's up?"

"I just want to talk to Star for a minute."

"Go ahead."

"I'll go after we put the groceries away."

"You know I'll get the prep done way faster without you."

"Oh, shut it," I say. "Like—"

But then he kisses me, and then I'm the one shutting it. Well, not literally, because my mouth has to open to let his tongue in, and then his hand is back on my hip, mine are on his shoulders, but when I dig my nails into his firm flesh, he breaks away. His lips, cheeks, and ears are all flushed.

"You should go talk to her," he says. "Before we contaminate the kitchen."

"Fine," I respond, but I'm smiling the whole time.

Star's in Tía's bed, covers pulled to her chin. I'm surprised she's not click-click-clicking through her phone. But then again, she hasn't been on her phone much lately at all.

"Hey," I say, in front of the screen curtain. "Can I come in?"

"Sure." She smiles, but again, it doesn't reach the rest of her face.

I sit on the edge of the bed. "You haven't been yourself lately."

Star shrugs. "Myself. I don't even know who that is lately."

"What do you mean? You're still you. Except. You moved here."

Star shrugs, but when I raise my eyebrows, she relents. "I haven't heard from Chamomila or Oak or even . . . Belle since I got kicked off the tour. Andro thinks I'm an immature jerk. Which, okay, I was. But then Mom . . ." Star closes her eyes really tight, like she's trying as hard as she can to not cry.

"She hurt you," I finish. I slide into bed and her hand finds mine.

"I don't know why, all these years, I tried to convince myself she wasn't as bad as she was. But all these memories keep coming back. Times when she'd be so cruel. To you, mostly. And I'd brush it off, every time."

"We did what we had to do, to survive."

The tears are coming now. "I'm not the good Christian I thought I was. It's a lot."

"Star, don't—"

"I was selfish, Moon. And it's a lot to take in. To admit. Whatever. But I want to be different." She shifts and looks me right in the face. "I'm going to be different."

"Okay," I say. "That sounds like a good start."

Star nods and then smiles. "You and Santiago had sex this morning, right?"

My skin prickles instantly, like it's growing thorns. "That's none of your business."

She reaches for the hand I've pulled back. "I'm not judging, Moon."

"Yeah, right."

"I'm trying to be better, remember?" I sit up in the bed, and so does she.

"What does it feel like?" She won't look me in the eyes as she asks.

"Are you serious? Is that really what the Virgin Mary would do?"

She sets her mouth in a firm, straight line. "You know what? Forget it."

"Oh, stop." I say. "Fine." And I look around for inspiration. Because it really does feel like the Virgin Mary just asked about sex.

"If the guy is careless, it could hurt or feel like nothing," I say. "Even if he does care, it could feel not great, because he doesn't know what he's doing."

Star looks a little disappointed. What I've said is basically a nicer version of Mom's warnings. Minus all the blood-eating STIs and mortal-sin details.

"But," I add quickly, "if he's slow and thoughtful and receptive"—I pause, thinking about how my morning with Santiago went—"it's the best feeling ever."

"Is that all?" Star still sounds disappointed.

"Sorry. It's hard to explain. It's not just the orgasm. Which feels like . . . I mean, it feels like you're dying in the best possible way."

"That doesn't sound all that great."

"Trust me. You pretty much never want it to stop. Anyway, besides that physical part, there's also feeling like you're, I don't know. Completely alive. The most alive you could ever feel, all with someone you really care about. Or love."

Star has kind of a small, distant smile on her face. "Well, that does sound nice." She takes a long breath. "Have you ever been . . . with a girl?"

I shake my head. "No. I've never wanted to with a girl before."

Star's voice is so quiet, I have to lean my ear really close to hear. "I've never wanted to with a boy ever."

"But you have wanted to . . . with a girl?"

"One girl." She's crying. "I'm scared, Moon. If anyone found out, they'd be so disappointed in me. The church, my followers. But at the same time . . ." She takes in a shuddering breath. "I'm in love with Belle Brix."

"Wow." I didn't realize she loved Belle back. Holy crap.

"I thought I knew about everything . . . thanks to Mom and the church." She gasps a little and covers her face with her hands. "I don't know if I want to wait for marriage anymore. If I'm being honest, that's a thought I've had for a while."

"Wow."

"And then . . . at some point I realized that I didn't know if I ever wanted to wait to begin with. I realized that choice was made for me, you know? It was made for me hundreds of years ago by some European dude who hated women."

"Wow." I never, not in one zillion years, thought I'd hear Star get this real. My brain is stuck on *wow*.

"And I'm mad and I want to be different than that. But then again, I'm scared of being disgusting and loose." She's full-on sobbing now, and I can barely understand her.

So I wrap my arms around her and smooth a hand over her hair until her breaths are a little calmer, and I say, "We've been brainwashed, Star."

"Yeah."

"And it's going to take time—a lot of time—to figure out what we believe is real and what's been decided for us nine hundred years ago by some white dude who hated women."

She sniffles. "Yeah." She pauses. "I'm also kind of freaked out about La Raíz." She turns to me. "Does it hurt? When the weird, bad miracles happen?"

I shake my head. "Star . . . no. It's never hurt. In fact . . ." I stop because I'm realizing how true what I'm saying is. "When it happens, I've never felt closer to God."

And that's exactly what it is. I think about all of it—from fireflies to ladybugs, red feathers to butterflies. When they surround me, fluttering, soft and tickly. How somehow I become the center of the universe. Somehow, I fall in love with it a little bit more.

We sit in silence for a few minutes, and then I clear my throat. "So what's going on with Belle?"

Star shakes her head. "She won't respond to my texts, comments, DMs. She said she knows I'm never going to be with her for real."

"Is that the truth?"

"I don't want it to be."

"Did you tell her you love her?"

"No."

"Why don't you?"

Star shrugs.

"Be honest with her. She's really cool. And whether or not it works out, Star, remember that I'm so proud of you, okay? No matter what happens, I'm proud to be your sister."

She hugs me tight. "You're the best sister I could've asked for." Star has told me nice things before, but it never really felt like she meant them until now.

"Thank you, sis," I say. I'm choked up, so we hug in silence. But I'm also practicing. What it means to accept a compliment and not deflect. To bloom into who I really am—soft and squishy, dark and smooth, warm, warm, warm like the fireweed all over my bedroom.

55.

The Best Dinner in All the Universes, Even Those Still Unknown

WHEN I GET into the kitchen, it smells like vanilla and honey, and Santiago is huddled over a cutting board, trimming some blooms off a fireweed stalk.

"Excuse me," I say. "But those are my flowers you're mutilating."

He narrows his eyes. "It's for a good cause."

"Oh? What cause is that? Because, if you didn't know, some guy totally brought those for me all the way from Alaska. They're worth a fortune. So what's this cause that's worth destroying what's basically pure gold to me?"

"Cake." He looks at me and grins.

"Well, then. Carry on."

"Not so fast." He stops me as I turn to leave, grabbing me by the waist and pulling me in, lifting and plopping me on the counter while I screech like an owl. And then he steps between my legs and kisses me like it's our first kiss all over again. He's shy and then more confident, and pretty soon all I can think about is how quickly I can rush him to my bed.

I have no coherent thoughts when he pulls back, so I start chanting "Bedroom" like I'm in some weird sex cult.

His eyes get really dark, almost like a forest at night, but then he shakes his head. "Help me candy the fireweed."

"Bedroom," I say in response.

"Later. I want this dinner to be perfect."

And I can see how important this is to him, so I groan and say, "Fine." And smile when he helps me off the counter and his arms are trembling a little. You'd think we didn't just spend the whole morning doing it. The way we're acting, it feels like it's been years.

But somehow we focus on the tasks of slicing onions, mincing garlic, browning the beef and the pork. I layer the lasagna until Santiago can't help but take over. But he lets me frost the cake.

"What kind of cake is this?" I ask.

"Hummingbird."

I turn to him. "Are you serious? This is a hummingbird cake?"

"It's not as bad as it sounds, or so I've heard."

I run and jump on him, not even caring that he's got a spoon of Bolognese sauce in his hand. We kiss and kiss and then he says, "I will make you hummingbird cake every day, I think." And I love that he says that stuff all the time, and he never, ever thinks about the amount of carbs anyone's eating.

I slide the cream cheese frosting over the round cake as smoothly as I can, and then Santiago places the sugared flowers on top. I'm completely mesmerized by this process: giant, muscly, beautiful guy bending low over a cake so he can arrange the pink-petaled blooms perfectly. I have to grab my camera to photograph him, and the cake, too, when he's done. It's too pretty to neglect documentation, the petals flitting all over like butterflies. I want my wedding cake to look just like it. One day.

Finally everything is ready and we all sit down to eat. Tía is head over heels for Santiago already. "When are you moving in?" she keeps asking.

Even Star seems more like herself in the presence of delicious food. "This is the best lasagna I've ever had," she declares, and though Santiago won't change the unexpression on his face, I can tell he's happy. He slides his hand up my thigh under the table to prove it.

"So," Tía asks after a while. "What's the occasion?"

Santiago wipes his face with a napkin, then stands.

I furrow my brow. "What are you doing?"

"I intend to court your niece," he tells Tía.

Star almost spits out her food. "Like, what? Court for marriage?"

"No," Santiago says. "Well, maybe someday. But right now I'm announcing my intentions to date her."

Tía looks so amused. "Okay, son, I hear you. You can sit."

Santiago sits. I think he's finally realizing how extra this whole thing is, because his ears and neck are pink.

"What about your family?" Star says. "Are you going to live with them and have a long-distance relationship? Or are you going to that culinary school downtown?"

I frown. Like. Should Santiago and I be having this conversation in private? I guess not, because he says, "Culinary school downtown."

"What?" I say. "You decided to go for sure? You're serious?"

"I start next week." He can't help the smile in his eyes. He's proud, and Lord, so am I. So I leap into his lap and put my arms around him.

"What made you change your mind?" I ask.

He shrugs and smiles, this time with his whole face. "Somebody." And then he says, "Ow." Because I'm hitting his arm.

"You're so freaking arrogant. You said yes to the institute knowing we'd get back together? You were that confident?"

He's still smiling. "Well, no. But I was really, really hoping that you loved me back."

My breath is caught. "Loved you *back*?"

Santiago nods.

"But that means—"

"Oh, stop being so dense, Moon," Star yelps. "He's loved you for ages. Since he first saw you."

"I wasn't even there and I believe that," Tía says.

"He didn't love me since he saw me," I say. "I was a jerk."

"The most beautiful jerk I'd ever seen," Santiago agrees, and I hit him again. But he stops my arm, cups my face, and we're just looking in each other's eyes and smiling like total dorks.

"Okay," Tía says. "I'm kicking the two of you out. Eat your dessert out back. It's hot enough in here as it is."

Before we leave, I stop because Star's got the biggest smile on her face.

"What's up?" I ask.

"She wrote back." Star is giddy. I haven't seen her this joyful and alive in so long, tears sting at my eyes.

I reach out and give her a hug. "I'm so glad, Star. I'm so happy for you."

It's humid and cool out. Santiago and I balance our dessert plates and café con leche in our laps. "So where will you be staying?" I ask.

"Andro's helping me get an apartment near campus."

I raise my eyebrows. "So you're accepting Andro's help now?"

"Yeah, well." He shrugs. "It's like you said. Foolish of me not to. And I can always pay him back when I make it big."

"I bet he doesn't want you to."

"Yeah. Doesn't matter, though. I'll pay him back."

I realize I've been a little too distracted to eat. So I put a bite of the cake in my mouth and moan.

Santiago grins. "Knew you'd like it."

"Like it? I only want to eat this forever." I smack his thigh. "Go back inside and make me another."

As soon as I finish the last bite, Santiago pulls my plate and mug away and tugs me into his lap. "Do you think your aunt will be okay with you staying the night with me?"

"Probably," I say. "After a birth control lecture."

He kisses my neck and slides his hand down to my hips. Hip man, this guy is. I inhale. "Give me . . ." I trail off when his lips reach my collarbone. "Give me five minutes to pack a bag."

56.

How I Become My Own Moonflower Miracle

LATER, THAT NIGHT, after Santiago is asleep in the giant, creaky hotel bed, I grab a glass of water, then stop at the window. And I think about what Tía said. That people could help me all they wanted, but the only person who can save me is me.

I place the glass on the windowsill, the one overlooking the courtyard filled with sweet-smelling pansies and alyssum flowing out of big clay pots like water. And then I open the window so I can hear the fountains outside, and reach in my bag for my deck.

The first card I pull is the Moon. Then the Sun. Last is the High Priestess.

The High Priestess is the card Tía hates the most, because she represents the unknown. Not just what we haven't figured out yet, but that which can *never* be known.

Isn't that why religions all like to fight? Because each one wants to be the one that knows it all.

But we can't know everything. We can't. Some people might say only God knows, or only the universe knows it all. Either way, we humans aren't the ones who've figured everything out. The more I learn, the more I realize that I know so little, it could be a fraction of a speck, and if you put the knowledge of all humans together, it might be two or three specks in the infinite and twinkling and wondrous universe.

I feel like the High Priestess is guiding me to go a little deeper, so I reach in my bag, take out my mirror stone, and face the window.

There are the little windows of the other hotel rooms across the way, framed by indigo shutters. There's the flowers overflowing out of the clay pots, the big fountain made of concrete with a texture like sand. The ivy along the walls, rustling in the wind. And everything bathed in the light of the moon. Everything all blue like cornflowers and lupine and bearded irises the color of night.

I look down at the stone, and this time I don't see him, but I feel him. I feel my dad. I feel his love all around me, so thick I could gather it in my hands like Spanish moss. I feel like he is a part of this universe, just like me, and we're both a part of what's ancient and holy. Me and Daddy and everyone else, too.

And that's when it happens, right when I'm thinking about the great mystery that is this whole universe, a moth lands on my chest. A luna moth.

It's huge. I want to scream, but my voice has dried up or something. Because, as mentioned, it is huge. Three or four inches in wingspan. "No," I whisper, because then I hear more flutters. More creepy moths' feet land on my arms, belly, even my freaking hair.

I almost turn to get Santiago, but then the image of him slapping moths off me, moth guts flying all over, roots me in place. I am a tree. My roots go deep into the earth. The leaves that are my hair can only be moved by the wind. The wind and moths, that is.

My eyes are squeezed tight. I'm about to ask myself once again, why is it me that always gets these little blessings, and that's when something clicks. I take a breath. My spine relaxes, my jaw unclenches, and the feel of the moth legs and fluttery wings starts to tickle. And then I bite my lips to keep from laughing.

Because it's okay. My mom can't love me. And that's okay. I'm still a size 16. And that's okay. My dad is gone, but I'll never stop loving him, and he'll never stop loving me, either. And that's okay.

I'm loved, I'm fat, I'm beautiful.

I'm Moon Fuentez, and I'm currently covered in luna moths. And that's all okay.

And as soon as I accept it, the moths, they fly up and out the window one by one like little spirits. Like they were feasting on their absolute favorite moonflower and had their fill.

Before I join Santiago and sleep, I keep thinking the same thing. Everyone is the center of the universe. Everything. Like Ana Mendieta said, how her art is connected "from insect to man, from man to spectre, from spectre to plant, from plant to galaxy." Moons to stars, fog to dirt. Weeds to nebulas.

I am the center of the universe. And that's okay. Better than okay. It's miraculous.

Acknowledgments

Believe it or not, *How Moon Fuentez Fell in Love with the Universe* started as a robot-and-cyborg traveling circus story set in historic Mexico.

I began the manuscript for National Novel Writing Month in November of 2018, and it took me over thirty thousand words before I realized the novel wasn't working. At the time, I didn't know why it fizzled, but now I understand that I was trying to combine two stories of my heart into one, and they were melding together in a way that just didn't work—too much honey, not enough pizza.

After I trunked the story, relatives came to visit, and we all took a stroll downtown where we lived at the time, in New Jersey. I was feeling pretty gloomy about giving up on thirty thousand words' worth of work, when I looked up and saw two young women taking photos of each other in front of a redbrick wall.

They reminded me of me and my sister, Jessica, when we were younger, and how differently we were treated from our white-passing primos. *What if we had grown up with social media?* I thought. I imagined all of us as teens with Instagram accounts, with the differences in the way we were perceived and approached so vivid in my mind—and how it would've affected our self-esteems, too.

Immediately, two characters formed in my imagination. Moon, from the manuscript I was working on, arrived first. Then there was her sister, Star. And finally, the story. Much of the plot was taken from the robots manuscript—except without robots, and now, it was a contemporary. It felt right, even though along the way, I had many doubts. But that is how it is when you write a story from your heart, of your heart—the doubts must be pushed through to get to the tender, vulnerable, and *honest* core.

I have so much gratitude to so many people who have supported me and the stories of my heart. First, my family: Jordan and Ansel. How I love you both.

My sister, Jessica, who helped me remember the pain of what we experienced. Thank you for always being there for me, and for your generosity, and your wide-open heart.

My mother, who has always helped me translate English into Spanish, and for all the gifts you have given us, especially unconditional love, and for your example of a strong, sustained faith.

My father, for teaching us all to fall in love with books and plants. My brother, for keeping us laughing even when it's difficult to laugh. Nana, for teaching us to speak with and thank the plants, and J.R., and Polo, always. And to my beautiful extended family: Matt, Oliver, Logan. Aries, Sophia, Daniella, Aria. Tod and Tina, thank you for being so understanding, so generous, and for loving us all and Ansel so completely.

So much gratitude to my agent, Elizabeth Bewley, for your belief in *Moon Fuentez* and all my work, and your ingenious ideas, and your friendship. I am so grateful I get to work alongside you.

Thank you to my editor, Jen Ung, for understanding and supporting this book so deeply from the start, and for making sure it was shaped to be its very best. I am so lucky to have you championing my stories.

To Laura Eckes and Veronika Grenzebach for creating a cover for *Moon Fuentez* that was more beautiful and majestic than I ever could have imagined. Thank you both for understanding the heart of this book, and Moon, so well, and conveying it, and her, in the most gorgeous way possible.

Thank you to production editor Rebecca Viktus and copyeditor Penina Lopez for your expertise in making this manuscript as clean and powerful as possible. I'm grateful for your input and advice.

So much gratitude to everyone at Simon Pulse. Everything you've done in making this world a more inclusive place for young adults and beyond, it will echo out into the universe forever. The good you've put out there will *never* be lost. I'm so thankful for our time together, and that you made my work at home from the start.

Thank you to the first readers of this (or, in one case, *very* early parts of this) novel, India Holton and Jenny Elder Moke. Your feedback was invaluable, and I'm thankful to call you both my friends. Also thank you to so many wonderful and talented people who have encouraged me, especially Sandra Proudman, Shannon Doleski, and Loriel Ryon.

Much love and gratitude to the Las Musas Collective,

especially Aida Salazar, Mia Garcia, Anika Fajardo, and Zoraida Córdova. Never in my wildest dreams did I think I'd belong to such a supportive and loving community, and every day I am grateful for the guidance, advice, and understanding Las Musas has brought me and my work.

At the time of this writing, it is not known whether the CWLA program at the University of Alaska Anchorage, where I received my MFA, will continue. I am brokenhearted about this uncertainty and want to extend enormous gratitude to those at UAA who have given me so much: David Stevenson, Elizabeth Bradfield, Linda McCarriston, Anne Caston, Erin Coughlin Hollowell, and Sherry Simpson, among many others. My MFA colleagues: Lisa Stice, Kersten Christianson, Andrea Hackbarth, Tara and Chaun Ballard, Marie Tozier, Jonas Lamb, Anne Haven McDonnell, Evan Tysinger, and Brandon Thompson. And, of course, love and gratitude to *Alaska*, which helped me fall in love with the universe so fully, I will always be connected to it through poetry and wild light and fireweed.

Thank you to the authors of *An Illustrated Dictionary of the Gods and Symbols of Ancient Mexico and the Maya*, Mary Miller and Karl Taube. This book first taught me about divination and mirror stones.

Gratitude to Craig Childs, whom I met through UAA. All of the adventuresome bits of William Fuentez were inspired by Craig, especially through his book *Atlas of a Lost World: Travels in Ice Age America*. If you're interested in what this continent looked like ages and ages ago, I urge you to pick his book up. It's where I first learned about wildflower pollen samples taken from the Bering Sea, and how amazing chert is!

To Marissa Lieberman and Lisa O'Shaughnessy, who gifted me the gold and gray elephant journal on which I began this novel. Thank you for welcoming me and Ansel with open arms to the EOPL, and making certain Ansel knew how magical libraries are from the very beginning.

Thank you to Jan DeBlieu, whose favorite word is "ocean."

I have lost two beloved family members to suicide: Margaret Villanueva and Ben Gilliland. Thank you both for how deeply you loved me and our family.

If you are experiencing suicide ideation, *please* phone the National Suicide Prevention Hotline: 1-800-273-8255. I may not personally know you, but I do know this: the world needs you, and your art, and your words. And the world—this whole, wild universe!—is *far* better for having you in it.

About the Author

Raquel Vasquez Gilliland is a Mexican American poet, novelist, and painter. She received an MFA in poetry from the University of Alaska Anchorage in 2017. She's most inspired by fog and seeds and the lineages of all things. When not writing, Raquel tells stories to her plants and they tell her stories back. She lives in Tennessee with her beloved family and mountains. Raquel has published two books of poetry. *How Moon Fuentez Fell in Love with the Universe* is her second novel.